As his mouth covered hers, Toby felt her lips open like a bud in warm sunshine.

She drew her hands around his neck, urging him to hold her closer. The intensity of Toby's reaction shocked Michael back to his senses, and he abruptly released her.

"Did I do something wrong?" Toby asked, hurt by his sudden withdrawal. "Tell me...."

"You didn't do *anything* wrong, but working next to you and keeping my distance has probably been the hardest task in my life."

"I know," she admitted.

"No, you don't know," he said harshly, and walked away from her. "I take full responsibility for overstepping the boundaries of our relationship."

"Just what are those boundaries?" Toby demanded. She had thought Michael found her attractive, but now, she wasn't sure what his motives were. All she knew was that she'd wanted him to kiss her, and he was acting as if that were a crime.

"We shouldn't mix business with pleasure. We're too good a team to ruin things by becoming temporarily cozy."

"Cozy? You make me sound like a bed warmer!"

Dear Reader,

As the green of summer fades into the warmer colors of fall, it's time to put away your beach chairs and think about curling up on the couch with a good book. With this month's four titles from Harlequin Historicals, we hope that every reader will find a story to pique her interest.

In *To Touch the Sun,* newcomer Barbara Leigh gives historical romance a new twist with a tale of a man and a woman who meet as enemies and equals on the field of battle. We hope you will enjoy this unique and enchanting love story set in the British Isles during the early 1300s.

Passionate Alliance, Lucy Elliot's sixth book for Harlequin Historicals, takes place in New York City during the closing days of the Revolutionary War.

Maureen Bronson's *Ragtime Dawn,* the lighthearted tale of a minister's daughter with her eyes on Broadway and a handsome music-hall owner, and *Tender Feud,* a fiery romance set in Scotland from Nicole Jordan, round out the month.

Coming up next month, look for Bronwyn Williams, Kate Kingsley, Nina Beaumont and Laurie Paige.

Tracy Farrell
Senior Editor

Ragtime Dawn

Maureen Bronson

Harlequin Books

TORONTO • NEW YORK • LONDON
AMSTERDAM • PARIS • SYDNEY • HAMBURG
STOCKHOLM • ATHENS • TOKYO • MILAN

Harlequin Historicals first edition October 1991

ISBN 0-373-28696-1

RAGTIME DAWN

Books by Maureen Bronson

Harlequin Historicals

Delta Pearl #32
Ragtime Dawn #96

MAUREEN BRONSON

is the pen name of writing team Antoinette Bronson and Maureen Woodcock. Old friends, Toni and Maureen live in Seattle with their respective husbands and children. Both are actively involved in their community and consequently treasure moments stolen from their hectic schedules to research and write.

Chapter One

Before entering the building, Toby Wells took one last glimpse at her reflection in the window and was perversely pleased. The image gazing back at her was perfect: fashionably sedate, unquestionably mature, and commonplace. What Toby fancied in clothing and hairstyle was unconventional, but today was not the time or the place for her to go against the traditional tide.

Women were supposed to wear their hair swooped into Gibson girl rolls, so Toby bent to fashion and pulled her butter-colored curls up and away from her face when she would have preferred to have tied her locks back with a simple ribbon. Ladies wore wing collars that strangled their necks and Toby obliged formality, buying a dress with a collar high enough to choke a giraffe. The simple serge skirt and tailored blouse she would have liked to have worn to this audition had been left hanging in her closet.

Today was the day to look elegant, sophisticated and artistic—not at all the real Toby, an unpretentious twenty-two-year-old who had never ventured farther than the outskirts of her hometown, Saint Louis, Missouri. Her ticket to a new life in New York City was going to be the songs she had written and now carried under her arm in the folding portfolio.

At the entrance to the music store, Toby hesitated. Sedaine Sheet Music Company had run an advertisement inviting, "Composers and Lyricists! Mark May 10, 1898 on your calendars! Bring your original compositions to us and we'll publish them."

Up until yesterday, when she'd read the bold-captioned proclamation, she'd assumed she would be one of a select few composers Michael Sedaine was meeting. It had been Mr. Sedaine's personal response to her letter that had given her the false hope. But since finding the advertisement, she'd been unsure of what would be waiting for her today at the piano store. Toby shrugged her shoulders in resignation and followed the signs down a narrow hallway to a door at the back of the building. The closer she came, the louder the hum of voices on the other side of the closed oak door grew. The raucous buzz was in direct correlation to her rising anxiety.

Toby's hand teetered above the doorknob, but she realized her hesitation was not from fear, not from any feeling of inadequacy, but from tingling anticipation. The instant she crossed the threshold, Toby was determined, no, *positive*, her life would never be the same. This was her first step toward independence, and she was ready to take more than a faltering, uncertain one. She was prepared to take a giant, surefooted leap—if Michael Sedaine offered to buy her songs.

Coming to this audition was one of the few well-planned acts in her life. After studying classical piano and composition, rhythm, melody, harmony, tempo and a myriad of other musical skills, she had painstakingly written three songs. By plucking out the measures on the keyboard and boring her family with unending modified renditions of each one, she had created what she was certain were upbeat, vivacious compositions. She had worked hard, and her debut as a composer had finally arrived.

Confident in her imminent success, Toby was consciously pausing at what she thought of as "fame's door." Failure? Rejection? They hadn't even whispered to her.

Silently she bid goodbye to her childhood and to her father's notion that she would someday leave his home to take up marriage and motherhood in another man's house. Her hesitation, an almost formal moment of prayer at the doorsill, surprised Toby and she smiled. She didn't usually reflect on why or what she was doing, she just charged ahead and did it. Contemplation was generally in hindsight and only if her action caused regret or pain.

Boldly Toby opened the door and prepared to meet Michael Sedaine, proprietor and chief buyer for Sedaine Music. Everything would be perfect as long as Mr. Sedaine wasn't a stodgy old goat whose taste in music ranged from the pedantic to the maudlin.

Toby stepped into pandemonium. Hopefuls lined two benches, and the overflow roamed the cavernous room. Like her, everyone clutched sheet music, and Toby suddenly felt as unique as a dandelion. Rather than facing her dream come true, she was confronted with a living, breathing nightmare.

Momentary shock was replaced in rapid succession by sympathy for an elderly gentleman seated at an upright piano. The victim—that was the only way Toby could describe the poor man—was attempting to play his songs at a piano centered in the room. Those in line for their turn talked rudely over his music, paying no respect to the composer's efforts, giving no heed to the man's feelings.

Reality took Toby's hopes and threw them out the window. Her illusions of walking in and captivating Michael Sedaine with her compositions had been naïve, and Toby was mortified—and angry. Angry with herself for thinking it would be easy, that she would be given special attention. But she was furious with the commotion the gathered lunkheads were causing while the poor miserable man played out his heart on the keyboard.

She searched the room, looking for someone with authority, and only found a balding, bespectacled little man scurrying around with a notebook clutched to his chest. His movements were nervous, jittery, as if he were terrified that all the aspiring composers were going to turn on him at any moment. Toby groaned as her last illusion died. Michael Sedaine was worse than a stodgy old goat; he was a twittering, ineffectual clerk!

Without thinking, she marched across the room and slammed her portfolio down on the piano top. The loud thud only caused the man who was playing to halt in the middle of a delicate crescendo while the rest of the group continued its impolite babbling.

Determined to put an end to the bedlam, Toby placed two fingers in her mouth and gave an interminable, ear-piercing, nerve-shattering whistle. It was effective, as always, and all conversations were amputated in midsentence.

"Now that I have your attention, ladies and gentlemen," she addressed the gathering, "continue to hold your tongues while you find your manners. There's no excuse for this shameful display of disrespect."

The sudden silence was not amazing. It was precisely what Toby expected when she took command. The bewildered faces staring at her in stupefaction didn't disturb her, either. She was used to being looked at as if her audience didn't understand the English language. Her ten-year-old twin brother and sister, Cleo and Mo, often stared at her in such a manner when she abruptly ended one of their childish squabbles.

"Now," she said, "I, for one, would like to hear this gentleman's lovely tune. Please, sir, start over from the beginning." Toby placed a gloved hand on the stunned man's shoulder. He smiled up at her but looked unsure. "Please," she cajoled, "we're all anxiously waiting."

In the doorway, Michael Sedaine remained motionless. The chaos, the noisy, packed mass of humanity, the cacophony he faced, had left him momentarily paralyzed. Reginald, his assistant, was supposed to have organized the day's appointments into a semblance of order but had lost control of the mob again. Briefly Michael considered turning around and taking the next train back to New York. This was the third city where he had held his talent search, and the mayhem, thanks to Reginald, was only becoming worse.

Michael pondered his choices. Should he endure another endless round of sugar-sweet pabulum from novices or fire Reginald for incompetency? Before he could weigh the merits of his only two options, a young woman who Michael had never seen in his life took control as if she were running the whole shebang. He wasn't sure if she simply had an innate authority or if she was a potential dictator. Either way, she was a hell of a lot more competent in restoring order than Reginald could ever be.

Competent and prettier, too. Except that she looked precisely like every other young lady nowadays. Why did every blasted one of them study the fashion magazines with such unerring accuracy and then copy the women between the pages? It was as if all the females he met subscribed to the same collective mind, the same communal taste and the same prim dress ensemble.

Not realizing what he was doing, Michael stripped the forthright blonde's stiff bombazine dress away and replaced it with a soft gown of lightweight lawn. He pulled the pins from her hair and let her curls fall naturally down her back and, for good measure, added a wide-brimmed straw hat tilted pertly to one side.

His criticism wilted the moment she looked up. Everything faded from his mind but her enormous blue eyes, eyes like twin seas. And like the water, they sparkled, making the light dance in their depths. But calling them just blue wasn't accurate. Lapis lazuli was closer, but he conceded even comparing her eyes to that deep blue gem didn't do them justice.

Toby didn't know why she looked up, why she instinctively knew a man was watching. Everyone in the near-silent room was still staring at her, so one more pair of eyes should have made no difference—but they did.

If she had been like her sister Rosie, Toby thought, she would have swooned at the sight of the elegant man poised in the doorway. Rosie would have delicately melted like a chocolate bonbon left in the sun. But then Rosamond was seriously demented when it came to men, and Toby prided herself on her sensible, logical attitude toward the opposite sex. Possibly having three strapping brothers made her immune, but most likely, she admitted, she was wary for much more practical reasons. Being attracted to a man—and having that attraction reciprocated—would mean settling down, getting married, having babies, cleaning house, having babies, cooking, having babies....

Still he *was* smart looking, and she allowed herself a flash of fantasy of what it would be like to have him as her beau. Rosie would turn pickle green with envy.

Toby watched him amble gracefully across the room and, as ridiculous as it seemed, the music being played seemed to have been written just for this moment, this man. The tempo was languid, and the mood, like the tall, graceful man, was poetically seductive.

As he advanced, Toby studied him as a painter would, instead of the musician she was. He had a strong curve to his jaw, an aquiline arch to his nose, and a luxuriant head of hair the color and texture of sable. Fortunately he was rescued from perfection by a small gap between his two front teeth, which appeared as he smiled at her.

Flustered, she realized she was gawking and dropped her gaze, playing with the buttons on her gloves. Ordinarily she never fiddled nervously and Toby clenched her hands together to still them. Her entire day was rapidly disintegrating along with her future, and she silently willed herself not to lose her dignity, even in the face of bleak reality.

The song ended and, with it, the last of Toby's confidence. As she edged her way to the back of the room, she tried to appear as pleasant and unobtrusive as possible. She hadn't meant to butt into the proceedings; she hadn't meant for herself, her personality to stand out. Only her music was supposed to speak, dominate. It was none of her business how Sedaine Music handled its affairs or how boorish the others in the room behaved.

"Thank you, Mr. . . . ?" Michael Sedaine started to address the gentleman at the piano but realized he hadn't checked Reginald's notes to see who the first person on the list was. He held out his hand for the notebook and Reginald willingly relinquished it. Michael glanced at the top and said, "Thank you, Mr. Wilson. That was a very pretty piece, but I'm not looking for sweet songs today."

Toby quit staring at the tiles on the floor and jerked her head up. The skittish clerk couldn't possibly have such a deep, calm voice. She had expected him to squeak when he spoke, like a frightened mouse. Toby's courage withered and floated away as she realized the timid little clerk was not Michael Sedaine. The man she'd been ogling was!

Her only hope was that he hadn't witnessed her entrance, hadn't observed the way she had barged in, making a fool of herself. Her father was always, and rightfully so, admonishing her to mind her own business. He also reprimanded, "For pity's sake, Toby, wait to see which way the cat jumps before you do."

Like a scolded kitten, she slipped to the farthest corner of the room to hide until it was her turn at the keyboard. Someone with a jot more sense, and a whit less courage, would have gone home, but she was determined to bear the humiliation and remain. She had waited too long for this rare opportunity to let her pride send her scuttling away.

Michael Sedaine introduced himself and, as he spoke, he tried not to look in the direction of the dauntless girl who had demurely retired to the corner. "This is going to be a long day for all of us. Unfortunately—" he paused and glared at Reginald "—my assistant ran an advertisement implying I was holding open auditions. That was not my intent, but the milk has been spilled, so to speak."

Lord, but I sound stiff and awkward, Michael criticized himself. He hated giving speeches, but what he abhorred even more were open auditions. Not because he was forced to listen to dreadful compositions for hours but because he had to tell the creators their songs were awful. Well, he never said "awful," but he did have to send the majority of people away, and it was always a struggle to do so without pulverizing the person's ego. "You can spare yourself a long, fruitless wait," Michael continued, "if I tell you now what I am looking to buy. Then, perhaps, you can judge whether or not your compositions are appropriate."

He explained what he wanted were variations on the "cakewalks," the snappy march or promenade music made popular by American Negroes. A friend had once described the new musical form as the happy gospel of syncopation. The French referred to it as *le temps des chiffon,* but American musicians called it "ragtime."

Toby noticed the awkwardness dissipate in Mr. Sedaine's voice when he began talking about this new kind of music.

It was obvious the man loved his work and held a special place in his heart for ragtime. She wasn't sure if her tunes would be close to what he was searching for since she'd never heard a true ragtime artist play.

What she did know was that her music fit the general description, especially her latest song. Toby had heard rumors the New York-based company was scouring several major cities for compositions to feed the voracious public, hungry for innovative music. The latest craze, pianolas, was bringing popular tunes into an extraordinary number of American parlors. Although her father wouldn't allow a pianola in the house, dubbing it "a crackpot contraption," Toby personally knew a dozen families who had purchased them.

Toby had revised the rhythm of her last piece until she'd shifted the accent and stressed the weak beat rather than the strong one. Her professor had described ragtime in great detail and Toby had taken careful notes.

Michael heard a few people groan softly at his speech and watched as they left the room; but the bulk held their places in line. He looked at the swell of eager, expectant faces and inwardly shuddered. Tonight he was going to have another talk with Reginald.

"Mrs. Peterson," Michael said, and smiled at a plump, middle-aged woman, "please begin."

Sitting down on a ladder-backed chair, he closed his eyes to listen to the woman's song. Clamping his eyes shut served two purposes. It eliminated distractions, allowing him to focus on the music, and it also masked his true reactions. He could control his facial gestures, the small smile never wavering, but he couldn't hide the horror people might read in his eyes. So many songwriters were guilty of plagiarism that he was frequently tempted to name the tune they were presenting as their own. But he never did, for he was convinced half the poor souls didn't realize they were cribbing from another artist.

"Thank you for coming to see me, Mrs. Peterson," Michael said, and opened his eyes. Standing up, he shook the woman's hand. "But, I'm not interested in lullabies today. Next, please."

Twice Toby watched Mr. Sedaine ask a composer to play the piece again, but each time, after hearing the song played through once more, he shook his head. What he said to those two people was quite different though. "You're close, very close. Keep trying. Here's my address in New York. If you create another song you think I might buy, send me a copy and I'll give it consideration. Good luck."

"Miss Wells," he said, reading the next name from the list.

The instant she heard Mr. Sedaine call her name, all Toby's insecurities flooded over her. After listening to a score of rejections, she wondered if she stood any chance at all of selling her songs. But she hadn't come this far, worked this hard to give up without at least trying.

Even though the room was sweltering, Mr. Sedaine intimidating, the mood in the studio oppressing and the temptation to race back down the hall almost irresistible, Toby stood and walked to the piano. With each step, she reminded herself why this moment was so important. If she established a career, nothing would drag her back home. She would never have to wipe her younger brothers' and sisters' noses again, never be happy cleaning up after her absentminded father again, or ever be willing to cook another chicken-and-dumpling Sunday supper.

"Good morning," Toby said as she set her scores down. "My first piece is titled, 'Only the Wind Knows.'"

"So, you are Miss Wells. Thank you for silencing this crowd. You have my undivided attention, Miss Wells, just as you gained theirs," Michael said, and swept the room with his arm.

She heard the amusement in his tone and closed her eyes to stifle her panic. There had been good reason to justify her impetuous actions, and if Mr. Sedaine's assistant had been doing his job she wouldn't have been placed in this embarrassing predicament. And since Mr. Sedaine obviously approved of what she had done, Toby lifted her head back up and opened her eyes. There was no way her pride would allow her to pass up this opportunity. At least, she knew Michael Sedaine wasn't likely to forget her. Now if she could only convince him she could write music half as well as she could whistle.

Adjusting the small wooden stool, she took a moment to flex her fingers to dissipate the tension. Toby blocked out the line of people still waiting and hesitantly played the opening bars. As she acquainted herself with the unusually stiff response of the keys, her confidence grew and she stopped concentrating on the mechanics of playing and focused on the more poetic interpretation of the notes.

Although she never thought of herself as having a particularly good voice, Toby had spent years in the church choir and could carry a tune well enough to give Mr. Sedaine a vague idea of how the lyrics worked with the melody. She breezed through the first number and, without pausing, began her second. This was a livelier, almost slapstick, piece, and she dropped her voice nearly an octave to suit the mood.

Toby had given a great deal of thought to this song's lyrics, basing it on her older brother Alexander's first date. He'd taken a young lady on a picnic, and a series of disasters virtually ruined the day and any chance he had of impressing the girl. Glancing over, she saw Mr. Sedaine grin as she described, in song, the skunk who provided the ultimate insult.

Her last piece was purely instrumental with complicated, uneven rhythms. She'd worked weeks perfecting it, but it still required concentration to translate the notes she heard in her head onto the keyboard. As she lifted her foot off the piano pedal and her fingers away from the ivory keys after the final note, she looked over at Mr. Sedaine to read his reaction.

"Although your second song was amusing, unfortunately, I bought a piece quite similar not too long ago," he said sympathetically.

Toby's heart shriveled.

"And the last song was unique, the syncopation was evident, but you need to study ragtime more thoroughly. It's not something I can describe. A song either works or it doesn't."

Michael had momentarily considered buying the last piece of Miss Wells's work, for it was fresh, but he had to be fair. If anyone else in the room had played that tune, he would have passed it by with just a few words of encouragement. He was on guard, knowing his judgment was influenced by the impish young woman hiding underneath the matronly garb. Michael would have wagered a month's royalties Miss Toby Wells wasn't anything like the image she was projecting, and he found the possibility of discovering who she was really enticing. The unbidden fantasy jolted him. Speculating about Miss Wells was ludicrous, and he said brusquely, uncharitably, "Next, please."

"Thank you for your time," Toby whispered, barely able to control her disappointment. This wasn't a day she would be commemorating in her diary with a row of bold stars.

She held her head up and passed by the twenty or so people still waiting their turn. But rather than flouncing out of the room in a huff like others had done, Toby waited. She wanted to hear just what kind of music, if any, Mr. Sedaine would buy. Next time, and there would definitely be a next time, she'd sell a piece. There was no way under heaven she would give up after one rejection. No one ever said making dreams come true was easy.

Toby had been so consumed with her own audition, she hadn't noticed the people waiting behind her until now. Three spaces back was a tall, thin black man accompanying a stunning woman. The lady's skin was several shades lighter than her escort's, and she wore an elegant navy silk dress with ivory ruching on the bodice. Toby had never seen a woman who carried herself with such a regal air.

A few minutes later when the lanky musician played his song, Toby knew Mr. Sedaine's day had been worthwhile. For the first time in her life, Toby listened to a piece of real ragtime and was immediately captivated by the upbeat music, the adventurous breaks, the unexpected, odd flourishes and the dashing style.

Ragtime was not the traditional supplication most people associated with Negro music. It had a dignity lacking in the glorified plantation tunes Toby had heard, and she found the element of risk in breaking classical rules exciting.

"Congratulations, Mr. MacRae," Michael said, and jumped out of his chair to shake the man's hand, "you've just sold a song."

"Thank you, Mr. Sedaine, but when you say 'sold,' does that mean you'll publish it with my name or someone else's?" Mr. MacRae asked suspiciously.

Michael wasn't surprised by the question. He was well aware of the practice of stealing an unknown composer's work and putting a recognized author's name to the sheet music. "Your contract will stipulate, Mr. MacRae, that you will receive full credit."

Grinning, the musician said, "Please, call me Caleb."

"And I'm Michael. Are your other songs as good as the first?"

"That was my least favorite of the bunch," Caleb said. "Couldn't decide which three to bring so I let Chantelle," he said, indicating the smiling woman with him, "pick out her favorites."

"You have excellent taste, Miss..." Michael floundered.

"Chantelle Reynard, Mr. Sedaine," she said in a low, throaty tone with a hint of an accent.

Toby couldn't place where the woman was from, but her slight slur had a faintly French sound and was charmingly unaffected. She watched Caleb MacRae squeeze Chantelle's hand affectionately.

"Play the others you brought," Michael directed him.

Caleb instantly obliged. The joy of being recognized as a serious musician gave him a lift and his playing reflected his excitement. Even so, he never lost control of his songs but played them with energetic discipline and panache.

"Let me see how your scores work," Michael asked. "I'm curious how you've indicated the breaks and pauses in the last combination. They were different from anything I've ever heard."

Michael sat down at the piano, but, even though he was a fairly proficient pianist, he couldn't reproduce the melody from the handwritten sheet music. Doubting his own skill,

Michael tried again, but there was no way what was written down matched the song Caleb had just played. To verify his suspicions, he tried all three of Caleb's songs and found they all missed being faithfully transcribed.

"We have a slight problem, Caleb," Michael said. "Your music and your songs don't match."

"It's my song, I wrote it myself," Caleb said defensively.

"I'm not accusing you of anything," Michael explained. "But I can't publish these. I need accurate scores, pieces other musicians can use."

Toby had already plunged in once today without thinking. Taking the risk of making a fool of herself again in front of Mr. Sedaine, she hesitated before leaping into the frigid waters of uncertainty. But she'd always excelled in translating music to paper, having practiced hour upon hour. Ragtime was complicated, but she trusted her skills enough to take the chance. And there was no way she could allow Caleb MacRae to lose his chance just because his ability to transcribe tunes didn't match his talent for composing them.

"Mr. Sedaine," she said, and watched as he turned to look at her. "Maybe I can be of some help. If you'll just take a moment to glance at my music, you'll see that, although the pieces are not what you want to buy, I can transcribe what I play. I could make some minor corrections on Mr. MacRae's pieces for you." She turned to the looming man and said, "That is, if you would like me to try."

"Any lady who could tame a mob could probably tame my music," Caleb teased. "Just don't go losing what I have here in my head and what I can do with my hands."

"Play the first bar, Caleb," Michael directed. "Miss Wells, you adjust the score."

Michael had forgotten about Toby Wells in his excitement over Caleb's music, but she had a surprising penchant for speaking up at odd moments. He wondered if she was always this outspoken or if there was something in the air today.

He watched Reginald offer her a pencil and was tempted to peek over her shoulder to see if she was really as good as she claimed, but he didn't. Michael contented himself with waiting for the verdict.

"Try it again, Mr. Sedaine," Toby said, handing Michael the sheet of paper. "It's perfect."

"Confident, aren't you?"

"Confident this is the best music you've heard since you opened your company."

"Are you always this sassy, Miss Wells?"

"Yes, Mr. Sedaine, I am."

Her honesty was refreshing. New York women were hothouse flowers compared to this midwestern blossom. Although he was tempted to tease her and keep up their lighthearted bantering, Michael rejected the idea and sat down at the piano. He studied the corrections she'd made and played the music. She was right, it was perfect. "And you're also a very good musical mechanic, Miss Wells."

Toby ignored his comment and said, "Let me work with Mr. MacRae and we'll have his songs fixed up before supper time. There's not very much work to do, really. Just a few finishing touches he neglected to add."

"Reginald," Michael said, "is there somewhere they can work?"

"In the practice room next door."

As they filed into the tiny room, Toby eliminated the formalities; in minutes, the diversified group was on a first-name basis.

A battered, scarred piano was facing the wall in the far corner and Michael wondered if it was even tuned. "Is that all the better you can do?" he asked Reginald.

"I didn't foresee the need for two instruments," Reginald said, defending himself.

"Suits me just fine," Caleb said. "I've played on lots worse. Honky-tonk owners even muffle the strings of some of their pianos just so they sound tinny." Caleb pulled the piano away from the wall and tested it. "Think it'll work, Toby?"

"Your magic can be played on any instrument," Toby said with a touch of envy. Hearing Caleb's creations helped her understand why Michael Sedaine had not bought her work.

Four hours later, Toby and Caleb finished the final song. It was hard work, but it had also been a great deal of fun. The three of them, Caleb, Chantelle and Toby, had fallen into an easy raillery. An outsider seeing them for the first time would have guessed they'd known each other for years.

While Toby and Caleb had been working, Michael had finished the audition and dismissed Reginald. He joined the small group and said, "Thanks, Toby," after he studied the scribbled and corrected scores. Nodding his head, he indicated his approval of the way she'd altered each measure, if necessary, to mesh with Caleb's music. "You're very talented."

"But not original." Toby found it impossible to pass up the chance to needle him for not buying one of her songs. Michael's formality had vanished and she wasn't intimidated by the owner of Sedaine Music. Now he was just another man.

Or was he? With a delightful spark of understanding, she realized no other man in her realm smelled as good as he did, not of bay rum but a faint, citric aroma she identified as lemon. Michael didn't treat her like other men did, either. He wasn't vague and distracted like her father, nor was he bossy and domineering like her older brother Alexander. And he wasn't too forward, like the young men from her classes at the university.

"I'm positive you'll publish your songs, Toby," Michael said. "Another company might jump at them. They are good. I really mean that. They're just not what I'm looking for."

"You're not patronizing me, are you?"

"I wouldn't insult you."

"Would you let me hear them again?" Caleb suggested. "Maybe I can give you a few ideas on how to snap them around."

Toby was grateful for the unexpected reversal of roles and gladly accepted Caleb's guidance. He listened carefully and pointed out several different ways she could change them. "I see what you mean," Toby said when they were finished. "Thank you."

Having enjoyed watching Toby's enthusiasm, Michael forced himself to pull the conversation back to business. "I'll be back in New York in three weeks, Caleb. Can you meet me there?"

"If you give us the address and a date," Chantelle said, speaking for both of them and sounding like a business manager.

As definite arrangements were made, Toby found herself envious of Caleb's success. She did not begrudge him his moment, she just wished Michael was extending the same invitation to her.

"Goodbye, Toby," Caleb said, and shook her hand.

"I hope we'll see you again," Chantelle said with sincerity.

"Yes, I'd like that very much." Even though something special had transpired among all of them this afternoon, Toby didn't know how or when they would ever meet again. The winner, Caleb, the man who had caught the music world's brass ring, was going on to New York while she was stuck in Missouri.

Trying to keep her chin up and not look like a sore loser, Toby started to follow Caleb and Chantelle out the door.

"Toby," Michael said, stopping her before she left, "may I have a moment?"

"Change your mind about my songs?" she teased.

"Not exactly."

Toby knew it wasn't proper for her to be alone with a man she'd met just a few hours ago, but she didn't care. Nothing could have dragged her away before she heard what Michael had to say.

Chapter Two

"I watched you take control today," Michael said to Toby, "and I was impressed. You have a unique way of handling people."

"I've had a great deal of practice, that's all." Raising a passel of children would give anybody the gumption to control a rude mob, Toby thought offhandedly.

"Would you consider helping me for the next two days?"

"Here?"

"I'd pay you, of course," Michael hurried to explain. "Ten dollars a day." He realized the wages were outrageously high, but he didn't care. If he could have two days of organized auditions, it would be worth twice the price.

Toby hesitated, absentmindedly rubbing the face of the cameo pinned on her bodice. If she did a good job for Michael, the next time she had a song suitable for his company, he'd remember her and maybe he'd be more inclined to give her work serious consideration. "What time should I be here in the morning?"

"Nine o'clock."

Mentally juggling her schedule, she wondered how she'd ever get the twins out the door to school, have the beds made, cookies baked for the Ladies Guild meeting, dirty laundry washed and supper organized, but somehow she'd do it. Nothing was going to stop her from taking this snippet of a chance.

Michael said good-night to the owner of the piano store and walked Toby to the corner where she'd catch the streetcar. As they strolled down the avenue in the late-afternoon sunshine, he wondered what Toby's family was like. He didn't know her well enough to ask for a biography but assumed she still lived at home.

"Will your parents object to you working for me?" he asked.

"No," she answered, realizing she'd never given a moment's consideration to her father's opinion. Robert Wells had always allowed her a great deal of latitude in managing her own life, and Toby had never abused the privilege. "My father trusts my judgment. I have one question about our arrangement, though."

"Yes?"

"What about Reginald?"

"He's an excellent clerk," Michael explained, "but his help at auditions is worse than no help."

"What will you do after Saint Louis?"

"I'm not sure, but it's bound to improve. Reginald handles the tedious details of my company with amazing accuracy, things like financial records. In fact, he's already on his way back to the office in New York. He told me he'd be no good at this, but I pressured him into coming. I should have listened to him."

Relief washed over Toby and she grinned hopefully. "Then you didn't fire him?"

Michael hadn't considered that Toby would think she was responsible for costing Reginald his job. "Absolutely not," he reassured her.

With her last reservation lifted, Toby said good-night to Michael, and after she'd hopped onto the streetcar, she cheerfully waved to him.

As the trolley rounded the corner, Toby sank back into the seat and planned how she would squeeze an entire day's housework into one evening. By roping Charlie and Gwen into doing the wash, she and Rosie could work in the kitchen. Toby wouldn't hesitate wielding her authority for the next few days. They could all pitch in and do their fair share.

The moment she opened the front door, Toby was greeted by a chorus. "We're hungry. When will supper be ready?"

The ten-year-old twins were good-natured, easy children under most circumstances, but they were conditioned to having their meals at a set hour and depended on Toby to maintain the schedule.

"As soon as it's cooked," Toby said. "Cleo, go get Gwen and Rosie. Mo, you find Charlie. I need everybody's help."

When they had all gathered, Toby explained, before she handed out assignments, why she wouldn't be home for the next two days. "Charlie, you and Gwen start scrubbing the dirty clothes. Cleo, dust the front parlor. Mo, fill the wood box and water the planters on the front porch. Rosie will help me fix dinner and do the baking."

Exactly as she had predicted, the only whiner was Rosie. But Toby didn't listen to her sister's complaints. At nineteen, Rosie was consumed with finding the right man and thought of little else. But then, Rosie had never thought of anything but boys since she'd turned thirteen. Toby found Rosie's preoccupation extremely annoying and had to continually fight with herself to be fair and evenhanded with her sister.

"You have a choice," Toby said, and grinned wickedly. "Do the wash or help me fix supper and bake cookies." She watched Rosie flounce across the room and pull an apron over her dress without answering.

No one else objected. Even at twenty, Charlie didn't challenge Toby.

It was nearly midnight when Toby finished hanging up the last of the clean clothes to dry on the lines strung from the low rafters in the basement. Her father had briefly noted Toby was working later than usual but didn't question why.

Robert Wells noticed very little except the book propped in front of his nose or the faces of his congregation on Sunday morning. Over the years, Toby had adjusted to his preoccupied form of love, for she relied on the fact that if she ever really needed him, he'd be there. She simply had never seen any reason to intrude into his world. As her mother had explained to her, and Toby had relayed to the other children, their father was a biblical scholar whose opinion was respected, whose books, although not frequently read, were well researched and insightful and whose business it was to minister to the world, not just to his family. It was his wife's duty to tend to everyday realities.

And Irina Wells had been a loving mother who filled the house with music, laughter, classical literature, Russian folklore and a sense of humor. Toby's mother had loved children, children of all ages, and she had paid the ultimate price for her love. At only thirty-seven, Irina died while giving birth to the twins.

That night Toby had dragged the twins' cradles into her bedroom and hadn't slowed down since. She never considered the task of assuming her mother's role too demanding for a twelve-year-old and, because Toby never doubted herself, no one else did.

Toby only resented her premature responsibility when she was forced to defend her brothers' and sisters' names to the other children who taunted them. Her mother had made odd choices and Toby was annoyed with the burden. Although she understood her mother's fascination with classical literature, Toby never appreciated Irina's penchant for christening her children after historical and fictional characters. Alexander, the oldest, had been named for Alexander the Great. Toby was supposed to have been a boy and was her father's only effort at naming one of his children. He'd picked out Tobias, meaning *God's goodness* in Hebrew, before she was born, and simply amended it to Toby after her birth. She'd always been grateful for her father's interference. But Irina prevailed on the remaining five—Charlemagne, Rosamond, Guinevere, Cleopatra and Mozart, or, Charlie, Rosie, Gwen, Cleo and Mo.

In spite of her late night, Toby arrived at the music store ready to face another mob. What she found was Michael waiting for her with two mugs of coffee and a bag of pastries.

"I didn't have time for breakfast," he said, and held out a sweet roll.

"Neither did I." Toby sipped the steaming coffee. "I have an idea of how we might organize the audition. I could review the sheet music before the people get to you. If I have any doubt, I'll let you decide, but I think I know enough about what you want to eliminate at least a third of them."

Michael slapped his hand on his knee and said, "We're going to make a good team. That was my plan, too."

Peeking over the rim of her cup, Toby watched Michael take a large bite of muffin and once more noticed the slight gap between his two front teeth. Without that one flaw, his looks would have been too close to perfection. Toby enjoyed real people with small idiosyncrasies and foibles much better than paragons of beauty and pompous virtue. And, although Michael was handsome, he was not arrogant or self-righteous, a refreshing change. She guessed his age to be around thirty, not too old but more confident than the young men her brothers kept parading home for her to notice.

The past twenty-four hours had been a whirlwind, and Toby relished this small moment of inactivity to consider just what type of man Michael was. She already knew he was well respected, a good businessman, kind and generous, but all these characteristics were simply a reflection of his public image. Who was the private man? The thought that Michael might be married, possibly even have children, had never occurred to her, and Toby looked at his hand to see if he was wearing a wedding ring. He wasn't, but neither did many men.

"Do you travel frequently?" she asked.

"Not often. I'm seldom gone for more than a few days."

"Who's taking care of business back in New York?"

"I have several employees who can hold the fort while I'm gone," Michael answered. "Have you forgotten Reginald already?"

Ignoring his question, Toby persisted. "Do you have a partner?"

"No."

"Where did you inherit your love of music?" she asked. "From your father?"

"Hardly," Michael said, laughing. "I don't mind discussing my family, but is there a purpose behind this sudden curiosity?"

Toby's cheeks flushed and she admitted, "I just want to know what type of a man my boss is." It was only half the reason behind her interrogation, but Toby wasn't about to blatantly ask Michael if he had a wife waiting at home for him.

"Well, then, I'm happy to oblige your professional concern. My father couldn't tell a clef sign from a bass signature. I'm the rogue in the family. He was a glorified tailor."

"Was your father displeased when you didn't take an interest in his business?"

"Why should he have objected?"

"Oh, I suppose because my father, who is a minister, was delighted when my brother Alex went to the seminary. All his life Alex has walked in our father's footsteps. Compared to good old predictable Alexander, I'm a rebel."

Michael smiled. "Oh, yes, I can see how you flout convention," he joked, flicking at the lace ruffle on her cuff. "Your dress is a touch masculine. Shades of George Sand? Or, perhaps, you have a pseudonym like George Eliot?"

"Heavens, no." Toby was enjoying the game. "Wearing men's clothing and using masculine names is old hat. If I am ever famous, I would name myself something exotic like Eloa Cassandra, or Electra Eloa, or maybe Cassandra Cellas."

Michael nearly spewed the coffee he was drinking. "Those are awful. They suit you like lead boots." He stared into her magnificent eyes and was reminded of the small light blue flowers he'd once seen. They were called bluets or angeleyes. "I'd call you Angel Eyes," he blurted out, and then immediately regretted it. His preoccupation with Toby's beauty was out of character, and he began shuffling papers to cover his embarrassment.

Toby blushed, not only at the compliment, but at the tone of his voice. There was a low, intimate catch in it, signifying something special was happening between them. It was as if Michael had whispered a secret, and a peculiar, delightful shiver started in her toes and raced through her body. Whatever it was, it had frightened him and he had immediately discouraged any further conversation.

The sudden shift in his manner was as easy to read as a grade-school hornbook and Toby took the cue to be less personal. She'd made him skittish and struggled to say something neutral. But before she could speak, Michael asked, "Just you and one brother?"

It was Toby's turn to choke. "Not quite. Three brothers and three sisters. My mother and father planned one of us for each day of the week."

He laughed at her joke and encouraged Toby to tell him about her family. She recited the history behind each of her siblings' names.

"They all sound interesting. The Sedaines are a very average group in comparison."

"At times average has a distinct advantage over eccentric. I'll never forget last summer when Mo had the chicken pox and was inside for weeks while all his friends were outside playing, catching frogs at the pond, swimming and enjoying the hot weather. After he recovered, he was embarrassed by his untanned skin and plastered himself, head to toe, with shoe polish. I had to scrub him raw to get all of it off."

The vision of the little boot-blackened boy created an amusing picture, and Michael grinned as he envisioned it. He wondered if his own son, Paul, would ever have the spunk to pull such a prank. Michael worried about his eight-year-old son but couldn't seem to get close enough to the boy to discover what was bothering him. On the other hand, Suzanne, Michael's six-year-old daughter, was cheerful, loving and voiced aloud every doubt or fear that crossed her pretty head.

Forcing his attention back to Toby's colorful description, Michael nudged his concerns aside. As he listened to Toby continue to mimic Mo's objections to the whitewashing, she was even funnier. This young woman had a carefully honed sense of humor that was both whimsical and brilliant.

"Did he survive?" Michael asked when he finally quit laughing. Too bad his grandmother couldn't accept Paul's occasional childish escapades with such grace.

"Barely."

"Poor little boy."

"What do you mean, 'poor little boy'? By the time he was flesh colored again, I was covered with polish. My hands were stained for two weeks and I had to wear gloves everywhere I went."

Michael knew he shouldn't touch her, but he did anyway and picked up her hands, turning them over. "They look fine to me." Toby's slender fingers were dwarfed by his larger ones, and he was amazed he hadn't realized how delicate she was before this. She was such a dynamic, outspoken young woman, and yet so beautiful. Since hearing her speak, he'd been intrigued by her personality but never overlooking her appeal. Toby's femininity, as well as her personality, claimed his concentration, and Michael found his usual, normally controlled response to a pretty face raging.

As accustomed as she was to a man's touch, for Toby had always enjoyed romping with her brothers, she was unprepared for the sudden clenching of her stomach when Michael took her fingers. To her, one man's hand had been no different from the next, but all her preconceived notions vanished the moment Michael's broad fingers stroked hers. The sensation was both pleasant and disturbing all at the same time, and Toby didn't know whether to jerk free or savor the warm flush that radiated all the way up her arm.

Michael gently set her hand down and took a big gulp of coffee. The echo of footsteps had alerted him that the day's influx of people was starting.

They wouldn't be alone for more than a few more seconds, and Toby searched for a lighthearted quip to ease the tension bouncing between them, but nothing came. Her usual glib humor failed her, and she silently chastised herself for letting this man knock her completely off kilter.

The room was sweltering long before midafternoon, and Toby was grateful she'd worn a lighter weight skirt and waist today, but, even so, she still felt wilted and wrinkled. She noticed Michael had shed his jacket and tie, removing his starched cuffs, rolling up his shirtsleeves and exposing the tanned skin of his forearms, which were a warm gold color. The sprinkling of hair on his arms and at the unbuttoned collar of his shirt caused her to imagine what he would look like bare chested, working in a garden the way Alexander did. It was a pleasant image and Toby's eyes closed as she mentally placed him behind the house, sinking down onto the clipped grass as she approached with a glass of cool water for him.

"Miss Wells? Miss Wells?"

Her eyes snapped open, and Toby realized Michael had called her several times before she'd heard him. "Excuse me. What did you say?"

"Pardon me, ma'am," Michael said to the woman standing next to him. "We will be right back."

He took Toby by the elbow and escorted her out onto the fire escape, where a small breeze stirred the air. "You looked as if you were about to faint. Are you feeling well?"

"I'm fine, really. I just didn't get quite enough sleep last night."

"If you're not melting, I am," he said, and smiled gently. "We should be finished in less than an hour. How about having supper with me this evening?" It wasn't exactly the way he had planned on asking her, but the invitation just blurted itself out—he seemed to do a lot of blurting in her presence. Michael rationalized his impulsive invitation by telling himself she had worked hard all day and deserved a quiet meal.

Toby was sorely tempted to say yes. Mercy, but it would be glorious to have someone else do the cooking and wait on her. Dessert would be having no dishes to wash—but she couldn't accept. She'd made no arrangements for the family and, if she relied on Rosie or Charlie to feed everyone, they would go to bed hungry. "I'm sorry but I can't. I have prior obligations, Michael."

He nearly asked what she defined as "obligations" but didn't. It was the polite way women had of saying they already had a date with another fellow. Michael hadn't realized that he had even been counting on having dinner with her until she said no. In fact, he was almost angry at her answer, but he was even more irritated with himself. Logic told him it was natural for a beautiful young woman like

Toby to have a parlor full of suitors, but logic lost out to his unexpected resentment.

Through the rest of the workday, Michael carefully studied this whimsical young lady to define what there was about her he found so engaging and precisely what was undermining his normally detached attitude toward women. He was at war with himself. He wanted to draw her close, study her flawless skin and kiss her smiling lips, but every ounce of his common sense was screaming at him to run the opposite direction. Maybe he could dispel some of his fascination if he watched closely and found a fatal flaw in her character. Michael was too well aware of the consequences of not knowing a woman well enough before he fell victim to her charms.

With clear and calculating objectivity, Michael watched the way Toby treated each person. All he could see was a manner of respect and kindness, regardless of how abhorrent the person's music was. Toby took the time to offer words of encouragement, sincere praise or gentle criticism. No one left the room feeling they had been rejected by Sedaine Music, only that they had to try just a bit harder to sell their next song. Not only was she the hardest working, most organized woman he'd ever met, but she had a kind heart. Michael realized he would have found her attractive no matter what she looked like, but her long hair, which resembled buttercup velvet, and lips that were continuously set in a sweet smile created a nearly irresistible package.

She looked tired, and Michael worried about her until he realized she was probably exhausted because she'd been out late the previous night with a beau. "Have I overworked you?" he asked peevishly the first moment they were alone, hinting she shouldn't burn her candle at both ends.

Toby was puzzled by his obvious displeasure and was quick to deny her fatigue. She didn't want Michael to think she wasn't up to snuff. "No, not at all. I could still work for hours," she lied. Even if she had been ready to drop, she wouldn't have let him know.

It was the end of the day, and he hadn't bought a single song. Plopping into a chair, Michael sighed, "I guess Saint Louis has only one Caleb MacRae."

"If you wait to find another man as gifted as Caleb, you're going to have a long vigil," Toby said.

He looked at her and became serious. "You could be as good as Caleb, Toby, but your music is too strict, too confined. Be a bit daring, unconventional."

"Mr. Sedaine," Toby feigned formality, "in all my days on this precious earth, no one has ever been reckless enough to accuse a Wells of being conventional."

The strain of the day and Michael's unwitting assumption combined to send Toby into a gale of uncontrollable laughter. If Michael had witnessed her just last week, hitching up her skirts, running for first base when she played baseball with Charlie, Cleo and Mo, he wouldn't have made such an outlandish statement. Or if he had seen her climbing the apple tree to nail together a tree house for the twins, he would have been forced to reconsider his opinion. But since he didn't really know her or anything about her family, except the few tidbits she'd shared, he was judging her by a completely standard set of values. And the one thing Toby knew she wasn't, was a typical young woman of the 1890s.

"Would you care to explain what's so amusing?" he asked.

"You would never believe me."

"Yes, I would."

"Trust me," she said. "You would think I had taken leave of my senses, and neither one of us has enough time for me to do justice to my family."

Michael's curiosity wasn't simply piqued, he was annoyed. She was in a hurry to meet her beau again and couldn't spare any time for him, but he hid his feelings as Toby collected her handbag. When she walked out the door, he went to great pains to graciously say good-night.

The following day was much like the previous one, but, rather than feeling relieved the job was almost finished, Toby was strangely melancholy. The hours she'd spent with

Michael were the happiest ones of her life and she didn't want it to end. If only it could last just a little while longer. She wasn't ready to go back to contenting herself with classes, the church choir, the Ladies Guild and taking care of the family.

"Toby," Michael said, interrupting her thoughts, "would you join me for supper?" He hoped he didn't sound too eager, but it was his final night in town and he steeled himself for her answer. His pride was tender, but it wasn't so fragile he wouldn't venture another rebuff.

"I'm sorry but I can't."

"Oh, I see, you're busy again." Despite his common sense, Michael vented his irritation. "Why don't you just say you don't like my company and spare me the embarrassment of repeated rejections?"

"My family is expecting me." Toby intentionally remained calm.

"I understand," he said sarcastically.

"I don't think you do. If I don't put supper on the table, no one else will."

"Is your mother an invalid?"

"No, but she finds it hard to be ambulatory from her coffin."

Michael was speechless. Toby's answer was so irreverent, especially coming from a preacher's daughter, he didn't know whether to laugh or offer an apology.

"Sorry," Toby said, "but I hate telling people my mother died ten years ago because it invariably leads to a long, sympathetic speech. Mama had a wonderful sense of humor and I have always known she would understand my attitude."

"Oh," was all he could manage to say. He knew exactly how she felt. After his wife, Lillian, died he had despised telling anyone he was a widower and enduring the predictable condolences.

"I've been in charge of my brothers and sisters since then. My father is a bit too preoccupied with his work to tend to everyday chores and, on a minister's salary, we can't afford a housekeeper."

He realized she had been spending all day working with him and then running a household and cooking for a family of eight after hours. Michael was consumed with guilt for having taken two days of her time and was grateful he hadn't scheduled a week in Saint Louis. The girl would drop in her traces at the pace she was keeping.

"I had no idea," he said. "Why didn't you tell me?"

"Because you wouldn't have hired me—and I wanted this job almost as much as I wanted to publish a song."

"Don't your brothers and sisters help?"

"Alex is on his honeymoon trip, Charlie is never around, Rosie is too self-centered and a terrible cook, Gwen tries very hard but she needs more experience, and the twins are too young to do anything without supervision. I'm all they have." Impulsively Toby asked, "Would you like to meet the conventional Wells family? I can guarantee you won't be bored."

"I would enjoy that very much, thank you," Michael managed to say contritely. He felt like a jackass for being jealous of a suitor that didn't exist.

"Just don't ever say I didn't warn you," Toby said, and smiled as Michael followed her out the door.

Chapter Three

Michael hadn't known what to expect, but when Toby opened the front gate guarding a two-story, neatly painted, shuttered home, this tidy house wasn't it. The yard was groomed, the porch was swept, flower boxes bloomed across the railing and pristine lace curtains hung at each window. How had she managed to maintain such order, create such an impeccable home at such a young age? Toby had been no more than a child when she'd tackled all this, and he wondered what price she'd paid for her accomplishment.

As he trailed behind Toby into the house, he noticed that although the parlor rugs were a bit frayed at the edges, the floors shone with a high gloss and the furniture gleamed from layers of beeswax. In short, everything was in absolute order.

"Toby," a young boy with blond hair and sunburned cheeks said as he bounded into the room, "you'll never guess what Cleo and I did today."

"Mind your manners, young man," Toby scolded. "We have a guest."

"Pardon me, sir. I'm Mo Wells," he said, and stuck out a rather dirty hand for Michael to shake.

"Michael Sedaine. Toby's told me a great deal about you, Mo." Releasing young Mo's hand, he couldn't help comparing him with his own son, Paul. Paul was a couple of years younger than Mo and always scrubbed spick-and-span by his grandmother until he resembled a miniature gentleman, not the child he was. Nor did Suzanne, his six-year-old daughter, ever have a ringlet out of place or a wrinkle in her starched pinafore.

"You're the fella Toby's been working for, aren't you?"

"Yes."

"How come you didn't like her songs?"

"Enough," Toby said, flushing with embarrassment. "Go get the others so they can meet Mr. Sedaine. He's staying for supper."

Although Toby had tried to prepare him for her family's individuality, Michael's head was spinning in less than ten minutes. Without any hint of pretension, Toby deposited Michael at the kitchen table while she supervised Cleo and Mo in setting the dining room table, helped Gwen roll out biscuits, nagged Rosie into slicing a plate of fresh tomatoes and reheated a giant pot of green beans.

The choreographed bustling seemed to be chaotic and haphazard, but well within minutes, Toby had the table groaning under a load of tantalizing dishes. Throughout the final preparations, each of the Wells vied for her attention. They related anecdotes about their day, sought Toby's judgment in settling minor squabbles and obviously tried to impress their guest with outrageous recitations of Toby's outstanding achievements in the one-act plays she'd produced for the church.

Michael was fascinated with the open affection displayed among the Wells and noticed Toby frequently stroked Cleo's arm, ruffled Mo's hair or patted Gwen's hand. Without thinking, she was continuously but silently reassuring and affirming that each one of them was special and loved. The way she had innocently touched him over the past three days, gently resting her hand on his arm or leaning over his shoulder to peer at a piece of music had been minor in comparison to the physical affection she lavished on her family. If he and Toby had worked together any longer, Michael wasn't certain if his restraint could withstand such a pleasing, intimate onslaught.

But Toby's unthinking, natural tenderness was blatantly opposed to Rosie's simpering flirtation. Rosie never missed a beat, never ignored a chance to brush past Michael and never masked her interest. Toby's sister's actions screamed,

"Look at me. I'm much prettier than Toby." Rosie begged for his attention and Toby was oblivious to it.

Sitting at the kitchen table, Michael was struck by how real, how alive this family was. He looked at the gleaming blue enameled pots and pans hanging from hooks on the wall and realized he didn't have the faintest idea what the kitchen looked like in his mother's house. It was the servants' domain, and none of the family were ever encouraged to step foot into it, much less sit around the table and relax. Or did Suzanne and Paul escape Grandma Laura's overbearing care by hiding with cook in the kitchen and sipping hot cocoa?

There was a great deal he didn't know about his own children, and watching Toby's complete involvement with her family made him feel as if he had abdicated his responsibilities—and forfeited the joy, as well.

"You always this quiet?" Cleo asked Michael, propping her elbows on the table and cradling her head in her hands. She stared intently into his face, waiting for an answer.

Michael mimicked her pose. "Why? Does silence scare you?"

"What an odd thing to say."

"I get the feeling the only time this house is quiet is when everyone is in bed," Michael elaborated.

Toby looked up from her work and smiled. "Not even then," she said. "The Wells are notorious for talking in their sleep."

"Hope you're not pointing a finger at me," Gwen said, picking up a platter of meat. "At least I don't sing in my sleep like some people I know."

Michael watched Toby's cheeks color and was surprised at her embarrassment. Her little secrets, small idiosyncrasies being exposed flustered her more than anything he had seen. "It beats snoring," he teased.

"Enough," Toby scolded happily. "Supper is ready."

Once they were seated, Toby fetched her father and he ambled into the room with a large, well-thumbed book held in front of his face. Michael had formed a mental image of Robert Wells, and the man was both very similar and in direct contrast to Michael's picture. The Unitarian minister was short and rotund when Michael had expected him to be tall and angular. But Toby's father was as vague and distracted in manner as she had described. Michael was quickly learning Toby did not exaggerate. If anything, she underplayed reality.

"Good evening, Mr. Sedaine," Robert Wells said. "We don't often have the opportunity of having such a distinguished guest."

Michael was prepared to respond to the compliment, but his reply was cut off when the man bowed his head to say grace and immediately afterward propped the book in front of his face and silently began eating. Robert never said another word as the conversation swirled about him.

Staring across the table at Toby, Michael could see she was unfazed by her father's actions, just as everyone else seemed to be. When she had described her father as being distant and distracted, Michael had thought she meant on occasion, not perpetually.

Despite the Reverend Robert Wells's fixation with an abstract text about Buddha, and his using the tome as armor to avoid socializing, Michael felt at home. Each of Toby's siblings made a point of drawing him into the conversation, asking his opinion, begging him to describe New York and hounding him to tell them about his travels in Europe when he was a student.

He had never been the center of so much attention in his life. The exuberance was so intense, Michael was sure if there was a scale to measure vitality, the reading would hit the highest mark.

"Has my presence," he whispered to Toby while the others talked over one another, "caused this uproar?"

"The truth is," she answered, "they're on their best behavior. Do the incessant questions bother you?"

"No. Not at all. New York society could take a few lessons from the Wells," Michael joked but also meant it seriously. "The art of polite conversation is dull."

Toby couldn't imagine anything about New York being boring. It was the greatest metropolis in the country, the center of the arts, the home of the nation's wealthiest financiers such as J. P. Morgan, the Vanderbilts and An-

drew Carnegie. Saint Louis was a poor relation to its big
sister on the Atlantic.

"Don't you find the atmosphere in New York exciting?" she asked.

"As an adult, yes. But never as a child. I longed for a
family like yours with lots of other children around all the
time."

"Really?" Toby had thought Michael would be appalled by the down-to-earth Wells brood, and instead he
seemed to be enjoying every second.

"Absolutely."

Before the dishes were cleared, Cleo batted her pretty
little eyes at Michael and pleaded, "Mr. Sedaine, do you
know any good games we could play?"

"Well," he hesitated, teasing the little girl, "hmm, how
about charades?"

"No," Mo vetoed, "I never guess right."

"How about *tableaux vivants?*"

"Never heard of it," Mo sneered. "Sounds like a disease."

Overriding her twin's objection, Cleo took Michael by
the hand and led him into the parlor. Followed by the rest
of the family, even the elusive Mr. Wells, Michael explained the game's simple rules. Two people would team
up, go out into the lighted hall and decide what book they
could portray. Meanwhile, the lamps would be turned very
low in the parlor so the doorway from the hall was illuminated like a stage.

Mo was paired with Michael as the first team and they
left the room to choose their book. "What about *Tom, the
Bootblack?*" Michael suggested.

"No fair. Toby put in the squeak, didn't she?" Mo accused.

Keeping a tight rein on his smile, Michael played innocent. "What could she have told me?"

"'Bout my chicken pox."

"Not a word, my man."

"Still, I'd rather do 'The Emperor's New Clothes.'"

"Who is going to stand naked?" Michael laughed. "Not me. Pick another story, young man." Mo's mischievousness delighted him.

"Spoil-pudding," Mo grumbled. "Let's try *Through the Looking-Glass.*"

"Good choice."

The game was like pretending to be a statue frozen in movement; no words or actions were allowed. Mo's selection was a perfect one to begin with, and Rosie and Charlie shouted out the title. Some of the most successful representations were suggested by Robert Wells. He used many biblical stories and they were great fun to portray.

It was a wonderful interlude after the strain of the past few days, and Michael basked in the simple pleasure. He was like a child himself, totally caught up in the frolic. Normally on one of these business trips he didn't miss his children, because he was too harried to think about them. But not tonight. Tonight he wished Paul and Suzanne were with him, romping and laughing with Toby's family.

As an encore, Rosie suggested, "I'd like to sing a song for Mr. Sedaine. Toby, will you play the piano?"

Toby objected. "Michael spends all day long listening to amateurs." Besides, Toby thought, I want Rosie to stay as far away as possible from him. As soon as she realized what she'd thought, even if it had only been in her mind, she was shocked. Michael had become more important than a boss, more important than a possible publisher for her music. He was the first man she had ever wanted to know better, know intimately. It was the most exhilarating and frightening revelation in her life.

Pursing her lips into a childish pout, Rosie said sweetly, "But I'm not trying to sell myself like you are, Toby."

Michael saw the fury spark out of Toby's eyes. He'd heard of competitive sisters, but, having none himself, he'd never witnessed such rivalry. Rescuing Rosie, sure Toby was likely to strangle her at any moment, he said, "I'm never too tired to hear another lovely woman sing."

Rosie smiled triumphantly as Toby grudgingly sat at the piano.

Seeing the two of them side by side, Michael noted their family resemblance, but he was also acutely aware of their differences. Both had blond hair, blue eyes and lovely figures, but Toby's beauty was natural. When she moved, smiled or laughed there was nothing artificial or calculated about it. Rosie, on the other hand, strained to be elegant and amusing.

Rosie's affected mannerisms toned when she started to sing. Her voice was strong enough to remove any pretense and she relaxed. By the end of the recital, Michael was impressed with her talent. "You have a charming voice, Rosie. Have you had any formal training?"

Glancing at Toby, Rosie said, "No, some of us are just born with talent."

Michael desperately wanted to laugh but knew Toby found nothing humorous about her sister's snide remark. "It's amazing that one family should have *two* gifted women," he said diplomatically.

Finally Toby sent the younger children to bed, and Mr. Wells went back to his study. Toby hoped to have a few moments alone with Michael but, of course, Rosie had a different plan.

"Would you like to see our grape arbor?" Rosie asked Michael. "Mother planted a hardy variety, which people find quite interesting."

"It's your night to wash dishes," Toby said before Michael could answer.

"Yes, but Gwen offered to trade chores."

"I did not," Gwen said.

"But Guinevere, it's our responsibility to be kind to Mr. Sedaine," Rosie wheedled. "I'm sure you wouldn't want our guest to think we're rude, would you?"

"No," Toby said, ending the brewing argument, "we wouldn't. That's why Mr. Sedaine and I are going to have coffee on the front porch while you do the dishes, Rosamond."

Toby considered pinching Rosie's arm to add emphasis to her unspoken warning to leave Michael alone, but she rejected the idea. Michael Sedaine was a grown man who didn't require her protection.

"A cup of coffee sounds perfect, and a taste of night air is too inviting to pass by," Michael said, grabbing Toby's offer like a drowning man clutches a log.

"Make yourself comfortable on the porch swing," Toby said. "I'll be right with you."

The moment Michael was out of earshot, Toby whirled on Rosie. "If you so much as poke your head out the front door, Rosamond Annabelle Wells, I promise you'll regret it."

"What's wrong, Toby? Jealous?"

"Mr. Sedaine and I only work together. But, I find your fawning over him to be personally insulting. Act like a lady, not a Jezebel."

Rosie stomped out of the kitchen, slamming down a stack of dirty pans in her anger. Toby had never understood her sister's venomous attitude and had long since given up trying to mend the chasm between them. Rosie was self-centered but, at least, pleasant with all the other children.

Toby fixed a tray to take onto the porch and, when she joined Michael, he was lazily drifting back and forth on the glider. The instant she appeared, he jumped to his feet.

"I need to apologize for Rosie's behavior. She's a bit trying at times," Toby said, hoping Michael wasn't offended by Rosie's flirting.

"There's nothing to apologize for. She's just young and impressionable."

"And a test of my patience."

"You've done a wonderful job, Toby," Michael said, taking the tray from her and setting it down. "Each one of those kids knows they're loved. They are secure enough to risk being honest and open with the world." She handed him a cup and took one herself and sat beside him.

"We are a unique bunch."

"That's what I like about your family, the diversity, and that's what I was trying to tell you earlier. Small families can't compete with the joy of a large one. It's just not possible."

"I suppose you're right," Toby said, "but you've only seen us on our best behavior. Wait until Cleo and Mo start arguing about the last cookie. Then I'm not so certain you'd be as thrilled."

"Oh, I don't know. There are a couple of children I'd love to see fight once in a while."

"What children never fight?" Toby asked, not believing there were two such creatures on earth.

"Paul and Suzanne," Michael answered, unconsciously giving the glider a little push with his foot. "They're..."

The swing's sudden movement caused Toby's coffee to slosh over the brim onto her lap. She jumped up and shook her skirts while Michael grabbed a napkin to mop up the spill.

"Sorry," he said. "I didn't expect this blasted thing to move so easily."

"No harm," Toby assured him. "Have a cookie. They're safe."

"You bake these?" he said after he tasted a gingersnap. She nodded and sat down again.

"They're even better than our cook's." Michael pretended to concentrate on the cookies while he considered what he was about to say. He had been hatching a plan ever since Toby had started working for him but, after this evening, he was positive she wouldn't consider the proposition. Even so, Michael couldn't leave without trying.

"Toby," he said, "I've really enjoyed working with you. You're efficient and have a good ear, you're bright and well educated. I know I've said it before, but we make a splendid team."

"Thank you. I respect your opinion and I've learned a good deal working with you."

"I just wish you could come to New York with me, but I understand completely why you can't."

Toby planted her feet on the porch and halted the swing in mid-arc. "What did you just say?"

"I was planning on making my temporary job offer a permanent one, but I knew you would refuse to leave Saint Louis."

"What kind of a job?"

"Doing just what you've been doing when I visit Chicago, Detroit, Columbus and Richmond. Once we were back in New York, I would have put you in charge of song revisions, negotiating contracts and interviewing people.''

"What kind of salary were you considering?" Toby asked softly. Her heart was dancing a wild jig, but she ignored it and attempted to sound poised.

"One hundred dollars a month."

Vaulting off the swing, Toby sent the tray and cookies scattering across the porch. "What makes you think I wouldn't want the job? I'd love to work for Sedaine Music."

Michael was both elated and perplexed. He'd assumed her family was completely dependent upon her, unable to function without her, and yet, she was willing to move to New York. It didn't make sense. "But what about your family?"

"Alex and his bride, Mary, plan on moving in with us anyway. They want to save their money to buy a house and furniture. Mary can take my place."

"Aren't Cleo and Mo too young to leave?" Michael couldn't believe he was discouraging her. He needed a competent assistant desperately, but here he was playing devil's advocate.

She quit bouncing around on her toes and sat back down next to him. "Have you changed your mind?" she asked. "Don't you want me to come? You don't have to pay me nearly that much money."

"Money has nothing to do with it," Michael said, and picked up her hand, leaning close to her. "I just don't want you to make a rash decision you'll regret. I want to be certain you'll be happy."

It was hard to think clearly when Michael whispered in his deep baritone. She couldn't distinguish if it was the night breeze or his warm breath brushing her cheek that was sending shivers skittering up and down her spine. What she knew for certain was that with her fingers clutched between his two palms, Toby felt the exact same cuddly feeling she'd had when he'd first held her hand.

But Michael wasn't discussing a personal relationship, he was outlining a business one, and Toby forced herself to focus on the latter. Besides, she didn't have time for a man in her life—at least not for years and years.

"You're probably going to think what I'm about to say is very selfish," Toby began, "but it's the truth. I've devoted myself to this family for ten years. They're my brothers and sisters, not my children. I made my mother a promise and I've kept it. Now it's my turn to finally do what I want.

"I want more from life than just scrubbing floors, weeding gardens, washing dirty clothes, preserving vegetables and baking bread. Consequently, I've avoided getting married when many of my friends already have children of their own. Right now, marriage would be like indentured servitude."

"Thousands of women would disagree with you," he said, amazed at the degree of Toby's conviction. Lillian had been quite content as Mrs. Michael Sedaine. Content and boring.

"But I don't want to be just like every other woman. I want to be someone special."

Michael sympathized and was pleased he was giving her the chance she deserved. It was obvious she'd sacrificed her youth to a grown woman's responsibilities and was chafing for the freedom she'd missed. If she was determined to leave Saint Louis, he wanted to protect her when she ventured away from her sheltered environment out into the world.

Tenderly Michael brushed a lock of hair off Toby's cheek. "You don't have to leave right now. Think about the job for as long as you need. I'll leave an itinerary and you can wire me with your answer."

"I should stay until Alex and Mary arrive. Where will you be in four days?"

"Chicago."

"I'll meet you there—and I won't change my mind."

"I think I should speak to your father. Reassure him."

Toby stood up and walked across the porch. Being close to Michael was dangerous. "Let me handle my father. He loves me, but he doesn't have the vaguest notion who I really am. Besides," Toby grinned impishly, "he never questions my decisions, and he might not even notice I'm gone if we don't tell him."

Michael would have doubted that about any other father but Toby's. "If you're positive you want to go, I should let him know you'll be safe. Once we reach New York, you can stay with my mother as long as you like. I'll wire her before I leave town."

Toby was moved by Michael's concern, but, unaccustomed to any nurturing, she didn't know how to react. "You don't have to do that. I can stay in a hotel."

"After living out of a suitcase for three weeks, my mother's home will be a welcome change."

This conversation about traveling, hotels, the Sedaine home and a completely new life didn't overwhelm Toby. She'd been waiting for a chance, any chance, to escape Saint Louis and foster the career her family and friends had said would never happen. Now that she had this opportunity, nothing would stop her. Nothing.

"I can't tell you how much I appreciate this," Toby said. "Thank you doesn't seem adequate."

He nearly wrapped his arms around her and showed her precisely how he wanted Toby to thank him, but Michael held back. It was true he'd offered her a job because she was the closest thing to perfection he'd ever find in an assistant, but the fact that he found her attractive troubled him. She was hard to resist, but if he had learned anything from Lillian, from marriage, it was that physical attraction wasn't enough.

His ground rules for hiring Toby were unspoken but clear in his mind. He'd foster their friendship, work with her, travel with her and dine with her, but each night he'd leave her at the door of her solitary hotel room. Michael had no intention of capitalizing on his attraction to Toby or fostering a more intimate relationship. He hadn't been looking for a woman to complicate his life when he'd come to this city, and he'd be damned if he'd leave with one.

But he also realized keeping his hands and his thoughts to himself was going to be the closest he hoped he would ever come to the fires of hell.

* * *

Toby rose earlier than usual. Even the barn swallows nesting in the eaves above her window hadn't let out a good-morning peep when she dressed, made her bed and headed for the kitchen to start breakfast for the family. Because of her decision to follow Michael, she was as giddy as a clown and just as unable to remain still.

In her exuberance, she whipped up a batch of waffle batter, scrambled a huge bowl of eggs, sliced a slab of bacon and opened a jar of her prized strawberry preserves. When she gave the family the news of her great fortune, Toby wanted to ease their reactions with a celebration feast.

The table, the family meal, was the one place when all of the Wells were together. Eating was more than a necessity, it was a ritual where everyone took the time to share in each other's lives. As the food was passed around, dreams were revealed, goals were discussed, benign gossip was bandied about, and, sometimes, troubles were eased by simply getting them out in the open.

"Mmm." Charlie sighed at the delicious smells emanating from the wood-burning Monarch stove. "Is it Christmas morning or am I dreaming?" He kissed the top of Toby's head and then rested his chin on her golden crown of curls as if she were a pillow, as if he were still tired and not quite awake.

"No, but it might as well be," Toby almost chirped.

"What's my big sister brewing?" he asked, and spun her around to look down into her eyes. He may have been almost a foot taller than Toby, but he would always think of her as his big sister.

"It's wonderful news, Charlie, but you'll have to wait until everyone is down for breakfast." He hadn't been home last night and hadn't met Michael, so there was a lot to tell her brother.

Charlie stared at her quizzically, trying to figure out the reason for her gaiety. "Saints preserve us—" he laughed "—but you haven't gone and fallen in love, have you?"

She put both her hands on his chest and shoved him away. "Hardly, Charlemagne."

"Oh, that's right," he said as he pretended to pout at the brutality of using his given name, "you plan on being a spinster."

"I do not!" Toby was certainly reluctant to be wed, but she had no intention of being an old maid. Someday a special man would come along who was liberal, supportive, romantic yet strong.

Someone like Michael Sedaine, she thought and then blushed. Michael was all those things, but he was just her employer, her means of getting to New York. New York men were probably all like him—urbane, educated, good mannered and advanced in their attitude toward women. Those qualities alone made a man "romantic" to a midwestern girl like her.

"Watch out, pip-squeak," Charlie taunted, "or you'll deny yourself right into marriage." He ducked the flick of her towel and ran off to rouse the rest of the family.

"Pip-squeak?" Toby shouted after him. "I can still take you over my knee!"

She had no favorites among her brothers and sisters, but Charlie owned her heart. He was a rascal who made her laugh, and he could insult and charm her in the same breath.

The family filed in one by one and dove into the sumptuous meal. But it wasn't until her father was seated that Toby sat down herself.

"Papa," she said, spooning a dollop of whipped cream onto his waffle.

"Hmm?" he answered, but continued to read the morning newspaper.

"Papa?"

"Yes, daughter, I'm listening."

"Michael has asked me to work for him. I will be meeting him in Illinois. He's leaving today without me, but I'll catch up after I pack my things and tie up some loose ends."

Loose ends were the whole family's needs. Alex and his new wife, Mary, were due back in four days, and Toby had a volume of notes to make so the reins of the family could be handed over without causing a disruption. There were

Mo's piano lessons, Cleo's school party, Papa's socks, which still needed darning, Charlie had been nagging her to help him decide which classes to take for the fall semester at the university, Gwen probably needed spectacles, and a hundred other matters to tend to before leaving.

"We'll hold auditions all the way back to New York. After we arrive, it will mean a great deal of work publishing all we've bought."

"That's nice, dear," Robert Wells mumbled. "It will be good for you."

"Oh, Papa," she bubbled happily, "I thought I was going to have to persuade you to let me move to New York." Toby leaned over and kissed him on his whiskered cheek.

"Persuade me to do what?" he asked, finally lifting his eyes from the newspaper.

"Why, go to New York. I just told you I've been offered a wonderful job."

"I think it's swell," Charlie piped up. "New York's the place to make your name... or change it." He winked at Toby.

"You'll be able to see the latest Parisian designs before they reach Saint Louis," Rosie exclaimed. "I'll visit you and have a gown made up in one of those fashionable shops."

"What are all of you babbling about?" their father asked irritably.

"New York," Mo answered. "Toby is moving to New York."

"What in heaven's name for?" Papa demanded. "Your family is here."

Toby watched her father begin twirling her mother's wedding band, which he kept on his watch chain. He only toyed with the gold ring when he was annoyed and struggling to master his temper or was deep in thought. Long ago, Toby had learned the secret of reading his moods from this habit.

"To marry Mr. Sedaine," Gwen teased.

"Hush up," Toby warned her. "I have no intention of marrying him. He's my employer and that's all."

"Well, Mr. Rogers was only Beth Carroll's butcher *until* she married him," Gwen countered.

"If you don't want him," Rosie scolded, "I'll take him."

"You'd marry Dorian Gray," Toby said, referring to the scandalous book of Oscar Wilde's. Everyone was talking about the handsome but evil hero.

Robert Wells stood and slammed the flat of his hand on the table. "Not another word out of any of you. Now, Toby, what is all this ruckus?"

She had expected her father to be startled, but he was more than surprised—he was angry. His temper only served to put steel into her resolution.

"Michael Sedaine has offered me a job with his music publishing house in New York City. It's a perfect opportunity to learn more about composing and to eventually sell my own songs."

"Are you just going to abandon your brothers and sisters?"

Guilt was a powerful weapon to use on Toby. Normally she buckled under its weight but not this time. "Mary has already said she's looking forward to helping out here."

"Mary is an outsider."

"Mary is your daughter-in-law, Alexander's wife, and therefore, a Wells. She is also going to take my place in this house."

"You don't have my permission," her father announced firmly.

Toby flinched. "I'm not asking for it, Papa. I'm telling you."

The other children gulped audibly. Their father was a kind, quiet man, but none of them ever dared to challenge him. Toby's defiance was the first time any of them had countermanded him.

"A woman's place is with her family. She should stay with her mother, if she was still alive, with her father who's still standing here, and with her brothers and sisters who still need her. Someday, she will go on to her husband's family and raise children of her own."

Toby's anger reached a pitch she had never experienced. "Preferably with one of those pasty-faced divinity students, I suppose? Have a dozen sniveling little monsters, too?''

''Is that what you think of your siblings? Monsters?''

She looked at Mo, Cleo, Charlie, Rosie and Gwen and regretted her angry words. ''Of course not, Papa. They are blessings, just like you've always said. But I want a life of my own.''

Why does he have to start interfering now? she wondered. For years he had drifted along, letting her do things her way. Why decide to meddle today?

''Papa, it's a different world than when you and Mama married. Women have choices now. Women have careers.''

''Beware of what you choose,'' he scorned. ''You need a father or husband to guide you.''

Toby rose from her chair and faced him. ''I do not need anyone, father. I *am* going to New York.''

They stared at each other in silence and each knew the other would not bend.

''Sit down and finish your breakfast,'' Charlie said, attempting to placate them.

''I'm not hungry,'' Robert Wells answered. He turned and left the room for his study.

''Neither am I,'' Toby said. In tears, she darted out of the kitchen and ran upstairs.

The bedroom she shared with Rosie suddenly seemed claustrophobic and childish. The first-place ribbon she had won in the high school talent show now mocked her. Did her father really want that to be the last time she would prove to the world what she could do? The dolls she had given up when the twins were born still sat on the bay window seat. Her music books were stacked on the bookshelf along with all her compositions.

Looking at the leftovers from her childhood, Toby realized that if she didn't leave this minute, she never would. In four days her guilt would dilute her ambition, her sense of responsibility would weaken her need to escape, and her love for her father would erase her determination.

Wiping her tears with the back of her hand, Toby pulled out her portmanteau from the closet. Michael's train would be leaving in less than an hour, but she could catch him at the depot if she hurried. She flung clothes into the suitcase, not bothering to carefully fold them.

"What are you doing, Toby?" Cleo asked from the doorway.

"I'm going to New York."

"Now?" Mo had come up behind his twin.

"Yes."

"When you make a lot of money, will you buy me a new wagon?" Mo asked. He didn't appear to be the least upset about Toby's departure.

"It'll be the first present on my list."

"I want anagram tiles," Cleo said.

Toby had expected the twins to cry and cling to her skirts, but they didn't. Like all children, they adapted quickly and with surprising flexibility. "Be good for Alex and Mary, will you?"

"That would be boring," Charlie said as he joined the group. "We want to make Mary feel at home, don't we?"

Rosie pushed her way through the jam at the door. "Who's going to fix dinner tonight?" she demanded.

"You, my darling Rosamond," Toby answered. "For a few days you're going to pull your weight around here."

"And we're going to lose weight," Charlie joked. "Rosie is about the worst cook in the state."

The packing was done and Toby turned to Charlie. "Will you drive me to the station?"

"I'll get the carriage."

She kissed the twins goodbye, hugged Rosie and Gwen before going downstairs to her father's study. Ordering her tears to stem themselves, Toby knocked on the door.

"Come in," her father grumbled.

Toby toted her suitcase into the room, letting it tell her father of her decision.

"I see you've made up your mind," Robert Wells grunted unhappily.

"Yes."

"Do you have money?"

"I've been saving my pin money for years."

He rose from his desk and paced angrily. "I could stop you. I could call the sheriff and tell him you're disobeying me."

"I know, Papa, but you won't." Her father would do everything within his power but never use an authority outside of the family to control his children.

"If your mother was still alive, she would be able to put an end to this madness."

"If Mama was here," Toby said angrily, "she would have seven more children to handle and would be too busy to worry about me."

It was a cruel thing to say, but her father's ire was cruel, too. Why couldn't he let her go, give her his blessing and be happy?

"If it had been God's will," Robert Wells said sadly.

"I have a will, too, Papa."

"A mighty stubborn one, daughter. Be off with you, then."

She turned without crossing the carpet to her father. It was the first time in her life she had ever left the house without hugging and kissing him goodbye.

Charlie tried to cheer her up on the drive to the depot. He kept up a monologue, reassuring her she was doing the right thing. Still, by the time he left her at the boarding gate, Toby was on the verge of turning back home. But the sight of Michael climbing up the steps to the coach changed her mind. He was her future, he was the man who would change her life.

"Michael," she almost wailed to get his attention. "Wait for me."

He turned at the sound of her voice, a voice that was prettier than any music he had ever bought. "Toby? What are you doing here? Come to see me off?"

She wiggled through the line of other passengers and faced him. Glints of sunlight danced in the tears cradled at the corners of her eyes.

"No. I've decided to come with you now."

"But what of all the things you had to finish before you left?" he asked, feeling helpless seeing her weep so quietly.

"They're done with," she whispered. "There was no point in waiting."

He felt selfish, but he was pleased to see her, to have her accompany him, no matter what the reason—and, obviously, the reason she had moved up her departure was painful.

"Come along," he coaxed, taking her by the shoulder. "I'll help you get settled."

He wanted to do more than help her. He longed to pull her close to his chest, wrap her tightly in his arms and steady the trembling he felt when he touched her. Toby Wells, the little firecracker of a woman, the lady who could conquer a mob, rule a home, tame a wild score, was frightened. It touched his heart and he felt himself tremble, as well.

Chapter Four

Three weeks of auditions had taken their toll, and Toby struggled against the increasing temptation to burst out laughing at the young man who was playing his music. Peeking at Michael, she saw he too was on the edge of hysterics and was attempting to smother it by clamping his hand over his face. The composition was not any worse than many others they had heard, but nearly a month of listening to scandalous creations had worn down their ability to remain impassive.

Toby prayed she and Michael could smother their laughter for just five more minutes. This audition in Richmond was the last one on the tour before they headed back to New York, and she didn't want to be the one who marred their success by acting incompetent. Michael had made too many remarks about how much he appreciated her professional manner to risk spoiling her perfect record now.

At the end of the piece, Michael sent the young man on his way with kind words and waited until the door was closed and the retreating footsteps silent before he unleashed his laughter. "A wheelbarrow could have made better music."

"You're too complimentary." Toby giggled.

She stood up and shrugged her shoulders to loosen the knots in her muscles while Michael collapsed into his swivel chair. "I'm exhausted," she said, sighing. "How do you feel?"

"Like celebrating. Shall we go to a fine restaurant and order champagne?"

Since she'd left Saint Louis, Toby had done nothing with her free time but eat sumptuous meals in restaurants. She would never have thought it possible, but a plain home-cooked supper sounded appealing.

"No," she hedged. "I'd like to go for a long, leisurely stroll instead."

"The park? It's still light."

"Capitol Square. It's supposed to be beautiful." Toby felt giddy and free. It was the first time since she'd left home that she'd had an opportunity to see anything more than crowded audition halls, monotonous hotel rooms, dreary railroad cars and unending miles of train tracks.

"Then the Capitol Building it is," Michael said, standing up and grabbing his coat. Toby's enthusiasm was contagious—everything about her was. Her laughter infected his sense of humor, her beauty influenced his vision, and her innocence swayed his judgment. If she wasn't so guileless he would have kissed her, but how would she interpret his motive? Would she see him as a miscreant, a depraved employer? Or would she accept it for what it was? A sign of friendship and affection. There was no way Michael could read her thoughts.

As he was straightening his collar, Toby stepped up to him until the flounce of her bodice almost brushed his shirt studs. Michael sucked in his breath as he always did when Toby came so close, which she had an unnerving habit of consistently doing! She was repeatedly leaning over his shoulder to scan the music he was reading, brushing her cheek near his ear. Her proximity reduced his determination to bewildering chaos, and why not? She owned skin like smooth porcelain, possessed a fetching profile, which was dominated by incredible eyes, blue angel eyes, and all of it was framed by hair like velvet.

"Here," Toby said as she took a handkerchief out of her sleeve, "you smudged ink on your face." Standing on her tiptoes, she tried to buff the streak from his forehead, but he was too tall. "Bend down a little."

He was afraid to lean down. If he so much as relaxed one nerve he would swoop her into his arms. After all, a man could only resist temptation for so long before he succumbed, and each moment he had spent with her had fueled his desire. Toby's beauty, sense of humor and provocative mien were driving him mad, and the promise he had made to himself was fading.

Back in Saint Louis he had vowed to only think of Toby Wells as an efficient and organized employee. What a fool he had been—he had made a pact with the devil and now he was roasting.

"Please, Michael," she insisted, gently tugging on his lapels.

He relented, and Toby inhaled the sweet lemon fragrance that always permeated his breath. Unlike so many men who smelled of a stale cigar, Michael had a penchant for lemon drops, and he kept a supply cached in his shirt pocket. As she rubbed away the ink, she found her own breath mingling with his, and a moist, warm air swirled between them. There was something magical about sharing the same space, the same moment and she trembled ever so slightly.

"Cold?" he whispered, but he was really questioning his own shaking.

"No, I'm too warm," she said, confused by the sudden flush she was feeling and the way her knees were wobbling.

His reserve crumbled like a dry, brittle leaf, and he drew her into his arms. Her caress, her touch was no more than a sisterly action, but it was one touch too many. Weeks of honorable, gentlemanly behavior was discarded without a second's hesitation and even less thought of the consequences.

Michael was confident she wanted to be kissed as much as he wanted to kiss her, for he could read the beguiling look in her wide, expectant eyes. All his intellectualizing and ignoring his reactions to this beautiful lady fell to his emotions. This moment was what he had been dreaming about since she'd flashed those marvelous angel eyes at him in Saint Louis.

As his mouth covered hers, Toby felt her lips open like a bud in warm sunshine. This flowering in Michael's arms was unexpected, and she was defenseless but welcomed his intensity. She had been kissed before, but what Michael was doing to her wasn't within the realm of her experience. Divinity students had pecked at her cheek, planted their dry mouths on hers, but Michael was creating an unfamiliar desire she adored.

He felt her response and boldly tasted her sweetness with his tongue, sensing her brief hesitation before she began her own exploration. She drew her hands around his neck, urging him to hold her closer. The intensity of Toby's reaction shocked Michael back to his senses and he abruptly released her.

Was she responding to him or just to being kissed for the first time in her life? It didn't matter. He had stumbled down this dangerous path before, this blind alley of passion that led to disillusionment and estrangement once the novelty faded. After Lillian's death Michael had promised himself he would never repeat the mistake. Love didn't last. Enduring relationships were based on common interests, shared goals and mutual respect. Everything that had been missing from his marriage.

Why did he have to feel so guilty every time he thought about his wife? Lillian had been a lovely young lady intensely in love with love, and Michael had simply been the initial object of her infatuation. Long before she died in the train accident, they had both known the marriage was over. One year of happiness followed by three of misery. The price they had paid for maintaining the sham of happiness had been too steep for the fleeting rewards.

He would never marry a woman because he thought he loved her. If he ever proposed to a lady, it would be for sound, rational reasons that might one day turn to love. Better to have a reliable, levelheaded wife at your side than a gorgeous lady in your bed. Michael had been a fool to believe he could be close to Toby's beauty and not be tempted to touch it, taste it and hold it in his arms.

During the four years since Lillian's death he hadn't been celibate, but he had been careful not to become seriously involved with a woman. Toby was the first threat to his precious independence, the independence he must preserve.

"Did I do something wrong?" Toby asked, hurt by his sudden withdrawal and the lengthy silence. "Tell me...."

"Shh," he hushed. "You didn't do anything wrong, but working next to you and keeping my distance has probably been the hardest task in my life."

"I know," she admitted.

"No, you don't know," he said harshly, and walked away from Toby. "I take full responsibility for stepping over the boundaries of our relationship."

"Just what are those boundaries?" Toby demanded. She had thought Michael found her attractive, but now she wasn't sure what his motives were. All she really knew was that she had wanted him to kiss her, and he was acting as if he had committed a crime.

"We shouldn't mix business with pleasure. We're too good a professional team to ruin by becoming temporarily cozy."

Toby couldn't stop her anger from surfacing. "Cozy? You make me sound like a bed warmer!"

"I wasn't implying such a thing." Michael was shocked by her frank analogy.

"You weren't? Thank you, Mr. Sedaine. I'm certainly pleased to learn you're not the type of man who has never just used a woman and then walked away and forgotten her," she goaded sarcastically. After the way he kissed her, she would be hornswoggled rather than believe he didn't have more than just business relationships with women.

Toby's accusation flooded him with shame, and the women he had known over the past few years mocked him. Bed warmers! He had never thought of them in such ugly terms. "That's unfair. Since my wife died I haven't—"

"Wife?"

"Yes, Lillian. She died in a train accident four, almost five years ago."

Toby was torn in opposing directions. Part of her was livid he had never mentioned being a widower, but she tried to rationalize his omission by telling herself Michael didn't owe her his life's history just because they worked together. Regardless of how levelheaded she tried to be, Michael's surprising revelation spurred a dozen more questions, but it wasn't her place or the proper time to ask any of them.

"I'm sorry, Michael," Toby finally said. "It must have been very hard for you."

"Yes, yes," he answered brusquely, irritated at once more fending off condolences he didn't deserve.

His abrupt dismissal of her sympathy was confusing. The only explanation was that Michael was still deeply grieving for his wife. "Were you injured, too?" she asked, hating herself for prying but still needing to know what happened.

"No." Michael sighed and gathered his papers together, "I wasn't there." How many times did he have to go through the story? The multiple renditions didn't ease his conscience or his guilt for not missing Lillian. He couldn't very well admit to people that her death hadn't left as big a hole in his life as they assumed. "She was in Belgium visiting relatives and was on her way to Paris. Fortunately, Lillian left Paul and Suzanne with their nurse and they weren't on the train when it derailed."

"Paul and Suzanne? Nurse?" Either the two people he was talking about were elderly invalids or, to Toby's total dismay, Michael was the father of two children.

"My children," he answered, smiling for the first time since this conversation began. "Suzanne is six and Paul is eight."

"Don't you think you could have mentioned them before this?" She was beyond editing her queries or her feelings.

Michael didn't need an interpreter to detect Toby's anger. "Why? Is it necessary for an employer to submit a biography when he hires an assistant?"

"I thought we were friends, not just boss and flunky. When you visited my home, my family, you just might have made a comment or two about yours," Toby countered.

"I started to several times but something, or someone, always interrupted me. You must admit that getting a word in edgewise in your house is a trick. Besides, I was about to tell you when I spilled coffee in your lap that night on the porch swing. The opportunity to bring it up again didn't occur." Having to defend himself was galling. He didn't owe her explanations or excuses. All he owed her was a weekly paycheck.

"Now that you have my undivided, uninterrupted attention, is there anything else you'd like to tell me?" How could the first man she had ever been interested in have children? It was as ludicrous as a teetotaler being attracted to a souse. Toby's dreams never included children, not even her own, and she had almost made a fatal mistake of falling in love with a man who already had two.

"Since you've asked, yes," Michael said icily. "I'd appreciate it if you would not be so informal when we're alone."

"Informal? You have the nerve to accuse *me* of anything?"

"I've struggled to behave like a gentleman despite your casual manner."

"And what manner is that? Please, Mr. Sedaine, explain it to me in detail so there won't be any further misunderstandings."

"You can't deny you're free with your touch. How many times have I brought my cheek up next to yours while *you* work? How many times have I adjusted your collar?"

"You have a vile, base mind, Mr. Sedaine," she retaliated. "How dare you accuse me of being a flirt!" In her whole life no one had ever had cause to criticize her morals. It was an insult that had always been reserved for Rosie. "If you feel that way, perhaps I should exchange my ticket to New York for one back to Missouri?"

"Do what you wish. If you feel like a schoolgirl, you might as well act like one." He dropped his stack of papers onto the desk and they resounded like a bomb, emphasizing his frustration.

His papers slid every which way and Toby reined in her fury. Stiffly she walked over to the desk and restacked them. She would never give this man the satisfaction of running back home. Toby had left Saint Louis with a purpose and had been temporarily sidetracked, but she was back on course with her goals firmly in sight. If her boss didn't have enough self-control to handle anything more than a cold, detached relationship befitting two adults who merely work together, then she would show him she was highly capable and willing to follow his orders.

"I think that's an excellent suggestion, Mr. Sedaine. Thank you for pointing out my carelessness. Next time I will let you spend the entire day with ink stains all over your face. Obviously I misunderstood your motives when you kissed me, but please don't distress yourself. It won't happen again."

Michael walked over to her and tried to take the sting out of her temper. "You're twisting my words," he said, raking his fingers through his hair. "I should never have kissed you, but you don't understand that men and women who work together just don't act the way you do."

"I realize that I don't have nearly as much experience as you do," Toby said through clenched teeth, "and I apologize for my shortcomings. What time does our train leave in the morning, Mr. Sedaine?"

"Seven o'clock."

"Fine. I'll meet you at the station."

Michael walked Toby to her hotel room without ever saying a word and left her at her door as if she were a package being delivered by an indifferent messenger.

Leaning against the solid strength of the heavy door, Toby finally released the tears that had been threatening to disgrace her ever since Michael mentioned Lillian. The joy, the anticipation of their stroll around the capital was forgotten as she sank to the floor in a crumpled heap. But much worse than the minor loss of a short jaunt was the realization that the exhilaration she had harbored about going to New York had been destroyed.

Chapter Five

For Toby, the train ride from Richmond to New York was like making the journey alone. Michael had not literally abandoned her, but he had emotionally deserted her. While she caught up with the entries in her diary in the crowded coach, Michael spent his time in the club car with other men. She mourned the loss of their previous friendship and made a few attempts to regain the old warmth, but Michael persisted in remaining distant but dutifully courteous.

If his mother had not wired an invitation urging her to stay in their home until she found adequate lodgings, Toby would have happily registered in a hotel. But it would have been impolite to have changed plans so suddenly, and she was forced to accept Mrs. Sedaine's hospitality.

On the way from the busy station in New York through the crush of traffic, Toby tried one more time to convince Michael she should find other accommodations. "I think it would be much less bother if I registered at a hotel. Your mother is busy and I'm certain a houseguest will be an inconvenience."

"It's not a problem. The servants won't mind," Michael said, never taking his eyes off the passing scenery.

"But...I," Toby tripped over her own words, unable to think of a politely phrased excuse and finally bowed to Michael's determination. But first thing tomorrow morning she would start looking for a respectable boardinghouse. One more night of Michael's practiced civility and cold, clipped replies to every comment she made was all she could tolerate.

Rather than allow Michael to spoil every facet of her arrival in New York, Toby concentrated on the parade of brightly painted wagons rolling down the cobbled streets, the tiny arch-roofed wooden bus pulled by two plodding horses and the little stone houses placed side by side with patches of grass in front of each. Everything in this city seemed to be crammed together, vying for space: people, houses, wagons and the myriad wires crisscrossing the street. This city was nothing like Saint Louis.

Toby alighted from the hansom cab and stood as still as a doe who suddenly finds itself startled in a strange forest. The Sedaines did not live in one of the brick houses they had passed but owned a fabulous residence in a building called the Dakota. The apartment building was like nothing she had ever seen, either in Saint Louis or all the other cities she'd visited with Michael.

The yellow-bricked eight-story edifice was edged in chocolate-colored stone. Its slate roof was trimmed with copper, and its silhouette was broken by hundreds of dormers, gables, turrets and peaks. Huge fireplace chimneys pierced the skyline, wrought iron balconies decorated main windows, and the whole structure was centered around a wonderful courtyard with spectacular bronze fountains.

"This is where you live?" she asked Michael. "It's not a home but a cathedral."

Michael nodded. "I moved in with Mother after Lillian's accident. This whole building is a bit heavy for my taste. I was happier with my modest home across town, but Paul and Suzanne needed a woman to care for them."

"I thought you said your father was just a tailor?"

"I said he was a glorified tailor. My father built his business into one of the largest men's clothing and haberdasheries in the country. He left Mother a wealthy woman."

"Then, then," Toby stumbled, "you're rich!"

"No, I'm not. I have nothing to do with my mother's business. Disappointed?"

"Not at all. Compared to my family anyone is wealthy."

The sun was angling toward the western horizon, and it cast a pale crimson aura onto everything, lending the scene a warm, abstract mood. Michael tried not to stare at Toby but he couldn't help himself. She was beautiful standing there looking up at the Dakota in awe. He'd always thought of her as small and delicate, but here in New York, she appeared even more diminutive and vulnerable than ever.

He felt inextricably guilty for taking her away from her family where she was protected from harm. New York could devour Toby if she wasn't sheltered from its dark side. There wasn't a city in America that was as sophisticated or as seamy as his hometown.

Toby wasn't conscious of Michael's staring. She was only aware of how provincial her clothing was in comparison to the elegant ladies coming in and out of the apartment building. One woman in particular caused Toby to inwardly shrivel at the simplicity of her own costume. The young lady was elegantly outfitted in a lovely but small draped hat trimmed with iridescent bird feathers. Her jacket and skirt had wide braid trim on the wrap-over panels, and the narrow skirt saucily flared at the hem like a bell.

Michael nudged Toby and she followed him into the foyer, her heels echoing in the cavernous room. They waited for the elevator in silence for Toby didn't dare speak. She was sure her voice would crack.

"Michael," she finally whispered, "I've made a mistake. Please, can we leave?"

"What happened to the sassy young lady from Saint Louis? You're not going to let an overdecorated building intimidate you, are you?"

Before Toby could answer, the elevator arrived and the attendant held back the highly polished accordion grille, allowing Michael and Toby to enter. Michael started up a light bantering to ease her tension and she was grateful for the distraction. From the way the elevator man critically raised his eyebrows at her, she was certain that if Michael hadn't been with her, the attendant would have mistaken her for a servant and insisted she use the back entrance.

Michael fitted his key into the brass lock and opened the door to a luxurious apartment. Toby stepped across the threshold and couldn't resist saying, "This is beautiful. How many rooms are there?"

"Thirteen or fourteen, I think," Michael said.

"For four people?" she almost yelped.

"Yes, except for the servants," a dignified older woman said as she swept into the room and extended her hand. "Welcome, Miss Wells. I'm Laura Sedaine."

"It was kind of you to open your home to me," Toby answered. The resemblance between mother and son was remarkable. It was hard not to stare at Mrs. Sedaine, for Michael had the masculine version of his mother's features. She was an impressive lady with a strong chin, a classic nose and thick black hair that was turning gray.

"Michael, dear," his mother said, turning to him, "I've planned a little dinner party to celebrate your return. Ansel is joining us at eight and so are the von Feldmans."

Michael swallowed his irritation and said, "On our first night?" He was certain she had arranged this gathering because he had brought Toby home with him. His mother had always disapproved of the people he associated with, calling them "riffraff." She went to great lengths to surround him with what she considered respectable company, and it made Michael's life a test in diplomacy.

"If you would like to freshen up, Miss Wells, I'll call the maid to show you to your room," Laura offered.

"Has my valise arrived?" Toby asked. "If not, I'd like to see the rest of your home."

Mrs. Sedaine blanched at Toby's two gaffes. Michael understood only the servants would know if luggage had been delivered and that his mother considered it an exceedingly forward request to ask to see the rooms. He jumped in to rescue the moment, knowing that in Saint Louis it was considered good manners to be impressed with a host's home but in New York it was improper to show such a blatant interest.

"Mother, I'll be happy to give Toby a tour while I wait for Paul and Suzanne to get home from school."

Laura almost derisively sniffed but didn't. "Thank you, Michael," she said as if he had offered to do a dirty chore. "Again, welcome to New York, Miss Wells."

Toby watched Michael's mother leave but was too distracted to notice the woman's disdain. She was unsuccessfully trying to hide her enthusiasm but couldn't help bubbling over at everything she saw. Marvelous portraits hung from heavy silk cords in the entry while delicate French furniture filled the parlor. In every corner Belgian lace doilies covered highly buffed rosewood tables and thick Persian carpets muffled their footsteps.

However, it was the telephone that intrigued Toby the most. She had certainly used one in Saint Louis, but it had always been a public telephone. No one she had ever known had one installed in their home. It was a luxury reserved for the very rich. Not just because they were expensive but because only harried, overtaxed businessmen had any need for a telephone in their parlors.

"I wish I knew someone to call," Toby said, laughing as she picked it up.

"If my office were open, you could call Reginald," Michael said, enjoying Toby's untarnished astonishment.

The elderly housekeeper overheard Toby's remark and scowled before flouncing out of the room. Watching her leave, Toby asked Michael, "Did I do something wrong?"

"In New York," Michael explained, "people don't normally express their opinions about other people's possessions."

"Oh." Toby sighed. "I've embarrassed you."

"No, your candidness is a pleasure. People buy all this stuff—" he swept the room with his arm "—to astound their guests, but everyone plays a game of indifference."

Despite Michael's reassurance, Toby knew she had committed a faux pas. His mother and now even the servants were probably whispering about the yokel who had followed him home. She mentally promised to be discreet and not shame Michael or herself again.

Toby's vow was broken almost immediately when the housekeeper escorted Toby to her room. "This is called a water closet, miss," she haughtily informed Toby, "and if you need instructions, I'll be happy to offer them."

Incensed, Toby spoke without mincing her words. "Regardless of what you may think, we do have indoor plumbing in Saint Louis. We're not exactly savages in the Midwest."

"Oh? Really? Too bad they don't have dressmakers, as well," the housekeeper sneered, disparagingly eyeing Toby's traveling suit.

Toby reddened. Was it good manners to tell servants to go boil their heads? Probably not, but she didn't care. "Our tailors can't compare with yours, but our hired help is superior," Toby said with dignity. "At least they know how to keep their tongues."

By the time Toby was alone in the mammoth bedroom, she more than regretted her stay in the Sedaine home, she loathed it. She sat down on the edge of the bed and glanced around the perfect room. There was nothing out of place, no table with a nick, no speck of dust on the lamps or window with a fingerprint smudged on the panes. But all the wealth and pretty gewgaws in the world couldn't make up for the lack of warmth. If it wasn't for Michael, for not wanting to offend him, she wouldn't even bother unpacking her bags.

There was a polite rapping at her door and Toby answered, happy to be distracted until her luggage arrived. "Yes?"

"Mr. Sedaine," a young maid said, "asks that you please join the family for tea in his den."

Toby followed the girl and found Michael alone, sorting through his mail near the window. The room was so reserved that it seemed to have infected Michael. There was little resemblance between the formal man standing in front of her and the relaxed man who had played games with Mo in Saint Louis. She had liked Michael then, but she wasn't sure she did now.

"Thank you for coming," he said primly. "The children will be arriving momentarily," Michael glanced at his pocket watch before snapping it closed.

Toby was aghast at the distracted, indifferent way he mentioned his children. They had been separated for over a month, but he acted as though they'd been absent for only hours. "I've seen you show more excitement over the arrival of a train," Toby scolded.

"Not all of us enjoy mayhem."

"True," Toby conceded, "but mayhem allows room for laughter. I doubt anyone in this house is allowed to giggle without permission."

Michael controlled the temptation to wince. Toby was closer to the truth than she knew. Everything in this house was done by the book, the calendar and a diary of appointments. Very little spontaneity existed here, and he wasn't sure who was guilty. His mother? Himself? Or just boring habits?

The door to the study opened, and Laura Sedaine entered with her grandchildren demurely in tow. "Children," she said, "please say hello to your father and his new assistant, Miss Wells."

Toby watched Michael pick Suzanne up and hug her, but he merely ruffled Paul's hair, earning an immediate scowl of disapproval from Paul, who quickly used his fingers to recomb his hair.

"I have a present for each of you in my luggage. Did you behave yourself while I was away?"

Toby sighed at his inane question. She doubted if Suzanne or Paul ever considered doing anything that was not befitting a lady or gentleman. How sad!

"Call me Toby," Toby said, offering her hand to Paul when the children finished with Michael. Paul had red hair like his little sister, although his eyes were chestnut brown, not hazel like Suzanne's. But it was more than the color that was different. His gaze was haughty while Suzanne's was bright and full of happy curiosity.

"Miss Wells will do," Paul said, succinctly rejecting Toby's offer of friendship.

"I'll call you Toby," Suzanne piped up. "Toby's a funny name."

"Yes, it is. It's better than my sisters' though, Rosamond, Cleopatra and Guinevere."

"You have that many sisters?" Suzanne said in awe.

"And three brothers."

"Well," Paul said, "I'm glad my mother and father had the good sense to have just two children."

Toby was shocked at the young boy's cheeky comment and was even more astounded that neither Michael nor his mother corrected Paul. "I enjoy coming from a large family. We have a wonderful time when we play games, for there are always enough people."

"You play games?" Suzanne asked. "What kinda games?"

"Charades, jacks, baseball, and checkers. Your father taught us a new one when he came to dinner. *Tableaux vivants.*"

Paul shot his father an odd, criticizing look. "How juvenile," he said. "I refused to play that silly game after I was six."

"Shall we?" Laura asked, raising the teapot aloft and ending the dialogue. She waited for Toby and the children to sit down at the table. "I'm sure Miss Wells doesn't enjoy reciting her family history for strangers, Paul. Now, we're having guests in tonight, so I want you to be on your very best behavior. No loud giggles, either of you, and you mustn't wait until this evening to do your practicing. As soon as we're finished here, I want to hear you, Paul, working on your scales until it's time for Suzanne's lesson."

Michael remained silent throughout the afternoon ritual and studied his children and his mother. Why hadn't he noticed that his son was a pompous whelp, his daughter starved for the attention of a young woman and his mother an inflexible matron? Suzanne's hunger was understandable, and Laura's attitude could be attributed to raising a family when she should have been free of responsibility. It was Paul's manner that shocked and worried him. His son was a hostile, angry young man. If Lillian had raised them, would they have been happy, outgoing children like Cleo and Mo?

He took a sip of his tea, not tasting its sugared flavor. Toby's mother had died, so why hadn't the Wells suffered the same fate as his own children? The answer was sitting directly across from him. Toby. Toby, who had only known Suzanne for a few minutes, and was leaning down, intently listening to his daughter tell a story, without showing a trace of boredom the way Laura did when Suzanne droned on. And Toby had told Paul that she would be equally interested to hear about his school day as soon as Suzanne finished. No, his children had not had anyone like Toby to heal their wounds and it showed.

Toby noticed Michael's pensiveness, and she had a clue of what he was thinking by the way he stared at Paul. It was as if he were seeing his son for the first time and was not pleased. Granted, Paul was only eight, but he had already developed an extremely annoying personality. Something had to be done and done soon, or Paul Sedaine would grow to be a wretched, miserable man.

Realizing she was fretting over a problem that didn't concern her, Toby stood to excuse herself. These were Michael's children and Michael's family—not hers.

Toby politely slipped away, using the arrival of her valise as an excuse. It was too early to dress for dinner and her head was a jumble of mixed impressions. The untroubled Michael she had known and liked had been supplanted by a subdued, if not outright dour, man.

Adding to her anxiety were her surroundings. Even though the Sedaine household was beautiful and appeared perfect to outward scrutiny, it lacked the tumultuous joy of the Wells's threadbare home. Alone in her bedroom, Toby slowly unpacked her good dress and pondered how she would go about injecting some life into this drab, regimented family.

"Great Scott, girl," Toby said to herself in the mirror over the ornate chest of drawers, "remember why you left Saint Louis. To escape!"

"Who are you yelling at?" Suzanne asked, tugging on Toby's sleeve.

Nearly a year of Toby's life was startled out of her by the little girl's unexpected appearance. "Are you a fairy?" Toby asked.

"Oh, no. *Grand-mère* says I'm a, a magpie. Why would you think I'm a fairy?"

"Because you appeared like magic."

"Uh-uh, I knocked. You just didn't hear me. Is that who you were screaming at? Fairies?"

The child's imagination was so easily sparked that Toby wanted to hug Suzanne. She didn't but kept up the whimsy. "No, fairies are lovely people and I'd never yell at them."

Suzanne crossed the room and rubbed the blue satin gown Toby had hung up on the armoire door. "Are you wearing this to dinner? It's so pretty."

"Yes. What are you wearing, Suzanne?"

She lifted her starched pinafore and frowned. "Oh, children aren't allowed to eat in the dining room when we have guests. Paul and I have our meal with cook in the kitchen."

Another rush of sadness swept over Toby. How could Michael shuffle his children off when he hadn't seen them for so long? "I wish I was eating with you. I'd feel a lot less nervous."

"You'd like cook. She always fixes us something special that *Grand-mère* and Michael never get."

"Michael?" Toby tried not to squeal while saying his name. Was allowing his daughter to use his Christian name another means of distancing himself even further from her? "Don't you call him 'Father' or 'Daddy'?"

"Sometimes. What do you call your father?"

"Papa."

Paul pounded twice on the door before he shoved it open. "Thought I'd find you here," he said, scowling at his sister and grabbing her hand. "It's time for your piano lesson."

"Bye, Toby." Suzanne smiled and obediently trailed behind her brother.

Suzanne's brief visit made Toby feel less awkward in this house, knowing that at least one person liked her, but it also increased Toby's doubts about Michael's love for his children. He had known her for one entire month without breathing a word of their existence. It wasn't as if they were dim-witted monsters he would be ashamed to claim. They were both bright and beautiful little people who needed a father to love them and buffer them from their grandmother's stern regimentation.

Sitting down on the overstuffed chair placed next to a large window, Toby thought about Michael's wife. She wondered what kind of woman Lillian had been. Obviously she had been a lovely redhead, for both children looked nothing like their father. But, had she been gentle and affectionate with her two babies? Or had she relegated their care to nurses while she flitted from luncheons to parties, between benefits and the theater? What type of woman had Michael loved so much he still grieved for her? It was becoming harder and harder to define the man she had thought she knew.

Whenever Toby was perplexed she found solace in writing her thoughts down in her diary. It was a habit she had started the year her mother became ill. Needing to vent some of her frustration, Toby rummaged through her bag of miscellaneous personal belongings until she located the bound tablet of ruled paper she used as a journal.

The words sprawled across the paper, but her thoughts raced ahead of her pencil. So much had happened in such a short time, it was nearly impossible to keep it all straight. Michael had treated her like a leper ever since Richmond, but she had seen a glimmer of his former self. The way he had tried to make her feel welcome in his home when they first arrived had been a sign he wasn't completely immune to her feelings. Still, there were all the other times he had shut her out, isolating himself. It was all jumbled into a complex maze, and Toby couldn't find any markers to show her which way to go. All she was certain about was that Michael had been articulate and specific about their personal relationship—they had none.

It was early evening before she finished filling almost eleven pages and a sense of clearheaded purpose returned. Michael had his life and she had hers. Nothing had changed, including her oath to build a life for herself in New York free from the past.

Glancing at the growing dusk outside her bedroom window, she realized it was time she started thinking about

dressing, not that she had anything appropriate for a fancy
dinner. The best she had was that simple gown of cobalt-
blue satin Suzanne had admired.

After she scrubbed the grime off her skin, she brushed
through her hair, wishing she had enough time to wash it.
But her hair was too thick and took hours to dry, so she
settled for just rubbing her head with a damp towel.

Wishing she had something more sophisticated to wear,
she took her gown off the hanger and stepped into it. The
shoulders slipped down around her upper arms, leaving a
delicate lacy yoke from the neck to the bosom. The rest of
the dress, bodice and skirt, were left unadorned.

For a crazy moment she considered styling her hair into
some elaborate fashion to compensate for her dress's understatement. Short on time, Toby abandoned the idea and
merely piled her curls on top of her head. Tiny wisps sprung
loose and framed her face in a golden halo. She wasn't satisfied but didn't dare dawdle or she would annoy Laura by
being late for dinner.

Ansel Prescott-Moore was the first to arrive. As Lillian's
brother and the only uncle Suzanne and Paul knew, Ansel
was included in most family gatherings. The von Feldmans had known the Sedaines for nearly thirty years, and
Hugo had wisely counseled Laura on her business invest-
ments ever since Michael's father died over fifteen years
ago. They were all gathered in the parlor before Toby appeared.

Michael had his brother-in-law at his elbow and was telling stuffy Mr. von Feldman about the tour while continuing to look for Toby in the doorway. Finally she entered the
room, trying to slip in without drawing attention to herself.

Michael stopped speaking in midsentence and took a
fleeting moment to secretly admire her. Toby's beauty was
an ever-changing kaleidoscope, it didn't matter where she
was or what she wore. She was breathtaking indoors or
outside, under lamplight or bright sunshine, draped in
gingham or brocade. But, he reprimanded himself, he
would never act on his feelings and, in time, this ephem-
eral fascination would fade. It always did.

"Well, Michael," Ansel said, breaking the silence Toby's entrance caused, "aren't you going to introduce me?"

Like a rubber band, Ansel snapped Michael out of his reverie. Michael rushed forward and escorted Toby around the parlor, introducing her to the elderly von Feldmans and to Ansel.

Ansel made no mystery of his admiration for Toby, and Michael bristled. A large auburn-haired man who tended toward the plump side, Ansel preened whenever he caught sight of a lovely woman. Ansel Prescott-Moore, dressed in an ice-cream suit, was a notorious rogue with the ladies, relying on his glib tongue, insincere compliments and money to impress every eligible female he met. Usually Ansel's tactics made a striking impression on the ladies, and Michael feared Toby could easily become another one of Ansel's trophies if he didn't intervene.

"This is the rascal I claim as a brother-in-law, Toby. Beware. No matter what he says, don't believe a word."

"Aren't we being sanctimonious tonight," Ansel said. "As I recall, Emily Lucas spent a year believing the stories you told her and I never spoiled your game."

Toby watched Michael's face turn white with only twin spots of color left on his cheeks. He never uttered a word but turned on his heel and began talking to Mrs. von Feldman.

"When Michael lets you out of the cage, Miss Wells, I'd be honored to show you the finer places in our city," Ansel offered.

Laura took over Michael's role and defused Ansel by poking fun at him, hinting at his questionable reputation. "I doubt Miss Wells would be interested in seeing the inside of some gambling hall or one of those dreadful vaudeville theaters."

"Dear Laura," Ansel said, "those dreadful theaters have the most beautiful women gracing their stages, with the exception of Miss Wells, here."

"Besides," Michael said, inevitably pulled back into the conversation, "vaudeville is an eminently respectable form of entertainment. It's also the bread and butter of Sedaine Music."

Toby felt invisible. Everyone was talking about her and around her as if she were not in the room. "I'm perfectly capable," she announced, "of deciding where I want to go and what I want to see."

"Wonderful!" Ansel said. "An independent lady. How in the world did you ever hook up with this stuffy character?" he asked, jabbing his finger at Michael.

"He offered me a job and I accepted," Toby explained. "I—"

"Ansel, dear," Laura interrupted, "why don't you escort Miss Wells to the table and she can tell you all about it during dinner."

"Mother," Michael said, "I would prefer to stay with the original seating arrangement as discussed." Without another word, he tucked Toby's arm through his and guided her into the dining room.

He seated her next to him, which left Ansel with Myrna von Feldman as his dinner partner and Hugo von Feldman at one end of the table while Laura Sedaine took her place at the other end.

During the first course when the maid offered Toby a platter of raw oysters on half shells, Michael saw Toby hesitate. He knew that having been raised in the Midwest she probably didn't know what they were.

Before he had a chance to speak, Toby asked the maid serving them, "What are these?"

The maid was startled by being directly spoken to and didn't answer.

"Have you ever tasted one?" Toby asked softly.

"If you have a question, Miss Wells, please ask me. The servants are trained to be unobtrusive," Laura Sedaine lectured. "Those are exquisite Chesapeake Bay oysters. Quite a delicacy."

Toby fell silent and took two of the unappetizing lumps. From under her eyelashes, she peeked at Laura and knew, even if she had been purposely trying to offend her hostess, she couldn't have been more successful.

As the meal progressed, Michael realized Toby was unusually silent and it took him a second to realize why. Myrna von Feldman was speaking in French, which was common when the two families gathered, but it was leaving poor Toby out of the conversation. The Sedaines were of French extraction and so was Mrs. von Feldman, despite her German married name.

"Please, Mother," Michael said in English, "we're ignoring Toby."

"Everyone knows how to speak French," Laura chastised.

Michael turned crimson and withered at her rudeness. "Mother, we're being inconsiderate."

Toby commiserated with him and found Laura's barb offensive, just as she found Michael's mother petty and shallow. "I'm afraid I'm not fluent in any foreign language. I only know a little Latin," she said demurely. Toby quoted Horace to prove her minor boast.

Michael laughed at Toby's wit, recognizing the quote, "The people hiss at me but I applaud myself."

"What did you say, Miss Wells?" Laura asked.

"Why, I'm surprised, Mrs. Sedaine. Doesn't everyone know how to speak Latin?" Toby goaded.

Laura sputtered at her own affront being turned back on her, and Michael enjoyed watching his mother flounder.

"I suppose even a parson's daughter has had a rudimentary education," Laura finally said.

Her tone was condescending, and Toby suddenly had her fill of bad manners. "Yes. One of the first things Papa taught me was to wear my education like a pocket watch, something to be kept private and special. You don't constantly pull it out and look at it just to prove you have it."

All the dinner guests, with the exception of Laura, laughed heartily.

"You'll do well in this city, Toby," Ansel said, toasting her with his wine. "Anyone with such a quick tongue is at the top of my list."

"Then you must have a very short one, Mr. Prescott-Moore," Toby said, verbally cutting him down. She was tired of being the novel toy of pompous people with double names and single-celled brains.

The entire table stared at her as if she had trampled every convention into the dust. Laura Sedaine remained quiet but her face was hardly impassive. She scowled at Toby as though she were a distasteful entrée.

Michael had been aghast at how rude everyone was, but he was horrified at his mother's behavior. He had never known her to treat anyone, much less a guest, with such acrimony. When he had spent the evening with the Wells, he had been treated with the utmost charm and made to feel as if he were a member of the family. Toby had faced nothing but ridicule and censure since stepping foot through the door.

"Toby has a delightful family," Michael said, intending to shame his own. "The evening I spent with them was a pure pleasure."

"How many brothers and sisters do you have?" Myrna von Feldman asked.

"Six."

"Tsk, tsk," Myrna said. "How does your poor mother manage so many?"

"I suppose in the West families need to be large to tend all the fields," her husband suggested.

"We live in the city," Toby said, squelching the speculation. "My father is a minister, not a farmer."

"How quaint, Son," Laura sniped. "It must have been amusing to be feted at a parson's table."

Toby had been drawn into an untenable situation, and she knew she was a fool if she remained for more abuse. "Excuse me," she said, standing up. She considered begging off and fleeing to her room with a feigned headache, but the duplicity rankled her. She did not like these people and didn't owe them the consideration of a social lie. Without saying another word, she left the room to pack her things.

"What an impertinent young woman," Laura said.

Michael stood and threw his napkin onto the table. "Mother, I blame you for this fiasco. It's your duty to make all your guests welcome and you've failed. Your condescending manner gave license for everyone here to insult and badger Miss Wells."

"Michael," Hugo von Feldman said, "I think you should apologize to your mother."

"For what? Being honest? You're just as guilty. Sitting here and remaining silent gave your tacit approval to your wife and my mother."

He didn't wait for any further reprimands but stalked out of the dining room. At Toby's door he rapped lightly, not blaming her if she refused to answer.

"Who is it?"

"Michael. May I come in?"

"Not if you're going to try and talk me into staying here tonight."

"I wish I could leave with you."

Toby opened the door and looked up at him. He looked like a repentant little boy, and her heart went out to him. "I've embarrassed you again, haven't I?"

"No," he said, "I couldn't be more proud of you. It's about time someone set that group back on its heels."

She stepped aside and let him enter. Closing the door, she sighed. "Why do they hate me so?"

"They don't. They're just threatened by outsiders."

"Is that what I am? An outsider?"

"Someone from Long Island is an alien." Actually he didn't have a clue to his mother's hostility but couldn't admit that to Toby. "May I help?" he asked, after seeing her clothes hastily flung into her suitcases.

"Yes. Suggest where I can stay."

"I'll take you to the Windsor Hotel." It was the only logical offer he could make, but what he really wanted to do was kiss away all the insults she'd endured.

"I've had enough of hotels, Michael," Toby said. "I'd like to find a decent boardinghouse that I can make into a home."

"We didn't scare you back to Saint Louis?"

"I haven't come this far to be frightened away by an acerbic witch," Toby said, surprised Michael had even thought she was leaving New York.

"Are you referring to my sweet mother?" he said, and traced his fingers across her cheek. "Don't ever change and don't listen to what other people say. They're just blind to perfection."

He took back his hand, afraid he might do more than just touch her cheek, afraid of the feelings she awakened by just being in the same room. All his worrying about New York devouring Toby was unfounded. Toby Wells would not be consumed by anyone—not even himself.

Chapter Six

Michael heard Toby before he saw her, because she was whistling a jaunty tune as she bounded up the stairs to the office. Toby had retained a marvelous childhood quality—playfulness. Even though she was a lady, she still took the steps two at a time when she thought no one was watching, sang under her breath when delighted and displayed her feelings on her pretty face without any attempt to disguise them. She was as easy to read as a grade-school primer, and he found being close to her turned a normal day into an adventure.

"Oh, Michael," she trilled happily the second she swooped through the door, "I found a wonderful new place to live." As was her habit, she unpinned her bonnet and flung it at the coatrack in the corner. It missed the hook by an inch and plopped to the floor. "I'm going to make that toss one of these days."

Watching her and listening to her, Michael knew why Ansel conveniently stopped by the office nearly every day. His brother-in-law didn't try to hide the fact that he couldn't get enough of Toby's refreshing beauty and happy disposition. But Ansel's repeated visits had begun to wear thin, and Michael had more than once asked him if he wasn't supposed to be at work.

"Try snapping your wrist a little faster," Michael coached as he picked up her hat and hung it on the brass knob.

Even though she was unconventional, it would be wrong to accuse Toby of immaturity. True, she did love games, challenges and, most of all, bending convention until it was less rigid. On the other hand, she was responsible in her work, mature in her dealings with people, punctual, reliable and astute.

"Did you find the rental agent?" he said, returning to his desk and lounging back in his carved oak chair. The springs creaked as he rocked slightly to and fro.

"Yes. I met him at the brownstone and he let me inspect it."

"And?"

"And—" she sighed as she sat behind her own flattop desk "—it's perfect except it's more than I can afford without someone to share the rent."

Being Toby's roommate! What joy that would be, he thought; waking up in the morning and seeing Toby's bright face across the breakfast table, spending quiet evenings reading to her in front of a blazing fire. His flight of fancy ended as soon as he realized where his mind was wandering. They were not pleasures he would ever experience, and Michael sprang forward in his chair, pulling out a contract to review and distract his mind.

"What's the matter, Michael?" Toby asked, seeing him suddenly shift positions. "Forget an appointment?"

"Not exactly."

"What then? Did I say something wrong?"

"I need to examine this contract before I sign it, that's all."

"But it's our standard agreement," Toby said. "You don't need to worry."

He didn't respond to her reassurance, keeping his head bent over the sheaf of papers. What had she said this time, Toby wondered? She had been working in New York for nearly three weeks, and nearly all of Michael's previous hostility had faded. But even though his animosity had dwindled, he was still an enigma. At odd, unpredictable moments, he would turn sullen, burying his face behind a book, or claim he had an urgent errand he had forgotten.

At other times, he was open, friendly and more than willing to share his thoughts. Michael didn't hesitate asking her opinion, quizzing her for a reaction to a song's impact or increasing her responsibilities on a daily basis. And Toby was proud of the fact that he often listened to her advice and trusted her judgment. Even so, when he was smiling, there was a guarded look in his eyes, a look that couldn't lie. Michael was hiding from her, and she was tired of chasing after him through a transparent fog of contradictions.

"Michael."

"Yes?"

"Are you unhappy with my work?" She hoped the question was unnecessary, but it might start him talking and then she could establish the reason behind his sudden mood shifts.

"Certainly not. I haven't fired you, have I?"

Toby was tempted to shout and scream, but she had learned Michael's armor of silence was too thick to penetrate unless he wanted a person to pierce it. In fact, not just talking, but everything, was done on Michael's terms. She came to work to suit his schedule, she worked late when he asked, she had picked out a place to live close to the office, and she even dressed in a manner she thought he would appreciate. It was all in vain. Every time they started having a little fun, Michael turned back into the almighty sphinx.

Toby didn't have a chance to pursue the subject, for someone rapped on the opaque glass office door.

"We made it," Caleb said, opening the door and peeking in the room.

He wore a grin that would have illuminated a large stage, and behind him Toby could see the feathers of a stylish bonnet.

"Caleb. Chantelle," she cried, and jumped up from her chair. With no ceremony or pretense, she pulled them into the office.

"Toby?" Chantelle said, amazed to see her. "What are you doing here?"

"Caleb wasn't the only one who was offered a job in New York. I work for Sedaine Music."

"How wonderful," Chantelle said, and hugged Toby.

"Shoot!" Caleb said. "I've been fidgety ever since Saint Louis about how I was going to write my music to satisfy Michael. You could have saved me a lot of grief, Michael, if you'd told me Toby was going to be here."

Toby could hear the laughter in Caleb's voice and responded. "Didn't you read the tiny paragraph at the bottom of your contract that states Toby Wells is the only person capable of taming Caleb MacRae's music?"

"Am I invisible?" Michael stepped between Toby and Caleb and stuck out his hand. "Great to see you. Any problems getting here?"

"Not a one unless you count the hundred trunks Chantelle insisted I tote across country."

"You're exaggerating," Chantelle objected with her strange lilt Toby was unable to place. "I only brought four."

"Four the size of baggage cars."

Toby laughed at the bantering. "What did you do, Chantelle, bring all of Missouri?"

Chantelle's answer was quite serious. "No, just a few of my best dresses."

"Thirty-five to be exact," Caleb said caustically.

Chantelle pulled herself up to her full height and retorted with an equal amount of sarcasm. "You know they're my best advertising. It's how I make my living, Mr. MacRae, sewing costumes and ball gowns. What if I'd insisted you leave all your music behind?"

Toby glanced at Michael and saw that he was as baffled by the tension as she was. A chilling silence filled the room, and Toby was tempted to make some boisterous joke the way she used to do with the twins, Cleo and Mo, when they quarreled. But these were adults, not children, and Toby held her tongue.

Michael turned to business to defuse the strain. "Ready to go to work, Caleb?"

"You'd better keep me as busy as you promised," Caleb needled. "I just left one of the sweetest little jobs in a honky-tonk I've ever had."

"Your days playing in gambling halls, pool rooms and saloons are over, my friend. In one year every theater owner in this city will be begging for one of your songs," Michael reassured him.

"Better than booing," Caleb said. "When do I make my big debut?"

Taking his watch out of his vest pocket, Michael flipped open its lid. "In twenty minutes," he said.

Caleb blinked. "Truly?"

"Yep. I wasn't expecting you today. I planned on walking over to Joel Greenpasture's hall and playing one of the pieces I bought from you in Saint Louis," Michael explained. "You're just in time to rescue your career."

"*The* Greenpasture?" Caleb's voice rose an entire octave.

"No, the other one," Michael teased. "He might as well hear this masterpiece from the maestro. It's time New York was introduced to Caleb MacRae."

After the two men left, Toby and Chantelle chattered about all that had happened since they last saw each other in Saint Louis. Toby was thrilled to see Chantelle and realized she had been lonely for a female friend. All her life Toby had been surrounded by family and lifelong friends until these past few weeks on the road and in New York, and it had been a lonely burden.

"Where are you and Caleb staying?"

"*We* aren't staying anywhere. He has a friend on Lenox Avenue who's going to let him use a spare room and I'm going to find a place of my own."

"You two aren't going to share..." Toby dropped the sentence then started another. "I thought you and Caleb were..." She left off again, stumbling for the appropriate words.

"Don't get flustered," Chantelle said. "I know most people assume I live with Caleb, but I don't. I just don't bother to correct them, because their opinion doesn't matter."

"How long have you known Caleb?" Toby asked, thoroughly confused.

"Six years."

"Don't you love him?"

"Completely. You're as curious as Eve, but I'm not handing you any apple," Chantelle said with a laugh. "That's all I want to say about Caleb. Do you have any idea how tedious it is being locked up in a railroad car day after day with a nervous man?"

Chantelle dismissed Toby's snooping with humor, and Toby took no offense. She recognized it as an effective tool. It was more difficult to penetrate the defenses of someone who relied on laughter than it was to deal with a person who bluntly informed you it was none of your business.

Although Toby had not known Chantelle for very long, the two women had several common bonds. They were both in a strange city, both had roots in Saint Louis, and both of them needed a place to live. Toby had a solution to their mutual dilemma, providing Chantelle agreed.

"When you said you make your living sewing costumes, did that mean you plan on staying in New York?" She hoped this was a safe question that Chantelle would be comfortable answering.

"Wild horses wouldn't drag me away. I'm going to make a name for myself by designing the greatest costumes for the theaters New York has ever seen."

Toby realized she wasn't the only one who had dreams. Chantelle obviously did, too, but there was something more to Chantelle's ambition that Toby couldn't define. There was steel behind her words and, whatever the cause, Toby decided not to pry. Instead she asked, "Would you be more comfortable in a moderately priced brownstone than a hotel or boardinghouse if you had someone to share the rent?"

"A what?"

"A little house. I found a very nice one this morning and once you see it, I know you'll love it. It's all furnished and available for the next year."

"Does it have a big kitchen?" Chantelle asked, standing and picking up her small purse. "I love to cook and I would like to have a sunny kitchen."

Toby grabbed her hat and added, "There's even room to have a small garden in the back. I'm so pleased you came to New York with Caleb."

"So am I. When can we move in?"

Toby scribbled a note for Michael and said, "The minute Reginald returns from the bank, we'll find the rental agent and give him our money. Then we'll make the arrangements to have your luggage delivered."

When they returned to the office, giddy after signing a one-year lease, their spirits were dampened by finding two dejected men waiting for them.

"Did someone die?" Toby asked.

"Yeah, my career in New York," Caleb muttered.

"That's not true," Michael objected. "Joel Greenpasture is not the beginning and end of vaudeville. He's just one of many owners we're going to approach."

"That wasn't the tune you were singing two hours ago," Caleb grumbled.

"I was hasty," Michael said, taking no offense at Caleb's remark. "I'm sorry I made it sound so easy. Nothing in this business is."

Chantelle mediated. "All Michael promised to do was publish your music, Caleb. The audition today was just a bonus. We won't starve."

"If we take the next train to Missouri," Caleb said, "I could get my old job back at the saloon."

"A year ago you said all you cared about was me and getting your music published. What happened? Greedy so soon? Besides," Chantelle said, taking a lighter tone, "Toby and I just signed a one-year contract on a house. I won't break it and leave her in a lurch. Until you become established, I can always sell my costumes to keep us from starving."

Toby saw Caleb bristle and tried to placate him. "Just think, Caleb, when you're a headliner she can get even by lounging in bed until noon, munching cucumber sandwiches."

Michael winked at Toby, silently thanking her for being optimistic, and Caleb rewarded her with a smile.

"That sure my name will be on a marquee?" Caleb asked, beaming at her confidence.

"Just don't walk past me on the street and pretend you don't know me when you're famous," Toby happily scolded.

* * *

"Why are you spending so much money on her?" Paul asked his father as their carriage followed behind the delivery wagon.

"Because she's Michael's friend," Suzanne answered before her father could.

He reached over and stroked his daughter's soft curls. "You like Toby, don't you?"

"She's nice. I like the way she smiles all the time and listens to me."

"And you, Paul. How do you feel about Toby?"

"I'd rather be at the park playing with my soldiers."

Every Saturday that the weather permitted, Paul spent the afternoon staging elaborate battle scenes with his miniature soldiers. He never invited any other boys to join him and seemed quite content to act out his solitary versions of famous battles. Lately, though, Michael had begun to wonder about his son's fascination with war, and he'd noticed that Paul's friends had quit including Paul in their activities. Maybe Toby could suggest a way to stir Paul out of his solitary pastime and back into more social activities.

But not today. Today he and the children were delivering a creative incentive to Toby.

Toby was still wearing her percale housedress when the brownstone's doorbell rang. She tucked the dustcloth into her apron pocket as she hurried to answer it. With Caleb and Chantelle off for the rest of the day, she had planned on spending the remainder of the afternoon settling into her new home.

"Michael!" Toby cried, and grabbed at the white cotton turban tucked over her hair. "And Paul, Suzanne. How, how nice to see you."

Michael stood on the stoop and shook his head in wonder. Lord, but this woman looked wonderful even in cleaning clothes. The smudge of soot on the tip of her pert nose added to the winsome domestic picture.

"I wasn't expecting company." Toby reached up and dragged her fingers through her tangled curls.

"I tried to tell Michael it wasn't proper to call on you when you weren't expecting us," Paul explained, wickedly grinning. "I'm sure you would prefer not receiving guests, wouldn't you, Miss Wells?"

"Good friends are always welcome in my home, Paul. Please, come in." Toby realized Paul would have rather been taking a mathematics examination than visiting her, but she knew Michael would not appear with his children on her doorstep without good cause.

"Excuse me for just a minute, Toby," Michael said, and tried to hide his smile, "but I need to tell them you're at home."

"Them? Are your mother and Ansel with you?" she asked in horror. Laura Sedaine already thought she was no better than hired help and, if Laura saw her dressed this way, it would be like being pronounced guilty by a vindictive judge.

"No," Michael said, reading the panic in her eyes, "but you're keeping four fellows from making a delivery."

"But I didn't order anything."

"I did and it's something you need," Michael said. "Show us where you'd like it placed."

Michael waved to the movers, and Toby watched as an upright parlor grand piano was hoisted up the stairs. She was stunned and couldn't force herself to move out of the way.

"Plan on leaving this in the hall?" Michael said, prodding her into action.

Quickly Toby pushed a chair and drop-leaf table aside in the parlor, making room for the gorgeous piano against a wall. She stepped back and stared in silence as the burled-walnut instrument was gently slipped off the dolly.

"For me? This is for me?" she whispered in awe.

"Yes, for you. I waited this week for you to get settled before having it delivered."

"Michael let me pick out the stool," Suzanne said proudly. "He said a lady always has better taste than a man."

"You did an excellent job," Toby whispered. "Both of you."

Words were inadequate, and Toby threw her arms around Suzanne's neck and hugged her. "Thank you."

"Why are you thanking her?" Paul asked. "She didn't pay for it."

"That's right," Toby said, and promptly embraced Michael. "Oh, thank you, Michael. I don't deserve such a lavish gift."

He tilted her chin so he could look down into her flushed, excited face. "Not unless you write some songs I can buy, Angel Eyes." The endearment slipped out, but he didn't regret it and gently tweaked her smudged nose.

Toby's mouth dropped open at his implication. "I—I— I don't know what to say," she stuttered.

"Nothing. Just play something for us." He grabbed her by the shoulders, spun her around and tenderly prodded her toward the piano while the delivery men slipped out.

"Something fast," Suzanne instructed.

After the first song, Michael sat beside Toby and they took turns testing the response of the keys, whether or not the piano needed tuning, the quality of its tone. It was the most superior instrument Toby had ever touched, and she was afraid to speculate on how much Michael had spent. Whatever it was, she knew the sum would be staggering.

"I can play a pretty song," Suzanne said wistfully.

"Then why don't you sit down beside me and teach it to me," Toby said. She had forgotten the children were in the room, something that never would have happened if Cleo and Mo had been in the background. Wells children might not be as well mannered as the Sedaines, but they were never forgotten.

"She plays like a baby," Paul said scornfully. "She only practices a half hour every day. I practice for at least a full hour."

Toby closed her eyes and scolded herself for wishing Paul wasn't along to spoil the pleasant spirit of the moment. Paul did make it hard to be kind, though. "When your sister has finished, I would love to have you show me how well you play, Paul."

"Not today. I don't want to."

The temptation to criticize Paul aloud for his surly tone almost overcame Toby's common sense. Instead she said, "Another day, then."

Michael glanced over at Toby and wondered if she would have been as tolerant with Mo had her brother talked to her like that. He doubted it but ignored the issue and concentrated on Suzanne's playing. When his daughter finished, he said, "That was lovely, Suzanne. You have been working very hard."

"Thank you, sir."

"Toby, I would like to hear something you wrote," Michael encouraged.

"Why the sudden interest in my songs? Aren't you the man who wouldn't buy any?" She put a playful note in her voice to assure Michael she was teasing.

He almost admitted he wasn't. The old Michael Sedaine had been changed forever. From the moment Toby Wells had turned around in Saint Louis and looked at him, his world had begun to spin in a different direction. "It was the best decision of my life," he taunted her.

"My music was that bad?"

Toby looked wounded and Michael rushed to explain. "No, but if I had bought a piece you would have merrily gone on your way and you wouldn't be sitting here with us today."

"So you didn't buy my songs just so you would have an assistant. What a devious nature. This piano is just a bribe to ease your guilty conscience."

"Suzanne," he whispered, "she's on to us."

Toby and Michael locked eyes over the little girl's head, and Toby gazed into his, daring to search them. They told her far more than she expected. No man had ever looked at her with such affection, and, instead of frightening her, the message she read in Michael's rich brown eyes gave her a magnificent sense of confidence. He believed in her, he trusted her and he would never do anything to harm her. Their misunderstanding in Richmond was finally put to rest.

Michael savored the sweet truce, aware of Toby's acceptance and forgiveness. He had never known another person capable of understanding what he was trying to say without being forced into a lengthy explanation. Toby

Wells was so attuned to the people around her it was uncanny.

Realizing that if they lingered, staring at each other for much longer, the children would wonder what was happening, he shifted away and said, "I'm starving. Would you like to go out with us to eat?"

"Would you settle for a cold roast beef sandwich and coleslaw?" Toby asked. "I really don't feel like going anywhere."

"Can we eat with you?" Suzanne asked, a worried frown on her face.

"Of course, sweet thing," Toby said.

"May I cut the crust off my bread?" Paul asked.

"You can trim your bread any way you like," Toby said, delighted to hear the first normal, childish response out of Paul.

"Do you have lots of mustard?" Michael asked, heading for the kitchen.

"Lots." Toby giggled to herself and took a minute to run her hand over the smooth surface of the piano. Again she wondered what had prompted Michael to purchase such a gift for her.

At Michael's suggestion, Toby turned the casual supper into an impromptu picnic. Although all three Sedaines were novices in the kitchen, she showed Paul how to slice the tomatoes and had Suzanne folding napkins into pretty shapes while Michael carved the meat. When they were finished preparing their meal, they sat together on the stoop, enjoying the twilight.

Couples out for an early-evening stroll passed by, and the men politely tipped their hats in greeting. This area was not the finest in the city, but it was respectable and quiet and Toby once again congratulated herself on finding the brownstone.

"I'm much happier here than I was at the boarding-house," she said. "Chantelle is a perfect roommate."

The mention of Chantelle made Michael feel ashamed of himself. Despite the promises he had made to Caleb, he hadn't been able to sell Caleb's talent to any vaudeville owner. Ever since Greenpasture's rejection, the others had followed suit. Poor Caleb and Chantelle! He had hauled them across the country to this hostile city that hadn't learned to appreciate true ragtime yet.

Refusing to let business ruin the perfect evening, he changed the subject. "Have you had a chance to explore your new neighborhood?"

"Not yet. Let's pile the dishes in the sink and go for a walk. Would you like to come with us?" Toby asked the children.

"What time is it?" Suzanne asked her father.

"Only six-thirty," Michael said. "Why?"

"You know I'm not allowed to stay up past eight o'clock."

"Tonight is special," Michael said. "You don't have to go to bed until I say so. We can't waste such a splendid summer evening."

He stood and offered one hand to Paul and the other to Suzanne, but Paul marched ahead without accepting his father's show of affection. Toby saw the hurt look on Michael's face and slipped her hand into Paul's place.

"My first exploring trip in New York," Toby announced as they set off down the street. "And I couldn't ask for better company."

As they wandered up one street and down another, she was aware of other women glancing at Michael and the children. She knew they all assumed Paul and Suzanne were hers, and she reveled in the attention. One woman boldly eyed just Michael, and Toby glanced over at him.

His face was relaxed, unguarded, and the grim little lines around his mouth had disappeared. He did have beautiful jet-colored hair and clearly chiseled features, yet that wasn't what held the most power over her. It was his quiet air of gentility and the security of knowing Michael would never let anyone or anything harm her.

She could have gone on walking for miles, saucy with pride. The streets were noisy with horses clip-clopping, squeaky wagon wheels, children yelling as they played games in the last few rays of sunlight, and neighbors calling to one another from porches. Toby heard none of it. She was only tuned in to Michael.

"Hey, kid," a scruffy little boy called to Paul as a rubber ball landed in the gutter at their feet. "Toss it back, will ya?"

A half-dozen children were playing stickball in the middle of an alley. Toby was reminded of her brothers and sisters and suddenly missed them a great deal.

When Paul didn't respond, Michael fetched the ball but didn't throw it to the boy. He bounced it from hand to hand a few times and winked at Toby. "Feel like joining them?"

"The girls against the boys," she challenged, and hitched up her skirts in one hand and snatched Suzanne's little fist in the other.

"We're going to play in the alley?" Suzanne asked in a puzzled, shy voice.

"And our team is going to win," Toby taunted Michael as she ran to gather her team together.

The ragamuffins were pleased to have the grown-ups join them, and everyone romped in the dusky alley as if the outcome were the most important victory in the world. Even Paul forgot his snooty attitude in the excitement and blended in with the other boys. Toby tried to break Michael's concentration by hooting benign insults at him when he was at bat with the broomstick.

"You couldn't hit a watermelon if it was thrown at you," Toby shouted.

"Oh, yeah," Michael whooped smugly, "watch this." He smacked the ball directly on center and sent it sailing toward Toby.

She knew it was coming at her like a speeding locomotive and bent to catch the missile between her hands. Her stance was short and she skipped forward to reach it, stumbling on the hem of her skirt.

Michael rushed to her as she jumped up and brushed the dust from herself. "Are you all right?" he asked.

"Of course," she answered, confused by his concern. She had taken a hundred tumbles playing in her backyard in Saint Louis.

Grinning at her dauntless spirit, he said, "Can't hit, can I? Well, you can't catch worth beans."

Toby opened her hand and stuck the ball right under his nose. "You're out, Mr. Sedaine."

They argued if it was a fair catch or not until the kids were laughing so hard they could no longer play seriously.

Exhausted, the teams disbanded and went home, leaving the adults, along with Paul and Suzanne, hot and thirsty. "Would anyone like a soda?" Michael asked, looking at the ice-cream parlor across the street.

"Yes. Two of them, please, plus a strawberry sundae with whipped cream and nuts." Toby wasn't really asking but was placing her order.

"For just yourself?" Paul asked in wonder.

"She has a healthy appetite, son," Michael said. He wrapped his arm around Paul's shoulders and for the first time in years, Paul didn't shrug away.

"Then I want a banana split," Paul said. "And a chocolate soda."

"Me, too," Suzanne said, bouncing up and down on her toes. "Me, too."

By the time the four of them made their way back home, twilight had turned to inky night with stars dotting the sky. A white crescent moon swung so low it looked as if it were rocking on the pointed steeple of Trinity Church. It was the ideal finale to a perfect evening and Toby didn't want it to end.

Michael had Suzanne draped over his shoulder, and Toby watched the little girl's head bob with each step. Suzanne's polished boots were scuffed and dusty and the hem of her dress was ripped.

"Why don't you come in for a few minutes so that I can clean the children up before your mother sees them," Toby suggested to Michael. "She won't be happy if she sees them like this."

"It's probably the first time Suzanne's hands and face have been smudged since the day she was born. Little girls and boys are expected to get dirty," Michael said defiantly.

"And if you want to keep peace in your family, you had better let me repair the damage," Toby said.

Toby scrubbed Paul clean at the sink before she took a washcloth to Suzanne's firm little cheeks. She couldn't mend the dress but both children were presentable when she finished polishing their boots.

"Can we go home?" Paul asked, and yawned. "I'm tired."

"Lie down on the sofa," Toby suggested. "Your father will be ready to leave in a few minutes."

Michael was curious about why she wanted them to stay longer. It wasn't that he objected, it was simply the tone of her voice, which hinted that she had something important to say.

Toby gently tugged on Michael's jacket and pulled him into the foyer where they were shielded from the children's curious glances. "Thank you for everything," she said. "I'm tempted to pinch myself to make sure I'm not dreaming."

"I didn't know you were that fond of ice cream," he teased gently.

"I'm fond of ice cream, beautiful pianos and handsome men," she said, lightly drawing her finger from the cleft in his chin to his Adam's apple.

Michael knew she was asking him to kiss her and he'd never had a more wondrous invitation. Perhaps other men liked taking what they wanted, but he preferred to wait until his affection was welcomed. Leaning down, Michael wrapped his arms around Toby's narrow waist and her hands automatically curled over his shoulders.

This time Toby wasn't surprised when Michael's warm lips covered hers. For days, she'd been unconsciously waiting for him to kiss her and had finally resorted to asking for what she wanted. When Michael's tongue charmed her lips apart, she hungrily accepted his entrance without reservation. His mouth moistened hers and she relished the taste of him. Their tangled kisses rose to a crescendo of passion, and Toby found her breath coming in short, labored gasps.

Unwittingly she pressed her hips closer to Michael, wanting to bridge the minute gap between them. No matter what she did, she couldn't get close enough and resented the clothing that was an unwanted barrier. She forgot everything, where she stood, her surroundings, the night. All Toby could think of was Michael. She couldn't get enough of him.

Cupping her face with his hands, Michael said, "If I accept what you just offered me, I'm afraid I'll get my face slapped."

"I don't know what you're talking about," she murmured, dancing her fingers across his chest. "It was just an innocent kiss."

Her flagrant denial was too great a temptation to resist. Grabbing her, Michael kissed her forcefully, probing her mouth aggressively until she was breathless. As their need for each other rose, he slid his hands around to her taut buttocks and kneaded them. Toby instinctively rocked back and forth against him in a primitive rhythm that begged for release.

Michael nibbled at her earlobe and then whispered, "Now do you understand? I don't want to stop at just kissing you."

If his children hadn't been waiting less than ten feet away, Michael would have spirited Toby up the stairs and into her bedroom. Grateful for reality checking his ardor, Michael stroked Toby's head and questioned how two people who were so perfect for each other could be so mismatched.

Dropping his arms, Michael opened the front door and turned to Toby. "It's time for me to leave." He eased Paul into his arms and pointed at Suzanne with a jerk of his head.

Toby followed his request and scooped Suzanne's featherweight into her arms. They carried the children to the waiting carriage and bundled them safely up onto the seat.

Before he left, Michael put his arm around Toby's waist and walked her back to the stoop. "I enjoyed myself tonight and so did the children. Can we come back for another picnic?" Without Toby's guidance, Michael wasn't sure he knew how to have fun with his children. But when they were all together, it was easy to be natural and loving with Paul and Suzanne.

"Anytime," Toby said, and leaned her head against Michael's chest.

"I wish I could stay," he said, and nuzzled her soft, golden hair.

"Handsome men are always welcome to stay," a feminine voice invited from the sidewalk.

"Rosie!" Toby screamed. "What the blazes are you doing here?"

Chapter Seven

"Well, you're not the only one who can run away from home," Rosie announced.

"I did not run away, Rosamond."

"That's not what Papa told Alex and Mary when they arrived and you weren't at home to help Mary."

Papa! Toby was sure her father's ire was now fanned into a rage with Rosie's flight to New York. "You did ask his permission, didn't you?"

Rosie put her valise down and exhaled as if the question were a tedious detail. "I left him a note."

"Brave of you," Michael said.

"Smart," Rosie quipped. "He would never have agreed to let me come, so why waste both our breaths arguing?"

Michael's eyebrows lifted in dismay. "Toby," he said, "why don't I stop by the telegraph office on my way home and reassure your father Rosie is safe?"

Toby nodded. "Thank you. Tell him I'll write tomorrow."

He heard the fatigue in her voice and felt sorry for her. Poor Toby, it seemed she would be eternally obligated to her family. Michael lightly wrapped his arm around her waist and gave her a reassuring hug. "If you need to take tomorrow off from work, I'll understand."

"I appreciate the offer," Toby said, sighing, thoroughly vexed with Rosie, "but I will be in early." She was determined not to let her sister interfere with her life.

After he left, Toby turned to look for Rosie and found her sister making herself quite at home in the parlor. Already she had tossed her hat onto the table, her cape across a chair and stretched out on the settee as if she had always lived in this house.

Furious, Toby demanded, "Just how do you plan to support yourself, Rosamond? Because I'm not going to."

"Keep spooning with Michael on the front porch and you won't need to work at all. You'll be too busy as Mrs. Sedaine to help him in the office."

"What I do with my private life is none of your business," Toby spluttered, humiliated at having had Rosie witness such a private moment. "But how you plan on making a living is my business."

"I'll get a job," Rosie answered blithely.

"Doing what?"

"Something."

"You always were a stickler for specifics," Toby snapped.

Rosie huffed indignantly. "Toby, you never like anything I do."

It was true, and for an instant Toby felt guilty. Her sister seldom did anything she approved of, but it was pointless to fight with Rosie tonight. There was nothing either of them could do about the situation. "I'll make up a bed for you in the spare room."

"I told Charlie you wouldn't mind having me stay with you. He said you would throw a full-fledged hissy fit when you saw me."

"If you don't gather your belongings up and put them away where they belong, Charlie's prediction will be right on target," Toby warned, and wearily trudged up the stairs.

Later Toby undressed and drooped into her own bed. The night had started out like a dream and ended in a nightmare. Pushing Rosie from her mind, Toby centered on the lovely hours she and Michael had shared. Remembering his sweet kisses, she was quickly lulled to sleep.

Toby sat bolt upright in shame. The dream caused a crimson flame to sear up her neck, spread across her cheeks and burn her ears. Was it considered sinful to have such fantasies? She was sure it must be, and there was no one to blame but herself. After all, she had enjoyed pressing her body into Michael's when he kissed her; she had adored being held by him, and she had allowed him into her bed— even if only in her fantasy.

She was furious with the betrayal of her subconscious and with the unbearable ache she was still feeling in her stomach. Confused by her need, Toby padded down the stairs to the kitchen and splashed cold water over her face.

Desperate to shove Michael to the back of her mind, she put the kettle on to boil for tea and sat down to write a letter to her father. It was difficult to write, because she was tempted to apologize for Rosie's impetuous behavior, and yet Toby didn't really feel she was to blame—or was she? Her brothers and sisters had always looked up to her as an example. Smiling grimly at Rosie's perverse nature, Toby realized this was the first time Rosie had ever copied her actions. Normally her sister went to great lengths to do exactly the opposite.

Deciding to take a different tack, rather than start the letter on a defensive tone, Toby told her father about all the nice things that had happened since she left Missouri. It was comforting to describe her new life, focusing on the positive while catapulting the negative—Rosie's sudden appearance and her disturbing dream—to the recesses of her mind.

As she filled the pages, Toby felt a bit homesick, picturing the twins' faces, remembering Charlie's raucous laughter and her father's habit of forgetting to change out of his slippers when he left the house.

Toby was still hunched over, working on the fifth page of her letter when she heard Chantelle's key rattle in the lock.

"I thought you'd be sound asleep by now," Chantelle said as she came into the kitchen.

"A noise from the street woke me," Toby said, blushing at the little lie. What sleep she had snatched had been filled with Michael.

"Are you all right? You look flushed."

"I'm fine. Just irritated with my sister."

"Get a letter from home?"

"A package."

"Oh? What was in it."

"Rosamond."

"Rosamond? Is that a flower?"

"No, a sister. A nineteen-year-old bundle of trouble."

Chantelle sat down at the table. "She's here? That's wonderful. I wish I had a family that could visit me."

"How would you like to adopt Rosie?" Toby said, laughing.

"Gladly."

Chantelle was wistful and Toby wondered what was behind it. She and Chantelle had been living together for over a week and not once had her friend mentioned anything about her past. The void in Chantelle's life caused Toby to suddenly appreciate the little vexations her family caused.

"Tell me why you're so upset," Chantelle encouraged. Toby summed up the story of Rosie's unexpected arrival, and by the end of it she felt a little silly for reacting so harshly. It was wonderful to have a confidante for a change instead of being the mother confessor.

"Now tell me what good thing happened today," Chantelle said.

"Good? Something fantastic happened," Toby said, jumping up and pulling Chantelle to her feet. "You must see it."

As Chantelle admired Michael's gift, Toby prattled on and on about the entire magical evening. Abruptly she blushed and became silent.

Even in the dim parlor light, Chantelle could see that Toby was flustered. "Ah, I suspect he kissed you goodnight."

"Yes, I guess so." Her answer was tentative.

"And?"

"Nothing," Toby said, wheeling around and returning to the kitchen.

"You didn't answer me, *chère*," Chantelle said, her accent more pronounced than usual.

"Yes, Michael kissed me and I kissed him back."

"Certainly you don't think that is wrong, do you?"

"No, but . . ." There was no way a decent woman could admit to a dream like hers.

"But what?"

"Oh, Chantelle," Toby cried, "what am I going to do?"

"Talk about it," Chantelle softly encouraged.

"I'm so confused." Toby sat back down at the table and propped her head on her hand. "Have you ever wanted a man so bad it hurt but, at the same time, you wished you had never met him?"

Before answering, Chantelle poured herself a cup of tea. Toby looked up and saw she was taking a long time stirring the sugar, apparently thinking before she spoke. For the first time, Toby realized Chantelle had more than a beautiful dark face. Character, wisdom, intelligence and sensitivity made her even more stunning than what nature alone had given her.

"You're talking about my life," Chantelle said, laying the spoon on the saucer. "I love Caleb so much that if I lost him, I wouldn't want to continue living."

"It would be hard loving a man who travels from one honky-tonk to another and never wants to settle down," Toby commiserated.

Chantelle shook her head back and forth and laughed quietly. "You have it all wrong, Toby. He's asked me to be his wife a thousand times. Maybe even two."

"And you said no?" Nothing in Toby's life made any sense. Had the entire world gone mad? "But, you said you loved him."

"I do, but I'm already married."

Myriad questions popped into her head, but Toby was determined not to make an insensitive remark. This was no time for hasty, foolish comments. Still, the questions were unlimited and she voiced the most urgent. "Where is your husband? What happened? Did he abandon you? Does Caleb know about him?"

Reaching across the table, Chantelle placed her long, slim fingers over Toby's hand and asked, "Can I be honest with you, woman to woman?"

"I'll never tell a soul."

She began the most amazing, as well as the saddest, story Toby had ever heard. In Haiti, Chantelle had married a wealthy mahogany grower and exporter, Dominic Reynard. It was a marriage her parents had arranged when Chantelle was only fifteen. They had assured their daughter that Dominic was a fine man and she would grow to love him in time. Unknown to her parents, Dominic had a sadistic nature, which he'd kept hidden until after the wedding.

For the first year, Dominic had only slapped his bride on occasion. Later his abuse escalated until his last beating left Chantelle nearly dead. She spent weeks in bed recuperating, secretly planning how she could escape. If Dominic had caught even a hint she was considering running away, he would have killed her. In Port-au-Prince a wife was no more than chattel, and Dominic's position and wealth left him above the law.

Chantelle might have sought refuge with her parents if they hadn't both died in a hurricane one month after her marriage. She knew no one powerful enough to protect her from her husband. Alone, and with no other recourse, she finally decided she had no choice except to leave Haiti forever.

One night when Dominic was carousing with his friends, Chantelle dressed in servant's clothing and bribed the housekeeper's grandson to take her to Cuba on his fishing boat. Afraid even Cuba wouldn't be far enough away from Dominic's wrath, she pawned her jewelry in Havana for passage to the United States.

Desperate to survive her new poverty, in New Orleans Chantelle learned how to sew for a living. As soon as she could, she left that city and sailed up the Mississippi to Saint Louis to put more distance between herself and Haiti.

"I was designing costumes for show business people when a tall man with the most brilliant smile walked into the shop. He wanted a special suit for his show at the Peacock Café and had heard I was the only person in town able to make heavily braided lapels lay flat," Chantelle said.

"Caleb, right?"

"Yes, *chère*. I tried to deny my feelings for him, but that man would not accept my rejection."

Toby was struck by how alike she and her friend were. They both had dynamic men who enhanced their very existence, and yet it was not a simple matter to include Michael and Caleb in their lives. Everything was all tangled together. Love, rejection, impossibility, desire, fear, hope...the list was endless just as the obstacles were immeasurable.

"Have you tried to get a divorce?" Toby asked.

Chantelle smiled. "*Chère*, I've spent hundreds of dollars hiring attorneys to force my husband to release me. Nothing works."

"Why not simply pose as Caleb's wife?" Toby suggested. "Who would know the difference?" Just last month, she would have considered such a proposal to be indecent, but she wasn't the same woman she had been.

What she used to define as a standard for morality had bowed to a greater principle—love. If a man and woman loved each other as much as Caleb and Chantelle did, it was wrong to keep them apart. Dominic's silence was just as evil as his battering.

"Maybe Caleb and I could live with the lie, but I would never do that to our children. He is a fine man," Chantelle said with pride, "and I want his children to legitimately own his name."

Toby couldn't argue, and there was no point in carrying on their conversation. Neither could change the rules to suit their needs. Silently they hugged, doused the light and went to bed.

Michael hardly slept at all, because he couldn't wait for morning to see Toby again. When he had left her at her door, he'd had a sense of what Adam must have felt when he walked away from Eden.

At the office, Michael arrived before anyone else, put an enameled coffeepot on the portable oil hot plate and then popped down to the corner grocery to buy a pint of fresh cream. Toby liked to heavily doctor her coffee, and Michael wanted to treat her to fresh, sweet cream.

By the time he returned, the coffeepot was percolating and the office smelled aromatic and inviting. He was certain she was up quite late sorting out Rosie's unexpected arrival and knew the small gesture would be appreciated. Toby acknowledged any kind gesture with sincere thanks, and she made it a joy to do tender little things for her.

When Toby walked through the door, she saw Michael grin with that priceless smile of his, showing off the small space between his teeth, and couldn't decide if she wanted to melt into his arms or run away. He looked so tempting, so handsome in the early-morning light, she nearly forgot her embarrassing dream and kissed him hello. What stopped her was the fear that if she gave in to her whim she would be encouraging a romantic covenant, and she didn't know if she could accept Michael's affection and his children. She had left Saint Louis to escape responsibilities, not waltz into another demanding set of arms.

Toby smiled warmly. "Good morning, Michael. How many appointments do we have today?"

"Who cares? The only thing on my calendar is supper with you tonight."

She tried not to stammer. "N-not tonight, Michael. I'm going to try and convince Rosie to return home. Also, Chantelle and I are going to start sewing a new dress for me. I need more clothes for the office." She kept bringing the subject back to business.

Toby's retreat frustrated Michael. Last night he had decided Toby was the logical, intelligent choice to be his wife. She was tolerant and affectionate with Suzanne, stern and levelheaded with Paul and could manage his home with skill and aptitude. Toby Wells was more than a competent assistant, she would make an outstanding wife.

He had made up his mind to start courting her today, and now she was using his own ruse to keep him at bay. Hiding behind work had been his personal game, and she had obviously learned the rules herself. Well, Michael vowed to himself, she wasn't going to get away with it. He would do anything he had to to budge her out of her complacency and into his arms where she belonged.

"Don't do this, Toby," he said, coming closer. "Don't pretend it's business as usual. We're just beginning to trust each other, learn what makes us happy, discover that merely touching makes our hearts rise into our throats," he said softly, placing his finger on her lips. "Don't lie to me or to yourself. Last night was real."

"I know it was," she admitted, "but I'm frightened. Can't we take our time?"

"Moment by sweet moment, Angel Eyes," he swore, tracing his finger around the lovely curve of her mouth. He stopped tantalizing her, quickly kissed her and said, "Let's get to work."

The morning was hectic and it was over before Michael and Toby knew it. There were still unfinished contracts littering their desks, and at noon they opted to skip lunch and stay in the office.

Caleb dropped by with Chantelle to read over his rewritten agreement with Sedaine Music. After carefully studying it, he said, "Don't appear you've hung my hide on a clothesline."

"Your hide isn't any good to me hung out to dry," Michael answered. "I want it plopped in front of a piano for the next ten years."

"Morning, noon and night," Caleb promised.

"Nights are mine," Chantelle said.

"That's the best proposition she's ever made. Say, Michael, how about writing that in for me? 'Chantelle Reynard must nurture, love and obey Caleb MacRae.'"

"You can sign a contract like that at city hall's marriage license desk," Michael chuckled.

"Tell it to her," Caleb said, pointing to Chantelle.

Chantelle smiled ruefully before she answered. "We'll set the date when the poor are fat and the rich are skinny. Until then I'll stay independent, thank you."

"A hex on Susan B. Anthony," Michael scolded. "All you modern women have abandoned hearth and home." He winked at Toby.

Toby defended not just Chantelle, but also herself. "Aren't we entitled to have ambitions, careers and dreams of our own?"

"Certainly," Michael said, "but you *can* have all of them."

"My exact words," Caleb agreed.

Before Toby or Chantelle could argue, a hullabaloo burst through the door. Laura Sedaine, with Ansel in tow, invaded the office. She was toting a pile of boxes almost as high as her nose and Ansel, too, was overloaded with parcels.

"Mother!" Michael was surprised to see her. "What's all this?"

"Our costumes for the party," she chastised as she placed her parcels on Michael's desk.

"What are you talking about?"

"The benefit on Saturday, silly."

Lord, but he'd forgotten all about the gala to raise money for his mother's pet charity. His mother had come up with an idea to invite all of their prominent friends to a ball to bolster the funds in the Arthur Sedaine Memorial Scholarship. After her husband's death, Laura had established the grant to provide schooling to bright, eager students unable to pursue their education without aid.

"Costumes?" he almost wailed. But then he changed his tone, unwilling to hurt her feelings after all the preparations she'd made. "I know you've worked hard, but must I dress up, too?"

"Son," Laura clucked, "where has your head been? I decided months ago to make this affair the talk of the city. You know how much I like to wear period gowns."

He groaned silently. His mother, like so many of New York's society ladies, relished flaunting what she considered to be her historical expertise. There were a dozen women's guilds where the members frequently hosted theme parties.

After coming up with the original idea for this benefit, he'd not given any more thought to it. It served him right. His negligence had allowed Laura to bastardize his good intentions.

"Smile," his mother said. "I've taken care of everything for you. Ansel was kind enough to donate his tailor's expertise in creating these fine costumes. Ansel, dear, put those boxes on the desk and I'll show Michael what he's going to wear."

"Poor sap," Ansel mumbled as he dumped his bundles. "I thought letting her convince me to come as Henry VIII was humiliating until I saw your getup."

"Thanks, pal," Michael hissed.

"Don't sabotage me, Ansel," Laura warned. "With your red hair you'll look just like Henry after we put a little pillow under your coat." She affectionately patted his stomach.

Toby was amused by the look of horror on Michael's face as Laura unwrapped tight cotton leggings, a soft tunic, a pair of kidskin shoes, a twisted cord belt and leather bindings to wrap around his calves. The tunic was thigh length, and the cotton of the leggings was so sheer every muscle in Michael's legs would be outlined.

"Good God, mother!" Michael said. "What is this?"

"You're going to be Macbeth, Thane of Glamis," Laura answered.

Toby couldn't resist needling him. "Put it on, Michael. I'm sure you'll look dashing."

"Thank you, Miss Wells," Laura said, misreading Toby's gibe. "See, Michael. Even your little assistant approves."

The insult infuriated Toby and she bit her lip, fighting the urge to counter with a snub of her own. Someday she would enjoy grinding Laura Sedaine under her heel like an old cigar butt.

"If you're insisting, Laura, on being so authentic you've overlooked something," Ansel said. "Henry always had a consort." He turned to Toby and bowed. "Miss Wells, would you consider being my Anne Boleyn?"

"What a splendid suggestion," Laura beamed at Ansel. "Ansel and Toby would make a lovely couple."

"No," Michael said brusquely, "they wouldn't. I already invited Toby to be my escort and she agreed. So sorry, Ansel."

"Toby will be the belle of this boring little undertaking," Ansel said.

"I'm flattered," Toby said, glowering at Michael for including her in his deception, "but I'm afraid I don't have a costume."

Michael was seething at Ansel. How dare he ask Toby to accompany him to this infernal party! The moment he had the opportunity, Michael would corner the rounder and warn Ansel to stay away from Toby. "Besides," he said, staring at Ansel, "I don't picture Toby as Anne Boleyn. She's more like Helen of Troy."

Ansel agreed heartily. "You're right, old man. Anne's beauty conquered one heart, Helen's launched a thousand ships."

"Launched or sank?" Laura sniped.

Michael's patience with his mother and his brother-in-law was quickly disappearing. Rather than directly criticize her in front of other people, which would send her into a dither, he decided to put her subtly in her place. "Give Hugo von Feldman this atrocious outfit," he said, fingering the limp leggings dangling out of the box. "Chantelle will design something appropriate for Toby and me to wear."

Laura Sedaine regally drew herself up and asked, "Who is this Chantelle person? I searched the entire city for a talented seamstress who was skilled at making costumes before I settled on using Ansel's tailor."

"Oh, pardon me," Michael said, "I've failed to introduce you to my friends." He turned to Caleb and Chantelle, who had remained as quiet and motionless as statues throughout this whole exchange.

"Your friends?" Laura scoffed.

The way Michael's mother's voice rose higher than normal, and the way both her eyebrows shot up, infuriated Toby. Any fool could tell she was aghast that Michael was close to Caleb and Chantelle, and Toby placed a wager with herself that Laura wouldn't even hire servants if they weren't white. She couldn't let the inferred slight pass without defending Caleb and Chantelle against the bigotry.

"Yes," Toby replied. "In fact, Chantelle and I are roommates."

"How liberated," Laura sniffed.

Until this second, Michael had never realized the depth of his mother's snobbery. Embarrassing him was forgivable, but snubbing three people he respected wasn't. "That's it, Mother," he said angrily, "I've had—"

Before he finished, Chantelle broke in, "I'd be honored to make you a costume, Michael."

Toby looked first at Laura, who was miffed by Chantelle's interruption, and then at Michael, who was still towering threateningly over his mother. She hurried across the room and snatched Michael's arm.

"I have a wonderful thought," Toby said. "Why don't we *all* dress up for the party? Caleb can give us a sample of his beautiful music and Chantelle will have an opportunity to show off her fabulous gowns."

Michael had to swallow his laugh. Toby was delightfully devious, and he thoroughly approved of her just retribution. His mother was already inwardly balking at Toby's being invited—much less at two people she considered servant material being added to the guest list.

Hugging Toby, he said, "Brilliant, Miss Wells. I've been looking for a way to introduce Caleb to New York." Peeking over Toby's curls, he looked at his mother and saw she was nearly apoplectic.

"But I haven't planned for all these extra people," Laura sputtered.

Winking at Toby, Chantelle said, "Why, Mrs. Sedaine, I'm surprised at how you ladies in New York prepare for such galas. When I hosted large parties in my home in Haiti, I always had my servants plan for at least twenty additional guests."

Caleb audibly gasped, not at Mrs. Sedaine's capitulation but at Chantelle's remarks. It was the first time he'd ever known her to publicly mention her life in Haiti, and he was pleased at the breakthrough. He and his lady might not be wanted at this affair, but nothing would keep him from escorting Chantelle if it meant she was beginning to reconcile her past. "Chantelle, can you come up with something for me, too?" he said, protectively wrapping his arm around her waist.

Thunder and lightning would have paled against Laura's wrath as she stormed out of the office and slammed the door so hard it shattered the glass inset. As shards crashed to the floor, she turned and yelled at Michael through the jagged gap, "None of this would have happened if you hadn't brought that little snit back from Saint Louis. She's turned you against me."

As Laura's back disappeared down the hall, Ansel shrugged indifferently and said to Toby, "Don't worry, she's prone to fits. A little cold water dashed in her face and she'll calm down."

Ansel followed Laura out but blew a kiss to Toby and winked at her. "Save the first dance for me," he said, and waved goodbye, neglecting to close the maimed office door.

"My pleasure," Toby said.

Michael wanted to stuff a fist down Ansel's throat. Nearly every day his immature brother-in-law found an excuse to fawn over Toby, and his unwanted attentions were pushing Michael beyond control. Women, any and all women, were a challenge, and Ansel was determined to add Toby to the bevy of single ladies who naively believed his babbling. Frustrated, Michael grabbed the battered door by the frame where the glass had been and violently shut it with a force that finished knocking it from its jamb. A sliver of glass nicked his fingers and they began to bleed.

"Here," Toby said, and tossed him the empty cream pitcher, "try smashing this if you're intent on having a tantrum. Your mother had first dibs on the door."

He carefully replaced the china on the tray and picked the sliver out of his hand. "Don't be so smug, Miss Wells," he said, taking his anger at his family out on Toby.

She ignored his misplaced fury and asked calmly, "Do you think I jeopardized the benefit?"

Trying to conquer his temper, Michael inhaled two deep breaths. He was unsuccessful and snapped his answer. "No. She'd rather die than cancel this ball after sending out all those invitations. We've just put a few twists in her plans."

"Michael," Chantelle said quietly, "we don't really expect to go to the party. It's obvious we're not welcome."

"Then I'm not going, either," Toby said.

"Wonderful," Michael roared. "You get me in this fix, then *all* of you," he said, glaring at his friends, "abandon me. Thank you for your support."

Crossing her arms as if she were studying Michael intently, Toby said, "Caleb and Chantelle, were you under the same impression I was that people in New York were soft-spoken, genteel folks?"

"Yep," Caleb said.

"My illusions have died, too. It's so easy to get these big-city people riled," she said, baiting Michael.

He bit. "Toby, you've done everything in your power to upset us."

"Honey," Toby crooned, "you haven't even seen me try, yet. My, but you Sedaines are a fragile bunch."

"Seems to me you were a little upset with *your* family last night," Michael countered.

"You're not going to win today," Caleb said to Michael, shaking his head. "But you're putting on a better show than anything currently playing at Greenpasture's." He started to clap and was joined by the ladies.

Michael and Toby turned and looked into the hallway where a cluster of people were staring into the room. Obviously the slamming, shattering glass and subsequent argument had attracted spectators from the other offices in the building.

"Show's over, folks," Chantelle said. She took Caleb by the arm and they dispersed the small crowd as they left.

Finally alone with Toby, Michael's temper abated and he admitted, "In the last hour, I have been angrier than in any time in my life. I have also made a complete jackass of myself, which, believe it or not, I don't enjoy."

Toby smiled sheepishly. "I wish I could say the same. I have embarrassed myself so many times I quit counting years ago."

Michael stepped up to her and brushed a blond wisp of hair off her forehead. "That's why I want you to marry me. I guess I was waiting for a feisty, opinionated, unconventional lady who could stand up to my mother."

She gulped. "Marriage?"

"Yes," Michael said, taking her hand and clasping it between his. "From the moment I first saw you, I've known we would make a good team. You agreed with me. Remember?"

Looking up into his dancing brown eyes, Toby realized that for the past twenty-four hours she had been trapped in an emotional mayhem. It was all caused because she had been struggling to deny the obvious—she was in love with Michael. But could she accept his platonic proposal?

Chapter Eight

Michael read the shock in Toby's eyes, and she burst into a bustle of activity. "Shouldn't we talk?" he asked, catching her by the arm as she madly grabbed her hat and purse.

"Later," Toby said. "I must get home and see that Rosie has packed her belongings. If I let her stay another day she'll never leave."

Adeptly Toby had shunted him aside under the guise of family obligation. As much as she protested her responsibilities, Michael saw Toby had a knack for using them as a powerful weapon that made any objections appear crass and jaded. Determined to impress her with the wisdom of their union, he left the office in Reginald's care and followed her home.

Neither of them was prepared for the commotion that greeted them at the door of the brownstone. Rosie was waiting on the stairs, ready to pounce on Toby the second she arrived.

"Chantelle told me about the ball!" Rosie said, nearly exploding off the stoop. "I can't wait to go."

"Calm down," Toby advised. "The only place you're going is back to Saint Louis. Besides, you weren't on the guest list."

"That can be corrected," Michael said, diluting Toby's objection.

"You are not going," Toby said.

"Toby?" Rosie was stricken. "You can't be serious. All my life I've dreamed of attending a fancy dress ball."

"I am serious and you are going to miss it. There's a train that leaves this evening," Toby said staunchly.

Rosie's shoulders dropped, her face went slack with disappointment and she began weeping. "How can you be so mean?" she whimpered.

Michael felt sorry for the girl. "Why can't Rosie stay for just a few more days? It can't hurt."

Toby scowled. She wasn't happy about his usurping her authority but had to admit that denying Rosie a once-in-a-lifetime opportunity wasn't fair. If the roles were switched, she would be just as miserable as Rosie.

"Go peel some potatoes while Michael and I discuss this," Toby told her.

Knowing she would win, thanks to Michael, Rosie hugged him enthusiastically, "Thank you, thank you," she said, and ran obediently inside.

"You have an admirer," Toby said dryly, entering the hall.

"Possibly you've been a mother for so long," he said, following her, "you've forgotten what it's like to be a little girl."

She turned on him abruptly. "First of all, you haven't looked closely at my sister. She isn't a little girl but a young woman. Secondly—" Toby sighed deeply "—I don't think I was ever young."

Michael found her admission poignant. Perhaps that was why Toby was often playful, trying to release the neglected child inside. Kissing her on the forehead, holding her tight to his breast, Michael said, "Then it's about time you stopped trying to mother Rosie. Let her live her own life and you live yours."

"I don't know how," Toby admitted, nestling into him.

"Stay with me and I'll teach you, Angel Eyes."

Darn him, she thought, he makes it so tempting to quit struggling against his love. With a start, Toby realized Michael had never said a word about love—all he had discussed was marriage. But no man would ask a woman to marry him without being in love with her, and she had successfully stalled giving him a direct answer.

Chantelle stepped out of the kitchen and intruded on the couple, "Still speaking to me, Toby?"

Releasing Michael, Toby turned to her. "Of course. Rosie was bound to find out."

"Am I making four or five costumes?"

"It's up to you, Chantelle," Toby said, leaving Rosie's fate in her friend's hands.

"Five it is. I haven't the heart to say no to her," Chantelle answered.

The piano came to life and Michael recognized Caleb's touch. Despite the hostile reception of New York, Caleb was still composing, bent on waking the city up to ragtime.

Toby and Chantelle left Michael with Caleb while they went to the kitchen to tell Rosie the good news. They found her diligently scrubbing and peeling potatoes, willing to do anything to insinuate herself into Toby's good graces.

"Well, Rosie, what kind of costume do you have in mind?" Toby asked.

Rosie squealed. "Marie Antoinette. Yards and yards of lace and brocade."

Toby laughed at Rosie's excitement and expensive request. "Cinderella in rags would be better."

"My fairy godmother wouldn't do that to me," Rosie chirped, hugging Chantelle. "Would you?"

"This one doesn't have time for five elaborate costumes. All of us are going to wear simple but nice ones," Chantelle promised. "Rosie, if Toby will parole you from the kitchen, I could use your help starting them."

"Go ahead," Toby said, holding up the pathetic nubbin of potato Rosie had pared. Her sister had barely left any meat on the poor thing. "Out of five pounds we'd be lucky to get an ounce of food," she yelled after her sister.

The security of doing mundane, familiar tasks allowed Toby's mind to sort through her jumble of feelings. The music in the next room, the sound of Michael's voice encouraging Caleb, the happy giggles of Chantelle and Rosie down the hall all helped to give her a sense of peace. It was as if she were home again, back in Papa's house—and she was shocked.

For years she believed she'd wanted to escape having people underfoot, mobs to cook for, a house to clean and the tumultuous confusion she'd had back home. Standing at the stove, Toby acknowledged that in less than a month she had instinctively recreated the same open, carefree home in New York. The question of why nagged her.

Grudgingly Toby owned liking the noise, the people and being needed. That left only ambition as the reason for coming here. Or was it? Blushing, Toby knew she was lying to herself. She had come because of Michael. If another man, one less attractive, less kind, less supportive had asked her to follow him, she would have quickly said no. Michael had a hold on her, and his grip terrified her.

On Saturday, Toby twirled in front of the mirror, admiring the Grecian gown Chantelle had designed and sewn. The way the fine white lawn of sheerest linen draped on Toby's body was almost sinful. Chantelle called the gown a chiton, which was a fancy word for two rectangular pieces of cloth equal in length to Toby's height. After the material was cut to size, the dress was constructed by sewing a simple seam up the sides and along the shoulders.

Two days ago, when Chantelle had pulled the chiton over Toby's head for the first time, it had hung lifelessly to the floor. Toby had been sure Chantelle had made a mistake, a flour sack would have been just as attractive. But her friend had known what she was doing and proved it. Starting at the back, Chantelle had brought a golden cord up over Toby's shoulders, crossed it under her breasts and wrapped the girdle around her waist, retying it at the back. The effect had been, and still was, astonishing.

Once more Toby marveled at how flowing sleeves were instantly produced with the cord, how her figure was accented by the cinching and how the fabric molded to her slender midriff.

During that first fitting, Chantelle had stood back and inspected her handiwork. "Saints preserve us, *chère,* but you are breathtaking," she had said.

Toby had groaned, feeling almost naked. What would Michael think? She wanted to do nothing to change their relationship, since the only word to describe the past few days was blissful.

After discovering, and admitting to herself, she was in love, she and Michael had spent every evening together. He would bring Paul and Suzanne along part of the time and they would stroll at the edge of the Hudson or romp in the park. Other times, he came alone and they would dine in intimate restaurants, talking for hours. They had shared secrets and whispered endearments, but the words Toby was waiting to hear were never uttered.

One night as they neared the brownstone, Toby had said, "Michael, I have an awkward question which is nagging me."

"You know you can ask me anything. What is it?"

"In all your rush to have me set a wedding date, you've never once told me the reason you want me to be your wife." Toby hoped her hint was obvious enough.

"I know how hesitant you are about making a lifelong commitment," Michael had said. "I'll try to be more patient and understanding, allow you time to adjust to our new relationship."

Toby looked at the costume and wondered why Michael couldn't bring himself to say the words, *I love you, Toby.* Was he still in love with Lillian and felt as though he were betraying his wife if he admitted his love to Toby? If his omission continued, Toby would have to confront Michael, but for now she was content with the way he showed her he loved her and didn't need to hear the words.

Besides, Toby had a secret misgiving of her own she wasn't ready to share with Michael. Every time she thought about telling Michael she was terrified of childbirth and couldn't face the risk of having children, Toby shuddered. He had made too many proclamations about what a joy it would be to have a large family to believe he would accept her fear and abide by her choice. Eventually she would find the right words, but there was no need to brood. They were a long way from being at the altar. Turning to Chantelle and forcing herself to think about her immediate concern, Toby had said, "I'd feel a good deal more comfortable if I was wearing Rosie's Little Red Riding Hood cape."

"Put those lovely arms down and stop hiding your figure," Chantelle had scolded.

Chastised, Toby had dropped her crossed arms from her chest and let them hang at her sides. "I'm not sure I'll have the nerve to go through with this."

"Hmm," Chantelle had muttered, ignoring Toby's anxiety. "I'm going to have to make you some very plain underwear. Ruffles and lace will only ruin the clean lines of this costume. And shoes. What are we going to do about those?" she had said.

By Saturday morning, Chantelle had solved the problems. A unique one-piece undergarment had been made, and she found a pair of white Crocus lambskin slippers for Toby to wear.

All that Toby had to do now was her hair. She piled her curls on top of her head and fashioned a cornet from the excess gold braid used on the dress. The result was lovely and some of Toby's misgivings faded.

Once more, she pirouetted in front of the mirror before she heard the doorbell. "Good luck," she whispered to her image and went downstairs.

When Michael looked up and saw Toby descending, he was speechless. He studied her with such intensity that Toby thought he was displeased with her costume, and all of her dread returned.

Searching for some way to dispel her uneasiness, she said as she reached the bottom step, "Michael, you look dashing." She wasn't lying. He made a splendid Paris to her Helen, garbed in a knee-length masculine chiton.

"No wonder Paris abducted Helen and I doubt she was half as lovely as you," he said, exhaling deeply. "If I start a war, will you run away with me?"

His compliment was reassuring and Toby relaxed. "Thank you, Michael. I was feeling a bit foolish."

"Stunning but never foolish. You'll start a new fashion trend."

Toby reached for a cloak to cover her gown, but he stopped her. "It's hot today and why cover up perfection?"

"If you insist," she said, and took his arm as he escorted her to his waiting five-glass landau.

Caleb was outfitted as a baseball player and Chantelle had altered one of her gowns and draped a shawl over it so that she looked like a Parisian noblewoman of 1812. They were waiting with Rosie, and Michael helped Toby up the one step to join them.

As they were chauffeured to the soiree, Michael asked, "Do you understand exactly what has been planned for the party?"

"Your mother sent a note explaining each of us was to prepare some type of skit, song or act. We'll put a slip of paper into a hat with the name of one of the other guests and an amount of money we're willing to donate to the scholarship," Toby said. "Is that correct?"

"And the top ten money-makers will provide the evening's entertainment."

"What have you prepared?" Caleb asked Michael.

"I have it easy. Homer wrote my lines and after I recite those dry old words everyone will be glad to shoo me off stage. What about you, Toby?"

"I have a little song ready but, since no one knows me, there isn't any chance I'll need to use it."

She was certain the hours she'd spent writing her comical version of Helen of Troy's story would be a waste. Still, she wasn't willing to take even a minuscule risk of not being prepared and end up looking like a ninny in front of Michael's friends.

"Whose idea was this little auction, anyway?" Rosie asked as the carriage threaded through the crowded streets.

"Ever heard of 'Kiss the Pig'?"

"Fortunately, no," Chantelle said, wrinkling her nose.

Michael told them how he had learned the game. "One summer mother took me to France where her grandparents still lived in a small village. Every year the whole town had a country fair. The main source of collecting enough money for new textbooks for the school was by playing Kiss the Pig. Villagers would pool their money, betting on the mayor, the headmaster or the priest. Whoever raised the most had to kiss the fair's prize-winning pig at the end of the day.''

It was a charming story and Toby could picture Michael romping on cobbled streets, guffawing at the sight of a grown-up being forced to endure the indignity of bumping noses with a sow.

"Enough of my family," Michael said. "We have a party to attend."

Toby looked up from his face and was surprised that they were at the hotel already. Michael's story had been one of the only times he had talked about his past, and she been so engrossed she hadn't noticed they were so close.

As the five of them entered the ballroom, Toby had to concentrate to keep from gawking. The glitter of the costumes was fabulous and she was dutifully impressed with the number of people attending. At least a hundred guests were draped as cowboys, pilgrims, Josephines and Napoleons, along with numerous other characters she couldn't fathom. The outrageously garbed patrons roamed the polished parqueted floor with glasses of champagne or punch.

"I'm glad you talked me out of Marie Antoinette," Rosie whispered. "I've counted three so far."

"You look lovely, dear," Toby reassured her. "Enjoy yourself tonight."

Ogling a group of handsome, unattached young men standing to one side of the dance floor, Rosie smiled. "I wonder if one of them is rich and available," she mused.

"Rosie!" Toby scolded. "Don't you think about anything but men?"

"No." Without waiting for another reprimand, Rosie talked Michael into making introductions, leaving Toby alone.

Toby lost Rosie and Michael in the crowd and searched for them. In a second she easily found him; his back was to her, but she would have recognized him anywhere. No one had hair like his, rich ebony and abundant with thick waves, and Michael's shoulders always seemed broader than any other man's. In fact, everything about him was larger than life.

She tried to work her way across the room to him, but Ansel took her by the elbow and guided her to the dance floor. "The first dance is mine," he said quietly but firmly. "After the other men catch sight of you I may not get another chance."

"Certainly," Toby graciously acquiesced.

The orchestra had just finished one waltz and quickly started another. Ansel was an excellent partner, surprisingly light on his feet for a man his size. Toby adeptly followed his lead, but she was not comfortable in his arms. He kept trying to draw her closer while she insisted on keeping a respectable distance between them.

Michael was talking to Joel Greenpasture when the theater owner stopped listening. Joel's gaze had drifted to the dance floor and he looked bewitched. Michael had never seen Joel this animated and was curious about the sparkle in, what was normally, the weary man's eyes.

"Who's the looker?" Joel asked.

Turning and following his stare, Michael saw Toby waltzing in Ansel's arms. Awe and jealousy struck simultaneously. The other dancers had moved aside, making room for the stunning couple. Ansel had never looked as proud of himself as he did at this moment. But Toby, dear Toby, was ravishing.

The chandelier's light frolicked in her golden curls, the soft breeze from the open terrace doors pressed her diaphanous gown against her supple body and her fair, unblemished skin was lustrous. Her beauty, which had always captivated him, was now magnified tenfold in her lovely costume.

Blast Ansel to hell, Michael silently cursed as he watched Toby struggle to keep her partner's hands from straying. Michael was the only man who had a right to touch her. Enraged at Ansel's vulgar groping, Michael left Joel Greenpasture unanswered and strode up to them.

Tapping Ansel on the shoulder, Michael said, "I'm sure you won't mind."

"Like the devil, I won't," Ansel warned him off. "Each man for himself."

Ansel attempted to spin Toby away, but Michael gripped the thick muscle above his collarbone and severely pinched it. He knew he was hurting Ansel but didn't care. "Leave like the gentleman you're not," he ordered.

"Let the lady choose," Ansel bartered.

"She has already chosen me."

Toby felt everyone's eyes on her and she cringed, her face turning scarlet. She was grateful for Michael's rescue, but why was it that every time they were near his family and friends a dismal scene developed? Still, she loved Michael's ferocious possessiveness and knew she would never grow tired of it.

"Please," she begged them both, "I'd just as soon sit down and have a glass of punch."

Between them, Michael and Ansel ushered her to a table, and in two minutes Toby was surrounded by a bevy of admirers. Michael decided to be polite and bask in Toby's popularity. He couldn't pick a fight with every man at the party, and she deserved the attention. Not a woman in the crowd could compare to her radiance.

The table in front of Toby was littered with glasses of punch, all brought by gentlemen eager to win an introduction. Their overwhelming interest left her head spinning, and she glanced at Michael every once in a while for reassurance that he was still at her side.

She was relieved when Michael finally freed her from the mob and led her back onto the dance floor. It was a relief to be in his arms, to be near him in the crystalline light and to be comparatively alone.

"I feel like a princess." Toby giggled.

"I'd better be your prince."

"Or what?" she teased.

"Or I'll have to slay all the imposters."

"Ansel first?"

"Definitely."

She drew him closer, throwing decorum to the wind, and whispered in his ear, "No need to harm anyone. You are my prince."

It was all so silly yet so lovely, and Michael's chest swelled at her words. The party, the costumes, the whole affair might be a charade, but what he and Toby were feeling was vividly real.

"We could make this last forever," Michael said softly.

"Wouldn't that be wonderful," Toby said with a sigh, "going through our lives with music and flowers and gaiety. Do you think we'd ever be bored?"

"Oh, I don't think we need worry," Michael said. "Just sitting in the same room with you makes my blood pressure soar."

Toby didn't know quite what to say. Hearing him voice such things caused her heart to pound. Afraid of divulging the intensity of her own response, she quipped, "Does that mean I make you angry or that I please you?"

"Come closer and I'll prove how well you please me."

He spanned the small of her back with his hand and pressed her against him. The jolt of feeling Toby's body, uncorseted, unmasked by yards of starched ruffles kindled his desire even further. It was a double shock to realize his own outfit was just as thin and they might as well have had only a sheet between them. He wondered if she could feel his hardening desire the same way he could feel her rigid nipples against his chest.

Michael could think of nothing else but his longing for her. If this had been their wedding day, he would have spirited her away to peel off the few layers of filmy fabric between them. For tonight, he was eternally grateful to Chantelle for designing the loose, shielding robe.

"Michael, I've been looking all over for you," Laura Sedaine said, shattering the erotic interlude. "You must pay your respects to our guests."

He tensed at the sound of her voice and apologized to Toby with his eyes. "Save another dance for me?"

"Go," Toby said. "I'll wait for you. You can't ignore all the guests who are here to support your father's memorial."

Smiling gratefully, Michael dropped his arms and turned to his mother. Laura was cloaked in a gown of heavy brocade typical of the eleventh century, and an unflattering veil shrouded her head. The headband gave her an ascetic appearance, and she looked more like a nun than a queen.

"Let's get this chore over with," he said to her.

"The company you've been keeping lately has done nothing for your manners," Laura reprimanded. "Smile."

The way his mother totally ignored Toby conveyed more insult than if Laura had slapped her. In this social circle, his mother's ostracism was a death knell to Toby's acceptance and it infuriated him. No wonder Toby felt as if she were in the presence of a predator when his mother was near. Watching Laura victoriously swagger through the throng, Michael devised a plan of revenge for her gauche behavior and a way to present Toby to New York society at the same time.

The highlight of the party, the time when the entertainment was presented, was still over an hour away, and Michael implemented his scheme. Every time he spoke with a friend, he asked them to vote for Toby. Many were happy to oblige but, to his chagrin, several had already been solicited by Ansel. With both men pushing Toby to the forefront, she was sure to be one of the contenders.

But rather than pleasing Michael, Ansel's usurping was grating on his nerves. At the first opportunity, Michael intended to corner Ansel and end the pointless competition. He was going to marry Toby and he wouldn't brook any more interference from his former brother-in-law. At times Michael doubted his sanity for trying to maintain a relationship with Lillian's family, but Laura had always reminded him that Suzanne and Paul had two sets of relatives, not just one. Was it his mother's means of insuring no other woman infringed on her territory?

At ten o'clock, Michael signaled the orchestra to stop playing. Six young boys dressed as pages ran onto the stage and blasted long medieval trumpets. The cacophony was deafening and so bad that Michael almost laughed at the overdone pageantry. Laura's fertile imagination had turned this benefit into a gaudy monstrosity.

"Ladies and gentlemen," Michael said, once again sounding stiff and uncomfortable in front of a large audience, "it's time for the festivities to begin. While we tally your votes for the top ten choices, you will have the unique pleasure of hearing Mr. Caleb MacRae entertain you with his original compositions.''

Michael paused, commanding himself to relax. He couldn't convince his friends to take Caleb seriously if he didn't sound confident. "I know I sound formal," he apologized, "but just talk to me after I've heard Caleb's magic and I'll be as loose as this dress I'm wearing." He shook the folds of his chiton and laughed with the crowd, who enjoyed the joke. With the casual opening complete, Michael left the stage to Caleb and took his place at Toby's side.

When the young people in the crowd couldn't remain still and started to move to the ragtime rhythm, Michael knew Caleb was a triumph. At first it was just a sway here and there, but soon it swelled into outright dancing. The couples improvised their steps, creating new ones to match the lively beat, until even the older couples mimicked them and joined the dance.

"I'll bet Joel is sorry he passed up the first chance on Caleb," Michael said to Toby.

"Is he here tonight?"

"Yes. Over there. He's the one with the slightly noxious look."

She followed Michael's direction and spotted the older man standing at the edge of the crowd. He was tapping his foot, but he definitely was not keeping time to the music. Joel Greenpasture's toe was pounding out his frustration, not his pleasure.

"He does have a bit of a scowl," Toby said, and giggled. "We'll have to make sure we tell Caleb about it."

Their friend's good fortune put Toby and Michael into a lighthearted mood. After Caleb's music, the guests were entertained by the evening's winners. They were treated to songs, a poetry recitation, a dramatic reading, a few mediocre piano selections and one juggling act. None of the talent was outstanding, but the audience wholeheartedly cheered everyone's efforts and, consequently, each person left the stage proud of his or her performance.

As the evening progressed, Michael could see by the smug look his mother had she was confident one of her friends would be number one. He secretly hoped his conspiracy would pay off and his mother would have a comeuppance, but he had to wait along with the rest of the audience. To keep the tension high, each entertainer was announced by an impartial auditor, so not even Laura or Michael knew who the next sacrifice to the evening's frivolity would be.

The pages heralded the number one choice of all the guests with a long, honorary broadcast.

"Now, the moment has arrived. The person to raise five thousand dollars for the conservatory is Miss Toby Wells," the man proclaimed dramatically.

Michael stepped back away from Toby for he wanted to watch her reaction. She blanched for a second and then promptly flushed bright pink at the honor.

"There must be a mistake, Michael," she gasped.

"Are you doubting my friends' taste? They know perfection when they see it," he said, and gently shoved her toward the platform.

Rapidly she overcame her momentary timidity and gracefully stepped onto the stage. She took a moment to speak to the conductor, who pushed a piano forward. Adjusting her gown, Toby sat on the bench and started to play.

Michael was not prepared for Toby's wit. She had written a lively tune that wasn't just a song about Helen of Troy but was a fabulous parody of the famous story. According to Toby's interpretation, Helen was never the Queen of Sparta but was just a simple working girl. Michael recognized Toby was poking fun at his mother's snobbery by rewriting the past and saying that the most beautiful woman in history had not been one of the elite but a commoner.

The myth of Helen's lineage, according to Toby, had been fabricated by jealous women who couldn't bear that a lowly servant girl had brought two empires to their knees. By using her wonderful musical ability, Toby made the music soar dramatically, lilt humorously, and then she twisted the refrains so they taunted the audience with unfinished chords. The effect coincided with the lyrics, creating a complex but delightful satire worthy of the best vaudevillian house.

The audience roared its approval and before the song and act were complete, they joined in singing along with Toby's chorus:

"One wink from mischievous Helen, Sparta's vamp,
And all the boys from Greece decamp!"

The crowd demanded an encore, and Toby obliged them with a repeat of the last verse. Michael watched her play the audience like a consummate entertainer and, if he hadn't known better, he would have wagered she was a comedienne and seasoned singer.

Her success and skill both thrilled and terrified him. He was compelled to admit that he really didn't know Toby as well as he thought he did. What he had seen in Saint Louis had been an unpolished girl; what he was seeing now would awe any professional in the business.

Joel Greenpasture was not the only legitimate theater owner at the benefit. He, and all of his competitors, converged on Toby the instant she stepped offstage. Michael observed them swarm around her and could hear them shouting over one another with offers as if they were bidding on a precious gem at an estate auction.

Michael was suddenly aware that he had provided Toby with an opportunity to write her own ticket in the theater if she wanted it, and he cursed himself for bringing her here tonight. Although his life was dedicated to fostering, discovering and encouraging exceptional talent, he didn't want her working for another man. He wanted her at his side, raising his children. The question was, was this what Toby wanted?

He tried to push his way through the throng of Toby's fans but was repeatedly stopped by guests. "Where did you ever find two such talented people?" several asked. "Ever thought of starting your own vaudeville theater?" others demanded. "If you opened a house you'd have Joel Greenpasture lying awake nights figuring out how to best you," a half dozen contended and laughed.

When Michael reached Toby, he heard Joel Greenpasture make a bid that floored him. Even though Michael was accustomed to the huge sums being offered to talented people, Greenpasture's proposition was staggering.

Instead of speaking to Toby, Michael remained silent. How could he compete with fame, money and the excitement Greenpasture was offering? A girl from Missouri who had left home to escape the drudgery of raising children, cooking meals and cleaning rooms was not going to turn down the opportunity of being a headliner to marry any man.

Or could he give her everything? Hadn't he been stopped by several shrewd businessmen who had all recommended the same thing? That many good minds couldn't all be wrong, and it was the only way to keep Toby. Quickly calculating all he would need to do, Michael momentarily doubted his sanity, but he had no choice—forge ahead or risk losing her.

Toby noticed him at her elbow and feverishly grabbed his arm. "Oh, Michael, isn't wonderful? Mr. Greenpasture actually thinks I could be a success onstage."

"I could make a star out of her," Joel said, "in six months or less. Just look at her, Michael, she sparkles like one now."

Any doubt Michael had about his insane plan evaporated when he looked at Toby's shimmering eyes. She was on the verge of accepting and before she could say a word, Michael grabbed the opportunity.

"We need to discuss this, Toby," he whispered in her ear. "There's a great deal to signing a contract that you haven't considered."

Toby nodded and excused herself. "I'll have an answer for you tomorrow, Mr. Greenpasture."

"Till then, Miss Wells. I'm scheduling a new show in Boston and the cast needs to be there next week. There's a lot to be done between now and then. Rehearsals, flyers, contracts and costumes are just a few of the details."

"Boston?" Toby said. The idea of playing Boston was exhilarating.

"Then we have an agreement?" Joel pressured. He was a good businessman and knew when to take advantage of someone's excitement.

"No, Mr. Greenpasture," Toby answered, shaking his hand vigorously. "I must think about it."

"Thank you, Joel," Michael said, ending the conversation. He wanted to get her alone before Toby did something rash. Grabbing her hand, he hauled her out of the circle of people and pulled her out onto the terrace.

"Isn't it wonderful?" Toby gushed. "I've dreamed of this kind of thing happening ever since I was a child."

"I don't think working for Greenpasture is a good idea," Michael said. He fought to hide his joy at his even better one.

Toby's reaction was volatile. "Why? Don't you think I'm good enough?"

Irritated with her attack, Michael dropped her hand and said coolly, "That's not what I said. Learn to listen, Toby."

"Listen to what? Someone throwing ice water on my good fortune?"

"You sound like a child," Michael snapped. "Wake up and face reality."

His words were as painful as if he'd slapped her. "Aren't you happy for me?" she asked, stunned by his vehemence.

"No, yes, oh, damn it!" he hollered.

"I don't understand why you're so upset."

"What happened to our wedding plans?" He couldn't outline his new scheme until he'd done some research. What could he say to stall her without sabotaging himself? "Have you forgotten you work for me?"

Toby had forgotten. "Actually, I did. Working with you has been so much fun it wasn't like a job at all."

Frustrated, Michael sighed deeply. "Then why spoil it all now? Marry me and I guarantee you'll be happy."

"Michael, in all our discussions about marriage, you have left out the most important thing. Why haven't you ever told me you love me?"

Michael had hoped he wouldn't have to explain the reasons behind his proposal, for it all sounded so cold, so calculating. But he knew she wouldn't settle for a quick evasion this time. "You're a beautiful woman, Toby, and my children need someone like you in their lives. We are compatible, our tastes and values are similar and we are definitely attracted to each other. Isn't that more than enough reason to get married?''

"No."

"But I need you."

"Need me?" Toby jumped on the word like a tigress. "Is that all you're worried about? Losing a clerk, an efficient flunky? Or is it my role as mother to your children, warm body in your bed, cook and chore woman that concerns you more? You don't want someone to love, you just want to trim the payroll."

"You're not looking at the facts. Love only complicates a relationship."

"Then I guess I like complicated relationships," Toby said, seething in anger. "You don't want a wife, you want a brood mare and an indentured servant."

"If that's how you interpret my offer, I guess we aren't as compatible as I thought," he answered curtly.

"You're a parsimonious, selfish man, Michael Sedaine. All these weeks you've led me to believe you supported my dreams. What was that piano for? A way of keeping me on the farm, of patronizing me while you played the benevolent master?"

"Good God, woman, you have an amazing talent for corrupting the truth."

"Or seeing it," Toby countered.

"You want truth," Michael said, "I'll give you some. If you work for Greenpasture—"

"Not if. When," Toby interrupted.

"When you work for him, you'll start at nine-thirty in the morning and go until at least ten-thirty at night. Just think of it, sweetheart, you'll have to do the same routine four or five times a day, seven days a week. Sometimes you'll be in a city for a week, then you'll have to pack up, sleep on the train and open that next morning. Your costume will get grimy, you'll share your cramped dressing room with a bunch of bawdy show girls, you'll be a slave to the stage manager's dictates and you'll never have time to even write a letter, much less have a private life."

Toby swallowed at the bleak picture he was painting. "I don't believe you. You resent my art."

"Art, hah!" he sneered. "Lunch-counter art is what we call it. The lunch is real but the art is vague, darling."

She fumed at his insults and spun on her heels to escape his barrage. "I don't have to take this abuse. I'll find Ansel and enjoy the company of someone who appreciates my talents."

As Toby started to leave, Michael swatted her on the fanny. "This is all Ansel appreciates."

His slap stung and Toby wheeled on him. "If you ever touch me again, Mr. Sedaine, you'll *never* sire any more children!" Toby boldly stared at the area below his belt to emphasize her threat.

Michael nearly staggered back at her blunt warning. This was the sweet little thing he thought he had to protect? If he hadn't met her family, he would have thought she'd been raised in the Bowery instead of a parsonage.

While Michael struggled to master his temper and shock, Toby picked up the hem of her gown and thrust her chin out defiantly. "Good night, Mr. Sedaine. Thank you for your company this evening. It's been quite enlightening." Toby didn't glance back as she marched from the terrace like a victor.

Chapter Nine

Two hours later, when Toby was trapped and alone in the carriage with Ansel, she regretted leaving the party without Michael and accepting Ansel's offer to escort her home. Even if she and Michael disagreed, or even outright fought, it was at least honest. Not like struggling with Ansel, who was a beau-trap, a dandy who relied on his stylish appearance to lure women into his arms.

"You dim the moon and stars," he gushed as the driver closed the door behind them.

"Can't you be more original?" Toby criticized. Ansel hadn't stopped drinking champagne since she'd sought him out, nor had he halted his battery of insincere compliments.

"But I'm in love."

"Then kiss a mirror," Toby said. "The only person you love is yourself."

He kept muttering about his undying devotion throughout the ride home until Toby felt like stuffing her shoe in his mouth. When the hansom cab drew up to her brownstone, Toby quickly jumped out. If she didn't get away from Ansel she would be ill. It wasn't just his syrupy compliments but also his liquored breath that was nauseating.

Ansel fled after her and caught Toby at the door as she was trying to unlock it. "You didn't fool me," he slurred. "Only reason you 'cepted my company was 'cause you had a fight with Michael. Thas fine. Probably went with Emily. She was there, you know."

"What in the world are you mumbling?" Toby asked, her ears pricking up at the name Emily. The first evening she had been in New York, Ansel had hinted that Michael's attentions had been devoted to a woman named Emily.

"Emily Lucas. Loves Michael," Ansel said.

Toby watched Ansel struggle to stand upright without swaying, and she felt sorry for the pitiful sight he made. "I really don't see that it's my concern who Michael spends time with."

"Good fer you. Wouldn't wan' him to ruin yer life, too. Lillian was perfect fer Michael. Didn' care what he did."

She wanted to but couldn't ignore Ansel's remark. "You mean I don't care what he does. Michael loved his wife."

"Yep, thas right," he said, and leaned against the building. "He jus' kep' givin' her money and she kep' spendin' it. My big sister was good at shoppin'."

"Many women enjoy buying pretty clothes."

"Whoee, Lillian was good, all right. Thas why she was in Europe. Stores here were boring, she said. Almos' broke Michael but he wouldn't say no."

Ansel went silent and Toby turned away, but he tapped on her shoulder. "Know what?" he whispered. "He told me he buried his heart with her."

All Michael's comments about his wife and his cool approach toward a second marriage suddenly made sense to her. He was only capable of loving one woman, and Toby would be a replacement, a convenience to fill the gaps in his life. Second best, Toby thought, I will always be second best. Michael still worshiped Lillian exactly the way her father still loved her mother. She was doomed to compete with phantom women. Impossible odds! Toby sighed and turned away to unlock the door.

"Here," he said, fighting to take the key from her, "let me."

"No, thank you and good-night, Ansel."

He swayed on the stoop, and Toby shook her head at his harmless drunken behavior. "Don't fall," she warned.

Turning her back on him again, she opened the door but was unexpectedly grabbed by the shoulders and jerked around.

"You haven' kissed me yet. Forget Michael. He doesn' love you."

Panting, Ansel roughly took her into his arms and leered at her. "Stop it, mister," Toby ordered, but he ignored her protest.

Ansel was too large for Toby to push away, and he had her pinned against the wall, waiting for her to acquiesce to his request. "Just leave and I won't tell Michael what a cad you were tonight," she said, adding an appropriately stern note to her voice. But Ansel wasn't fazed.

"Jus' one li'l peck," he said, and grinned. "I won' tell."

While Toby was wrestling with Ansel, Rosie was attempting to snuggle up to Michael in his carriage, but he was oblivious to her shameless behavior. His mood was foul and he could think of nothing but Toby. Not only had he been forced to watch her blatantly flirt with Ansel at the ball, but she had humiliated him when she refused to ride home with him, leaving Michael to squire Rosie.

"Toby just doesn't know how to treat a man like you," Rosie chattered. "I'm not like Toby."

"That's for sure," Michael grumbled, and slid as far away from Rosie as he could.

He wished he could have left the party earlier but, as the host, he had been obligated to remain. As he had smiled at his friends, all happy to donate to the scholarship, he had been silently fuming at Toby's criticism. Why had she insisted on tainting a respectable, pleasant relationship with her accusations? He would never understand women. What was wrong with wanting her to settle down, marry him, have his children and dabble in her music? It was logical and he knew they would both be content.

Rosie pointed to the street lamps as the carriage neared Toby's house. "Even the lights in New York are romantic," she said, and sighed wistfully.

Michael didn't notice the lights, all he saw was Ansel mauling Toby on the porch. She was fighting him off but

Ansel was winning. The shoulder of her gown was ripped, and her cries were muffled by Ansel's mouth.

Ordering Rosie to wait in the landau, Michael bounded up the stairs and pounced on Ansel. The drunken sot wobbled against the wrought iron rail, confused by the unexpected assault.

"What the . . . ?" Ansel mumbled.

"You filthy bastard," Michael bellowed.

"Jus' havin' a li'l fun," Ansel slurred. "You got Emily and I got Toby."

Instead of wasting words, Michael slammed a fist into Ansel's puffy face, and he sank slowly to the landing like an overstuffed rag doll. Rosie rushed to Toby while Michael loaded Ansel's inert body into the cab.

"Are you all right?" Rosie whispered as she vainly struggled to tie the ripped edges of Toby's chiton together.

"Fine," Toby said, grateful Rosie held her smart remarks for a change. "Where are Caleb and Chantelle?" Toby hoped they hadn't been an audience to this ugly scene, too.

"With some friends. Caleb was still floating from the offers he received. He said he needed to tell some folks about tonight," Rosie explained.

"You can go inside, Rosie," Michael said, returning to the stoop. "I want to speak to Toby in private."

His voice was soft, so quiet, Toby would have preferred to hear him yelling. She pasted a false smile on her face and turned to him, but it faded the moment she looked into his accusing brown eyes.

"Ansel is just a sample of the kind of suitors you'll encounter in show business," he thundered.

"I was handling him just fine."

He fingered the ripped edge of her gown and scoffed, "You look like a winner."

"I don't need you to take care of me. If all I wanted was a man in my life, I didn't need to leave home," she said, still angry with him. "I had four proposals of marriage before I even left Saint Louis." She was lying but didn't care. "Where's Emily Lucas? Did you abandon her at the party, too?"

"Emily? What does she have to do with this?"

"Then you admit you were with her tonight."

"You keep twisting my words," Michael said. "I said hello to Emily but that was all. Did you expect me to be rude to an old friend?"

Toby stepped right up to him and glowered. "Is that what you will call me a year from now? An old friend?"

"No," Michael said, and jammed his hands into his pockets to keep from shaking some sense into Toby. "Obnoxious, stubborn brat or distracting, petulant child but never an old friend."

"No one, absolutely no one, can make me as angry as you do, Michael Sedaine. Do you stay awake nights plotting how to goad me into losing my temper?"

Michael sighed at the sudden shift in their argument. It was true they seemed to disagree more than any other two people he knew but, even when they were fighting, he admired Toby's strength of conviction, which put fire into her life. He envied her sense of honor, which didn't sway to other people's opinions, and was fascinated with her active imagination, which turned the impossible into the probable.

"I can't even believe we're still arguing after all that's happened. For the second time tonight, please, Toby, I'm asking you to listen to what I have to say."

Toby felt beaten. First Michael verbally attacked her, then Ansel physically assaulted her, and now Michael was back for another bout. She sank down onto the stairs and cradled her weary head in her hands. "I heard you tell me I wasn't good enough for the stage, that I was living in a fantasy world, that you thought I was only suited for clerical work and that my music was lunch-counter art. Then you came back and invented an entirely new list of names to call me. What's left to say? I have bad breath?"

Michael chuckled and sat down next to her, took her hand in his, kissing the fingers lightly. "You don't have halitosis and I didn't say you weren't talented. I said working for Greenpasture wasn't a good idea, but you didn't let me finish."

"Finish what? All I asked was if you loved me. You couldn't answer that simple question. What more is there between us? Are we going to draw up a contract of what I can and can't do, like you do with your songwriters?"

"If you hadn't been so eager to give me the rough side of your tongue," Michael said, "I would have told you that I wanted you to headline *my theater*." He made the final decision out of desperation. Too afraid to commit his heart, he was pledging his financial security to keep Toby.

Toby almost quit breathing. "Your theater?" she finally managed to ask.

"Yes." Michael chose his words carefully, for he didn't want Toby to think he was delving into this new venture just to keep her from Greenpasture. Although it was partially true, he also had a niggling feeling he could expand his business horizons by investing in a theater that took risks, premiered unknown artists and set the trends of the future. "I was very proud of you and Caleb tonight and thought why the devil should Greenpasture have either of you?"

Both guilt and joy overwhelmed her while bittersweet tears rolled down her cheeks. "Do you really think we can do it? Wouldn't you be taking a tremendous gamble?"

"No. You saw the audience's reaction. They are this city's most critical group, and they'll act the same way every night with you and Caleb on stage," Michael said. "We're a guaranteed success."

Toby scooted across the brick step close to Michael. "But you still haven't answered my original question. We can't pretend tonight didn't happen." She waited for him to say something, anything, but all he did was stare at her with glistening eyes, a sad tilt to his head. "You're not in love with me, are you?"

"I'm not sure I even know what the word means, Angel Eyes. If it means I enjoy being with you, then, yes, I am. If it means you make my heart pound and turn my knees to custard, I am. But if it means always feeling this way, always believing our infatuation won't ever fade and grow stale, I don't know."

Toby stood up and took a ragged breath of the cool night air. Michael was infatuated with her but not in love. It was plain that he had loved his first wife so deeply there would never be anyone who could replace her. She couldn't settle for spending the rest of her life with a man who admitted he only panted after her and wanted a mother for his children.

"Thank you for finally being honest with me. I made a pretty big fool of myself, didn't I? But I suppose you're used to women fawning over you and assuming you're in love with them."

Michael let Toby's jab slide by unretaliated. Her pride was aching and he understood her need to soothe the hurt. "I guess we're back at the beginning. I can't give you what you need, but I can offer you an opportunity to satisfy a dream. Is that enough?"

"I guess it will have to be," she said.

Michael's decision to open The Pantheon Theater was like setting off fireworks in everyone's life. Caleb recruited several of his friends to fill out the ragtime portion of the program while Chantelle went crazy trying to design and sew costumes for the cast.

Toby was divided between helping Michael run auditions and assuming more of the work load at Sedaine Music. In between her doubled duties, she rehearsed and wrote new routines. Rosie avoided going back to Saint Louis by becoming a valuable roving assistant to everyone, helping Chantelle in the sewing room, running errands for Michael, who was swamped with details, and even donning an apron to help Toby with meals. The brownstone became the hub of all this activity, looking and sounding more like a madhouse than a home.

"Take this back to the printer and have him make the corrections," Michael said, giving the handbill to Rosie. "On your way back, stop at the butcher's for Toby."

"Any special requests?"

"If you don't have time to stop, don't worry," Toby said.

"It's no problem," Rosie answered. "I'm happy to do anything Michael asks."

Toby turned her back on Michael and Rosie and screwed her face into a frown, poking her tongue out just like she'd done when she was seven.

"Toby," Chantelle called from the landing, "I need your help."

Closing her eyes, Toby prayed Chantelle had not seen her childish gesture but doubted her plea would be heard.

"I thought you told me you and Michael were just friends," Chantelle scolded the minute they were alone upstairs. "So why is jealousy lifting its nasty head?"

"Have you noticed how Rosie caters to Michael's every demand? No task is too demeaning or too great for my baby sister but only if it's for Michael."

"Rosie doesn't mean anything special to him," Chantelle said. "She does a good job and she's your sister. Did you want him to slap her on the head once in a while to prove she's just an employee?"

"Of course not."

"Then let your childhood squabble with Rosie die. I couldn't get along without her help and neither could you."

"Just wait. One day you will all understand that I'm not exaggerating about Rosamond. The only person she cares about is herself."

"Toby!" Michael bellowed. "Come here, please."

Chantelle sighed and shook her head as she watched Toby hurry back downstairs. Ever since the benefit, Michael had been working on the theater, pushing each of them, including himself, for the earliest possible opening. A demon was nipping at his heels and he was determined not to slow down long enough to let it grab his leg. Poor Michael, as hard as he tried, Chantelle knew he would never escape. He was in love with Toby and couldn't face the truth. How ironic—Chantelle wanted to marry Caleb and couldn't, while Michael and Toby could marry tomorrow but wouldn't.

Later that evening, Toby was finishing the lyrics to a new song when Michael sat down beside her at the piano. It was the first time they had been alone since they had redefined their relationship.

"When is the gang due back?" he asked, uncomfortable in the silence of the near-empty house.

"Not for a while. They took in the new show at Greenpasture's to see what the competition is doing," Toby said.

"Doesn't matter how good it is, he doesn't have you."

"Is all this really for me?"

"And Caleb."

"What if I'm a failure?"

"Impossible, but there's always Caleb to draw a crowd."

"Then why use me?" she said, searching his eyes for the truth.

"This is vaudeville, lady, and that means variety. No matter how good a routine is the audience wouldn't sit still for hours of one style," he said.

Toby wanted to ask Michael what he was really thinking but didn't dare. He never veered from their one neutral topic, work. It was as if he had centered every particle of his mind on this project the way a house of cards rests on a few flimsy supporting cards. If she nudged too hard and shoved a card a little too far to the side, the entire house would collapse around Michael's ears.

"Do we have enough acts?" Toby asked, staying within Michael's confines.

"Just about. Tomorrow is our last chance to fill the gaps before we open next week."

Opening! The realization that in seven days her reputation, Caleb's future and Michael's money would be on the line—or stage—made Toby's stomach flip. "What if no one comes?"

"They will. It will be your job to insure they come back a second time," Michael said, and went back to writing down the names on the guest list for opening night.

Not knowing when they would be alone again, Toby used the opportunity to broach a sensitive subject, one that encompassed work but was a lot more personal than the people who would be invited to The Pantheon's first public display.

"Have you forgiven Ansel?" she asked, remembering the last time she had seen Michael and Ansel together—that dreadful night of the benefit.

"In a manner," he said without raising his head.

"Did you know he sent me an apology and a dozen roses?"

"Only a dozen?"

"His note was very contrite. He promised he was going to control his party behavior from now on," Toby said, surprised to find she was defending Ansel's behavior.

"He damn well better," Michael said. "I had a long conversation with him the next morning and let him know if I ever heard a whisper about him manhandling a woman, I would show him exactly what the word really means."

"Then the only reason he apologized was because you threatened him," she said. "I was ready to excuse his rude behavior."

Michael set the tablet down on the floor and leaned forward, resting his elbows on his knees. "He had already written the note and ordered the flowers. I didn't have to coerce him. I just added a bit of incentive to his gesture."

"Speaking of family members, why don't you ever bring Paul and Suzanne with you anymore? They're nice children and because you work here almost every evening, you aren't spending much time with them." She was worried about the winsome little girl and the angry young boy Michael was ignoring.

"They have my mother. They understand," he said, never looking up.

"I'm sure they do understand. Understand that their father would rather be doing just about anything than spending time with them. Understand that if they don't behave like a perfect gentleman and lady they will earn their grandmother's reproving comments."

"You are chock full of bits of wisdom, aren't you?" Michael said, and kicked the tablet across the floor before he began to pace back and forth in front of Toby. "I have my career on the chopping block with The Pantheon, and you want me to drop what I'm doing and run home at five o'clock every day." He stopped and stood in front of her. "If you feel I'm mistreating my children, why don't you volunteer for the open position as their mother? I can guarantee a good salary and wonderful fringe benefits."

Toby was shocked that her suggestion struck such a sore point with Michael. Obviously he was feeling guilty and she had been too accurate, but that didn't excuse Michael's venting his hostility at her. Her role was not mother to his children, nor was she willing to sacrifice her pride to act as Michael Sedaine's scapegoat.

"Did you say you were Ansel's brother or brother-in-law? You have so many character traits in common I must have misunderstood the family relationship."

Toby spun on her heel and raced up the stairs, slamming her bedroom door behind her. She couldn't be alone with Michael for over five minutes without fighting with him, and she was just as angry with herself as she was with Michael. Paul and Suzanne were not her responsibility and furthermore, she didn't even care for Paul. So why was she spending an inordinate amount of time worrying about them? Wouldn't she ever be free of children? Wasn't New York far enough from Saint Louis to escape?

She heard the front door click shut and peeked out through the curtains. Michael was on the sidewalk, his head bent down and a stack of papers under his arm. The bright evening moon glinted off his dark hair but left his face hidden in shadows. He walked slowly, his long legs in no obvious hurry to carry him home, his arms still and passive rather than swinging away from his body.

Michael was burdened by so many warring obligations that she felt guilty for reminding him that he was neglecting his children. After all, he was risking his reputation and a great deal of money to offer her a chance. From this moment on, Toby promised herself she wouldn't do or say anything to add to his load. She would bite her tongue whenever a criticism came to her lips and forget about Paul and Suzanne.

"Fudge!" she said, and threw her tiny boots against the wall. No matter how hard she tried, she would never erase the memory of Suzanne's radiant smile and she would never be able to dismiss the haunted look in Paul's wary eyes. And she was furious with herself for caring.

Determined to be the actress Michael expected her to be, Toby whisked into the theater the next morning and sat next to him as he called out the first act to audition.

"Patrick Casey?" he hollered out. Turning to Toby, he whispered in her ear, "He's my mother's butler. If I give him a job she'll disinherit me."

"I'll teach you how to live like a commoner," Toby teased.

"Cocky, aren't you?"

"Sassy, remember?"

"You never let me forget."

Patrick Casey was an astonishing tenor. He had a bagful of Irish ballads and Toby knew he'd be popular. "Michael, he's wasted as a butler."

Michael groaned. "Mother's going to have a fit."

Silently Toby thought, she has them anyway. Aloud, she said, "She'll recover."

By the end of the day, they'd added a juggling act, a trained dog show and a comic monologuist to fill in the program. They were exhausted from watching so many acts and only gleaning a few good ones, but it was a necessary task.

"That's all for today," Michael announced to his assembled cast. "Since tomorrow is Sunday, enjoy the day off. Rehearsals start Monday at ten o'clock and anyone who's late is fired."

He knew all too well the fickle hours entertainers kept and decided to nip his troupe's bad habits now, before any of them thought they could wander in whenever they pleased. The Pantheon's success depended on their reliability as much as their talent.

"Feel like polishing floors tonight?" Caleb asked, sliding into the row behind Michael and Toby.

"Are you crazy?" Toby asked, standing up in protest. "The last thing I want to do is go home and work."

Chantelle slipped in next to Caleb and laughed. "He wasn't talking about going home. It's Caleb's way of inviting you two to go dancing with us."

"Sounds good to me. Michael?" It had been weeks since any of them had done anything but work, and the chance to go dancing was too appealing to pass.

Michael knew he was mad for exposing himself to Toby's charm and setting himself up for an evening of delectable torture, but he couldn't resist. "Great. Lead the way and we'll obediently follow."

Caleb took them to his roommate's house, where a party was already in full swing. The music, provided by Caleb's friends who had come to New York to work in Michael's theater, was peppy and impossible to ignore. Michael grabbed Toby's hand and pulled her to the center of the room, where the rug had been rolled back so the couples could dance.

They tried to imitate the others, but years of formal ballroom dancing left them stumbling awkwardly on each other's toes.

"Whoa," Michael grumbled. "If I keep this up you'll need a cane to limp onstage."

Toby halted her bungled attempt to match the rhythm. Panting, she said, "Learning to walk had to be easier than this." She looked at the other dancers and was embarrassed at how easy Caleb's friends made the complex pattern of steps look.

Chantelle rescued them. "Let's switch partners," she said to Caleb, "and teach these babies how to do a proper cakewalk."

By shrugging to Toby, Michael signaled, why not. "Brave," he said to Chantelle as he took her in his arms.

"First," Chantelle instructed him, "link your arm with mine. This is a strut not a waltz."

Caleb also taught Toby the intricate promenade steps, and in a few minutes she was able to mimic him quite well. "Why, this isn't much different than a good old-fashioned schottische," she bragged.

"Think so?" Caleb said, winking. "Then try this." He spun her like a top and slid into a wild, fast-paced set of steps that left Toby gasping as she tried to keep up with him.

"My grandmother would have been shocked," Toby huffed.

"Are you?" Caleb asked.

"Not at all," Toby proudly boasted. "I'm having a wonderful time. This makes other dances I've been to seem stodgy."

The song ended and Toby fanned herself. Her tight bolero jacket was too warm and she removed it, tossing it onto a chair. Searching for Michael, she saw him taking off his coat, as well as his stiff celluloid collar. It was a splendid freedom to cast aside restrictions—both physical and social. The room was filled with laughter, with people who thought nothing of happily bumping shoulders, hugging each other in their delight of simply relaxing.

Only thirty seconds lapsed before the next song started and Toby sought out Michael. "Ready to try again?" she asked him.

"With you, I'd tackle anything. You're my lucky charm, so we can't lose."

Dancing with Toby to the uninhibited songs was like romping in a field of daisies. Not since he was a child had Michael felt so unfettered, so young. As a boy he had never thought twice about touching a beloved parent, holding hands with a friend, or frolicking gaily with his cousins in the grass. All of that had been lost with adulthood, and not until this moment had Michael realized how much he missed it. Toby had always kept that childlike love of touching and she was unaware of the effect she had on him, bending her body into his, molding her thighs against his thighs and pressing her firm breasts against his chest.

She wasn't trying to be erotic and therefore was immensely successful in stirring his desire. Women who planned their moves, who plotted romance, had always left him cold. It had taken the refreshingly natural Toby Wells to teach him that true happiness couldn't be forced, it was spontaneous. It was immoral to care about a woman as wonderful as Toby and not act upon it. But Lillian's lessons had been educational, and he remembered them well.

He could still hear her saying, "You're a very nice, generous man, Michael. It is a shame you're so boring." Time had blessed him with a degree of impartiality, and he admitted he couldn't place all the blame on Lillian. He had been equally disenchanted with her. She was beautiful, came from the proper background, could speak three languages fluently and hosted lavish parties with style. And after the first year of marriage, Michael had thought he was going to lose his mind. The prospect of a lifetime locked into a relationship with Lillian had been like facing a living, breathing, auburn-haired hell.

"You need practice, dear man," Toby teased him, and placed her hands on his hips. "Loosen up and wiggle. Like this." Her thumbs pressed against his hipbones while her fingers gripped the taut flesh of his buttocks. Shaking the stiffness out of him, she laughed. "That's better."

"My turn." Michael took her tiny hips in his large hands and duplicated her gentle massage. "You have the advantage," he grumbled, feeling the layers of fabric protecting her from his touch.

"How so?"

"You're wearing petticoats, a skirt and who knows what else."

Blushing, she felt him kneading her clothes, trying to feel beyond them. "What would you have me wear?"

He leaned down and whispered, "Nothing."

She couldn't answer his blunt suggestion without admitting she would love to see him undressed, too. "Good friends aren't supposed to fondle each other, are they?"

Michael read the desire in her eyes and guided Toby out of the stuffy room into the small quiet backyard.

"Come here, Angel Eyes," he groaned, and drew her tightly to him. His kiss was impatient and she responded, equally hungry for him. Aching with need, he pulled away and asked, "My God, woman, how long are we going to torture each other?"

Toby knew what he meant and didn't trust herself to speak. Her legs could barely hold her weight, there was a delicious craving building deep inside she desperately wanted to feed, and she trembled at his slightest touch.

"Oh, Toby," he said softly, "what am I going to do with you?"

"Be my friend?" Toby wanted to say love me, take me home with you and never let me go, but she couldn't. Michael had been blunt about his feelings for her and besides, he had two children. She wasn't ready to tackle another family, no matter how tempting their father was.

"I wish that was enough. How long will it satisfy either of us?"

As Michael's lips brushed hers, angry, familiar voices shattered the solitude. Caleb and Chantelle had come onto the back porch.

"Is it so hard to love me?" Caleb asked.

"No, but that's not what you're asking," Chantelle countered. "You're asking me to live with you."

"Yes. We should have our own place, not this stupid arrangement."

"I can't. You know I can't."

"Won't. You won't," Caleb snapped at her. "I'm tired of waiting for you to get a divorce."

"I'm not waiting," Chantelle yelled back. "I've tried everything to force Dominic to release me."

"Then forget him and live with me as my wife," Caleb said.

"That would be a lie."

"Which is more of a lie? Choosing to honor a marriage you don't have or pretending you and I aren't lovers?"

Chantelle cupped his face and held his gaze. "What are you asking me to do?"

"Choose me now or lose me now." Caleb coldly gave the ultimatum.

"What if I can't?"

"Then I'll do it for you, lady."

He waited for her to say something, but she didn't. Angrily Caleb stalked back to the house and left Chantelle weeping on the porch.

Toby made a small movement toward Chantelle, but Michael gripped her shoulders and shook his head. He was right. Letting Chantelle know they had innocently been privy to the fight would only add to the dignified woman's grief.

As they waited in the shadows for Chantelle to regain control, Michael wrapped his arms around Toby, gripping her fiercely. Was he taking the same risk as Chantelle and would he suffer the same fate?

The minutes passed, and they finally heard Chantelle's footsteps echo on the pavement as she escaped to the street by using the back staircase.

"I can't go home and face her," Toby said. "I wouldn't know what to say."

"Did you understand any of that?" Michael asked.

"Yes. It's a long, sad story and a private story. Michael, I've lost my enthusiasm for dancing, but I don't want to go home."

"I'll collect our things and meet you out front. I know the perfect place."

The stage was dark, the curtains missing and the aisles littered with paint buckets, drop cloths and ladders, but Toby felt at ease the moment they stepped into The Pantheon.

"I love this place," she said, wrapping her arms around a pillar. "It has personality, a life of its own like no other building I've ever been in."

"I can feel it, too," Michael agreed.

"Maybe it's the ghosts of all the other performers who loved working on its stage."

Michael laughed at her flight of fancy. "More like the ghost of the banker who wants us to pay him back the money I borrowed."

"I'll be right back," Toby said, switching on the house-lights and heading for the food she had stashed in her dressing room.

While he waited, Michael analyzed his undeniable fascination with Toby. What would happen if he ignored his common sense and proposed to her again? What if Lillian had been wrong and he could keep a woman happy? What if love didn't die of boredom after the first year and he was passing up his opportunity for a lifetime of happiness with Toby?

"Ta-da," Toby said, flourishing a tin of crackers, a can of shrimp and two apples. "A feast worthy of two talented dancers."

He laughed at her penchant for always having food at her disposal. "For such a tiny thing, you have the appetite of a logger."

"That's because I have a boss who works me too hard," Toby said, and unabashedly spread out the food. "If you insult me, I won't share any of these delicious shrimp with you," she said, and waggled one under his nose.

"My stomach wins."

After they had finished appeasing their hunger, Michael said seriously, "Toby, do you believe that two people can love each other year after year?"

"Absolutely. Mama and Papa were as much in love on the day she died as they were on their wedding day. Maybe even more so."

"But were they happy or had they just accepted their circumstances?"

Toby shuddered whenever she thought of the bitter price Irina Wells had paid for her love. She'd sacrificed her most precious gift, her life. Her mother had loved children so much, she had died giving birth to the twins. The doctor had been specific about cautioning her not to have any more babies after Gwen, but Irina had followed her heart, not his warning. The night Toby kissed her mother goodbye, she'd promised herself she would never love anyone that much.

"Mama loved every day like it was a special gift to be treasured and Papa loved his wife. Why are you asking me so many questions about my parents? You understand what it's like to be in love much better than I do."

"No, I don't."

"But you were married for four years."

"Just because you are married to a woman doesn't mean you are in love with her."

Toby gasped at Michael's admission. "You really do believe in that nonsense about making a logical choice for a wife, don't you? Even after she's dead, after she gave you two lovely children, the brick wall between your heart and your head is still intact.''

''I wasn't the only person guilty of contributing to our wedded bliss. I loved Lillian as much as she loved me. Our marriage died long before she did.''

''No wonder. Your attitude probably destroyed any tender feelings she had for you.''

''Why can't you clamp your lips together and listen to me instead of jumping to false conclusions? I loved Lillian with a deep passion when I proposed to her and I assumed, falsely so, that we would always be in love. She appropriately and tenderly began to bore me to death the moment the wedding ring was on her finger. Lillian never really did anything wrong—she just never cared for anybody but herself.''

''Michael, did it ever occur to you that I don't really want to hear all about your wife? Why don't you tell Caleb about her or explain your feelings to Chantelle, but spare me your late-night confessions. I can't accept a relationship on your terms, and maligning Lillian won't justify your attitude. I don't care what happened between the two of you and I don't want to know all the intimate details of your private life.''

He tried to joke his way back into Toby's good graces. ''I thought all women were curious about the other ladies in a man's life?''

''You're mistaken,'' Toby said, finding nothing humorous in Michael's comment. ''You assume I'm like the other women who clutter your nights. Go back to Emily Lucas. Or encourage Rosie a whit more and I'm sure she'd be willing to listen to you caterwaul about how boring Lillian was. But don't complain to me, because I don't give a fig.''

Michael bent over Toby's chair and trapped each of her wrists on an armrest. ''Is this the same sweet little girl who shocked herself by kissing me on the front porch? The same tenderhearted, caring young lady?''

''I've changed,'' she whispered, forcing herself to look him in the eye.

''No, you haven't.''

Michael wouldn't close his eyes as he lowered his lips to hers and locked her eyes in a battle of wills. He couldn't afford to let Toby win again, and he forcefully defeated her momentary denial. "You enjoy this as much as I do," he said, moving his mouth over hers.

"You only want me because you can't have me," she mumbled back.

"Maybe you're right and maybe you're wrong. Either way, eventually I'm going to satisfy my curiosity."

"Over my dead body."

"I'm a patient man, but I won't wait quite that long, Angel Eyes."

"You are such a romantic, Michael Sedaine," she said, wiggling free of him and marching up the aisle to the front doors. "Do you really think I find your logic endearing? Even your son could feign more affection than that pathetic display. You're just a spoiled little boy who would do or say anything to get his way."

Chapter Ten

The night air was crisp and Toby buttoned her coat against the chill. Even though the theater was a fair hike from the brownstone, she decided to walk, needing time to think. If she managed to avoid Chantelle, there was no way Toby could deal with Rosie tonight without bopping the girl on the head if she uttered as much as one positive statement about Michael. And, lately, Rosie had fallen into the annoying habit of droning on and on about Michael's amazing accomplishments. It was enough to make any rational person bilious.

Toby kicked a stone and watched it land in the gutter. Too bad she couldn't bounce Michael off the sidewalk just as easily. The man was intolerable. Why she had ever considered marrying him was a serious question of her sanity. He had no heart.

Just down the block, Toby spotted a bench on the edge of a pocket-sized park and crossed the street to it. Even though it was late and the streets were deserted, she didn't feel nervous, for this was a respectable neighborhood. Sitting down on the sturdy wooden seat, Toby tipped her head back and looked up at the lacy pattern of maple leaves outlined by the night sky. Fall would be here in a wink, and soon the streets would be covered with bright leaves. The exact same type of leaves Mo and Cleo would rake into huge stacks before they took turns jumping out of the swing into their neat pile.

The thought of the twins' happy faces brought tears to her eyes, and Toby didn't have the gumption to fight her melancholy. Every time she thought her life was on the right track, the train stopped at an unscheduled station and the conductor kicked her off. Once again she was stranded in strange territory with no guidebook.

Michael wanted her to be his wife but didn't love her. Chantelle loved Caleb but couldn't marry him because she was still legally bound to Dominic. Paul and Suzanne desperately needed a loving woman to guide them through their childhood, but Toby didn't want to accept the responsibility. The last item on her jumbled list of problems was the fact that even if Michael had been in love with her she couldn't marry him because she wasn't brave enough to give him the large family he wanted. By stirring in Rosie and Ansel to keep things simmering, it was enough to make her tear her hair out and run through the streets wailing like a madwoman.

"Fudge!" Toby said to the stars. "Why does it have to be so complicated?"

She remembered asking her mother the same thing when she was nine and didn't understand division problems. Irina had explained that nothing worthwhile was ever easy and people wouldn't take any pride in solving problems if there was no effort involved.

Well, Toby had exerted every ounce of energy trying to solve this dilemma, and she still couldn't find the solution. She couldn't make Michael love her, she couldn't win a divorce for Chantelle and she couldn't overcome her fear of childbirth. The last problem was the most hopeless and Toby cursed her body for betraying her.

Over and over again Toby had relived those last months of her mother's life and came to the same conclusion every time. Irina's body had been exhausted from producing seven children, and she had died when Mo and Cleo were three hours old. Ten years later Toby was still as resolute as she had been on the day of the funeral that she wouldn't match her mother's destiny.

Paul and Suzanne were perfect examples of what happened to motherless children. At best, they were raised by a woman who resented their presence. Toby had spared her brothers and sisters a similar fate but couldn't accept the obligation of raising another set of children. She knew it was selfish, but Paul was not an endearing young man who fostered any maternal instincts in her heart.

The entire scenario was bleak and hopeless, emphasizing her doubts about marrying Michael. No marriage could survive such a warped foundation, especially when the man plainly stated he didn't love his bride-to-be. She had made the right decision, walking out on Michael, but Toby wondered how long it would be before her heart understood what her brain was telling her.

Chilled from being out in the night air for so long, Toby headed down the block and glanced at the clock on the corner. She had been sitting on the bench for an hour and it was very late.

She hoped Chantelle and Rosie wouldn't be up at this hour and she could sneak into the brownstone without either of them realizing what time she came home. That hope withered the moment she unlocked the front door.

Tapping her foot on the entry tile, Rosie demanded, "Where have you been? I was worried sick and about ready to alert the police. Chantelle has been home for hours."

The reversed roles, Rosie the mother and Toby the errant child, stung. Unable to look Rosie in the face, Toby mumbled, "I couldn't come home. It's private."

"What does that have to do with the price of elderberries?"

Lying had never been part of Toby's ethical repertoire, but it was impossible to be honest with Rosie. "I needed to be alone and think."

"Don't try and convince me you've been at the theater this entire time."

Pausing, trying to find a delicate way to extricate herself from this predicament, Toby stammered, "I, ah, went—"

"Rosie," Chantelle interrupted, coming down the stairs, "why don't you fix some tea for us."

"Not until Toby answers my question," Rosie said adamantly.

Toby looked to Chantelle, pleading for help.

Smiling sadly, Chantelle hugged Rosie. "*Chère,* we women all have secrets. Honor Toby's and we'll honor yours someday."

Being treated as an equal appealed to Rosie. "All right, but I have one question. Toby, since you and Michael had a fight, does that mean he's available?"

"How do you know we had a fight?"

"He was here looking for you, silly goose," Rosie said. "I told him you enjoyed pouting and that you would forget all about it by morning. You might think of his feelings though. Try to be a little more considerate, Toby. I would—"

"Rosie," Chantelle said, "good night."

Rosie's predatory interest in Michael had never been more obvious. Toby had always suspected Rosie was attracted to him but, until now, didn't consider it a threat.

"Is every single, attractive man fair game?" Toby snapped.

Smugly Rosie said from the stairs, "Yes. Can you think of any better way for a beautiful woman to entertain herself?"

Her sister's conceit was galling. "Listen, Miss Vain, your inflated self-esteem may puff you up, but it won't support you in a real relationship with a man."

"What would you know of a real relationship?" Rosie countered. "You're so afraid of men you manufacture reasons to avoid them."

Chantelle verbally leaped between them. "Hush before you two say one more thing to hurt each other. None of us is perfect."

Rosie shrugged and Toby knew what her sister was thinking. To her, arguments were a game. She lost some, won some and the rest were a draw.

Exhausted by the strain of the past few weeks, Toby dashed by Rosie up the stairs to her room and threw herself onto the bed in a fit of tears.

There was a knock at her door and Chantelle asked softly, "May I come in?"

Lifting her head, Toby cried, "Only if you're a saint and can work miracles."

"I'm not a saint," Chantelle said softly, "but I'm a good listener. Sit up and dry your tears, then you can tell me what's really bothering you."

Sniffling, Toby said, "Everything. I thought I was in love with Michael, but then I found out he has two children." Toby squeezed her eyes shut to halt the tears. "I have been raising children since I was twelve. I don't want any more children."

"For weeks I've watched you and seen how you hold back. It's a logical reason," Chantelle said, unaware of the volley of fresh tears her words would cause.

"Have you been talking to Michael?"

"No."

"That's the exact word he used to describe our relationship. He doesn't love me but I'm a 'logical choice.' Just what I always wanted to be. I feel like a horse he's buying, sorting through all the other animals until he finds a healthy, well-mannered mare that fits his specifications."

"Michael is afraid of you. Afraid of the power you will have if he allows you to get too close."

"Then why can't he treat me like he used to? I'd be content to just work with him."

"My, but you are confused, aren't you?" Chantelle said, shaking her head.

"No, I'm not."

"Well, you certainly talk like a madwoman. You admit you are in love with Michael and try to tell me it won't bother you to be around him every day. Either you don't know the meaning of the word or you are lying to both of us."

"What can I do? Run home? Abandon him and The Pantheon?" Toby brushed her long hair away from her damp cheeks and stared at Chantelle. "That would be a terrible thing to do to anyone."

Chantelle managed a weak smile. "Running away is no answer. Some things can only be solved with time and patience."

Toby wished she could solve her friend's quandary. If Caleb looked half as miserable as Chantelle, she pitied the man. She admired Chantelle's composure and wondered what would happen between them now that Caleb had taken his stand. Would his pride make him honor his words, or would he continue to accept Chantelle's love on her terms until she could finally win her freedom? Toby couldn't express her sympathy without revealing her presence in the garden, and she wouldn't disgrace Chantelle by admitting she and Michael were both witnesses.

Feeling as though she had invaded Chantelle's privacy but unable to apologize, Toby said, "I'm sorry for burdening you with my problems. I think Michael and I were just overtired."

"Don't ever try to play cards," Chantelle said, and shook her head. "You couldn't lie your way out of a pickle barrel."

"I don't know what else to do but paint a smile on my face and go on. Any better suggestions?"

"I wish I had the wisdom to offer you an answer, *chère*, but I can't seem to even manage my own life. This theater is a big gamble for both Michael and Caleb," Chantelle said, her Haitian accent heavier than usual. "When the curtain rises on opening night you win every heart in New York while I keep the backstage running smoothly. It's all we can do for our men right now."

Before Toby could correct Chantelle and stress the point that Michael didn't belong to her, Chantelle turned off the light and left the room without saying another word. Didn't anybody but Rosie believe her when she said it would never work? Michael Sedaine and Toby Wells would never be husband and wife. Maybe if she took out a full-page advertisement in the daily newspaper, people might take her seriously. A small giggle wound its way past her misery at the thought of what Laura Sedaine's face would look like opening up the morning paper to read such a public proclamation. Emotionally exhausted, Toby curled up into a ball, hugging her pillow and burrowing under the blankets, and was blessed by sleep.

The first hour of rehearsal was a disaster, and Michael cursed himself for having ever considered opening a vaudeville house. He was certain that in one week he would be the laughingstock of New York.

It was bad enough that a quarter of the cast came in late, but Caleb hadn't even arrived yet. Michael hadn't heard a word from him since Friday night and was worried his major headliner had left town after fighting with Chantelle. If Caleb had vanished, Michael cursed, he might as well close down now.

Toby, on the other hand, had come early and was the epitome of efficiency. He couldn't fault her on her professionalism, her attention to details, her patience with the rest of the cast, her prompt response to his directives or her unwavering politeness—and it was exactly that condescending politeness that infuriated him. She used it as a weapon to keep him at a distance.

"Toby," he said, catching her attention, "may I have a moment of your time?"

"Yes, Mr. Sedaine?"

He fought the urge to shake her for being so damn formal. "I'd like to go over the third routine with you," he managed to say passively.

"Fine. I'll call Chantelle and have her join us. She knows more about the jugglers than I do," Toby said.

"Forget it," he barked, thwarted at getting her alone. "I'll handle it myself."

"As you wish, Mr. Sedaine."

"What I wish is for you to knock off the 'Mr. Sedaine' garbage," he yelled.

She remained unruffled. "The only thing I plan on knocking off, Mr. Sedaine, is the corners of this music hall."

"With your attitude, Miss Wells, there's no way you'll be that successful. You haven't the faintest idea of teamwork."

"You're wrong. I'm an advocate of teamwork but not of partnerships."

Michael felt the slap of her double entendre. Knowing that his temper was on the verge of exploding, he stomped into the wings and ran smack into Ansel. His brother-in-law was paying more attention to Rosie than the duties Michael had assigned him.

"Where's the rough draft from the printers for the program?" Michael demanded.

"Not ready yet, old boy," Ansel answered, not taking his eyes off Rosie.

"How about the tickets? Have you ordered them?" Michael persisted.

"Done."

"Ordered those flowers?"

"Of course," Ansel said, waving his hand in dismissal.

Ansel's laissez-faire manner pushed Michael out of control. "Then find something to do besides drool over Rosie."

"Here, Ansel," Rosie laughed, handing him the stained paint rag she'd been using on a set. "Wipe your chin."

Michael left them bantering, aware his reprimands hadn't slowed Ansel's ardor one whit. He needed some time alone and headed for his office near the stage door. Five minutes of peace would give him a chance to regain his composure.

But he was denied even an instant's respite. Caleb sauntered through the entrance, nattily dressed and dangling a gaudily costumed woman on his elbow. The creature was an insult to Chantelle and a caricature of the kind of woman who haunted cheap saloons and theater alleys.

"Is this why you're late?" Michael asked, rudely pointing at the floozy pressing herself against Caleb.

"I was busy," Caleb answered indifferently.

"Let's get a few things straight," Michael ordered. "You made a commitment to me and I expect you to honor it."

"Who pulled your chain?"

Michael stepped up to him until they were nearly nose to nose. The reek of liquor on Caleb's breath was unmistakable. Looking closer at him, Michael could see the fatigue in Caleb's bloodshot eyes. He almost yielded to pity, sensing that Caleb had been suffering all weekend, but Michael couldn't let personal problems destroy everything—whether they were Caleb's or his own.

"Let's forget it for now," Michael said. "Park your tootsie somewhere and get to work. You and I will talk later."

The woman took offense. "You gonna let him talk to you like that, sugar?"

She poured it on too heavy and Caleb shrugged her loose. "This man is my friend and he owns this theater, so he has the right to demand a good day's work out of me."

Michael was relieved Caleb hadn't totally lost his senses. "Come on, partner, let's get this show moving," Michael said, feeling better than he had all morning.

"Michael!" Laura Sedaine bellowed.

He had never heard his mother raise her voice to such a screeching pitch and reluctantly turned to face one more problem. "Yes?"

"This ridiculous idea of yours has gone far enough. When I woke up this morning, I discovered you'd hired *my* butler away from me. When I came here to force you to fire Patrick, I found your little Miss Wells out front running things as if she owned the place and Ansel making a fool of himself over a schoolgirl." She paused long enough to catch her breath. "All of this disruption just so you can consort with riffraff like that!" she said, directing her hostile stare at Caleb and his date.

Chantelle and Toby had followed Laura Sedaine down the aisle and into the wings. Laura's tirade made Chantelle blush in shame, and she fixed her attention on the tart. Pinching the woman's collar as if it were a piece of dirty linen, Chantelle marched her to the alley. "This man," she said, and pointed to Caleb, "needs to go to work. Just like you should go home and use a trowel to scrape that makeup off your face."

Toby had never seen such controlled anger. Her friend's voice held an underlying promise of threat and announced that she was not a person to trifle with—even Laura Sedaine seemed intimidated by Chantelle.

"And you," Chantelle spoke slowly to Caleb, "are an idiot. If you thought I'd be jealous of your rolling in the gutter with vermin like her, think again. I'm only insulted and disgusted."

"I'm sorry," Caleb said, hanging his head.

"I don't want to hear any apologies. Get out on that stage and prove you're at least a responsible man if not a faithful one."

Michael watched them walk away, Caleb slinking behind Chantelle. Now, if only his mother and Toby would disappear he'd be happy.

"This is all your fault, Miss Wells," Laura said, spinning on Toby. "Before Michael met you he was a rational businessman, and now he's a buffoon in the eyes of all of New York."

"That's unfair," Michael defended Toby.

His mother brought her attack back on him. "By involving yourself with these lowlifes you are jeopardizing your own family. How do you think Paul and Suzanne feel, knowing their father owns a vaudeville theater?"

"Mother, do me a favor. Shut up." Michael didn't wait for her to respond. He walked into the office and slammed the door. Leaning against it, he wondered if his mother was right. Was all of this a terrible mistake?

Staring at the door slammed in her face, Laura Sedaine took a minute to collect herself. When she did, she flew into Toby with renewed vengeance. "You're quite remarkable, Miss Wells. You've managed to ruin Michael's career, probably bankrupted him, shattered his social standing and alienated him from the bosom of his loving family."

After Laura imperiously swept away, Toby stood in front of the office and tried to think of what she could offer Michael. Maybe if she went home to Saint Louis he could recoup his losses and start again. Heaving a large breath, Toby walked in on him.

"I'm sorry, Michael," she said.

"When did you drop Mr. Sedaine?" he retorted.

"I deserved that. Would it help if I packed up and went back to Missouri?"

He jumped to his feet. "Oh, no, you don't! You wanted a job, I gave you one. You wanted to be onstage and I started a theater. If you leave I'll track you down, hog-tie you and drag you back here."

"I wasn't making a threat," Toby said, trying to explain her offer. "Your mother might calm down a bit if I left New York. The woman hates me and will continue to make your life miserable as long as I work for you."

"That's my problem, not yours. I don't need you meddling in my family affairs. All I want from you is the best damn performance of your life."

Toby had never heard Michael sound bitter and vindictive before and didn't know what to say. "Pardon me," she said. "I made a mistake coming in here."

Michael reached around her and slammed the door shut before she could leave and kept his hand on the knob, preventing her escape. "You are always running away. Every time we argue, you pick up your skirts and gently trip over anything in your way, leaving a trail of destruction behind you. Not this time, lady. We are going to resolve our differences, because I can't tolerate your attitude any longer."

All Toby's promises to maintain her composure evaporated the moment she turned and saw his determined stance. His jaw muscles were twitching in anger and his eyes glittered dangerously.

"You listen to me, Michael Joseph Sedaine," she said. "Nothing is keeping me here except my own sense of honor. No amount of bullying or guilt will force me to stay if I don't want to. You tried to buy me by opening this theater and it didn't work. The Pantheon was just a ploy to keep me away from Joel Greenpasture. And unless you have rewritten history to suit your personal needs, you offered me a job in Saint Louis. I never asked for one."

"Do you think I would go through all this," Michael said, "just to keep you in New York? Don't flatter yourself, little girl. This is a business investment. The women I keep company with don't require payment."

Toby's hand itched to reach out and slap Michael for his disgusting innuendo, but she fought the urge. "That surprises me. I heard it cost you nearly every dime you owned to keep Lillian happy." Before Michael could respond, Toby slowly walked out the door as if she were strolling down the Ladies Mile, browsing for a new bonnet.

Michael wanted to chase after Toby and shake an explanation out of her, but his pride wouldn't allow him to give her accusation any credence. Besides, where did she ever get such an erroneous idea? Had Ansel been filling her head with lies about his marriage to Lillian? None of it made a bit of sense, but Michael would find out where Toby had heard the rumors and take immense pleasure in stuffing them down the guilty party's throat. Then he would take even more satisfaction in watching Toby squirm as she apologized for repeating them.

He opened the door and yelled, "Ansel!"

Toby heard Michael screaming Ansel's name and, for all her verbal bravery and casual saunter, knew it was wise to stay as far away from him as possible. She wandered backstage, searching for a job until she eventually found Caleb.

"Caleb," Toby said, approaching him, "need any help?"

Caleb looked up from the piece of paper he was holding and smiled. "You mean you're still speaking to me?"

"If we don't all put our differences aside, this show is going to be a disaster."

"That bad?"

"I don't understand what you mean," Toby said.

He pulled out a chair and patted the seat for Toby to join him. "Your discussion with Michael wasn't any more confidential than mine was with Chantelle. Half the crew has put bets on whether you stay or go home. Gossip travels fast behind the curtains."

"Wonderful," Toby said, and sighed. "Isn't the word *privacy* part of entertainers' vocabulary?"

"No, it isn't. So?"

"So, what?"

"Are you staying?" Caleb asked.

"Of course. I work for Michael and wouldn't walk out on him this close to opening night."

"Michael is a good man, Toby. You should be careful of the tales you carry."

"Michael Sedaine is a good businessman," Toby said slowly. "Our relationship begins and ends on those terms."

"Is that so. I haven't met too many men who would do this for anybody—mother, father, or sweetheart," Caleb said, and craned his neck around to look all over the stage.

"Michael did not buy this theater for me. You are as terrible as he is, trying to make me feel beholden to him because of a business decision he made. You are as much to blame as I am," Toby said, and glowered at Caleb. "Why is it that nobody blames you?"

"Wait a minute. I'm not blaming you for anything. Michael is an adult with a good head and this is his decision, but I think you need to realize that the two of us were the catalysts. We both owe him more than a load of grief."

Toby sat down in the chair next to Caleb and picked up a bent nail left lying on the floor by the carpenters, twirling it in her fingers. "See this nail? It's like Michael. Strong and hardworking. Finely tempered and capable of doing far more than any of us ever expect of it. But someone came along before me and pounded on it, bending it. I can't straighten this nail without breaking it, and it still has some value to someone even though it's bent. It just doesn't have any use to me."

"You might get Michael to believe that speech, Toby, but not me," Caleb said, and started to chuckle. "Never thought I'd live long enough to see the day when I'd meet a female more demented than Chantelle, but my mama always said I shouldn't ever say never." His eyes grew serious and he covered her hand with his. "At least, be honest with yourself, Toby. That's what really matters." Caleb got up and slowly walked away, his laughter returning and echoing in the wings.

Caleb's laugh infuriated Toby and she went to find Chantelle. Toby was certain her help would be welcome in the wardrobe room, and for the rest of the day she hid from all the men in the world, sewing with Chantelle until they finished the last costume. The theater was dark and quiet when Toby finally left her sanctuary and hurried out through the back exit.

Michael never found Ansel and didn't catch sight of Toby. He knew Toby was evading him, but instead of being relieved, he was annoyed with her absence. Although

Rosie tried her best to follow orders, she didn't have the knowledge Toby had and, as vexing as Toby could be, he still wanted her by his side. Fighting with her was better than the void she left behind when she wasn't with him.

Walking slowly home, he considered stopping at a bar to have a drink but rejected the idea. Alcohol wouldn't make it any easier to fall asleep, and a drink wouldn't ease the dread he felt every night he climbed into his bed—a bed Toby would never share. It was equally devastating to realize he'd started this theater to keep her near and all he'd accomplished was to torture himself with her indifferent presence. Had any other man been as miserable or placed himself in such a predicament? He knew of only one and went to find him.

Caleb's roommate was home and went to fetch him while Michael waited in the parlor. With the musicians and dancers from the party missing, the room was empty and cold just like his life without Toby.

"Michael?" Caleb said, coming into the gloomy room and hitching up his suspenders. "Come to check that I was tucked in safely and alone in my bed?"

"Frankly, I don't know why I'm here," Michael admitted, nervously spinning his hat in his hands.

Hearing the noise of his roommate puttering around in the kitchen, Caleb asked, "Want to go for a walk?"

"Yes. Do you have the time?"

"I've got the rest of my life," Caleb said.

They walked in silence for blocks until they turned into Central Park. The path wound through the trees, and the night breeze sounded melancholy as it rustled the leaves.

"Do you understand women?" Michael asked.

"About as well as I grasp chemistry."

"Too bad. I was hoping you could tell me why Toby runs hot and cold."

A humorless laugh escaped Caleb. "Toby cut you out?"

"Yes."

"If those two women stay together much longer they might as well start a convent."

Michael simply nodded at the joke. "I know about you and Chantelle separating. Toby and I were in the backyard when you two fought. We couldn't go anywhere and didn't want to embarrass either of you."

"Makes no difference."

"Or sense. I never saw a better match than you two. The light sparks in both of your eyes when you're together," Michael said. "Am I being too nosy if I ask what's the problem?" He wanted to help, since he couldn't do a damn thing about Toby. Caleb and he had been denied the women they loved for reasons beyond their control. Stubborn women, prideful ladies and irresistible females, both of them.

"No, I'd like to talk about it to somebody." Caleb walked up the arched stone bridge, rested his elbows on the railing and stared into the water. "Did you know Chantelle is married?"

"I guessed something like that."

"It isn't a real marriage. Her husband in Haiti abused her and she ran away. She's spent every spare dime she has trying to get a divorce, but Reynard refuses to grant her one."

"And she won't live with you, right?"

"Right. I don't need a piece of paper to marry her. In my heart she's been my wife for years. I just want to start living together the way we should."

Michael sympathized with Caleb, but he understood Chantelle. If he'd learned anything about her, it was that she was a lady and would insist on a legal wedding before she'd publicly live with Caleb.

"I had this big plan to make Chantelle jealous," Caleb said. "You saw how well that worked. Sorry, Michael, I wasn't thinking when I dragged my personal problems to the theater this morning."

"Forget it," Michael said, waving the incident away. "It was stupid of you, but I was having a devil of a time with Toby and took my frustration out on you."

Caleb nodded. "I used to think music was my whole life until I met Chantelle. Now it doesn't mean as much."

"Great!" Michael sighed and walked down off the bridge. Caleb followed him and, without looking back,

Michael ranted, "First, Toby wants to quit and now you're telling me you don't care about ragtime anymore."

"There's a world of difference between quitting and being distracted. I know Toby was bluffing."

"I hope so. I'm counting on both of you to give the best damn show New York has ever seen."

"Then you'll have it," Caleb promised. "Anything else I can do?"

"Set a good example for your buddies you brought from Saint Louis," Michael said. "I need you, Caleb. Not just your talent but your contacts. How does ten percent of the net receipts as an incentive sound to you?"

Caleb halted in midstride. "You don't need to bribe me, Michael. I'll do a good job and show up for work on time."

Bribe? The word shook Michael, for two people he cared about had accused him of precisely the same corruption. Was he guilty of buying people? Certainly. In his business it was important to pay higher than the competition for the best music. Yet, material things held little value for him, probably because he'd always had money. Michael didn't consider paying Toby above-average wages a bribe but a fair salary for the amount of work she did. Nor had he invested most of his money in the theater just for her but because he really believed Toby and Caleb could bring in large crowds. Making money was a game not a necessity.

"I was just trying to show you how much I appreciate you, Caleb."

"Then find another way. I make enough money to keep me happy. Besides, money won't buy Chantelle's freedom."

"Mine won't buy Toby, either."

As they headed back to Lenox Avenue, Michael was struck by how much alike he and Caleb were. His mother wouldn't agree, pointing out their differences in backgrounds, race and social standing, but Michael knew she was wrong. Caleb was more than an employee, he was one of the few men Michael felt genuinely comfortable with.

When they reached Caleb's stoop, Michael shook hands with him. "Thanks for the stroll and the talk."

"Did we solve anything?"

"No, but at least I don't feel alone in my misery."

Caleb grinned his marvelous smile. "In show business, pal, you're never alone—just crazy. By the way, someday you need to ask Toby if you're an eight-penny or sixteen-penny nail. I'm going in now and get some rest. Good night."

Michael scowled at Caleb's odd comment but knew Caleb wouldn't say anything further. He puzzled about it all the way home. The only explanation was that Caleb was just trying to be funny and give validity to his observation that they were all, Toby, Michael, Chantelle and himself, deranged.

It was nearly dawn before Michael thumped his pillow for the last time and, at peace with his decision, closed his eyes. He wasn't going to let Toby make false accusations and then slip out of his life. She was the perfect woman to fill every gap, and it would be a gratifying vendetta to prove to her what a mistake she had made.

The day before opening was a madhouse, and Toby prayed the old adage was true, "If the dress rehearsal is a flop it guarantees a great show." Chantelle was on the edge of tears and Toby tried to help. The magician's girl had gained ten pounds and her costume couldn't be hooked up. Another dunce had thought she was doing Chantelle a favor by ironing her velvet gown and scorched the bodice.

"Tell me what to do," Toby asked Chantelle as she held up the ruined dress.

"Nothing. You've enough to do. Rosie is quite competent at making a spray of silk roses to hide the damage. The child is a wonder," Chantelle said, stitching gussets into the side seams of the chubby assistant's dress. "Go to your dressing room and start on your hair."

Alone in her tiny cubbyhole, the only wonder in Toby's mind was how her sister, who couldn't even darn a sock two months ago, was now so indispensable. Toby felt her irritation and realized she was critical because her own life had changed dramatically. Once, everyone had depended on her to do everything, but recently she'd been replaced by a competent and efficient team. Chantelle was a better cook and seamstress than Toby would ever be. Rosie had become Michael's right hand, freeing Toby from numerous tedious details while Caleb had brought in remarkable talent, bolstering the show's cast.

Looking at her contribution, Toby conceded she was important but not indispensable. At least there was one area where no one could replace her—in her routine. It was a skit she had created and perfected, adapted to her voice, sense of humor and personality. Even with their differences, Michael had complimented her, saying, "You have the marvelous ability of putting your unique stamp on an act."

Michael voiced his approval in many ways, verbal and physical. Toby couldn't take issue with him for he made every incident seem so guileless it would have been like reproving a faithful friend for being kind. But she knew him too well to believe he was as innocent as he was pretending to be.

All week Michael had stayed close, using any excuse to rub her shoulders, brush a wisp of hair off her cheek or simply pat her knee when they were watching a scene, and he was pleased. Each time he touched her, she gritted her teeth to control the tremble that started in the pit of her stomach and raced through her body, bringing a flush to her cheeks and a glimmer to her eyes. And every day it was becoming increasingly difficult to remain aloof. Just smelling his sweet lemon-drop breath reminded her of the time she had snuggled in his arms.

Toby closed her eyes and envisioned the night they had kissed on the landing. She wanted to recapture the mood of the moment, the feel of Michael's lips pressed to hers, the way his chest felt pressed against her and the luscious way he had of easing her lips apart. . . .

"Toby? Are you decent?"

She hadn't even started to change and jerked herself up out of the enfolding security of her overstuffed rocker at the sound of Michael's voice.

"Yes," she called out, fearing there was a last-minute problem he wanted her to handle. As he stepped in, she asked, "Do you need me out front?"

Michael wanted to say he needed her, all right—in his arms—but didn't. "No, I haven't had a chance to see your costume and wanted to check it before we start."

"A little late if it's wrong, isn't it?"

"Humor me. I like to check every last detail."

Toby gave in to his whim. After all, he was the boss. "Step outside and I'll put it on," she said.

"I'll just sit here," Michael said, dropping into the chair. He saw her blush but didn't budge. "Get used to working with professionals. There's no room for modesty when you only have minutes to change. But, if you're embarrassed, step behind that screen." He indicated the three-paneled folding divider in the corner.

She knew he was challenging her by pretending to have only a professional interest in her, but she was in a dangerous mood. Taking the dare, Toby stood her ground and unbuttoned her blouse, but when he didn't politely look away, her courage failed and she slipped quickly behind the screen.

Like a rascal, Michael grinned at her discomfort and flight. Bit by bit, he was winning the battle of wills. Toby thrived on direct confrontation but faltered at his devious tactics. She didn't know what to do when he turned the tables on her; Toby simply did not know how to handle the sensual tension sparking between them, and he wondered how much longer she could ignore it.

"Need any help with the buttons?" he asked.

"No, no, I'm fine," she said nervously. "I'm just about ready." Even though there was a partition between them, Toby almost believed Michael's gaze could pierce the thin wood. Disrobing in the same room with him sent her heart pounding, and as much as she swore she didn't want him, her body incessantly betrayed her.

When she appeared, Michael laughed at her outrageous yellow feather cape and matching hat. The effect was precisely what they had planned. Toby's opening number was a comical rendition of "The Ugly Duckling" and in that getup she looked like a fat, downy bird.

"Stop laughing," she pleaded, sure he was mocking her not the costume.

"Why? My reaction is exactly what you want."

Toby didn't know what she wanted. She wanted his approval and—hard as it was to admit—she wanted him. Defiantly she let the cape drop and tossed her hat aside, knowing it would still his laughter.

Her beauty never ceased to shock him. The simple, sleek white gown molded her body, accenting her long graceful neck. Even without her song, Toby had been transformed into what she really was—an exquisite swan.

Clearing his throat, forcing himself to control his desire, Michael said, "I don't know if we need those rhinestone straps. Your shoulders are quite lovely without the glitter. Let's see." He slipped the thin diamond ties down and rubbed her incredibly soft skin.

She almost cried out with pleasure. How could his fingers feel so good, fire such a heat in her? Toby was afraid if she spoke she'd beg him to hold her instead of telling him to stop the torture.

"Hmm," Michael said, running his warm hands down her arms to her hips. "The fit is perfect." Encircling her tiny waist, he squeezed her and complained, "Must you wear this horrible corset?"

Trying to back away from him, Toby simply nodded.

"Why?" Michael insisted, pulling her closer.

"Because, because," she stammered, "it keeps the dress up."

"Oh, well, we can't have it falling, can we?" Lightly he traced the sweetheart neckline with his fingertip, skipping across the swell of her breasts, dipping into her silky cleavage.

"Why are you doing this?" Toby gulped.

"What?" He trailed his finger up the hollow of her throat to her chin. Lifting it gently, he bent and kissed her.

She willed her stomach to stop flip-flopping, her heart to stop throbbing, her arms to remain at her sides, but her body disobeyed. All Michael had to do was part her lips with his, trace his tongue across hers and her resolve vanished.

Michael felt her surrender, and instead of taking advantage of it, he released her. "Are you going to continue this farce that we simply work together?"

"No," she said, taking a deep stilling breath. "I can't."

"Finally." He smiled, picked up her feathered cape and hat, handed them to her and said, "After rehearsal, we'll talk."

Chapter Eleven

It was late, the rehearsal over and the last-minute changes noted. Michael hurried to his office to clear off his desk before Toby joined him. He glanced around the room and sighed in disappointment. It was not the setting he would have preferred, but there were no other choices. Finding a place to spend time alone with Toby had become impossible, and his office was the only alternative. At work they were surrounded by people, in the brownstone Rosie hovered within arm's reach, and it was ludicrous to consider taking Toby back to his mother's apartment.

Standing next to the bookcase, Michael tucked his hands into his pockets, afraid that if he didn't imprison them he would reach for Toby and pull her into his arms the moment she walked through the door. The past week of tormenting Toby with his physical affection had tested his dwindling reserve of composure. And, tempting as it was, they needed to talk before they touched. There was no denying the intense attraction that sparked between them. But Michael wanted more than physical gratification; he wanted a commitment.

Toby had made cruel accusations, tried to push him away with angry words, but he knew she had been merely mouthing them. Her lips said one thing, but her eyes told a completely different story and Toby's clear blue eyes couldn't lie. After they had made peace, he would resolve their differences in a calm, adult manner. Tonight he was thrilled just to know she was willing to speak with him.

"Michael?" Toby said, and knocked on the door. "Are you in there?"

"Yes."

Toby nervously smoothed her skirt and wished she had something more flattering than her navy serge and plain lawn waist to wear. She didn't know what to expect from Michael, but looking her best would have given her a trifle more confidence.

He could tell she was nervous by the way she thrust her chin out and the determined manner in which she walked across the room. She looked like a schoolgirl called in for a scolding after being found guilty of breaking a classroom rule, and Michael tried to ease her tension. "You've been doing an excellent job and I want you to know your extra efforts haven't gone unnoticed."

"Thank you," Toby said. She knew he hadn't set this meeting to discuss business and didn't have the strength to wait for him to wander through inane pleasantries before he got to the point. "I thought we were going to talk, not just exchange compliments."

"Do you think we can without ending up in an argument?" he asked.

Toby strolled to his desk and toyed with the metronome he used as a paperweight. She wound the key, unwittingly causing the pendulum to start ticking at the same rate as her fluttering heart. Facing his direct question added to her agitation. "I don't want to fight with you, but you are so frustrating, Michael."

Michael stopped the irritating clicking of the metronome. "Try. Other people say I'm a good listener."

"It isn't you," she answered, turning and looking him directly in the face. "There is nothing wrong with you. It's me. I had all these plans, step by step, of how my life would go. Getting married wasn't one of them, at least not for a long time."

"Sorry I'm so inconvenient."

His sarcasm grated on her nerves. "Are you going to become defensive? If so, I'll leave right now and spare us the inevitable quarrel."

He yanked angrily on the slipknot of his four-in-hand necktie and sighed audibly. "What am I supposed to say? I'll come back later when you have the time for me? Call me in ten years? Or should I just trail behind you, begging for a favor like a lovesick puppy?"

"Why ask for permission?" she countered. "You haven't bothered any other time this week."

"Listen, lady," he said, clipping his words, "I'm not doing anything you don't want me to. You haven't voiced one objection. I'm attracted to you and find nothing wrong with admitting I'm a man with human needs and desires. You're only angry because you enjoy every minute of my attention. You can't wait until I touch you, kiss your lips, wrap my arms around you. What is the problem? Why turn your back on something that works so well?"

Michael added emphasis to his claim by skimming the tip of his finger up the side of Toby's neck across her cheek and circling her lips. He watched her bodice rise and fall and saw her hands clench. "Tell me you don't want me to kiss you."

"I, uh . . ." Toby stammered but couldn't finish the sentence. Every other thought raced from her mind except the consuming need to feel Michael's lips against hers again.

She stood on her tiptoes and leaned into his body. With his collar and tie tossed aside, there was an exposed triangle of skin just below his throat, and she placed her lips against the pulsating hollow. He smelled of clean starched linen and she nuzzled her face into his chest, savoring his unique essence. Without thought, her arms wound around his waist, and she found herself tugging his shirt out of his trousers, desperate to stroke the hard muscles of his back.

The war Michael fought with himself to withstand Toby's amorous gestures was fierce, and he felt no shame in failure. Obviously she found it easier to show him how she felt rather than admit she had been wrong. He'd had his fill of denying his craving for this woman, and there was no point belaboring the indisputable with unnecessary words.

"You are so beautiful," Michael whispered as he pulled the pins from her hair and raked his fingers through the saffron curls.

Sitting down on the edge of his desk, Michael lured Toby closer, wrapping his legs around hers and his hands around her waist. "I won't ever let you go again."

"Promise?" She looked into his twinkling brown eyes and found her answer.

Content being trapped in Michael's embrace, Toby traced his back hairline where the short barbered hair gave way to his smooth skin. If she was bolder, she would have leaned just a smidgen forward and pressed her lips against his, but she couldn't bring herself to bridge the few inches separating them. She could feel his warm, sweet breath brush across her cheeks, could almost taste the lemon drops and could nearly feel the soft velvet of his mouth.

Toby sighed contentedly when Michael cupped her face with his strong hands and lowered his lips to hers. Nothing mattered except the ecstasy of Michael's kiss, and Toby parted her lips, begging him to caress her tongue with his the way he had done before. The warm, tight tingle that started in the pit of her stomach and spread up to her pounding heart was the most delicious sensation she had ever experienced. How could she have denied her love for him?

When Michael tried to pull his mouth away, Toby greedily denied him. He could feel the firm nipples of her breasts pressed against his chest and wanted to kiss more than her lips, but she moaned softly when he started to pull away.

"There is so much more to making love than this, Angel Eyes," Michael said against her lips. "Let me show you."

Toby followed his directions and tipped her head back, her eyes closed as Michael unbuttoned her blouse to the waist. She gasped aloud when he burrowed his face in the valley of her breasts and then gently brushed his mouth back and forth across her skin. The sensation of his tongue surrounded by the shadow of his whiskers grazing across her skin was decadent, the contrast incredible. Her heart was pounding and her legs were ready to buckle when Michael quickly stood up.

"I want to lock the door. I don't want anyone disturbing us," he said.

Toby watched him cross the room and marveled at her good fortune to be in love with such a handsome, exciting man. He was every woman's dream and he was hers, all hers.

When he turned and hurried back to her outstretched arms, Toby couldn't keep quiet any longer. "I love you, Michael Sedaine."

He smiled at her. "There isn't anything I wouldn't do for you. I know you'll be happy."

Toby waited for the words, the only three words she needed to hear to make her life complete, but Michael was silent. Didn't he realize how important it was to her to know he loved her as much as she loved him?

"I recall a speech you made about what a sensible decision it was to marry me, but you didn't believe in love," Toby said, her fear growing with each syllable. "Now are you willing to confess how wrong you were?"

"The only thing I'm guilty of is letting words get in the way. Every time we talk we get into trouble. So, hush, pretty lady."

"No, Michael. I won't be still." Toby knew her voice was rising, her words sounding shrill, but she couldn't gain control. "You haven't changed one bit, and I've made a fool of myself one more time."

He hugged her close, willing her to listen. "Sweetheart, you are everything I need in a woman. I want you to be my wife, mother to my children. I can't think of any finer compliment a man could pay a woman."

"I need to hear you tell me you love me. I believe in falling in love with the man I marry and I expect him to love me back. That is not too much to ask, is it?"

"You're asking me to give you the one thing I can't, while you turn your back on all the rest. We would be so good together, Toby. I want to teach you how glorious it can be between a man and a woman. I want to wake up every morning and see your shining hair spread across my pillow. And my children need someone like you in their lives."

She jerked free and didn't try to stop the tears. Clumsily she buttoned her blouse back up and tucked it inside her skirt. "Can't you understand, Michael, that people have been needing me for my entire life? All I want is to be loved, not because I would make somebody a good mother or because he likes the way I look or even because I invite him into my bed. I want to be loved because the man I marry can't possibly imagine spending his life with any other woman."

Michael dragged his hands through his hair, searching for the right words to explain. "I know it hurts, but you are asking the impossible. I don't trust love. It dies, but what we have will last."

"You don't love me, but you want to marry me. It doesn't make any sense."

He grabbed her by the upper arms and held her tightly. "Toby, please believe me. What we have is better than love. Trust me. I want to marry you and have a large family. Paul and Suzanne need more brothers and sisters."

"Yes, they do," Toby said, knowing what Michael wanted most from her was the one thing she didn't have enough courage to give him. She had offered her heart and her love, but she couldn't offer her life. "You want a house full of children, don't you, Michael? And you think it would be wonderful if I gave up the theater before I even started, moved in with you and your mother to raise babies."

Thrilled that Toby was finally agreeing with him, Michael was deaf to the flat tone in her voice. "Oh, we wouldn't live with Mother. I may not be wealthy, but I can certainly afford to buy my wife her own home," he said, smiling.

"But I don't want to give up the theater, Michael. I like what I'm doing and I don't want to have any children. At least, not yet."

"I will never understand what goes on underneath those pretty blond curls. What do you want? I can't believe you would be content being my mistress."

"Oh, yes," she said sarcastically, and swished her skirts back and forth, flashing her ankles at Michael. "Mr. von Feldman, I would like to introduce you to my mistress, daughter of the Reverend Robert Wells of Saint Louis, the famous entertainer, Toby Wells." Dropping her hem, she curtsied. "Thank you, but I'll pass."

"Then what?" Michael wanted to sweep her into his arms and carry her to the sofa, but he contained his emotions and clamped down on his rising sense of futility.

"Don't people in New York ever get engaged?" Toby asked with sudden inspiration. If she could stall long enough, she was certain she would be able to resolve their differences. The perfect solution to both problems. "We could meet somewhere in the middle of our disagreement that way."

"That would keep you satisfied? A modest little diamond on your finger and I'd have you on my arm?"

"Yes," Toby said, stunned that Michael didn't sound elated. "Yes!"

"What about this?" Without warning, Michael wrapped one arm around her waist and spanned the small of her back with the other. Pressing her close to him, Toby moaned softly as he nibbled the delicate spot behind her earlobe, whispering endearments as his breath tickled her neck. Her will to resist his passion had vanished, and when he cupped her buttocks, nearly picking her up off her feet, she fought the urge to lift her skirts and eliminate the shrouding layers of clothing between his wonderful hands and her body.

"An engagement would be denying nature, Toby. A cat hunts mice and roosters crow at the cock of dawn. They're following nature's laws. And sooner or later we'll follow nature's laws," Michael said. "You were raised in a churchgoing family. I doubt that you will be comfortable until we legalize our partnership. Let's get married tomorrow."

"Tomorrow? But, we open tomorrow." Toby's scheme of a long engagement was backfiring.

"Then next Monday. Our first day off."

"But..." Toby stopped. But what? She was in a corner and not sure if she wanted out. "There's too much to do. I don't have time enough to plan a wedding."

"How long?" Michael could tell Toby was purposely delaying setting a date.

"Enough to give your mother and me a chance to become friends, time for the children to adjust to me and for the theater to start running smoothly. Then I'd like a real wedding with my family present."

He resigned himself to her postponement, knowing Toby well enough to give her room. Push, and Toby either ran away or she shoved him away. "All right, little one. Mixing the Wells and the Sedaines will be interesting."

Toby was delighted he had accepted her delay. "Interesting or overwhelming?"

"I think we're pretty well matched. You've got Rosie and I've got Ansel. Cleo will have Suzanne to spoil and Mo can teach Paul how to play."

Realizing she'd have to tell Rosie that Ansel would be a relative made Toby giggle. The two hadn't stopped alternately bickering and flirting since they'd met.

It had been too long since Michael had heard Toby laugh and he hugged her. "Do you need me to get on my knees and make a formal proposal?"

"All I need is you," Toby whispered. She entwined her fingers in his raven hair and slowly pulled his lips to hers.

Opening day was a grand autumn day, made perfect by Michael's announcement of their engagement to the cast when they assembled onstage for last-minute directions.

"It's a good omen," Chantelle said, kissing Toby. "Your news means tonight will be a triumph."

Toby's step was light as air as she walked to her dressing room, and before she could close the door, Rosie came in to help with her makeup, hair and costume.

"Are there many people out front?" Toby asked nervously.

"Almost a full house. Ansel may be a nincompoop, but he certainly knows how to advertise."

Toby grinned. "Well, that's an improvement."

"What is?"

"Yesterday you were calling him a titmouse."

"Better than calling him a jackass."

"Rosamond!" Toby scolded. "Watch your language. Ansel will soon be part of our family."

"How soon?" Rosie asked cynically.

"We haven't set a date."

"And you never will."

"Of course I will," Toby objected.

"I know you. After ten years of coddling us, you're not about to harness yourself to a man and children."

The truth, warped as it was, infuriated Toby. "That's a rotten thing to say."

"Rotten? No, honest. But don't misunderstand me, Toby. I think you have played your hand beautifully."

"Now what are you blaming me for?"

"Manipulating Michael. You've gotten him to start this theater just so you could do what you've always dreamed of doing."

Abruptly standing up at the makeup table, Toby spun on her sister. "Is that what you think I've done?"

"Don't get your dander up, sister. I'm not criticizing. I admire your spunk."

"What you call spunk, I call deceit, and I'd never do that to Michael. Just leave me alone. I don't need your help," Toby ranted.

Rosie shrugged and grinned insolently. "Whatever you say, Toby," she said, and left.

In the wings of the stage, Caleb cornered Michael. "Congratulations, pal. Some of us have good luck and the rest of us are still waiting."

Michael had a secret, a plan he hoped would help his friends, but he was unwilling to share it with Caleb yet. He had contacted an attorney, a man he'd gone to school with who was familiar with international law. If Michael could, he was going to exert pressure on Dominic Reynard to grant Chantelle a divorce, but he didn't know what chance, if any, he had. Until he had something positive to report, he wasn't going to raise Caleb's hopes.

"How are things going between you and Chantelle?" Michael asked casually. He was interested but didn't want to pry.

"About as well as the Spanish did in Cuba," Caleb joked, referring to the recent news that Spain had surrendered to the United States.

"You and Chantelle have called a truce, then?"

"We've suspended hostilities but haven't resumed friendly relations."

Michael chuckled at Caleb's equating his love life to international politics. "You two need an arbitrator."

"Know a good one?"

"If I did, I'd hire him." Michael shrugged his shoulders.

The hum of the gathered crowd beyond the curtain alerted them it was almost time to begin the show. Caleb grasped Michael's shoulder and squeezed it reassuringly. "I may not be able to win Chantelle, but I'm going to conquer that mob."

"Never had any doubt," Michael said, punching Caleb softly in the arm. "Knock 'em down."

"Where will you be? Back here?"

"No. It's time I let you pros take over. I'll stand to the back of the hall and enjoy the show."

Joy wasn't the right word for what Michael was experiencing as he leaned against the wall and watched the curtain rise. *Gnawing anxiety* was a better description even though Ansel had informed Michael the house was completely sold out. His apprehension wasn't based on just the financial risk—although it was considerable. Seven thousand dollars a week just to keep the doors open was not a sum to sneeze at. The wages of two hundred people, counting actors, performers, backstage crew, custodians and musicians took a huge bite out of his pocket.

Still Michael was able to shunt the money aside for other concerns. What if he'd misgauged the public and subjected his friends to scathing reviews? He cared more about Toby, Caleb, Patrick Casey and all the others than he did for his bank balance.

The first routine was intended to loosen the audience up, and to Michael's eye it seemed the juggler who balanced a set of parlor furniture on the tip of his nose accomplished his goal. The crowd applauded his feat and laughed when the entertainer couldn't walk off the stage without tripping over his own feet.

Laughter was money in vaudeville. Every act battled to elicit the most hoots and hollers. If guffaws were not appropriate then the performer encouraged audience participation, whether it was getting them to snap their fingers or joyfully bounce in their seats.

After the eighth act Caleb took his seat at the piano and there was a shift in the mood. People didn't know what to expect. A single pianist usually meant a subdued classical recital, and the audience emitted a silent air of disappointment. It took only a few bars of Caleb's scintillating style to put them at ease. A couple more measures and everyone was enthusiastically tapping their toes to what the program billed as "ragtime."

Caleb exploited their approval and swiftly started the second set of tunes. By the end of his thirty-minute act the audience roared its appreciation by standing and clapping through three curtain calls. They chanted, "Caleb, Caleb, Caleb" until he had to raise his hands, begging them to calm down and allow the next act to proceed.

Michael was thrilled. All his worry vanished and he stepped out into the foyer to savor Caleb's moment of triumph. He'd known since Saint Louis that Caleb was gifted, but it was satisfying to have the entire city agree with him. Now, if only Toby could claim half as much applause.

He decided to wait until her turn, judging the rest of the acts by listening from the lobby to the responses of the crowd. Michael heard no boos or catcalls and began to relax. If the newspaper critics didn't rave about The Pantheon, they at least couldn't say it was a flop.

After weeks of rehearsals, Michael knew exactly when it was time for Toby to make her debut. The orchestra played the introduction and Michael slipped back into the darkened performance hall. His anxiety doubled. He knew how much this moment meant to her, how long she had dreamed, through her childhood and her adolescence, of the day when she'd be able to display her talent. Her dream had changed, taken a different road from the path of composer to that of singer, but all her hopes were still pinned on this evening. Whatever the verdict, Michael would stand by her, either brushing away her tears of failure or kissing her for joy.

Three seconds were all he could stand of the tension, and he fled back through the lobby and out the front of the theater. There was nothing he could do at this point but wait in the wings for Toby when she came offstage. He cut down the alley to the stage door and bumped into Chantelle as she stepped outside.

"Scared, too?" he asked her.

"It'll break her heart if they don't love her."

"Maybe I should never have encouraged her," Michael groaned.

"Holding Toby back would have been like trying to stop a locomotive."

"Noticed that, did you?"

Chantelle laughed her deep, rich laugh, the kind that warmed anyone within earshot. "People like Toby cause a stir wherever they go. Nothing's the same after she breezes by."

"I haven't been."

"No, you're not the same stuffy man I met in Saint Louis," Chantelle said, remembering how starched Michael had sounded at that audition. "Then again, Toby is no longer a little girl from Missouri."

"Was she ever? I don't remember seeing her any way but as a self-confident woman."

"Don't let her fool you," Chantelle warned. "Underneath her bravado, Toby is terrified."

"When she first came to New York I worried about her but, trust me," Michael said, "that lady isn't terrified of anything."

"I might be wrong, but I doubt it. Don't accept her word on everything, Michael. Even Toby doesn't understand Toby."

"And you do?" Michael was puzzled by her choice of words. First Caleb made his outlandish comment about the nails, and now Chantelle was talking in riddles.

"I only know enough not to believe she's as indestructible as she pretends to be. Hiding beneath quick tongue and spirited temper is a fragile young woman."

"I understand her fears," Michael assured Chantelle, "but our engagement resolved them."

"I hope so," Chantelle said, baffled at how his proposal could have alleviated Toby's anxiety about Michael's children. "I'm glad she finally told you about her misgivings."

"What all did she say?" Michael asked, wondering if Toby had really told him everything.

"Nothing specific," Chantelle stressed, seeing Michael scrub at the bricks with his toe. "Remember, she hasn't had a mother to listen to her or counsel her the way most young girls do. It's no different than when you and Caleb went walking and had your little chat."

"He mentioned it?"

"Yes, and I'm not the slightest bit offended."

Mentioning Caleb provided a perfect opportunity to suggest his idea. "Chantelle, would you be insulted if I tried to help you secure your divorce?"

"Insulted? No, but there isn't anything you could do. I have tried to convince Dominic to legally end our marriage, but he refuses to sign the papers."

"I have a friend who is a very good attorney in international law. I'd like to call in a marker he owes me and get his help with your problem. This man can be very persuasive."

Michael stressed the last word in a way that shocked Chantelle. "Are you talking about someone with enough power and influence to speak a language Dominic Reynard just might understand?"

"Exactly," Michael said and laughed.

Even if he failed, it was one of the nicest things anyone had ever offered to do for her, and Chantelle stared at him in openmouthed silence. Finally she whispered, "You'd do that for me?"

"For you and Caleb."

Tears stung Chantelle's eyes and she kissed Michael's cheek. "Thank you."

"Don't tell Caleb," Michael cautioned. "No point in getting his hopes up. We'll keep it our secret."

"Are you going to tell Toby?"

"No." Michael wasn't comfortable boasting about something that he might not be able to accomplish.

Caleb poked his head out the door. "Toby's just about finished. Come listen to the crowd."

As Michael mounted the steps, he heard the swelling roar of the audience and knew Toby had scored a hit. He wove his way through the people in the wings and greeted her as she skipped off the stage.

"They liked me, Michael," she squealed, bouncing up and down on her toes.

"They loved you," he said with a laugh, and gently pushed her back onstage. "Take another bow, Miss Wells."

Watching Toby curtsy on stage, Michael felt someone hook elbows with him. He glanced over and smiled at Rosie. "She's wonderful, isn't she?"

"She's pretty good," Rosie conceded. "But then Toby's always been good at getting her way."

Toby had told Michael that Rosie had a caustic tongue, but this was his first sample. "Do I detect sour grapes?"

"If you insist," Rosie replied, completely unfazed by his criticism. "Or, you can take it as a warning from a friend. You just lost your bride. She married a more satisfying lover tonight—the stage."

Indignant, Michael jerked away from Rosie and grabbed her wrist. "If you ever say a thing like that again, you'll be fired."

"All right, but someday you'll remember I warned you."

He watched Rosie flounce away and for a few seconds he fretted at her barb, wondering why she would say such a vicious thing. Shaking it off, Michael refused to let it eat at him and ruin the evening.

While the cast changed clothes, Michael telephoned the Buckingham Hotel and spoke with the maître d'. He asked the hotel to set the buffet for a cast party. It was common to have an opening night feast, and he wouldn't deny his people the pleasure of celebrating their success even though they weren't traditional theater but vaudeville.

He called the cast together to announce the surprise. After they assembled onstage, he said, "Thank you all for working so hard and I'd like each of you to be my guest at the Buckingham tonight."

Toby kissed his cheek. "That's a lovely idea, Michael."

As Michael draped a wrap around Toby's shoulders, Rosie joined them. "May I ride with you?"

"Have you finished checking all the costumes and made sure they're ready for tomorrow?" Michael asked coldly.

"Michael?" Toby intervened.

"When Rosie was hired, one of her commitments was to take care of the dressing rooms after performances. She may join us when her duties are completed." Michael knew he couldn't exclude Rosie, but he could damn well delay her fun.

"He's perfectly within his rights, Toby," Rosie said calmly, and walked away.

Climbing into the carriage, Toby grilled Michael. "What in the world was all that nonsense with Rosie about?"

He settled into the seat next to her. "Teaching her some respect. Rosie needs to be knocked down a peg or two."

His sternness was unusual and she was tempted to question him, but there was something in Michael's tone of voice that cautioned her to let the subject drop. Obviously the two had clashed—nothing unique for Rosie.

Michael and Toby shared the cab with Caleb and Chantelle. Everyone chattered like magpies about the performances, interrupting each other, praising one another and laughing about the minor mishaps.

"Did you see the one dancer lose his shoe?" Caleb said, and chuckled. "He kept right on going as if nothing was wrong."

"And the dog trainer," Toby said, laughing. "When his black mongrel refused to quit barking, I thought the poor man would expire."

"But the audience thought it was a singing dog act," Chantelle said. "People will expect it again tomorrow at the matinee."

The four of them were the first to arrive at the Buckingham, but most of the cast and crew were right on their heels. All through the party Michael never had an opportunity to spend a moment alone with Toby. His mother,

who had surprised him by coming to the opening, dominated his time with praise and congratulations.

"Michael, darling," Laura said, "the show was spectacular. I always said you had a good sense for what the public wants."

"You have an odd way of showing your confidence,
Mother," Michael said. "The last time we spoke, you said
I would be the laughingstock of New York."

"It was just misplaced motherly concern."

"So you trust my judgment?"

"Of course."

"Then you'll give me your blessing when I tell you Toby
and I are engaged."

Michael studied his mother's face. Laura blanched, her
cheeks lost all their color, but Hugo von Feldman, along
with his wife, grinned.

"Quite a lady, my boy," Hugo said, and shook his hand.
"I know you'll be happy."

"Mother? Don't you have anything to say?"

Before Laura could speak, Toby unwittingly broke into
the private conversation. "Michael, Joel Greenpasture just
arrived. I think he's jealous."

"Be careful. The old coot will offer you twice your salary to woo you away from me."

"Impossible," Toby said, and stood on her tiptoes to kiss
him.

"I just told Mother our good news," Michael said, and
took Toby's hand. "And since I can't seem to find a more
appropriate time, I might as well give you your ring right
now." He had planned to slip the ring on her finger in a
more private setting, but his mother's glowering stare baited
him to make a public presentation.

Toby looked at the diamond enveloped by midnight-blue
velvet and gasped. She'd read about women who received
engagement rings, but none of her friends had ever been so
lucky. Holding her breath, she tilted the gem and watched
how the light made the diamond dance with a blue-white
color. "This is too much," she said, awestruck at the size
and beauty of the ring.

"Try it on," Michael said. He slipped the solitaire onto her finger and then brought her hand to his lips. "We will make such a happy family, the four of us."

Snatching her hand away, Toby turned to Michael's mother to show Laura the ring, but inside she was wilting. Why did he have to ruin what was supposed to be one of the most beautiful moments of her life by reminding her she wasn't just marrying Michael but two other Sedaines?

"Isn't it beautiful?" Toby said, forcing herself to smile at Laura, and held her hand out for inspection.

"Lovely. Michael, did you have Lillian's diamond put in a new setting for Toby? It looks like the same stone."

Michael snapped the lid of the box closed with enough force to crush it. "Suzanne will have her mother's ring when she is old enough to appreciate it. I have it in the safe."

"How silly of me," Laura said. "Lillian's was larger."

Toby looked first at Michael and then at his mother. The two were waging a battle of wills, and she was a pawn in their skirmish. "I think we need to talk, Michael. Privately." She turned to walk away, but Michael put his arm around her shoulder and pulled her close.

"There's nothing to say, Toby. Mother is just so thrilled and surprised by our news that she's been a bit thoughtless. She's delighted. Aren't you, Mother?"

Laura knew when to fight and when to concede. "Why, of course. Toby, there are so many plans to make and so much to do, you and I'll have to get started immediately. First of all, we must find you a proper dressmaker and design your trousseau. I'm certain Michael will want to tour the continent for your honeymoon."

In one breath, Laura Sedaine had humiliated her, planned the wedding, insulted Toby's taste in clothing and dictated their honeymoon. If Toby allowed her to have full rein now, there would be no stopping her. "Chantelle is sewing my gown, my father will conduct the ceremony and we don't know if we'll be able to leave New York long enough for an extended trip."

"But why not?" Laura said, reacting to Toby's final comment.

"Mrs. Sedaine, Michael needs me onstage. I have twelve shows a week. We can't leave."

Even Michael hadn't really comprehended how busy Toby would be. How were they going to arrange any time alone much less build a life together?

"You can't possibly continue with your little hobby once you're my son's wife," Laura stated. "It wouldn't be proper."

"Mother," Michael said, halting her brewing tirade, "Toby and I haven't discussed our future yet."

"No, we haven't," Toby agreed. "But Michael has always supported my career. I'm certain he won't object to his wife performing in his theater."

They mingled with the other guests until Michael drew Toby aside and whispered in her ear, "Are you ready to leave?"

"Not yet."

"But I thought we'd go back to the theater and have our own private party," he said, opening his jacket and showing her the bottle of champagne tucked inside.

Toby hesitated, the luxury of spending the evening with him was tantalizing, but she was frightened of the consequences. The temptation of spending uninterrupted hours alone with Michael would have a definite effect. Neither one of them would be able to resist the delight they found in each other's arms. And, if she welcomed his lovemaking, there was the possibility of a pregnancy. Toby didn't dare tempt fate and turn her nightmare into reality.

"Oh, Michael, I'm exhausted."

He knew Toby was lying, for she was wound up as tight as a top and wouldn't run down till dawn. "Don't let Mother spoil our engagement party. She's never adjusted to changes well. Once she gets to know you, she'll treat you like a daughter."

"Spare me the good fortune," Toby said. "Michael, why didn't you tell your mother we weren't getting married for a long time? You made it seem as if we were planning a wedding for next week instead of next year."

"Next year? Who said anything about next year?"

"I just assumed you would want to wait until The Pantheon was making money and—"

"I don't give a damn about money."

Looking across the room, Michael saw that Rosie had finally arrived with Ansel. Her head was thrown back as she laughed at a joke he couldn't hear. Or was he the joke? He hated Rosie for planting a seed of doubt about Toby but couldn't help wondering if she had been telling the truth.

Chapter Twelve

"Father," Suzanne asked, "do you think Toby will be happy to see us?"

"Disappointed," Paul said.

"Toby enjoys both of you," Michael said, scowling at Paul. "She asks about you every day."

Michael had hoped this day off would give him some time alone with Toby, but his mother had effectively quashed his plans. In front of the children, Laura had challenged Michael about spending too many evenings away from his family, leaving him no option but to include Paul and Suzanne on the outing to the beach.

But there was another way, a much brighter way, to evaluate his mother's suggestion. Toby rallied to other people's needs and Paul and Suzanne definitely needed her. What better method to prove that than by bringing the children with him? Didn't familiarity lead to appreciation? Appreciation to tenderness? And tenderness was one of the main ingredients in a mother's love.

"If we are very quiet, we can surprise her," Michael said as he helped Suzanne from the carriage. "Toby!" Michael called out, ushering the children into the entry. "Are you ready?"

The sound of Michael's voice made her feel like a caged bird that had been set free, and Toby bounced down the stairs, ready to greet him with a kiss. She was even humming a little ditty as she twirled her parasol, intentionally making a grand entrance.

"Boo!" Suzanne said, and popped out from behind her father. "We're your surprise."

Toby had purposely been avoiding Paul and Suzanne, unable to be around the children and maintain an uncaring detachment. But Suzanne's freckled cheeks and turned-up nose were too angelic to resist and Toby hugged the little girl.

"What a wonderful idea to invite Paul and Suzanne on the picnic," Toby said. After she released Suzanne, she gently squeezed Paul's shoulder. "I have missed both of you."

"I told you she wouldn't be angry when she saw us," Suzanne said accusingly to her older brother. "Toby doesn't hate you."

Before Toby could step between them, Paul pinched his sister's arm just as Mo would have punished Cleo for such an outburst.

"Ouch," Suzanne wailed, and buried her face in Toby's skirts, avoiding any further revenge.

"Younger sisters can be very humiliating, can't they," Toby said to Paul as she stroked Suzanne's head. "I have a sister who loves to embarrass me, but I really don't think you should hurt Suzanne."

"She's stupid," Paul mumbled.

"She's not stupid," Toby said, "but she's wrong. I don't hate you at all. I think you're a very nice young man, except when you pinch your sister." She winked at the boy to add a merry note to her censure.

"The Sedaines are here," Michael finally said. He had never really appreciated what a fine actress Toby was until now. He spotted the flicker of disappointment that had made her shoulders droop for just an instant when she saw the children, and he was pleased to know that she had been looking forward to spending the day alone with him. But he was proud of the way she had rallied to the moment and hid her emotions.

"Paul, would you please get the basket out of the kitchen and, Suzanne, you can bring the blanket. They are both on the table," Toby said.

Hungry for her, Michael crushed Toby to his chest the moment they were alone. Days without tasting her special sweetness, without feeling her softness molded tightly against him, left him winded. "I have missed you so much. How can I work with you all day and most of the night and feel like I never get to see you?" he said breathlessly, setting her back on her feet.

"To quote one of our good friends, Mr. MacRae, 'There are no secrets backstage.' I think we need to keep our work lives and our private lives separate."

"I was worried you were changing your mind again," Michael said, twisting Toby's engagement ring around her finger.

"You will enjoy my apology for treating you like a boss all week," Toby said, nipping at his earlobe and then stealing across his cheeks to his lips. She could hear Paul and Suzanne arguing about which one was going to carry the basket and ended the kiss before Michael had the opportunity to reciprocate.

"My turn," Michael said, and pulled her back.

"Your turn will be later tonight when we are alone."

Shocked, Michael saw Toby's blue eyes twinkling mischievously. "What do you have in mind, little one?" he asked softly.

"Proper ladies," Toby said, "don't speak of such things in broad daylight." Unexpectedly she wrapped her arms around his neck, drew him closer and ran her tongue in the curve of his ear before whispering, "They just do them."

Toby's high spirits, her playfulness, her titillating words erased all the suspicions Rosie had sown. At this moment, Michael was more enchanted with Toby than with any woman he had ever known, even Lillian. The comparison was unbidden and unwelcome, but it replaced his certainty with caution, dousing his carefree mood with clearheaded logic.

"Let's stop dillydallying," Toby said, goading him to move. "We're wasting the day standing here making eyes at each other. Paul and Suzanne, are you ready?"

"If we don't hurry, we'll miss out on the last nice day before winter," Michael called.

He smiled as Suzanne's thin little legs hurried to keep pace with Paul's sturdy, longer ones, the picnic basket carried between the two of them with the blanket balanced on top.

"Michael," Paul said, "I told you Toby didn't want us along today. This basket has two of everything. Or did you just plan to eat in front of us without offering us any lunch?"

"Did you ever think that I wanted to leave enough room so that we could buy a few treats? Or don't you like goodies?" Toby answered.

No wonder he could never win an argument or best Toby when they were bickering, Michael thought to himself and shook his head in amazement. That woman's tongue was like quicksilver, fast and unpredictable.

Toby chaperoned Suzanne and let Michael handle Paul, for she was itching to tweak Paul's ears for being so imperious. If Mo had ever behaved like Paul did, she would have had him picking rocks from the garden patch until he had enough stones to build a wall.

Halting abruptly at a delicatessen, Toby said, "Are there any special requests? Suzanne, what is your favorite?"

"Pickles. Great big pickles."

"Paul?"

She gritted her teeth to keep the smile on her face as Paul made an elaborate display of considering his choices. She watched him scratch his head, chew on his fingertip, walk up to the window and peer inside before he turned to her and said, "Do you suppose they would have any fresh peaches or strawberries?"

"Of course not," Michael said.

Toby didn't say a word but marched inside and ordered enough meats and cheeses to feed ten people. She was determined Paul wouldn't return home to tell his grandmother she hadn't fed him. Two doors down, she gained Paul's cooperation as she let both the children select a dozen cookies and four tarts. At the foot of the staircase to the el, a newsstand caught her eye and she bought her favorite periodical. "This always has the most marvelous stories," she said, thumbing the pages of the magazine.

"While we sit on the beach and the children go wading, you can lay your head in my lap and I'll read aloud."

Toby refused to bend to Paul's attempt to spoil the day and her spontaneity was contagious. A flower girl was selling nosegays on the platform and Michael stopped to look at them. "Do you have any lilacs?" he asked the waif, wanting to buy the kind of flowers he always associated with Toby.

The child stared at him as if he were daft. "No, sir. Lilacs only bloom in May. You'll have to wait till next spring. I've some wild daisies, though."

"Perfect for a wild woman," he said under his breath. He chose one large bouquet and a small nosegay, presenting the daisies to Toby and the violets to Suzanne. "For the two special women in my life."

"Oh, they're lovely, but they'll wilt in this heat," Toby said.

"Stop being so practical," Michael said.

"I've never had flowers of my own before," Suzanne said, catching Toby's attention.

Toby looked down at the little girl and was struck by the look of rapture on the child's face. Her round, pink cheeks were bright and rosy, and a wide smile split her face as she buried her nose in the violets. If Toby was a painter, she would capture Suzanne on canvas and immortalize her joy forever.

"Oh, thank you, Michael," Suzanne said.

A hurt look crossed Michael's face, and Toby knew he didn't like his children calling him by his Christian name but merely tolerated it.

"Suzanne, very few little girls call their fathers by their names. Why don't you just call him *Papa?* That's what I've always called my father," Toby said.

"Thank you, Papa," Suzanne said hesitantly before she slipped her tiny hand into Michael's.

The ingredients for a perfect day were all present: beautiful weather, the day free of work, good company and delicious food, but Toby knew Paul was just about to let loose with one of his famous comments that could ruin the mood. Two jumps ahead of his devious brain, she averted his comment by saying, "The ferry is just about to leave. Last one there washes the dishes."

Michael snatched Suzanne into one arm and the picnic basket in the other while Toby clutched Paul's hand as they raced from the train through the ticket lines at the South Ferry Terminal. Other passengers laughed at them as they leaped aboard.

Toby ribbed Michael as she gracefully hiked up her skirts and jumped the small span between the dock and the ferry. "Come on, it's easy. It's no different than jumping a brook."

Suzanne squirmed out of her father's arms and easily landed next to Toby to prove Toby's point.

"We're city boys and haven't had much practice jumping streams," Michael said, but took one stride and lit next to her, juggling the basket. "Laugh all you want. You're the one who loaded me like a packhorse. Come on, Paul. You can do it."

Paul jumped across the gap and rammed into Suzanne, knocking her to the ground. "Very easy," he said, grinning at Toby.

"Paul, you didn't need to trample her," Toby said, and brushed the dirt off Suzanne's dress. "That was needless."

"But it was easy. Just like you said, Miss Wells."

Toby closed her eyes and counted to twenty. When she opened them, Paul was staring over the side of the boat and she decided not to make an issue of it.

Suzanne joined her brother and Toby rushed to the rail, nervous that Paul just might shove his sister into the churning foam. Protectively Toby wrapped her arms around Suzanne.

"He didn't really mean it," Michael said when Paul walked over and sat down on one of the benches.

Very soon Toby would have to insist that Michael discipline his son for his cruel behavior, but today was not the proper time to reprimand Michael for the way he allowed Paul to behave. She was determined not to let an eight-year-old spoil their adventure.

"Let's eat as soon as we get to the beach. I'm hungry," she said.

Kissing Toby on the cheek, Michael said, "Don't lose that appetite."

"These are just the hors d'oeuvres," she said with a giggle, poking at the corner of a sack sticking out of the basket. Tickling Michael in the ribs, she whispered seductively in his ear, "You're the entrée."

"Sedaine *sans vinaigrette?*"

"Hope that means Michael without dressing."

"Your French is improving."

The afternoon was perfect, the sun warm and no breeze to cool the air. Paul called a truce to his outrageous behavior, and Suzanne rallied to the occasion by agreeing to help him build a sand castle after lunch. Watching them pat the moist sand into turrets and dig a deep moat around the base of their crude building, Toby realized she had forgotten what fun children added to an outing.

Later Michael and Suzanne fell asleep while Toby read to them, and she closed the magazine. She watched Paul playing by himself, happy to wage his imaginary battle around the castle, lobbing rocks at the towers and accompanying his mock war with appropriate noises. Gently she shifted Michael's head to her shawl and joined Paul.

"Who is winning?" she said to Paul, bending down next to him.

"Nobody."

Toby watched Paul take a small driftwood stick and poke at the sand castle. Every time she tried to talk to Paul, her attempt was rejected with an angry rebuff, and she wondered why Paul disliked her so intensely. For Michael's sake, she was obligated to make peace with Paul and tried a different approach.

"My brother Mo has a sack full of marbles. He's quite proud of two of his special shooters."

"Oh."

"You enjoy playing war, but what else do you like to do, Paul?"

"Nothing."

"What about baseball? Don't you like to join your friends at the park and play a game or two? I'll bet you would be a wonderful first-baseman," she said, hoping flattery would soften Paul's acrimony.

"I don't like team games. You have to depend on other people," Paul said. "Someone always misses the ball or strikes out."

"It doesn't have to always be a competition," Toby said. "Just play the game for fun."

"Why?"

She floundered for an answer. "Because it makes you feel good to be outside on a day like this and spend time with your friends."

"I don't have any friends," Paul said.

"Well, what about reading? Do you like any special authors?"

"I do my assigned reading every night. Did Michael say I don't?"

Not willing to admit defeat, Toby went back to discussing Paul's one passion. "Your father says you have an entire army of toy soldiers. He says you have one of the finest collections in New York. Would you show them to me sometime?"

"They are not toys. They are miniatures, exact replicas. And why would you like to see them? It's not as if you were interested. Please, Miss Wells, you really don't have to pretend you like me. Suzanne believes you care for her, she's a baby, but I know you only want Michael to marry you."

Toby grabbed Paul's arm and pulled him around so he was facing her. "I don't just tolerate you. Suzanne is a sweet, loving little girl and you are a nice young man underneath that ornery mouth of yours."

She watched Paul stand up and calmly brush the sand off his clothes.

"Isn't it almost time to wake Suzanne and Michael?" Paul said before he turned and walked off down the beach.

"Don't you . . ." Toby quit speaking, knowing it was a waste of breath. Over the years she had looked after many children, friends of her brothers and sisters, students in Sunday school, but she'd never come across one who was as difficult to reach as Paul. Although she didn't understand him, she knew his fascination with soldiers was odd. But she wasn't Paul's parent, and Michael was the one who should have been guiding Paul, not her.

Thoughts of Michael made her eyes track to the beach umbrella where he and Suzanne were still napping. They made a contented picture, but it was getting late and she couldn't let the two sleepyheads doze for any longer. Tiptoeing across the blanket, she dusted Michael's nose with a daisy to wake him.

"Wake up, Rip van Winkle," she cooed. "Nap time is over."

He rubbed his eyes and saw that Suzanne was still asleep and Paul nowhere in sight. Free to retaliate, Michael wrestled with Toby until he succeeded in pinning her beneath him. She looked like an angel with her hair loose and spread out in a halo. "When will you marry me?" he whispered.

Pouting prettily, Toby hesitated, "I won't answer unless you let me up."

"When will you marry me? Give me a date."

"Guess," she taunted.

Straddling her little waist and hovering over her, he forced her to go through the ritual of watching him pluck daisy petals and reciting, "November, December, January," until the verdict ended on "October!"

"You cheated," Toby said. "It's impossible."

"Then set a date," Michael said, bending down and kissing her neck, her cheeks and her mouth. Devouring Toby was a temptation, but he let her free.

"You're wicked, Michael." Smiling, she stood up and straightened her skirt.

"Don't be mean to Toby, Mi—Papa," Suzanne said, sitting up and rubbing her sleepy eyes. "Boys aren't supposed to fight with girls."

"That's right, Michael. Listen to your daughter."

Michael grabbed one of Suzanne's bare toes and wiggled it back and forth. "Are you always going to protect Toby? Do all ladies stick together?"

"We're a team, aren't we, ladybug?" Toby said to the giggling little girl.

"Toby and me," Suzanne mimicked, basking in the attention.

Michael left the two ladies alone and joined Paul at the water's edge. "Find anything interesting, son?"

"Not much. Just a couple of rocks."

"May I see?"

Paul handed his father the small stones and asked, "Do you really like Toby?"

"Yes, I do."

"Well, I don't. She's common."

Michael knew the words coming from Paul's mouth were his mother's and cursed Laura for poisoning Paul's young mind. "You hardly know her. She's very nice and I expect you to be polite. Do you understand me?"

"Yes, sir."

"I love you, Paul," Michael said, suddenly realizing it had been years since he'd told his son how he felt. He leaned down and gripped the boy's shoulders and faced him squarely. "Just because I like Toby doesn't mean I don't love you. I know I have been busy lately and haven't spent as much time with you and your sister as I should, but that isn't Toby's fault. It's my work."

"Other fathers come home after work."

"And so will I, I promise. A lot of things are going to change," Michael said, and looked up to where Toby was holding Suzanne in her lap, brushing Suzanne's curls. "Very soon."

The four of them, hand in hand, waded in the shallow surf until the stars glittered in the sky like a diamond canopy. On the ferry ride back to the city, Toby bundled the two sleepy youngsters up in the blanket on one of the benches and begged Michael to follow her out on deck.

"I've missed seeing a beautiful night sky. In Missouri I used to spend hours lying on my back and studying the heavens." Toby sighed. "New York's lights make it difficult to find Orion or Virgo. I'd wager the city is full of children who have no idea what a constellation is."

Michael stood behind her, wrapped his arms around her waist and pulled her to his chest, encouraging her to rest her head against him. "You don't miss what you've never seen," he said. "I couldn't appreciate what you're saying if I hadn't traveled through the Midwest." What Michael wondered, but didn't ask, was what his life would be like if he hadn't stopped in Saint Louis.

"What's that cluster over there called?" he asked.

She searched to where he was pointing. "I don't know."

"Then I'm claiming it for us."

"What should we name our constellation? Something Greek or Latin?"

He pondered for a moment and then answered, "No. Don't you see the shape? It looks like a wedding party. There." He pointed again. "See all the attendants? And the groom? He's a bit dull compared to his bride. She's the brightest star so we'll name it after her, 'The Bride.' I never dreamed I would be lucky enough to find anyone like you."

She turned and looked at his strong, handsome face and wanted to cry. Even when he was tender, romantic, Michael could not trust her enough to tell her he loved her, but she knew she had no right criticizing Michael's shortcomings. She had agreed to marry him under false pretenses, and she wondered if their entire relationship was just a fantasy. Would she wake up one day to find it had all disappeared in a wisp of smoke? Was the ring on her finger just a way to avoid the pain of facing the truth? Michael wanted her, he needed her but didn't love her, and she couldn't ever be the wife he wanted. In the end she would disappoint him even more than Lillian had. At least Lillian had been woman enough to give him children.

As September closed, Toby found that the unlimited supply of energy she once had was diminishing. Two shows a day, six days a week was draining her physically and emotionally. The time in Saint Louis when she had cleaned house, taken care of the family, cooked and sewn, and worked a full day for Michael had been a breeze compared to her present schedule.

It wasn't only the hectic pace of the shows that was eroding Toby's stamina—it was her guilt. Every time she started to tell Michael that she didn't know how long it would be before she was ready to set the wedding date, she found a sensible excuse to delay. Her secret, the longer she kept it, grew into a hideous monster. Questions, agonizing ones, nagged her, and she found it hard to sleep nights. How could she love Michael so much and yet not want to marry him?

Alone in her dressing room, Toby sighed audibly. Michael had become more insistent day by day, and she couldn't keep putting him off. Eventually she'd have to tell him she wasn't ready to take the risk of having a family and doubted she ever would be.

Rummaging through her purse, Toby found the most recent letter from Gwen and reread the letter. It was filled with bits of news about the family and tidbits about Papa's parishioners. If she had had the good sense to stay in Saint Louis, she wouldn't be facing this impossible decision. And if, and if, and if...

Toby picked up her shoe and threw it against the wall. Her entire life had been shaped by other people, and she was tired of accommodating everybody but herself. It had started before Mama died, and the saga continued no matter how far Toby ran.

Babies had replaced her dolls when she was still in short skirts. She had been changing diapers and walking the floor with babies when her friends had been complaining about needlework and piano lessons. She had never been able to take the long way home from school when a boy asked to carry her books because she had to hurry, supper needed cooking. Schoolwork always came last, after the dishes were washed, the laundry scrubbed and the parlor dusted. It wasn't fair.

Throwing her other shoe at the wall, Toby began to cry. She was so frightened of repeating Irina's fate of leaving a child motherless, there was nothing she could do. She was totally powerless and clearly remembered what the doctor had said to her just before Mama died. Dr. Harris had said that Mama wasn't strong enough to have the twins and then he had stroked Toby's head, commenting on how Toby was an exact replica of her mother. His warning still rang in her ears.

Exhausted, she leaned her spinning head against the frame of her screen. There was one more fear, one more chilling reality. Either path she followed, she would eventually lose Michael. If she married him and managed to avoid pregnancy by modern means, he would become suspicious and learn the truth. Her deceit would kill their marriage, and he would probably resent her even more than he did Lillian. All along she had deceived him into believing she wanted a family.

But if she conquered her fear and gave birth to a child only to fulfill the doctor's prophecy, Toby would betray her deepest conviction. Every child deserved two parents and the opportunity to enjoy carefree years in the heart of a loving family. Either choice she made, she would betray a person she loved.

Michael quietly stepped into the room, thinking Toby might be catching a few winks before the show. She wasn't asleep but was standing in her sheer silk kimono, leaning against her dressing screen with her back to the door. He was shocked at how thin she was, her shoulder blades protruding through the sheer material.

"Toby?" he called softly. "Are you all right?"

She turned and stared at him as if he were an apparition. "I'm fine."

"You look like a wraith."

"Thank you very much, Mr. Sedaine," she snapped. "If you can't say something nice just go away."

"Why are you doing this to yourself?" He grabbed her by her skinny arms and spun her around so she could see how bedraggled she looked in the mirror. Toby had lost ten pounds—weight she desperately needed.

"In case you haven't noticed," she said, "I've been working hard."

"Too hard. Why have you been driving yourself like this?" He couldn't understand her fanaticism when he'd repeatedly pleaded with her to quit the stage.

"It's what I've always dreamed of," she answered weakly, wondering when she had altered her dream from becoming a composer to being a star of vaudeville.

"Well, it's turned you into a nightmare," Michael said.

"I'm your creation. Opening a theater was your idea."

He had no argument. By providing Toby a stage, by keeping her close to him instead of letting her go to Greenpasture, he had constructed a prison for her. "Quit, Toby. The Pantheon doesn't need you. We'll find another act and, besides, Caleb is expanding the program with more and more ragtime."

"Are you saying I'm dispensable?"

"No, I'm saying you're too valuable. Stop this nonsense and stop delaying our wedding. Let's get married and settle down to a quiet life, have another baby or two," he begged.

Grabbing her prop, a staff for her Little Bo-Peep routine, she whirled on him and began poking him in the chest. "Replace me, is it? Turn me into a brood mare, will you? What if I won't cooperate? Find another woman? Another headliner to dangle from your arm?"

Michael snatched the staff from her and threw it into a corner. "What in the hell has gotten into you?"

"I like being a star. I like the stage and my career, and you want me to give it all up," she cried.

"You're tired. This job is killing you."

Rather than be assuaged by his compassion, Toby held him at bay. "Once you said I could do anything I wanted. Nothing should stop me. Did you mean it?"

"Yes," he answered, remembering the talk they had had with Caleb and Chantelle when Toby first came to New York. He'd meant every word of it, but at the time he'd had no idea the price they'd pay for his encouragement. "I said a woman could have her ambition and a family at the same time. You've chosen only one—ambition."

"What do you call our engagement?"

"A stall. You've avoided setting a date for the wedding and all but climbed into my bed."

She tried to slap him, but he caught her swing in mid-arc.

"The truth stings, doesn't it?" Michael said. "What happened to the sweet minister's daughter who felt sinful for kissing me?"

Toby had never felt ashamed of her love for Michael. She had let him put words in her mouth to avoid her fear—a fear she couldn't overcome or admit. "Oh, Michael," she cried, brushing her tears away, "I will marry you but be patient. I made a commitment to this theater, and I can't change my mind just because I'm tired."

"But the owner has given you permission. The owner wants a wife, not a scrawny singer."

"Please, try to understand that this has nothing to do with you. If I quit, I'll feel like I'm running away and, for the rest of my life, I'll wonder what could have been if I'd stayed."

Michael searched Toby's eyes and couldn't bring himself to force her into choosing between the stage and him. Too many women, faced with similar decisions, ended up bitter with life and their husbands. He had been Lillian's scapegoat and he wouldn't be Toby's. He wanted a loving woman, a wife who was in his bed by her own volition.

Glancing at the clock on her dressing table, Toby said, "I'm on next. Give me a kiss for luck."

After she'd dressed and left to perform her act, he lingered in the small room, toying with her hairbrush, her gloves, and laughed sardonically at the irony of fate. Caleb had been jealous of his relationship with Toby, envious of their engagement, but Caleb had been mistaken. After all the fanfare surrounding the engagement, Michael was impotent against Toby's determination to keep performing and he felt as if he were in limbo.

No, it wasn't limbo, it was hell. His instincts were screaming at him that Toby was hiding something, and the harder he tried to nudge her into revealing her secret the further she backed away from him. He tried not to let Rosie's insinuation bias him, but his suspicions kept growing.

For the first time in weeks he noticed the enormous amount of fresh flowers in her room. They were all from admirers, men who hoped to win Toby's favor by sending her expensive bouquets. Michael had grown accustomed to the attention she received and never once felt threatened by it. But tonight it was different.

Michael crammed every single bloom into the trash, knowing he was being boorish but fed up with sharing her with the world. It was growing wearisome, struggling to steal a private moment together here and there. He was sick of sharing Toby with every man who bought a ticket or sent her roses, tired of being patient. He was through with being understanding, and he was finished with this illicit obsession that could only be satisfied between acts.

It was childish, but venting his rage made him feel better. Slamming the door, Michael finished unleashing the last trace of his temper and went looking for Chantelle. If his own life was a mess, at least he had something to be happy about for his friends. Chantelle and Caleb, thanks to Michael's lawyer, would soon be man and wife. Tonight he was going to tell them the wonderful news.

Pleased that there were some events he could control, Michael searched backstage and found Chantelle. Because she was harried, he spoke quickly and made arrangements to meet at the brownstone after the show. He was cryptic about his reason, but he could tell from the hopeful glimmer in Chantelle's eyes that she had already guessed the truth.

As the four of them entered the house after the show, Toby collapsed onto the sofa and immediately pulled off her shoes. "Aren't you tired, Chantelle?" she asked, intrigued by her friend's vitality.

"No, and I have a hunch you won't be either when Michael tells us why he called this conference."

Toby looked at Chantelle, then at Michael and Caleb, stymied about what exactly was going on. "Michael? What's she talking about?"

"Let's have a glass of sherry first. We have a reason to toast the future," he said, and put his arm around Toby. All evening he had prayed his news would inspire Toby to follow Caleb and Chantelle's lead.

"Toby, you and I are the only ones in the dark. Have any idea what your man has been up to?" Caleb asked.

"Hush," Chantelle said, and smiled at Caleb. "In due time." She poured four glasses of sherry and passed them around. "Michael, may Caleb and I have a weekend away from the theater? Do you think you could spare us?"

"Have you lost your mind, lady? We can't afford to leave," Caleb said.

"What weekend did you want off?" Michael asked, winking at her.

"You set the date," Chantelle said, taking Caleb's hand in hers. "We'll accommodate your schedule."

"Would you two stop playing cat and mouse with us?" Toby said, her curiosity raging.

"I think the middle of November would be a good time," Michael said, purposely ignoring Toby's frustration.

"You're both crazy," Caleb objected.

"Crazy to want to get married?" Chantelle answered, looking into Caleb's warm brown eyes. "Crazy to love you so much that I can't wait any longer?"

Caleb couldn't speak. He'd anticipated this moment for too many years and had spent too many sleepless nights trying to devise a scheme to win Chantelle's freedom to believe their chance at happiness had finally arrived.

"Will you marry me, Caleb MacRae?" Chantelle said softly.

Toby felt tears pool in her eyes as she watched Caleb pull Chantelle into his arms. She and Michael quietly left the room and, as they tiptoed out, Toby glanced at Michael, searching for confirmation. His eyes gave her a silent answer. Yes, Chantelle will be free by November.

"You're the dearest man," Toby said the minute they were alone in the kitchen. She bounded into his arms and hugged him. "How did you work such a miracle?"

"I just contacted a friend of mine who's a specialist in international law. Dominic Reynard had no motivation to release Chantelle until we found the right pressure. It suited his perverse nature to stand between her and happiness."

"What kind of pressure?"

"Financial, of course. A few importers persuaded the man that his income from exporting mahogany would drastically drop if he continued to hold Chantelle hostage."

"But when did you start working on this?"

"Several weeks ago. Chantelle didn't want Caleb to know for fear I wouldn't have any luck."

They heard the front door close, and Toby peeked out of the kitchen to see if it was Rosie. The parlor was empty and she looked at Michael and smiled. "I just lost a roommate."

"Shall we start looking for a house of our own?"

Toby cringed. Michael never let an opportunity to nag her slip by. How much longer could she hold him off? Pleased as she was for Chantelle and Caleb, it starkly clarified the impasse between herself and Michael. She resented the fact that not Michael's power, his influence or his money could erase her apprehension.

"I don't think it's quite the right time," she said, grasping for a way out of her predicament. "And you were right about my quitting. The Pantheon doesn't need me any longer and the audience is growing tired of my act."

Michael picked her up by the waist and twirled around in circles. "Fantastic! Can we get started planning our wedding?"

"Put me down, Michael," Toby said, pounding him on the shoulders. "You didn't let me finish."

He heard the gravity in her tone and dropped her to her feet. "Finish what?"

"I thought it would be good for you and Joel Greenpasture to exchange acts. I could go on the road with his company and you would have a fresh headliner."

If Toby had shot him in the stomach with a pistol, Michael couldn't have been any more stunned or hurt. "Say that again?" he demanded, needing to be sure of her intention.

"I want to go on the road with Joel Greenpasture," she articulated slowly and carefully.

"How long have you planned this?" he accused. "Have you already signed a contract with him?" Michael was amazed at his control. He was actually interrogating Toby when he wanted to throttle her.

"I've been giving it a great deal of thought lately," she lied. "I hoped you would handle the contract for me."

Michael stared at her. She was asking him to release her, send her out of his life and be gracious enough to negotiate her departure. "Damn you, Toby, what about us? When will you wedge a wedding into your schedule?" he shouted, already knowing her answer.

"Later, Michael. After I come back to New York, we can talk about it."

Rosie had been right, Michael swore. Toby never had any intention of settling down with him. She had used him to suit her own needs, just as Rosie had predicated. "There isn't going to be any marriage, is there?"

There was too much truth in his question. Feeling trapped, Toby coyly snuggled up to him and tried to woo him with all the feminine wiles she could muster. "We have our entire lives ahead of us. Why rush?"

Angry with her artificial, manipulative affection, Michael firmly, almost cruelly, grasped her blond curls and forced Toby to look him in the eyes. Barely able to control his fury, he said, "Such cheap antics belong on the stage. Whatever happened to the real woman I once met in Missouri?"

Toby slowly wrapped her arms around his waist, but Michael wanted no part of it. "Do you think a few kisses will pacify me? Keep me tame and in line? It'll take more than a few, lady."

Wildly he consumed her mouth, forcing his tongue between her lips. Without a word, Michael pushed Toby down onto the table and began tearing at the buttons on her gown. "You have been playing a game with me. Teasing me. Now it's time to pay the penalty, my dear."

"Michael!" Toby yelled. "What are you doing? Stop it!"

"Don't you want me? Isn't that what this whole farce is about? An engagement to salve your conscience."

"You're scaring me. What's wrong with you? Don't you know how much I love you?" Toby whispered.

Appalled at his behavior, disgusted with the state of their relationship, Michael's sanity returned. "Love? You're just like every other woman. You don't even know what the word means. At least, I don't claim to feel an emotion which doesn't exist. You want me to make love to you, not be in love with you and that is no more than servicing each other's needs. At least I want to legalize our lust by exchanging vows first.''

Put in those base terms, Toby was shamed into silence. Had it only been May, a few months ago, when she had been a naive girl from Saint Louis? Was this the life she'd dreamed of? All she'd managed to do was hurt and deceive the man she loved—and lose her own dignity in the process.

"I never meant to hurt you, Michael. Whether you believe me or not, I do love you."

"If you love me, marry me tomorrow."

"I can't."

Glaring at her for betraying everything between them, Michael said, "You may be free of me, but you're not free of our business contract. I own you, lock, stock and barrel, Miss Wells. You'll work on my stage or you'll never work again. I will guarantee that no theater owner or music publisher touches your work if you walk out."

"You'd do that?"

"Just like you used me, I'll use you. You have a matinee tomorrow. Get to bed and get some sleep. You look terrible and I don't want my customers being disappointed by a scrawny, lifeless mannequin."

"Don't worry, mister," she mocked him, repressing the urge to curtsy. "You've always had your pound of flesh and I won't disappoint you." Toby took off her ring and stretched her hand out to him. "Here. Take it."

"You keep it," he said cruelly. "Consider it payment for services rendered."

Chapter Thirteen

"**G**o straight to hell!" Toby cursed, slapping his ring down on the chopping block. Her eye caught a small ceramic crock filled with kitchen utensils and she grabbed a meat cleaver.

"This is what I think of you and your gift," she said, chopping at the ring as hard as she could. "Lilacs will bloom in December before I'll ever marry you."

"Lilacs, roses, weigela, or dandelions, who cares?" he shouted.

"I thought you did," Toby whispered, her anger quickly turning to horror at the undercurrent in Michael's voice.

"I never say things I don't mean, but if you're still interested we should retire to your bed. Let you earn your diamond, pay for it in full." Michael was beyond caring how deeply he hurt Toby. His battered pride had taken control of his temper, and he latched onto the first insult to come to his mind.

His declaration was total and Toby attacked the symbol of their love with renewed vengeance. The cleaver bounced off the diamond, not harming the stone, only denting the honed metal edge of the knife. Angry, she bashed it again several times and eventually the gold setting bent, but the diamond remained intact.

Michael crossed his arms, watched Toby's impotent fury and finally goaded her. "You're being silly, Toby. You might cut your finger off, but you can't hurt me by destroying something I've given you. You've already chopped my faith in you into a thousand pieces."

She brandished her weapon. "Maybe not, Michael, but it gives me satisfaction to destroy this symbol of the sham we shared."

Toby's blue eyes sparked cold fire and she started forward. Michael stepped aside, afraid she was going to attack him, but that wasn't her intention. She marched past him and directly into the parlor.

"You can take this piano," she wailed, tears running down her cheeks, "back where you bought it in pieces. I don't want anything in this house to remind me of you." Toby lifted the cleaver to begin hacking at the piano.

"Don't!" Michael hollered, wrapping his arms around Toby from behind and pinning her forearms to her chest. "Don't."

"Let me go," she ordered, but Michael held her tighter, even lifting her off the floor so her feet dangled helplessly in the air. "Put me down right this minute or I'll..."

"Or you'll what?"

"Or I'll break your legs." Toby kicked back with her heels, pummeling his shins unmercifully.

"Ouch!" he bellowed. "If I weren't a gentleman, I'd drop you and paddle your fanny with the flat side of that cleaver."

Bucking in his arms, fighting to free herself, Toby yelled back. "Gentleman? Hah! What gentleman randomly leaps from one woman to the next? You're just angry because I wasn't as cooperative as Emily Lucas about jumping into your bed."

"Toby? Michael?" Rosie interrupted the tirade. Ansel was next to her, and they stood paralyzed in the arched doorway of the room. "Ansel, stop him. Michael's attacking my sister." She rushed to Toby and started bashing Michael on the head with her handbag. "Quit hurting her."

"Enough, Rosie," Ansel said, and pulled her off Michael. "Looks to me like it's Michael who's in danger. She's the one with the cleaver."

Michael released Toby and wrenched the cleaver out of her hand. "Leave us alone," he bellowed at Rosie and Ansel.

"Toby?" Rosie asked, looking to her sister for direction.

"Don't take a step," Toby said, brushing back her hair, which had fallen down during the struggle with Michael. "Mr. Sedaine is just on his way out and we have nothing else to discuss."

"That's right," Michael said. "Do what you've done your whole life, use your family as a shield."

"What do you mean by that?"

"Poor little Toby," he said sarcastically, "the martyr. Whine about how hard it was to raise your brothers and sisters, how you couldn't wait to start your own life, but the minute you have to face the world like an adult, you surround yourself with family."

"At least I can depend on their love," Toby countered, hugging Rosie to prove her point.

"Good, because it's liable to be the only kind of love you'll ever receive in your miserable, barren life."

Ansel laughed nervously. "Calm down," he coaxed. "You two will never make it to the altar at this rate."

"We should never have made it this far," Michael said, trembling with anger. "The biggest mistake I ever made in my life was falling for her sweet-little-girl-from-Saint-Louis act." Accenting his feelings, he buried the cleaver in the door frame and stormed out of the house.

Ansel, Rosie and Toby stared at the quivering cleaver. Reaching out and stopping it, Ansel said, "I've never seen Michael this angry." He turned and studied Toby as if she were a oddity. "Whatever you've done to him, Toby, it was thorough. Even Lillian's death was less of a shock. I'm going after him."

Numb, Toby sat down on the piano bench and encircled her waist, rocking back and forth in silent misery. Her stomach was knotted in pain, but it hurt less than her heart. Losing Michael, even though she had sent him away, was more devastating than she could have ever imagined. How could they have said such ugly things to each other when just last night they had whispered tender endearments?

"Guess the engagement is over," Rosie said matter-of-factly.

"Thank you, Rosamond, I didn't notice."

"Cheer up, sis," Rosie said, waving away Toby's depression with a flick of her wrist. "Now you can start painting the town red with some of those anxious beaus hanging around the stagedoor. Up till now, I've had them all to myself but I'll share."

Toby sighed and shook her head. "Rosie, my dear, I do love you, I have to. You're my sister. But I don't like you, your clichés or your shallow values."

Insulting Rosie was like trying to drown a duck, and she shrugged in her usual manner.

"You're just testy. By tomorrow you'll be over Michael. He's served his purpose."

Rosie's accusation made Toby jump to her feet. "That's twice you've accused me of using him."

"Maybe it's the truth. I predicted you would break off the engagement, didn't I? I even told Michael you would."

"You what?"

"I warned Michael you would never marry him. No point in letting the poor schmuck get his hopes up."

Marching across the room, Toby grabbed Rosie and shook her like a rag doll. "How dare you interfere and fill him with lies!"

"Saint Toby can't admit she's no better than me, can she?" Rosie scoffed. "Who orchestrated this little tiff tonight? I'd wager every dime I have it wasn't Michael."

Defeated, Toby let go of Rosie. "No, it wasn't."

"Are you fired? If you are I'm sure you can find another stage," Rosie said practically.

Chantelle had walked into the room unnoticed and only heard Rosie's last comment. Her eyes darted to the meat cleaver still wedged in the door casing and then to Rosie and Toby who were nose to nose in the center of the room.

"Fired? Who's been fired? What's this doing here?" she asked, pulling the meat ax free.

"Toby can tell you all about it. I'm tired and I'm going to sleep," Rosie said, and walked upstairs.

"Well?" Chantelle asked like a disapproving parent.

Toby reacted poorly to her accusatory tone. All night long people had been interrogating her and she was exhausted. "I'm not fired and I don't want to talk about it. Good night."

Left standing in the parlor, Chantelle turned down the lamps and walked into the kitchen. She found Toby's mangled ring on the chopping block and picked it up. "Poor *chère*," she whispered, "your demons are still chasing you."

The weather turned cold, but Michael didn't really notice; he'd been chilled for weeks since the night he and Toby had separated. All through October and into November, he had avoided any extended contact with her, hoping the less he saw her, the less he would grieve.

Drawing his fur collar up around his neck to protect himself from the brutal wind howling off the East River, Michael shivered. Trying to deny the emptiness Toby had left was as futile as pretending it wasn't raining, and he could no more change the weather than he could change his feelings for Toby.

Through the drizzle, the terra cotta gargoyles on the facade of The Pantheon came into view and he slowed his pace. A queue of patrons was patiently standing in line, bumping umbrellas as they slowly moved forward to the ticket booth. Not even the wet gray day could dampen the success of the theater. But he was indifferent to the packed houses, the rave reviews or the fat bank account. None of it held any joy without Toby to share in the largess.

Toby. Just silently saying her name was hard enough; seeing her was impossible. More and more Michael had turned the reins of running The Pantheon over to Caleb and Chantelle, allowing them to pass on orders to Toby. Caleb had a knack for handling the performers, Toby was managing the books and, with Chantelle's gift for supervising the backstage, they were giving Greenpasture, their fiercest competitor, peptic ulcers. More important to Michael, the assignment of duties was freeing him to steer clear of Toby.

He wouldn't be here tonight if Chantelle hadn't asked him to come. Slipping in the back door, Michael tried to find her and settle their business before he ran into Toby.

"Hey, Michael," Ansel said, slapping him on the back, "where have you been hiding?"

"The office. Sedaine Music is still my first love," Michael said.

"Odd. I thought Goldilocks over there," Ansel said, gesturing at Toby's dressing room, "held that honor."

"Funny, but I'm in no mood for bantering. Just tell me how she is." He hadn't wanted to ask about Toby and cursed himself but couldn't resist the temptation.

"Go find out for yourself, old man," Ansel said, stressing the word *old* as if Michael were a decrepit relic.

"Never mind. Where can I find Chantelle?" He was irritated by Ansel's constant joking.

Ansel tossed his head toward the office and Michael started in that direction, but Ansel caught him by the sleeve. "Have you seen Toby lately? Puff in her direction and she'd topple over. I don't think she's eating much or sleeping, either."

"So?" Michael sounded more callous than he felt.

"So, she's working too hard."

"It's what she wants."

"Children want to eat all the candy in a sweetshop, but their parents love them too much to allow it."

"What do you do all day, Ansel? Dream up these platitudes? I'm not Toby's parent, so she can eat all the fame and fortune she wants." He didn't wait for Ansel's rebuttal and stalked into the office.

"Hello," Chantelle said, smiling at him as he came through the door. "Don't look so grim. The final papers arrived today." She waved her divorce decree as if it were a banner.

"Congratulations," Michael said, coming over and kissing her on the cheek. "Have you set the date?"

"Friday, if it's all right with you?"

"Impatient, aren't you?" he teased, knowing Caleb and Chantelle had waited years.

"Caleb was ready to get married today."

"Why didn't you?"

Chantelle stood up, stepped into the hallway and sent a stagehand for Caleb. Leaving the door ajar, she leaned against the wall. "We want you and Toby to stand up for us but needed to know first how strongly you'd object."

Caleb joined them and saw Michael frowning. "Looks like you're not too pleased at being my best man."

"Not pleased?" Michael forced himself to grin. "I'm delighted."

"Then you don't mind if Toby's maid of honor?" Chantelle asked.

"Of course not. How does she feel about it?" He detested himself for constantly asking everyone how Toby was, how Toby felt, what Toby was doing.

"She was pleased," Chantelle said.

"Really?" Michael found Chantelle's answer thin if not downright false. "Then she's a better actress than you are a liar."

Smirking, Caleb coughed softly. "Let's just say you wouldn't want Toby writing your epitaph."

It was an apt joke, closer to the truth than Caleb knew. Michael felt dead; he felt as lifeless as the leaves littering the ground in Central Park. The only interest he had was in not letting his gloom ruin Caleb and Chantelle's wedding.

"Tell me when and where I'm supposed to be and I'll be there with bells on my toes," he said, being as jolly as he could.

"Shoes and socks will be fine," Chantelle said.

"Ten o'clock at city hall on Friday," Caleb instructed him. "But that's not all we need from you. Remember your promise to give us a few days off?"

"Certainly."

"Well, this ship needs a captain," Caleb said, indicating the theater, "and you're elected."

It wasn't a request, it was a directive and Michael nodded. The power Michael had abdicated to Caleb had come home to roost. He was now giving Michael orders, insisting Michael take back the reins for a few days—a reasonable demand. Yet it worried him. Having to work closely with Toby made his resolution to force her out of his mind hopeless. Seeing her would be torture, but he was left with no alternative. "Have a wonderful time."

Chantelle and Caleb watched Michael leave and stood silently in the wake of his somber capitulation. Shaking her head, Chantelle reached over and held her man's hand, wanting to feel his warmth after Michael's cold detachment.

"I wish I could help them," she said.

"You can't," Caleb said, pulling her closer. "They have to find their own way out of purgatory."

"And that's exactly where Toby is. I hear her crying every night." Chantelle sighed and hugged Caleb tighter.

When Ansel arrived alone at the courthouse, Toby was angry. Michael had apparently reneged on his promise to Caleb and Chantelle and Rosie. Toby took her sharp annoyance out on Ansel.

"Don't tell us," she said, cocking her pert little hat at Caleb and Chantelle, "that Mr. Sedaine had sudden pressing business and won't be attending."

Ansel looked confused. "He isn't here? He left an hour ago and said he needed to stop at the office for some papers and then he would be right over."

"Papers? He certainly has his priorities straight. He could have waited."

"But he's never late," Chantelle said, defending Michael's tardiness. "Caleb sets his pocket watch by Michael's promptness."

"Oh, dear," Rosie cried melodramatically, "I hope nothing has happened to him." Working in vaudeville had exacerbated Rosie's penchant for affectation.

Toby scowled. "Why the sudden concern, Sarah Bernhardt?"

"You may not care for him, but the rest of us do," Rosie said.

Not care for him? Tears turned the room to a blur, and Toby had to pretend to stare out the window to regain the hard composure she'd donned for the seven weeks. It wasn't easy pretending she didn't worry about Michael, didn't care if he was seeing Emily Lucas again, never wondered how Paul and Suzanne were enjoying their new school term. Days without even catching a glimpse of his face and reassuring herself he was fine left her drained and vulnerable.

Looking down on the busy street, Toby silently admitted how defenseless she felt without Michael in her life. Not until he'd walked away had she realized how much she depended on his encouragement, how much she needed his strength and how much she would miss him.

The rare, precious moments that they carved out of their frantic days tormented her, leaving her cold and frightened. Would there ever be another man who could make her feel the way Michael did?

She had prepared herself to miss the obvious things about him—his touch, his laugh, his kisses. But the little things had sabotaged her self-control. The smell of lemon drops brought tears to her eyes. Seeing a man with his jacket off and his sleeves rolled up drove her crazy, remembering the times she and Michael had worked together at Sedaine Music. Passing children playing stickball in the street literally made Toby catch her breath as she relived the evening she and Suzanne had led the way to victory over the boys.

But lilacs were the worst offender. Rosie had bought some lilac cologne, and Toby couldn't bear to smell the fragrance. It mocked her vow to never marry Michael, and she wondered if Rosie had heard more of their argument that awful night than she would admit and wore it to spite Toby, to drive in the proverbial knife.

Toby decided she was getting nowhere brooding about what could have been and put her cheerful mask back on. Smiling at Chantelle, she said, "You look absolutely stunning." Chantelle hadn't let anyone see her dress until today, insisting it would be special.

"I wanted something that would be both functional and unique," she boasted. "Do you think I've succeeded?"

"Mrs. Vanderbilt would strangle you to own that dress," Toby said, admiring the rich burgundy-colored underskirt, tiered with a shorter skirt made from a rose fabric and trimmed with elaborate braiding.

"Well, Mrs. Vanderbilt may just show up at Cape May," Chantelle said, beaming.

"Toby," Caleb spoke, "thank you for the wonderful gift. Three days at Cape May in a luxurious hotel is going to feel decadent."

"You two deserve it. Your plan to just get a room in the city was nonsense. Come back and tell me what it was like," she asked. "I've heard the town is beautiful and many of the homes look like wedding cakes with lattices dripping like icing."

Ansel chimed in. "I've been there. The boardwalk is fabulous and, if you want, you can search for diamonds on the beach."

"Diamonds? Really, Ansel," Rosie scolded his fantasy.

He didn't bend under her criticism. "You're the most unromantic girl I've ever known. They look like diamonds, so what does it matter if they're only quartz?"

Toby smiled even though she would just as soon have any discussion about diamonds dropped. Pushing the memory of her mangled ring out of mind, Toby concentrated on Ansel's new pluck. He was taking less and less of Rosie's abuse.

A clerk notified Caleb that the judge was ready for them, but there was still no sign of Michael.

"Should we go on without him?" Rosie suggested.

Caleb asked the clerk, "May we have a few more minutes?"

"Only five. The judge is a busy man."

Michael's absence was disturbing. Toby fluctuated between being relieved he wasn't present and terrified something dreadful had happened.

Ansel decided to telephone Laura and then Michael's office to check on him. As he was about to leave, a disheveled and battered Michael came through the big double doors.

"Sorry," Michael grumbled, dabbing at a scrape on his forehead with a handkerchief. When he bent his arm, a sizable rent was apparent in the elbow of his jacket.

"You made it," Toby said with relief but frightened by his deplorable condition.

"Disappointed? Prefer I was killed in that damn carriage instead of just being inconvenienced?"

All his concern for his own mishap vanished the moment he caught sight of her, and he couldn't bear to look at her for very long. Ansel hadn't been exaggerating when he'd implied Toby was a shadow of her former vibrant self. As usual, she was beautiful, but her dress hung on her thin body and her eyes looked huge in her gaunt face.

"Of course not. What happened?" Toby desperately wanted to brush his ruffled hair away from his bruised forehead. Michael looked as though he'd been mauled by a wild animal and, as meticulous as he was, she knew he was embarrassed.

"I had to fetch these from the office for you," he explained, ignoring Toby and handing a sheaf of papers to Caleb. "They're a wedding gift."

Caleb didn't look at them. He was more concerned with Michael's welfare than with gifts. "What the devil happened?"

"A dray was racing along Broadway and lost its load. Unfortunately, it was my cab that was hit by falling crates." He didn't mention that his driver had been seriously injured or that he'd come close to being crushed.

Ansel swore. "Blasted avenue. If you can stand the noise of the traffic, you take your life in your hands driving on it. I always tell my driver to take another route. Accidents like this are all too common."

"Poor man," Rosie said, drawing Michael to a bench, forcing him to sit while she brushed the dust from his shoulders and lapels. "I was so worried about you. I don't know how any of us could get along without you."

Irritated, Michael shirked away from her fussing. During those few seconds when the hansom cab had rolled over and Michael had believed he was going to be killed, he had called out Toby's name, not Rosie's, not Emily's and not even his children's. He wanted Toby's caresses, and seeing her standing away from him, remaining aloof, increased his bitterness. "Take a look at your gift," Michael said to Caleb, pointing to the papers.

Chantelle leaned over Caleb's shoulder and they both read together. She exhaled sharply, "Michael, you can't be serious?"

"He is," Caleb said quietly, looking into his friend's sad eyes. "If Toby agrees, we'll sign, but it must be a fair deal. You hold the contract and we'll make monthly payments."

Caleb handed the papers to Toby and she thumbed through them. Her face was expressionless when she looked up.

"What is it?" Rosie asked, trying to have a peek.

"I'm turning The Pantheon over to Toby, Caleb and Chantelle. After Caleb and Chantelle return from their honeymoon, I don't want anything more to do with that hoof house."

Toby took his derogatory remark personally and flushed. What he meant was that he didn't want anything more to do with her, and everyone in the room knew it.

"The terms are extraordinarily lenient. What about a down payment?" Chantelle asked.

"That's your wedding gift," Michael told her.

"But I'm not marrying anyone today," Toby said. "I insist on paying for my third if you're going to be foolish and give away a gold mine."

"One woman's gold mine is another man's plague," Michael said. "I don't need your money."

"And I don't want your maudlin generosity."

Caleb took both Toby and Michael by the elbow and marched them over to the corner. "Can you two save your animosity for another time? This is my wedding day and I won't allow anyone to spoil it for Chantelle. Now I want you to smile, quit acting like enemies and put on the best damn performance of your lives."

When the three of them rejoined the rest of the party, Chantelle said, "Michael, your generosity is going to be hard to match when it's time to give you a wedding present."

Michael gave her a half smile, the kind a person uses when he doesn't find anything humorous. "That'll never be a problem you'll have to face," he said, glancing at Toby for emphasis. "Never."

Chapter Fourteen

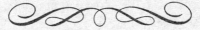

The day had been horrendous, and Toby wondered how she would make it through the evening. After seeing Chantelle and Caleb off at the train station, she considered going home for a couple of hours and sleeping before she was due onstage. But she nixed the idea of taking a nap even though her throat was sore, probably from too many performances. Or maybe it hurt because she was strangling on the tears she refused to let surface. Seeing Michael, being so close yet so far from him, was playing havoc with her determination to forget him.

It was against her nature to crawl under a blanket when she wanted to hide from the world, and Toby forced herself to go to the theater. She had made some changes in her music and needed to consult with the conductor, Saul. There was no problem presenting him with last-minute revisions; Saul was used to it and was always at The Pantheon early.

Saul took her score and studied it. "I've been admiring your work for months," he said. "Do you realize your talent is wasted in vaudeville?"

"The gallery mob would disagree with you," Toby said defensively. "They like what I give them."

"It was a compliment, not an insult. You should be doing serious composing."

Toby wondered if Michael had put Saul up to this. "Did Mr. Sedaine ask you to suggest this? I know he would rather I quit working here."

"I haven't polled him," Saul said sarcastically, "but I suspect he would agree with me. Mr. Sedaine is noted for recognizing superior talent and I'm quite sure he hasn't overlooked yours."

Toby huffed indignantly. "He had an opportunity to buy some of my work once and rejected it."

"Anton Rubinstein rejected Tchaikovsky's First Symphony, too. What if Tchaikovsky quit writing and became a circus performer?"

She threw her shoulders back. "Is that what I am? A circus performer?"

"Yes."

"Then what are you? The ringmaster?"

"A man with limited ability who's content to feed his family."

Humbled by Saul's honest admission and unwilling to justify herself, Toby said, "Please make the changes," and hurried away.

Rosie, juggling an armful of wigs, rushed past Toby. Her responsibilities were doubled with Chantelle's absence, and Toby admired how efficiently Rosie was handling her extra duties. It made Toby tired just watching Rosie bustle about, and she settled in the large chair in her dressing room to mend a small rip in one of her own gowns.

Tucking her legs under her skirts and wrapping a quilt around herself, Toby snuggled up and began to repair the costume. It was comforting to be warm and cozy, and she hoped her aching muscles would relax. Being on edge, tense, from struggling to ignore Michael all morning was the only explanation for the knots in her arms, legs and back.

The wedding ceremony popped into her head and, although it was beautiful, it had left her feeling melancholy. Her joy for her friends was overshadowed by her own misery. What was it that Michael had said about her life? Barren. At this moment she felt as barren as the Gobi Desert. The only consolation she had was that she was still needed by Chantelle and Caleb, Rosie and The Pantheon. Michael could sweep her out of his life like a piece of litter if he wanted to, offer the theater as a donation to a charity, but the others depended on her.

While she was working on the minute stitches, the monotony of the task lulled her to sleep and the needle dropped into her lap. Unaware of the bustle outside her door, Toby dreamed she was on the beach again with Michael. She could hear Paul and Suzanne laughing in the background; it felt as if the sun were pounding down on her and she tossed the quilt aside.

Michael discovered Toby had not responded to her fifteen-minute call and went looking for her. He rapped on her door, but there was no answer and he opened it. Toby was curled into a ball in the chair, looking like a little girl with her hair scattered around her face. Her cheeks were flushed bright pink, and it reminded him of the glow she wore after he kissed her. He had a deep-seated urge to skim his hands across her face and absorb that beautiful warmth. By thunder but he'd been cold lately, and he knew the only thing that could chase the chill away was Toby.

Watching her sleep so peacefully, exhausted and frail, Michael weighed whether or not the show could go on without her. But he didn't dare excuse her with Caleb's acts missing from the program. Caleb's replacement was a newcomer to New York, and there was no predicting the audience's reaction. Besides, this was no longer his theater nor his future to gamble with, and they needed Toby's guaranteed draw.

Tiptoeing across the room, Michael couldn't resist touching her. He wound one of her golden curls around his finger and marveled at how this woman, who looked so angelic, could be such a hellcat. Would he love her as much if she was a passive, sweet-natured woman, or was part of her appeal her feisty temper? Grudgingly Michael admitted he admired her spunk, but his life would be a lot easier if she was just a bit less spirited.

He felt himself softening toward her and applied the brakes to his affection. Toby was hard on him, never giving him an inch, and he would reciprocate equally. "Toby," he said, and shook her by the shoulder, "you're late. Get your fanny out of the chair and out on the boards."

Groggy, Toby looked up and saw Michael bending over her. A smile drew her mouth into a bow. "Michael," she said happily.

The ease with which she could twist his heart made him furious. "Wake up, Miss Wells. Get your costume and makeup on. You've only ten minutes."

Toby jumped out of the chair. Michael had made it obvious he didn't care what she did, who she saw or how she felt, and she wouldn't give him the opportunity or the pleasure of lecturing her.

"I'll be ready in five," she said hoarsely.

"What's wrong with your voice?"

She cleared her throat slightly. It felt like an animal was clawing it to shreds. "Nothing. I'm just not awake yet."

"Here," he said, taking a throat atomizer off her table and brusquely handing it to her, "spray it with this. Can't have you sounding like a frog."

Toby snatched it from him. "Your solicitude is touching."

"Just protecting the hired help."

"Hired help?" she squeaked. "Every day you sound more and more like your mother."

"At least my mother was brave enough to get married." He didn't wait for her retort but left, slamming the door behind him.

Trembling, Toby changed and looked at herself in the mirror. Michael was right—she was a coward. Growing up, she had dreamed of falling in love, believing it would fill the void in her life. No one had ever warned her of the dangers of loving a man so much it would tear her apart. Love had always been idealistic, divorced from the reality and the responsibility of that love. Why couldn't he have been content with their relationship, a nice long engagement? Why did he have to ruin everything by insisting she step right back into the same role she'd been playing for the past ten years?

Michael Sedaine was a self-righteous man who didn't appreciate anything she'd endured. He had been sheltered and pampered his entire life and didn't have the vaguest notion what her life had been like. Toby knew she was being unfair, but she felt so horrible, pity for herself welled up and threatened to claim her.

"Shake a leg, Toby. Michael's on the warpath," Rosie said, popping her head in the room and darting back out to rouse the next act.

Toby moaned and croaked at Rosie's retreating back, "Tell that vulture I'm coming."

Her sister stopped and returned. "Vulture?" She giggled.

"Worm, egg-sucking dog, skunk—"

"How about weasel or swine?" Rosie contributed, enjoying the game.

Toby laughed at their endless vocabulary of insults. "Is our father responsible for our ladylike language?"

"Blame it on Charlie. Or better still, why not blame everything on men?"

"Wonderful idea," Toby said, and picked up her props.

The next day was a blur and Toby felt as if she were staggering in a fog. She stayed in bed until it was time to leave for work, hoping the respite would cure whatever was ailing her. It didn't. She was unable to control the sudden bouts of shivering and bone-weary fatigue.

How she arrived at The Pantheon was vague. As she passed the crew, their faces were hard to separate, blending into a bewildering sea of strangers.

"Miss Wells," someone called.

Whoever it was might as well have been miles away. Toby couldn't concentrate on one word, much less an entire sentence.

"Toby?" Rosie said, rushing to her side and supporting her by the waist. "You're sick. Why did you let me leave the house this morning without telling me?"

"I'm fine," Toby tried to say, but no sound came out of her mouth. She tried again and still nothing. The effort consumed her last ounce of strength, and Toby sagged to the floor.

"Ansel!" Rosie screamed, and he came running. "Take her to her room and I'll find Michael."

Rosie found him high above the stage on the catwalk, adjusting the curtain pulleys. "Michael," she hollered, cupping her mouth, "Toby's sick and needs you."

He leaned over the railing. "Fix her a cup of tea and she'll rebound," he called down, assuming Rosie was like everyone else in the place finding excuses to throw the two of them together.

"I'm serious, Michael. She collapsed and Ansel had to carry her to her dressing room."

Michael slid down the ladder and ran to Toby. He found her stretched out on her chaise longue with her eyes closed. She looked as pale as snow and her breathing was rapid.

"Call the doctor," he ordered, covering her with his jacket.

Ansel responded to Michael's command while Rosie wrung her hands. "She overslept this morning and I just thought she was tired," Rosie explained.

"Didn't you check on her?" he snapped.

"No. She hasn't exactly let people close to her lately."

He felt guilty. Yesterday he should have recognized she was ill but hadn't. Instead he'd badgered her, and now he was placing the blame on Rosie when she was less at fault than he was.

"Michael," Rosie said, "with Toby sick, there's a huge gap in the show."

Michael didn't want to think about business and sloughed off her concern with a feeble solution. "See if the magician can add a few more tricks to his routine."

"I could do it."

"Do what? Magic tricks?"

"No. Toby's songs. Her costumes will fit, I know the act and you've heard me sing. You know I could do it."

He looked at Rosie suspiciously. Was she taking advantage of Toby's illness? No, Rosie was really trying to help. "Get dressed," he said, "and bring the house down, kid."

The doctor arrived and examined Toby. While he was taking her pulse, she roused and attempted to answer his questions, but her throat was on fire and she still couldn't speak.

"Laryngitis?" Michael asked hopefully, not wanting anything to be seriously wrong.

"Along with anemia, I'd venture, and influenza. This young lady," the doctor said, shaking his head disapprovingly, "has worn herself down to a skeleton. What has she been doing besides working too hard and not eating?"

"Is she going to be all right?" Michael asked while holding her hand.

"If someone gives a damn enough to see she rests and doesn't contract pneumonia."

"I'll take full responsibility and personally see she's taken care of," Michael assured him.

"Good," the doctor said, handing him an envelope. "Take her home and give her a quarter teaspoon of this powder every few hours. Call me if there's any change for the worse and keep her away from older people and children. This influenza is especially hard on them."

Michael took the packet and asked, "What's this?"

"Salicylic compound, a wonderful new remedy for fevers. The Germans call it aspirin."

"Anything else I can do for her?"

"Get her to eat rich food like custards and raw liver for her anemia, if she'll cooperate."

After watching Toby consume any kind of food placed in front of her, Michael thought raw liver might finally be the one item she would refuse. "Any alternatives to liver?"

"Yes. A little sweet red wine might help."

An hour later Michael had Toby at home in her own bedroom. She was semiconscious, as pliable as a rag doll and quite content to let him carry her up the stairs.

"Come on, little one," he coaxed, removing her clothes.

He had no difficulty sliding the skirt down over her hips, unbuttoning her blouse and slipping her arms out, but his fingers fumbled with the hooks on her corset and he couldn't get her free.

"Damn it, Toby," he mumbled. "A summer breeze would blow you away and you still lace yourself up in this armor."

She was beginning to shiver again, and Michael searched the room for a solution. Spotting a pair of small scissors, he laid her down on the bed and snipped her loose.

When he turned her over, he saw a long gold chain dangling around her neck and his mangled ring was cradled between her breasts. Michael lifted the diamond and felt his throat tighten. Even after their terrible row, she had secretly kept him close to her heart. Choking back tears, he scolded himself for forgetting that Toby often said one thing but felt or did another. Wearing his engagement ring was a perfect example of how valiantly she worked at obscuring the truth.

"I'm sorry, Michael, for being a pest," she managed to whisper.

He lifted her up off the coverlet to slide her between the sheets, but she didn't cooperate. Toby rested her head against his chest, sighing contentedly. Michael was struggling to get her nightgown over her head, but she was making it difficult by pressing so near and gripping his waist. He finally gave up and held her, feeling her naked softness.

Kissing the top of her head, he tried to persuade her to release him. "You'll get chilled if you don't let me put this gown on you."

"But I'm so hot. It feels good," she whimpered.

"Shh, I know. Don't try and talk."

He attempted to pull away, but she clung tighter. "I'm not going anywhere," he promised, and she finally allowed him to tuck her in bed, but he never did get her gown on.

Hours later, Rosie and Ansel peeked in the bedroom. "How is she?" Rosie asked.

"Sleeping soundly," Michael said, and yawned. Not wanting to disturb Toby, he motioned them into the hallway. "How did it go tonight?"

Ansel bragged, "Rosie was unbelievable. She didn't bungle one line and the audience loved her. Four curtain calls, Michael. She had *four* curtain calls."

Michael grinned and looked at Rosie. "Ready to aim for five tomorrow?"

Rosie didn't blink. "Or six," she said confidently. "But I can't handle both Toby's and Chantelle's jobs. What are we going to do for the next few days?"

"Survive," Michael said, and shrugged. "Ansel, I might be a little late in the morning, depending on how Toby feels. Tell the cast they'll have to be responsible for their own props and costumes until Chantelle returns."

"Anything else I can do? No need to hurry in. I'll take care of things if you need to stay here."

"Thanks," Michael said, touched by Ansel's consideration. His childish brother-in-law was outgrowing his adolescent self-centeredness and becoming a reliable man at last. "Tomorrow morning have Reginald give you tonight's receipts and make the bank deposit." A few months ago, Michael wouldn't have trusted Ansel with cab fare, let alone a whole night's earnings from the theater.

Grabbing Michael's hand, Ansel shook it vigorously. "Right," he said, lowering his voice a notch to sound properly forceful and quietly walked back down the stairs without saying another word.

Rosie watched him leave and then turned to Michael. "Why is he in such a hurry?" She pouted. "I usually have to ask him to leave."

"You've been replaced," Michael said.

"How?"

"By power. Ansel has just discovered a force that is sweeter than a fickle woman." Michael took a childish joy in sticking the barb to Rosie for a change.

He left her standing on the landing with her mouth open and went back to Toby. Rubbing the screaming muscles in the small of his back, he looked at the chair he'd been sitting in and didn't fancy spending the night there. Longingly he wished he could strip, crawl between the sheets and curve his body around Toby. It was out of the question but so was leaving her alone and going to another room for the night. Compromising, Michael slipped off his shoes and jacket, found a quilt in the cedar chest and stretched out on top of the coverlet.

Around midnight, Toby started thrashing when her fever rose, and he gave her another dose of powder. He wrung out a washcloth in cold water and bathed her feverish forehead, her fiery arms and legs the way he had seen his mother do with Paul and Suzanne, until she relaxed and could sleep peacefully.

The tension and fatigue of the day robbed Michael of his will to resist Toby, and he didn't pull away when she rolled over and draped her arm across his chest. He was grateful her breathing was regular, and he wrapped his arm around her, nestling her waifish body into the crook of his arm. A warm relief flooded over him when she mumbled, "I love you," and he pulled her closer, kissing her damp curls.

The years of battling Lillian's spiteful legacy, his fear that he was incapable of loving a woman, vanished without a trace, and Michael bolted upright. Worried he might have disturbed Toby, he listened carefully before he inched out of bed and went to the window, pulling the curtain aside. Wind-whipped leaves skipped across the sidewalks unfettered by horse's hooves, wagon wheels and pedestrians, but Michael didn't notice the deserted street. All he could think of was his marvelous discovery.

He loved Toby and knew without any doubt that he would love her until his heart quit beating. Silently Michael cursed himself for being such an idiot. The things he had said to Toby about logically selecting a wife, her qualifications being well matched for the job, were asinine.

As soon as she was well, he would confess his idiocy and they would resolve the issue. He had done everything he could think of to convince Toby he was sincere and his reasoning sound, but she had been right to insist on her due. With all she had to give the man she married, she deserved to be loved and was entitled to every ounce of his devotion. No wonder she had kept him at arms' length. He had made a terrible mistake misinterpreting her stalling their marriage as anything more than a demand for her future husband's love.

This was all his fault, and guilt brought him to his knees. Staring at the small mound beneath the covers, Michael said, "I'm sorry, Toby. Sorry I didn't listen to you and couldn't hear what you were saying. I do love you. I was just too stubborn and ignorant to recognize the truth. As soon as you're well, we'll start over again."

When Chantelle and Caleb returned from their honeymoon, an awkward situation developed that Michael hadn't considered. The brownstone was the perfect first home for the newlyweds, but that left Rosie and Toby without a place to live.

"I don't mind staying in a boardinghouse," Rosie said. "But what about Toby? She needs someone to take care of her and we are all busy."

"She can stay in the guest room at Mother's," Michael said, without consulting either Toby or Laura.

Rosie and Caleb accepted Michael's solution with relief, but Chantelle frowned at him.

"Do you think that's a wise decision?" Chantelle said. "Your mother may be too busy for the extra burden."

"The servants won't mind and neither will Mother," Michael stated, oblivious to Chantelle's unstated warning that neither Laura nor Toby would welcome Michael's decision.

But when Michael explained his plan to Toby she was less guarded with her words. "Absolutely not. Your mother hates me and I'm not overly fond of her."

"First, she doesn't hate you," Michael said. "Second, it won't be any bother as the servants will do any necessary work and the most important fact is, what choice do you have? There is no place for you to go where you can receive the proper care."

Toby sank down onto the mound of pillows and pulled the covers over her face, groaning loudly. The doctor had been blunt in his warning that she would have to spend at least another two weeks in bed recovering, but the thought of even one night in Laura Sedaine's house was almost more than she could bear.

"Have you told her yet?" Toby asked, hopeful that Laura would overrule Michael's plan.

"She was delighted," Michael lied.

He had been forced into threatening his mother with moving himself and the children into their own house before she agreed to having Toby stay with them. Suzanne had been overjoyed at the news and had even offered her favorite doll to keep Toby company, but Paul never said a word.

The next afternoon when Michael and Caleb helped Rosie move her belongings, Chantelle packed for Toby. The two women were alone in the house and Chantelle seized the moment.

"I'm going to miss you," Chantelle said as she folded a petticoat and piled it on the foot of the bed.

"We'll see each other every day at the theater," Toby said. "Remember, we have a business to run."

"It's your business, Toby. Caleb and I convinced Michael to put only your name on the papers, and you need to sign them as soon as you feel well enough to see the lawyer."

Toby was astounded. "Why did you do that? It was a wedding gift for you and Caleb."

"It was Michael's way of escaping you, my friend."

"Well," Toby said, sitting up straight and yanking on the quilt, "you're wrong. Michael knew what he was doing when he gave the theater to the three of us."

"Yes, I believe he thought he did. But he was really trying to escape misery and heartache. He was giving away something he loved to someone he loved. He was admitting defeat in the face of an unmovable, stubborn woman. Besides, it wouldn't be right to list Caleb and Chantelle MacRae as the official owners, because New York society would never accept the idea. All of our hard work would be for nothing when the theater went bankrupt."

"Don't do this to me, Chantelle," Toby wailed. "I can't handle it all by myself."

"Toby, do you really think so little of me?"

Toby wiped her eyes and sniffled. "What do you mean?"

"I love my job and so does Caleb. We have everything in the world we ever dreamed about but, even if we hated The Pantheon, we wouldn't desert you. From the first moment we met you and Michael, you opened your arms to us in friendship. You didn't question our backgrounds or our lives. The world has very few people like Toby Wells or Michael Sedaine.''

Toby started to cry again but this time from happiness. "You make it impossible to fight back. That's the nicest compliment anyone has ever paid me."

"You're wrong. The nicest compliment you've ever had was when Michael asked you to be his wife. He's a good man, Toby, and, believe me, there are not that many."

"I'm so confused," Toby said, and started crying again. She was annoyed with herself for feeling so weak and blubbering over every shift in the conversation, but she couldn't seem to get control of her emotions.

"That's because you talk constantly but seldom say what's really on your mind," Chantelle answered, deciding it was time to begin prodding Toby into discussing why she still wore Michael's ring but acted as though he were an irritant.

"What's that supposed to mean?" Vexed, she punched her pillows into a ball and sat back with her arms crossed defiantly in front of her.

"Exactly what I said." Chantelle sat on the bed next to her and tugged on the gold chain around Toby's neck until the ring was exposed. "The Jabberwock made more sense when he spoke than you do."

It hadn't occurred to Toby that anyone knew about the ring and she gulped back her retort. The excuse she had for wearing the ring would sound just like that—an excuse. Chantelle would never believe her if she claimed she was keeping it safe because of its monetary value.

"All that business of going on the road with Greenpasture was just a bluff, wasn't it?" Chantelle said. "You're hiding something from Michael and probably even yourself. You love him as much as he loves you."

"And you're full of pickle juice," Toby said. "Michael is only saying he loves me because he feels guilty. I fainted because I was overly tired, and he panicked."

Chantelle jammed her hands on her hips and said, "Who are you talking to? I know it couldn't be Chantelle MacRae, because you wouldn't insult my intelligence by expecting me to believe what you just said."

"It's the tr—"

"Now Miss Wells," Chantelle said, her voice taking a deep, serious tone, "you clamp those lips together and keep them that way. I don't want to hear you say another word. Listen and think but don't talk, because I'm tempted to give you a good shaking. And, the doctor wouldn't like it if I abused an invalid.

"You've given Michael laughter, love, tears and happiness. Now, you need to have enough faith in this man to believe what he says and to tell him the truth."

Toby tried to speak but Chantelle interrupted her. "No, not a word. I don't want you to utter a peep. Do some serious thinking and when you have solved your mystery, I know you will do the right thing."

Everything Chantelle said was valid, Toby thought. How would she have reacted if Michael had shut her out of his life without an honest explanation? Betrayed, exactly the way he had felt.

Chantelle wiped the tears off Toby's cheeks. "Some people define love only in joyous terms, *chère*. That's a mistake. Love also means taking the good with the bad, and you've had some silly notion that Michael's love was conditional. It isn't. It just took him a bit longer than some to believe he was worthy of your love and that he deserved another chance for happiness. If two people were ever meant to spend their lives together and raise a house full of children, it's the two of you. Michael gave me the gift of freedom from Dominic, but he can't banish your ghosts the way he did mine. Only you can."

Toby watched Chantelle leave the room and closed her eyes, privately begging for the same wisdom Chantelle had and the guidance nothing but her own conscience could provide. She knew if she took the wrong path, she would never, ever forgive herself, just as surely as she knew she would never love another man the way she loved Michael.

The realization of what Michael had done by giving her The Pantheon smacked Toby in the face as surely as if Michael had detailed his plan on a piece of paper. He was presenting her with a dilemma and forcing her to choose. Michael had handed her the opportunity to be one of the most important women in the music industry or she could elect to become his wife. But he would be no part of the theater and if she chose The Pantheon, she would lose him. No matter what she did, Toby would lose, and she doubted she would ever be brave enough to face the consequences of her choice.

Chapter Fifteen

"If you need anything," Laura said, "just ring this bell. One of the staff is bound to hear you."

Toby forced herself to smile. "Thank you, Mrs. Sedaine. I'll try not to bother anyone." Toby made a promise to herself that she would die before she touched the silver bell.

She rummaged under the covers for her journal and propped the notebook on her lap. The entire time she was ill she hadn't made one entry in the diary. So much had happened between herself and Michael that she was anxious to sort out her feelings on paper.

Some minutes later, Toby heard a tiny knock at the door. "Come in, Suzanne. I'm alone."

"How did you know it was me?"

"I recognized your knock. Special people sound very important when they rap on a door."

"Really?"

"Really." Toby smiled and patted the bed. "Come sit down and tell me how your day at school was."

"*Grand-mère* said I couldn't stay very long because you're sick. What's wrong with you?"

After Toby told Suzanne what had happened, the little girl asked, "Do you like Margaret?" Suzanne picked up a porcelain doll dressed in sky-blue velvet and sat her next to Toby.

"She's very nice," Toby said seriously. "She was telling me all her secrets."

Suzanne giggled. "Dolls can't talk."

"Margaret? A doll?" Toby pretended to be shocked. "I thought she was a short friend of yours who was just waiting in my room until you came home."

Toby smiled as she watched Suzanne wrap her arms around her middle and double over in an outburst of laughter.

"Are only girls allowed?" Michael said, walking in through the open door. "What's the joke?"

"Papa, Toby is silly."

"And beautiful," Michael added. "How would you like to have tea in Toby's room today?"

"Does *Grand-mère* know?"

"She went shopping," Michael said, lowering his voice to a conspiratorial whisper. "We just won't tell her."

Toby's heart warmed as she watched the two of them plotting the unspeakable crime of having tea in her bedroom. It was obvious this was a rare occasion, and Suzanne basked in her father's playful mood. They dashed away whispering to each other to set the tray.

While they were gone, Paul solemnly arrived on the pretext of looking for his father. At the first opportunity, he said, "How long will you be staying with us?"

"For just a little while, Paul. Until the doctor says I may get out of bed."

"Are you going to marry Michael?"

Michael's son had a direct approach to life and wasted few words on pleasantries. Ordinarily Toby found this attitude honest in an adult, but she found it irritating in a child. She tried to hide her vexation as she said, "Have you asked your father?"

"Of course not. Michael doesn't confide in his children, but I know that you two were engaged. He told us you were going to be our new mother. Are you still going to marry him? I don't see a ring on your finger."

"I'll make a bargain with you. When I can answer that question with complete certainty, you and Suzanne will be the first two people, besides your father, to know the answer. Is that fair?"

"Not quite as good as a simple no, but do I have a choice?"

Paul's animosity was not surprising, but Toby was determined to conquer it before she resorted to his tactics. "You really miss your mother a lot, don't you? I know I still miss mine."

"Was your mother killed in a train accident, also?"

It was the first time Paul had ever used a civil tone of voice when he spoke to Toby, and she saw the scared little boy hiding behind the obnoxious young man's veneer. Willingly she shared the story of her mother's death and the loneliness she still felt at times.

"But your father loves you very much, Paul."

"I know that. Michael always brings me a present when he returns from a trip."

"Like soldiers for your war games?"

Paul stood up ramrod stiff and glowered at Toby. "They are not games, Miss Wells. They are enactments of actual battles. I research the details and carefully set my soldiers and weapons in proper order."

"Paul, Paul, we're having tea in Toby's room," Suzanne said, bursting into the conversation. "Come help Papa carry the tray."

"Won't we get crumbs on the bed?" Paul said. "I really don't think we should bother Miss Wells."

"But Papa said we could," Suzanne said. "And he said he's going to be home every day when we get through school. Hurry, Paul. Come on."

The astonished look on Paul's face matched Suzanne's earlier look of surprise, and Toby was relieved when he hurried after his sister. Maybe there was hope for this starched Sedaine group after all.

While the audience ate their snack, each one of them took a turn at being the afternoon's entertainment. Toby sang songs, Michael told stories, Suzanne did a dance and Paul was coerced into reciting a poem. There were spells of senseless laughter, frequent hugs and an entire platter of cookies consumed as the four of them bounced on Toby's bed.

It was nearly five o'clock when Michael finally said, "Who is going to help me clean this mess up?"

Both children immediately jumped up and collected the scattered dishes. It had been a long time since Toby had enjoyed herself more, but she was tired and grateful for the opportunity to rest.

When the crumbs had been brushed from the bed-clothes, Suzanne tried to straighten the covers. "May I visit you tomorrow afternoon? I wouldn't want you to be lonely."

"I'll look forward to it," Toby said, and wiped a smudge off Suzanne's cheek.

Paul didn't say a thing as he left the room, but Toby noticed his intense look of concentration had been replaced by a calm childlike look of happiness. She'd bet her best pair of boots that Paul would be back for another afternoon of tea as long as Laura didn't meddle.

The next afternoon Paul knocked on Toby's door first, and she cautioned herself not to read too much into Paul's appearance. The best way to damage their emerging friendship was for her to push Paul.

"Did you learn anything new today?" Toby asked.

"Nothing important. My teacher is making us keep a daily diary and turn it in at the end of each week. She grades us on spelling, penmanship and grammar."

Toby lifted her journal up and said, "That's wonderful. I've been writing down my personal thoughts and dreams since I was about your age. It's a great deal of fun to look back and see how much you've grown, how different your ideas were."

"If I did that, the teacher would rap my knuckles. I just say what she wants to hear."

She wondered what Paul would write down if he was given complete freedom to express his thoughts with no risk of reprisal. Toby knew that within his malicious mind there was still a happy, loving child waiting to be set loose.

Without any planning or forethought a new routine was established, and by Friday, Michael and the children never questioned the timing but simply joined Toby for tea every day. Toby enjoyed the relief of the monotonous days in bed but was curious as to why Laura went shopping every afternoon. In fact, Toby realized she rarely saw Laura at all.

Every few days Michael's mother would stick her head in the door and ask if Toby needed anything before she left as rapidly as she could. Rather than look too deeply into Laura's absence, Toby accepted it as a special gift.

The nutritious food, excellent care and cheerful company made Toby's convalescence much less trying than it would have been had she been alone in a boardinghouse room with just occasional help. She realized Michael had been right insisting she accept the Sedaine's hospitality, but now that she was able to get out of bed, Toby felt she should start looking for a new place to live.

The day Toby had the doctor's permission to leave the house, Michael came home from work early to take her on a brief outing. "Where would you like to go for your maiden voyage?"

"The brownstone," Toby said immediately. "I've missed it, and Caleb and Chantelle are expecting us. I talked with her earlier today."

Toby felt odd climbing the steps and waiting on the stoop for Chantelle to answer the door, rather than fitting her key into the lock. It was an affirmation that she had nowhere she could call home.

After the initial hugs and greetings, Chantelle said, "Come with me. I want to show you what I did with your old bedroom."

The men followed the women with their eyes until they were left standing alone in the parlor. Caleb clapped his hand on Michael's shoulder and said, "That was prearranged. I wanted to talk with you privately."

Michael looked at his serious face. "Is something wrong?"

"Maybe. Let's go get a beer out of the icebox."

Closing the oak door of the refrigerator tightly, Caleb unsnapped the spring-loaded lid of the bottle and poured two glasses. When he remained silent, Michael finally said, "What's the problem, Caleb?"

"Rosie."

Since Toby's illness and the MacRaes return, Michael hadn't been to the theater and had no idea of what was happening at The Pantheon. In fact, Rosie had only seen

Toby twice, and Michael had heard through Ansel that Rosie was seldom at her boardinghouse, darting in and out for a few minutes to grab some personal items or to simply sleep and be gone again.

"What has the little vixen done?" Michael asked suspiciously.

"Nothing wrong. She's a great hit with the audiences, that's all. Our sales at the door have doubled since she stepped onstage."

"Ouch."

"Ouch, is right," Caleb said. "Toby's ego is going to be shattered when she finds out how popular Rosie has become. The rivalry between them is already bitter."

"Ansel said Rosie brought the house down, but I thought he was biased."

Caleb paused to take a sip of beer before continuing. "Ansel understated it. Toby was good but Rosie's better."

Angry, defensive at the honest appraisal, Michael said, "Toby wrote the damn songs!"

"Yes," Caleb said calmly, "she did and they're wonderful, but Rosie makes them come alive. Their talents are split with both sisters equally gifted—just in different areas."

"Toby wasn't exactly a flop," Michael grumbled. "What are you going to do?"

Caleb shook his head. "I have no idea. Toby is the boss, and I'm worried she won't be able to see how good Rosie is. Do you think she would share a billing with Rosie? The competition between them will be brutal, but anything else would not be in the best interest of The Pantheon."

"Well, I'm not going to make a decision for Toby or try to talk her out of going back onstage. It's not any of my business, legally or morally."

"I could let Rosie go. Greenpasture would sign her in a flash," Caleb suggested.

"Not a smart move, pal. Toby would never want you to cut The Pantheon's financial throat to save her pride."

"Would you consider taking back my portion of the theater?" Caleb asked. "I see a bank of black storm clouds in the distance."

Michael laughed at Caleb's predicament. "I haven't regretted my decision for a moment. The Pantheon was conceived from my desire to promote your career, yours and Toby's. Now, Mr. MacRae, you are paying a price for being talented and successful."

"Then you have the dubious honor of breaking the news of Rosie's success to Toby so it won't come as such a shock."

"Not asking much, are you?" Michael said.

The beer suddenly tasted bitter, and Michael poured it down the sink. He popped a lemon drop in his mouth and leaned against the zinc counter. Rosie. Good old Rosamond. She could be a pain, a royal headache, but he would grant her a smidgen of credit that she hadn't sashayed through the door and boasted about her success to Toby. The girl had some sensitivity even though it was most often invisible.

Up in Toby's old room, Chantelle watched Toby's face for a reaction. "Like it? I can spread all my fabric out, make a mess and close the door behind me. Caleb thinks it's a wonderful way for me to work at home part of the time."

Toby had known she had nowhere to call home, but seeing every trace of her belongings missing from her room hammered it deeper. "You needed this," she said, forcing herself to smile. How much longer would she have to live with Michael's mother before she found something as perfect as the brownstone? Probably never. The future had taken and reshaped her life, and Toby wasn't happy with the consequences. Although she didn't begrudge Caleb and Chantelle their happiness, she wasn't thrilled at trying to find another place to live.

"Toby, you look wonderful," Chantelle said, sensing Toby's gloomy thoughts. "Just a few weeks ago you looked like a wraith and now you're nearly recovered."

"Tales of my impending death were grossly exaggerated."

"So why do I still feel so worried about you? A piece of advice?" Chantelle asked.

"No, thank you," Toby said, standing up. "I know what I need to do and why I must do it. You had your reasons for not marrying Caleb even though you were in love with him, and I have mine for not marrying Michael.''

Toby was leery, afraid Chantelle would shatter the equanimity she was fighting to maintain and couldn't take the risk of letting Chantelle speak too candidly.

''I promise to be brief,'' Chantelle said. ''And it's only because I care so much about you that I keep trying to ease you around the potholes I had to wade through all by myself.''

''I know you care,'' Toby said, her voice softening, ''but I don't need any more lectures from you or Caleb about what a wonderful man Michael is. I know that.''

''This isn't about Michael,'' Chantelle said. ''It's about you and storms. When I was a little girl, hurricanes would strike Haiti, and the hardwood trees like the mahogany would be uprooted because they couldn't bend. But the tall, limber coconut palms snapped back after the storm.''

''Thank you for swallowing your advice. And I'm not rigid,'' Toby said, tensing every muscle in her body.

Chantelle disarmed Toby's defensiveness by laughing. ''Not stubborn either, are you? I remember that day in Saint Louis when everyone who'd been rejected hightailed it out the door and you stuck around. Or how about the times you've stayed up all night to finish writing a song and went to work the next day without sleep?''

''You're confusing dedication with stubbornness.''

''It's called dedication when used for a good cause and obstinacy when it interferes with your happiness.''

''I swear,'' Toby cursed, ''you have a short memory. Aren't you the lady who kept Caleb at bay for six long years?''

''Don't fool yourself,'' Chantelle warned. ''If I could have married Caleb sooner I would have. Nothing, absolutely nothing would have stopped me.''

''Then, ask me how I feel six years from now. For today, I have a request, a test of our friendship.''

''Anything, *chère*.''

''Be my friend, work as my partner, but don't plead Michael's case every time we are together.''

"Not another word," Chantelle said. "If we hurry there's enough time to convince Caleb and Michael into going for a drive before we let them buy us supper." Her cool tone made it clear their serious chat was over.

"Let's go dancing tonight," Toby suggested to the others before they left the restaurant. She would have done anything to prolong the evening.

Michael looked at Toby's thin, pale complexion and teased, "You're not going anywhere except home to bed. If you were a horse they'd have to shoot you."

"Why, thank you, Michael," Toby said. "Do you write books of poetry as a hobby? You have so many tender endearments just waiting for the right moment."

"And you are exhausted even if you're not willing to admit it," Michael said. "Say good-night to the nice people, Toby."

"At least let me walk back to the brownstone. We have our own carriage waiting there and I'm perfectly capable of walking five blocks."

"Michael, quit arguing or she'll make you stand on the corner all night until she wins," Caleb said, siding with Toby. "I'm an old married man now, remember? Listen to me, I know what I'm saying."

Chantelle punched Caleb's arm and said, "You may be old, Mr. MacRae, but your wife isn't."

"Caleb, we both lost," Michael said, and started laughing.

Toby linked her arm with Michael's, pulling him forward in the direction of the brownstone. As they began to walk, she reveled in the feel of his body, his hip innocently brushing hers. And she envied the freedom marriage had given Caleb and Chantelle. Her jealousy only accented the longing she felt for Michael, the agony of knowing he was sleeping just two doors away from her.

"Why so quiet suddenly?" Michael asked, patting her hand resting in the crook of his elbow.

Closing the minute gap between them, Toby hugged his arm tighter. "I was just thinking that we need to talk about my living arrangements. I can't go on staying with your mother."

"It does make it impossible for us to spend any time alone," Michael said, misinterpreting Toby's reasons.

"I'm going back to work at least for a few hours tomorrow," Toby said, not correcting Michael's assumption. It had been a lovely day and Toby couldn't spoil it by pointing out to Michael how uncomfortable she was living in Laura's home, how fond she had grown of Suzanne and even Paul and how painful it would be if she stayed longer. If Toby didn't leave soon, she would never have the nerve to abandon the children.

Chapter Sixteen

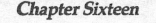

When they reached the brownstone, Toby was startled to find Rosie waiting in a carriage for Chantelle to return. Toby gawked at Rosie's magnificent white fur cape as she climbed out.

"Is that rabbit?" Toby asked, knowing it had to be something much finer, much more expensive.

"No, darling, it's arctic fox," Rosie whispered, and grinned before she hurried up the stairs and into the foyer.

Darling? Rosie's new affectation irked Toby, but she refused to take the bait. After growing up with her, Toby had finally learned that half the fun for Rosie was getting a rise out of her big sister. Two steps behind her sister, Toby said, "How could you afford it?"

"Why, I didn't have to spend a dime. It was a gift."

"From whom?"

Rosie swiveled around and smiled demurely. "One of my admirers."

"Excuse me," Chantelle interrupted. "There must be a reason you were camped on my doorstep, Rosie."

"Can you repair this?" she said, and showed Chantelle a large hole in one of Toby's costumes. "I ripped it last night and I'm afraid I'll ruin it if I repair it myself."

"We might have to take these in a bit when I return," Toby said, picking up the Little Bo-Peep costume and inspecting the tear. "At least temporarily."

"Before you make any alterations, Toby," Rosie said, "be sure to talk with Caleb."

"Since when is Caleb in charge of costumes?"

Michael impatiently pulled the curtain of the long entry window aside and nodded toward the elegant carriage waiting at the curb. "You shouldn't keep your gentleman friend waiting much longer, Rosie," he said, trying to hurry her out the door before she said too much. "He looks a bit ruffled."

"I adore men who are temperamental. It adds spice to life."

"Is that your admirer?" Toby asked, spying a dapper gentleman pacing beside the brougham.

"One of them," Rosie replied, as blasé as a woman who was counting eggs instead of suitors. "Listen, I have to hurry. William is taking me to dinner before the show. Oh, Toby, I think it might be interesting for you to see the new show. Why don't you come tomorrow. Please?"

"All right," Toby said, wondering what Rosie meant by "new."

"Great," Rosie said. "I almost forgot. Here's a letter from Charlie. He had some exciting news."

Without any further explanation, Rosie kissed Toby goodbye, wiggled her fingers at the others and left.

Once Michael and Toby were alone in their carriage, she touched her cheek where Rosie had kissed her and smiled. "It's been years since she's done that. Michael, I believe Rosie is happy. I may not approve of everything she does, but I'm glad she is content."

"You're not suspicious of why she was so pleasant?" Michael asked, wrapping his arm around her waist and pulling her close.

She snuggled back and relaxed into his body. "A little, but I'm pleased she's happy."

"It doesn't bother you that by stepping into your shoes she's reaping all kinds of attention?" What he didn't say was that Rosie's success was at Toby's expense.

"To be honest, I hadn't thought of it in those terms." Toby moved out of his grasp so that she could see his face. "No, it doesn't matter. Rosie is enjoying her brief stint in front of the footlights."

"And you didn't?" Michael asked hopefully.

"Certainly I did, but there's a difference. I loved performing my work, but the extraneous benefits didn't interest me."

"That's because you've had all the extraneous benefits you wanted right here," Michael said, and squeezed her hand.

As much as he wanted to do more than hold her hand, Michael couldn't afford to be more affectionate. If he relaxed his guard he wouldn't be able to keep his desire in check. Besides, Toby still didn't understand the impact of Rosie's popularity, and there was almost no time left to explain it.

"What if her appearance at The Pantheon isn't brief?" he persisted.

Toby realized Michael wasn't indulging in a casual conversation. He was earnest. "You've been trying to tell me something. Be specific."

"You have some stiff competition. Rosie has doubled the receipts."

Toby shivered. If what he said was true, the indispensable kid from Missouri had been booted off the stage. She had been replaced, and that hurt more than being rejected. Placing Charlie's unread letter on her lap, Toby shuddered again.

"You're cold," Michael said, rubbing her upper arms. "When we get home, I'll build a fire. I had a fresh load of wood delivered yesterday."

"The Pantheon doesn't need two similar acts and one of them inferior to the other," Toby said, not being diverted from the subject.

"What happened to the sassy Miss Wells? Where's your spunk?"

"What do you expect me to do? Ask Caleb to sack Rosie? That would be a selfish and an ignorant business decision."

"Do you believe you could be better than she is?"

It was easy for Toby to answer him. "No. I gave it all my effort, and without even trying she's still more talented."

"Because you did half the work for her, damn it. You wrote those songs and you're not taking any credit."

"I'm tired." She sighed, rubbing her temples. "Right now I can't think clearly. Every time I decide what it is I want, whether it's leaving home, being a songwriter, working for you or running The Pantheon, I get pushed in another direction."

"The past few months have been hectic," he said, rubbing her shoulders, forcing her to relax.

"Strange, but the greatest thing that's happened to me was the one thing I didn't want—to fall in love with you."

"Does this mean that we're getting married? You've made up your fickle little mind to finally believe that we could be happy together?" Michael asked, hardly able to grasp the fact that Toby had given up fighting him.

"I know we would be happy, Michael, but I still won't marry you."

"What?" Michael wanted to shake some sense into her but forced himself into remaining outwardly calm. "Quit talking in riddles."

"You would eventually end up hating me the same way you hated Lillian. I think the only way to handle this is to enjoy each other's company until the day one of us needs to leave. The door will always be open."

Toby saw Michael's stunned look and went on to explain. "I can't restructure my life to satisfy you. You're pushing me to give up the stage, settle down with you and have babies. I feel like I'm being backed into a corner without any way of escaping."

"I didn't mean we'd start having children right away," Michael said. "I was talking about someday, not immediately."

"And I meant forever."

Michael was reeling from Toby's words. It wasn't the words she'd used but her tone of voice; she'd been quiet, firm and nauseatingly precise. He'd done it again! It was his destiny to give his love to a woman incapable of returning it with any permanency.

"I will not allow you to leave me," Michael said, clenching his teeth to keep from shaking Toby so hard he rattled hers.

"I love you, Michael. I just can't marry you."

"Can't or won't?"

"That's just a matter of semantics," Toby whispered, noticing the dangerous glitter in Michael's eyes.

"And this is an anatomical one."

Michael pulled Toby onto his lap before she could utter a word of protest and crushed his lips against hers. Always before he had been cautious with his lovemaking, afraid of hurting or frightening her. But not tonight. Tonight he wanted to hurt her, wanted to make her body beg for him to love her and then deny her. Michael wanted to brand her soul with his passion so that no matter how long she lived or how many other men she kissed, Toby Wells would always compare their lovemaking to his.

"I'm the first man you ever loved," he said, sliding his hands up the warm skin of her thighs and pulling her stockings down. "And even if I'm not the last man to love you, you'll never forget me because I'll damn well be the best."

A man of his word, Michael tortured Toby with his lips and brought her to the brink of passion with his hands. He could hear her breath coming in short, tormented gasps, but every time she tried to speak, he ended her objection with his lips.

Michael was firm, aggressive and discreet with his lovemaking—the driver never suspecting anything was happening under her skirts—but Toby wished they were alone in bed together. In her daydreams she had tasted Michael's body, the delicious flavor of his mouth taunting her, relished touching his taut muscles and had spent hours picturing how his stomach muscles would quiver at the slightest touch of her fingertips. Sighing with impatience to end her dreaming about making love with Michael, she pulled at his tie, moaning softly in his ear, pleading with him not to stop.

Before she could entice Michael into even unbuttoning his shirt, the horses came to a rest and Michael pulled her petticoats back into place. "Here we are," he said sweetly, offering his hand to help her out of the carriage.

He paid the driver and walked her right up to her bedroom door before he pulled Toby up to him and traced the outline of her sensitive breasts with his thumbs, circling the nipples repeatedly. "Sweet dreams, Angel Eyes."

Without another word, Michael walked away and left Toby frustrated and abandoned at the moment she had expected to invite him into her room. She had known it was risky, but she had been willing to take the chance just to experience the sublime ecstasy of feeling Michael cover her body with his and show her how well they fit together.

Toby flopped down onto her bed and pounded her fists into the pillow. "Michael Sedaine," she screamed, her words muffled by the mattress, "I hate you."

Alone in his room, Michael kicked his boots off and stretched out on his bed. He popped a lemon drop into his mouth and locked his hands behind his head, staring at the shadows dancing on the ceiling. Toby was going to have a bitter dose of her own medicine, and he would enjoy teaching her what wanting a man really meant. If he couldn't convince her with words that she couldn't live without him, it was going to be a unique pleasure showing her how desperately she needed him.

Charlie's letter, which Toby finally retrieved from her pocketbook the following morning only added to the confusion that had kept her tossing and turning all night long. It was full of family gossip, but one piece of news was particularly unnerving. Her brother hinted that Papa might be remarrying, and Toby was dumbfounded.

The Widow Simpson, according to Charlie, was fattening Papa up with her apple pies. "He told me," Charlie wrote, "that he's escorting her to the next church social. You know what that means around here. It might as well be a public declaration of their engagement."

Toby allowed the letter to settle in her lap. She never expected her father to remarry. For years he'd worn his grief for Irina as a cloak and now it seemed he had shed it. Only Toby clung to the past, unable to close the book on her mother's death and afraid to move into the future.

Michael was in the den working, and he watched Toby refold the letter and put it back into the envelope. Without saying a word about her family, she crossed the room and stared out the window. After a few minutes she reached across the small gap between them and rested her hand on his shoulder, lightly clenching and unclenching her fingers.

He was accustomed to Toby's normal display of affection. It was one of the first things he'd ever noticed about her. But today she was more than just casually touching him as she passed by, she was clinging to him.

"Where are the children?" Toby finally asked.

"In school."

"It's too quiet when they're gone."

"Do you want to tell me what Charlie wrote that is so upsetting?"

"Nothing much," Toby said, taking a deep breath. "He just said that he thinks Papa is going to propose to a woman named Ruth Simpson."

Toby's fingers dug into Michael's arm and he reached up to cover her hand. "Don't you like her?"

"I suppose she's a nice lady but I've never met her. I didn't realize Papa was even keeping company with a lady."

Michael stood up and joined Toby at the window. The traffic on the street was light, the weather clear and crisp, a beautiful Friday morning.

"You sound skeptical. Rather like Paul when he mentions your name."

"Oh, no," Toby said, "I want Papa to be happy. I'm just surprised. I never thought he would marry again."

"Why? He's been alone for ten years, Toby."

"I don't want to discuss it." She brought up another question that was nagging her. "Do you know why your mother asked me to have lunch with her today?"

"I suppose because she would like to get to know you better. Even though you two live in the same house, you rarely have a chance to talk. Give her a chance, Toby. She's really not a dragon."

"I wish you were joining us."

Tucking one of her stray curls behind her ear, Michael said, "Sorry. I've left Reginald on his own too much lately. I need to be in the office on a regular basis."

"Meet me at The Pantheon?" Toby rested her cheek against his lapel.

"I'll be there. Are you feeling up to this much activity?" he asked, worried about her sudden dependency.

"I feel fine," she said, not knowing how to tell Michael of her decision. Suddenly she blurted out, "I'm going home to Saint Louis tomorrow."

"Running away from me again?" Michael had expected Toby to bolt and wasn't surprised.

"No. I need to go home and talk to Papa."

"About his wedding? Do you want me to go with you?"

"Not this time. I need to do this alone. Will you be here when I return?"

Michael could feel her fear and nodded. "I'll be here. How long will you be gone?"

"I don't know. As long as it takes."

"I have to go scouting for a week, myself. I'll make my trip while you're gone. We'll meet back here before Christmas."

"Thank you for understanding."

"Whatever you decide, I'll always be behind you. Now," he said, "if we don't hurry, we'll both be late."

Toby collected her things from her room and thought about how calmly Michael had accepted her announcement. She had been ready with a long list of arguments to convince him it was necessary to go home, but he had squelched her defense before she could offer it.

Looking in the mirror, she pinched her cheeks to add color to her face before she joined Michael in the foyer. When he arrived, he pulled up Toby's collar, making sure she was protected against the stiff wind, and she said, "I don't know what to say to your mother, Michael. It's difficult making small talk with a woman who wishes you would get run over by a trolley."

"You've only had to put up with her for a few months," Michael said, and grinned. "How do you think I feel after a lifetime?"

The tearoom where Michael dropped Toby off was excessively warm, and Toby immediately removed her heavy outer clothing. A waitress led Toby through a forest of exotic plants, palms, ferns and other strange varieties Toby didn't recognize, to Laura's table.

"You look a little flushed," Laura commented after their initial pleasantries. "Did your late night with Michael overtax your strength?"

Laura's politely phrased criticism increased Toby's apprehension. "Healthy as a Missouri filly," Toby said, regretting her folksy comment. She never went around saying things like that unless she was nervous. Changing the subject, she tried again. "I'm fine. It's just a little close in here." Toby batted at a palm frond that was tickling her cheek.

"I'd forgotten they keep this place like a hothouse for all these plants," Laura said, dabbing at her brow.

Throughout the first course, Laura made trivial comments about Paul and Suzanne but never pried once. Toby felt as though she had a tenacious bee crawling across her skin, knowing she would get stung eventually but not quite certain when the pain would strike.

"Mrs. Sedaine," Toby said, finally unable to tolerate the suspense any longer, "why did you want to meet with me?"

"To see if we might find a way to wave the white flag between us."

"We're not at war," Toby said. "You've given me a home when I had nowhere else to go and I'll always be grateful for your generosity."

"Generous enough to leave you alone every afternoon with the children."

Toby lifted her eyes up off the damask cloth and studied Laura. "You were gone on purpose, weren't you? I thought it was rather odd that you had that much shopping to do."

"Michael believed me. It was the only excuse I could invent."

"Why not join us?" Toby watched Laura nervously dab at her lips with her napkin. "You were welcome to join us, Laura."

"Was I? How many times have you seen Suzanne laugh when I am in the room? How often does Paul smile if he's speaking to me?"

Toby couldn't respond. There was nothing she could say without condemning Laura.

"I may be foolish, Toby, but I am not a fool. I stood in the hall outside your door and listened to the children on that first afternoon. I heard them warn you not to tell me they had tea or cookies in a bedroom."

"They only wanted to avoid upsetting you," Toby explained.

"I love my grandchildren, Toby, and I don't want to lose them. I also have taken stock of the way they are being raised and it isn't right."

"Maybe if you just relaxed a bit more..."

"Do you know that I was purposely trying to drive you away so that I wouldn't lose Paul and Suzanne?"

The idea that she might have been a threat to Laura was comical. Toby saw herself about as intimidating as the chicken salad she was eating, but Michael's mother was genuinely frightened.

"I could never come between you and your grandchildren. They love you too much."

"Do they? I'm not so sure. I've held them so tight, afraid of doing the wrong thing that I think I've stifled their youth."

"It's been a great deal of work for you, raising two rambunctious children. I know how tiring two active kids can be."

"I am tired," Laura agreed. "But if I couldn't handle them, I was afraid Michael would send them to Lillian's parents in Belgium. Michael, Paul and Suzanne are all I have."

Toby put her hand over Laura's. "Michael would never send his children away."

"Not now he wouldn't," Laura said, nodding her head. "But at one time, we discussed the advantages of Paul and Suzanne having a large family. You know they have fourteen cousins in Europe. In New York, all they have is their father, grandmother and a flighty uncle."

"I don't care how many relatives they have or what country these cousins live in, Paul and Suzanne need their father."

"And they need a mother. I'm too old to raise them and I haven't wanted to admit it, even to myself."

Toby had too many problems of her own to sort through, she didn't want to have to tackle Laura Sedaine's. "If you relaxed just a bit, it might be easier."

"I know," Laura said. "I've tried, but Paul is a trial to my patience. I know how fond you are of him and so I can say this to you, but if you quote me, I'll deny it. I think it's a bit odd how preoccupied he is with his soldiers and destroying the enemy."

The waiter cleared the table and poured coffee, giving Toby a chance to phrase her response. Their privacy restored, Toby said tentatively, "Paul does have an active imagination. And he's very angry that his mother left him."

Toby had wondered if her dislike of Paul was that she saw too much of herself in him, but she didn't have the emotional strength to resolve all her problems with Paul. In fact, she didn't feel like she had enough energy to survive the next twenty-four hours.

"Laura, I'm sorry, but I can't solve Paul's problems," Toby said. "I can't even find my own answers."

"Like whether you're going to marry my son?"

Toby simply nodded her head.

Laura continued as if Toby's silence were nothing untoward. "When I met you I saw myself thirty years ago. That may be hard to believe now, but I was once as fresh and unaffected as you, my dear."

"It's not hard," Toby said, but she had difficulty believing Laura had ever been anything other than a sophisticated lady.

The older woman's face crinkled into a gracious smile. "I can see why Michael adores you. You lie so believably. As I was saying, I hope I haven't prejudiced you against all the Sedaines. We really can be quite nice once you get to know us. It's just getting to know us that can be painful at times."

It was the first hint of humor Toby had ever heard from Laura, and she started to giggle. "I won't tell your secret to a soul."

"Thank you, Toby. I have over half of New York frightened, and I enjoy watching them shake when I walk into a room."

Laura paid the tab, and as the two women left the restaurant, she hooked arms with Toby and said, "You're not only charming, diplomatic and lovely, you're also much wiser than Michael's mother. My son's taste in women has improved with age."

As Toby walked to the theater, she found her feet dragging with fatigue. Every person who talked to her was pushing her into marrying Michael for their own selfish reasons. Michael wanted her to quit the theater and Rosie had probably left her with no other option. Still, she owned a third of The Pantheon and would continue to manage it.

Michael also wanted a mother for his children so he wouldn't have to worry about them. And, to be fair, Toby knew he genuinely loved her, at least he thought he did. But was that enough? Would it make up for everything she would sacrifice by marrying him?

Now she had Laura Sedaine trying to shirk her responsibilities off onto Toby. Why was everyone so convinced Toby had been born with *Mama* tattooed on her forehead? It was as if they all assumed she had no other talents, no other goals except for raising another woman's children.

By the time she reached the theater, Toby was tired of thinking and wanted to lose herself in activity. She wandered backstage and was encompassed by the usual mad bustle, and her trepidation vanished. Being surrounded by creative, energetic people was wonderful and she realized how desperately she had missed it. Wanting to be a part of it again, to be a help, Toby searched for Chantelle.

"Hello," Toby said when she found her friend in the prop room.

"Hi," Chantelle answered, quickly snatching up a small table. "Wish I had time to visit, but our new act is screaming for this." She rushed past, leaving Toby feeling as if she were a stranger.

The others were equally distracted. Saul, the conductor, was in a flurry to collect his music, and Rosie was practicing a new dance step in the wings. No matter who she tried to talk with or who she stopped and offered to help, they didn't have time for her. They barely broke their stride long enough to be polite.

"Toby," Caleb called, catching her wandering aimlessly. "I reserved front row center seats for you and Michael. Why don't you wait for him in the lobby?"

Toby smiled at Caleb but shriveled inside. Caleb wasn't intentionally cruel, but he was telling her she wasn't needed on this side of the curtain. Pacing the lobby, waiting for Michael, Toby wondered if she belonged anywhere.

Chapter Seventeen

Toby had never had the pleasure of watching the entire show from a paying seat. Her experience, until now, had been of small snippets viewed from the wings or fractured segments spied during rehearsals. It was surprising to discover how many old routines Caleb had dropped and how many new ones he had added. This was not the same production she and Michael had launched, but she happily conceded it was better and that The Pantheon was flourishing.

"I'd never have gambled on this comedian," Michael whispered in her ear, "but you should be grateful Caleb did. Listen to this crowd roar."

She could barely hear Michael and simply nodded while she glanced at the people behind her who were wiping merry tears from their eyes. Earlier, when she and Michael had taken their seats, she was stunned to see the house was packed—a rare feat for a Friday night.

As much as she was enjoying herself and as proud as she was of the way Caleb and Chantelle had guided the theater during her illness, Toby's anxiety rose. Rosie was next on the program. The detached critic in her wished Rosie the best, but the competitive sister that lingered in Toby had her fingers crossed that Rosie would make a minor error. One little sour note or missed step would satisfy Toby's ego enough to salvage her pride. After the applause faded for the comedian, Michael took Toby's hand in his and asked, "Is this hard for you?"

"Which would you pick if your back was sore, a feather mattress or a bed of nails?"

Michael chuckled loudly at her joke and felt the eyes in the quiet hall turn on him. It only added to his mirth and he mumbled to Toby, "They must think I'm a numskull to have taken so long to catch the gag."

She giggled, too. "Or crazy."

"I am—about you."

"Then you are a numskull."

He had succeeded in dissipating her tension and when the curtain rose, Toby settled back in her seat to judge what Rosie had done to the routine she had created. She sat up straight after only a few minutes of the first song; Rosie's rendition was superb. Toby forgot Rosie was her sister, caught up in the magic where reality and rivalry were suspended.

Before the set was completed, Toby's hope of ever coming back to The Pantheon as a performer died. She felt like a fool for having believed she was talented. It had been a grandiose delusion, which Rosie was presently shattering with her fantastic performance.

Toby thought she had been prepared for this, but she wasn't. It seemed so unfair, after all the work she'd invested, for Rosie to be reaping the accolades. Fighting her jealousy, Toby stood with the rest of the audience and gave Rosie her due, a standing ovation—but Toby was the only one in the hall crying while she clapped.

She and Michael left the theater directly after the curtain fell. He hailed a cab and as they rode home, Michael said, "When you come back from Saint Louis, I don't want you to marry me because you think you're a failure and I'm your last option."

"Do you really think I'd use you like that?" Toby asked, startled by his statement.

"Not on purpose," he said, patting her knee. "But you're hurt right now and I can tell you're doubting yourself. Don't. You have more talent in your baby finger than Rosie has in her whole body."

"Ha!" Toby scoffed. "I don't believe that and neither does Caleb."

"Standing up on a stage and singing for your dinner is ridiculous when someone has your gift for composing. Write some songs, sell them to me, have Rosie perform them and turn them into popular tunes. You can do all that and still have time left to pull your share of duties at The Pantheon. Do you think Ibsen performs in his plays or that Strauss wastes his time playing a violin anymore?"

"Oh, I see," Toby said sarcastically, "I'm too creative to bother with vaudeville."

"Damn right. I've been telling you that for months, but you had it in that pretty little head of yours," Michael said, lightly tapping her temple, "that vaudeville was the beginning and the end. The rest of us knew you were squandering your time. Saul, Caleb, Chantelle and I all shook our heads at your choice."

Toby slumped against Michael. "All my life people have been dictating what I should do and what I shouldn't do. Tomorrow I'm going home and try to figure out exactly what *I* want."

He grasped her face firmly and said jubilantly, "Hallelujah! It's about time you took control of your life. Get rid of the ghosts, the guilt and insecurities that prevent you from being happy."

Smiling at Michael's unwavering confidence, Toby teased, "What if I decide I don't want you, Mr. Sedaine?"

"Hardly," he said. "You may not want me, but you can't resist this." He loosened the scarf around her neck and sampled the sensitive point behind her ear with his lips. As if he were devouring a delicacy, he nibbled his way to the soft hollow at the base of her throat.

She tried to withstand his magnificent assault, but her will dissolved under his blazing kisses. Toby moaned and squirmed, guiding his mouth to hers. As her tongue danced with his, Michael slipped his hands under her cape.

"If this is rejection," Michael whispered, "I love being a failure."

"Oh, dear, sweet Michael," she said with a sigh, running her fingers through his luxuriant hair. "You always make failure seem like a victory."

"I wish we could go home and celebrate our disasters," he suggested, molding her breasts in his hands.

"Someday," Toby said.

"Promise?"

Toby hugged Michael and wished she could say yes, but all she whispered was, "Maybe."

As the train neared Saint Louis's depot, Toby realized she'd spent the entire trip from New York dreaming of Michael. Seven months ago she would never have believed she could have been so obsessed with a man, but Michael had taken her world and thrown it into a different orbit. Once, the center of her universe had been Papa, her brothers and sisters and her composing; a simple, orderly world, but now it was all different.

She owned a theater but had no place to call home, she had been a successful performer and a flop, and she was in love with a dynamic, handsome man who was the most frustrating individual she had ever had the pleasure to know. Michael showed her a dozen times a day how much he loved her but refused to accept her on any terms but as his wife.

Before Toby placed a foot on the platform at the depot, Charlie and the twins were waving their hats and calling her name. "Toby! Over here!"

Seeing Cleo, Toby was astounded at the spurt in her height. She was no longer a little girl but a child just about to step into adolescence. Mo, on the other hand, still retained his impish little-boy charm. The twins were at the stage where they would mature at a much different pace just as she and Charlie had done. At one time, Charlie had been like her twin, and then she had outdistanced him for a time.

"Where's Gwen?" Toby called to them.

"Working," Charlie answered, coming up to Toby and swinging her off the coach steps. "Our little sister has a job at a millinery shop."

"Everyone is growing up," Toby said, kissing the twins and enjoying Mo's grimace. "Too big for kisses, young man?"

Mo wiped his cheek with his jacket sleeve. "Women. They always have to be smooching."

"Just wait a few years and you'll like them again."

Cleo poked her brother. "Miss Cavanaugh says that when he dips Sarah Jean's pigtails in the inkwell it's because Mo's sweet on her."

"I am not," Mo complained, punching Cleo in the arm. "Sarah Jean is a wart."

Toby laughed. Some things hadn't changed and it made her happy to be home again. Hugging Charlie, she asked, "How about you? Dipping any pigtails?"

"As many as I dare," he said, winking. "Let's grab your luggage. Papa's anxious to see you."

"I can't wait to see him," Toby said, both chomping at the bit to talk to her father and dreading the conversation.

At the house, Alex informed them Papa wasn't home yet, and Toby's reunion with her father was forestalled. "Where's Mary?" Toby asked her oldest brother. "I haven't seen her since the wedding."

"In the kitchen. She's been slaving all morning over your welcome-home dinner."

Mary, showing her advanced pregnancy, came into the room, wiping her hands on her apron. "Hello, Toby," she said, kissing her sister-in-law on the cheek. "Keeping this family fed is a major chore. I don't know how you did it for so many years."

"I don't think I did as good a job as you are," Toby said. "Everyone has sprouted up at least a foot since I left. Well, not everyone grew up. Some of you grew out," Toby said, and smiled. "When is the baby due? I've lost track."

"Two months," Mary answered, laying a hand on her rounded abdomen. "Either I have an acrobat in here or Cleo and Mo are not going to be the only twins in the family."

"What does the doctor say?"

"He said if they ever invent a way of telling a woman how many babies she's carrying or if it's a girl or a boy, it would take the glorious mystery out of having a family."

Some mysteries were glorious, Toby thought, but others were frightening. She hoped that someday she'd be as optimistic as Mary about the unknown future.

"Is Papa always this late?" Toby asked Alex, recalling Papa used to be so prompt for dinner.

"Recently," Alex answered, smiling cryptically.

"Charlie hinted that he was seeing Mrs. Simpson."

"Courting is a better word. He would have met you at the depot, but one of his parishioners was ill and he called on the family. Mrs. Simpson went with him to deliver a basket of food."

"He actually has his nose out of his books and is practicing what he preaches!" Toby exclaimed. For years Papa's ministry had only been theoretical.

"Thank Mrs. Simpson," Alex said. "I hope Papa marries her. He'll never find a better lady."

Gwen, Papa and Ruth Simpson arrived almost simultaneously. Toby lapped up all the hugs and kisses, giving back a huge measure of her own. Papa was exuberant, his anger at her leaving with Michael long forgotten.

"Stand back," Papa said. "Let me look at you."

Toby did as directed and twirled to show off her New York gown. "Like it?"

"Like the woman in it," Papa said. "You're as beautiful as your mother was."

Gwen started babbling about what kind of hat she could make to go with Toby's dress. "You need something pert with an arching feather."

Cleo fingered the rich hunter-green wool skirt and said wistfully, "When I grow up, can I borrow your clothes?"

"I'll send you a lovely new dress made of this when I return to New York," Toby promised.

Ruth Simpson played with one of Cleo's ringlets and said, "You'll look as elegant as Toby does."

"When I wear it, will you put my hair up like you did last Sunday, Ruth?" Cleo begged.

Watching her little sister and Ruth, Toby saw they had developed a warm relationship. Her father had found a nice lady to complement his family. And Ruth had given Cleo what she never had before—a mother. Hard as she had tried, Toby had always remained an older sister, and she wondered whether or not that was as it should have been or if she'd just done a poor job.

"Since no one has introduced us," Ruth said, extending her hand, "I'll do the honors. I'm Ruth Simpson and I already know you're Toby. I've heard outrageous stories about you and someday we'll have to sit down and compare notes. I suspect your exploits have been exaggerated."

Charlie piped up. "Not so. You'll discover we understated things."

"I find that hard to believe," Ruth said, looking at Toby and smiling warmly. "This sophisticated lady doesn't look like the type to give her unsuspecting brothers and sisters string sandwiches."

Toby covered her face with her hand. "It's true," she admitted.

"It was April Fools' Day," Papa explained. "She rose early, made these fancy sandwiches but twirled long twine in between the meat."

Mo contributed his recollection. "I kept trying to bite through this tough roast beef until my mouth was full of string."

"Were you always so inventive?" Ruth asked.

"Always," Papa answered for Toby.

Looking at all her family, Toby found herself on the edge of tears. She had missed them, but she was glad to see they were all doing so well: growing up, falling in love, starting families and moving ahead with their lives. During the long lonely days when she had been ill, there had been many times when she had doubted her decision to leave them.

"Dinner is ready," Mary called from the swinging door to the kitchen.

"I'll help," Toby said, starting to move forward.

"No, dear," Ruth insisted. "You're the guest of honor. Mary and I will serve."

Throughout the meal Toby wished Michael was with her. He would have enjoyed the way the table was bowed with wholesome food, the way the walls of the room nearly burst

with gaiety and the way everyone chattered over one another to tell a story.

After supper they moved to the parlor, but Papa pulled
Toby aside. "How is my little Rosamond?"

"Very happy, Papa. You should see her onstage. Come
to New York and I'll take you to the theater. You'll be
proud of her."

He stroked his chin. "Funny you should mention that.
Ruth and I were thinking of taking a little trip."

"A honeymoon?" Toby whispered.

"Do you object?"

She had never heard her father sound nervous, but he did
at this moment. "No, I think Ruth is a great woman and
I'm happy for you both."

"Are you?" he asked, lifting her chin and looking into
her eyes. "Your approval sounds a little flat."

"I'm sorry, Papa. I'm just tired after the trip."

"Rest and we'll talk later."

Toby didn't have another chance to speak to her father
for the remainder of the evening. Between catching up on
what was happening in everyone's life, a few songs around
the piano and a serving of the rich pecan pie Mary had
baked, the night slipped away. After retiring to her old
bedroom, which was now Cleo's domain, Toby found her
exhaustion was deeper than even she knew and was relieved to let her questions wait another day.

But it was two days before Toby could corner her father
in his study. The man who used to burrow in his den like a
mole now spent most of his time mingling with his congregation.

"Do you have a few minutes?" Toby asked, worried that
his schedule was too full for her.

"Is it important?"

"Yes."

"Then," he said, sitting down behind his desk, "the
church budget can wait."

"Thank you, Papa." She sat in an old cane-backed
rocking chair, the one Toby remembered her mother nursed
Gwen in. "I never understood why you kept Mama's chair

in here," she said, rubbing the delicate arms, "when it's so feminine compared to your other furniture."

"I like having it right there. It makes me feel as if she's near," he answered in a soft, sad tone, playing with Irina's ring on his fob. "For years after she died, I pretended she was still sitting right where you are and I'd read my sermons out loud to her like I did when we were first married."

It was a touching image of Papa and Mama as a young couple sharing their lives, lending support and encouragement to each other, and Toby empathized with her father's loneliness. Ruth had miraculously filled the void in his life, and he deserved all the joy she would give him. Toby regretted having suddenly dredged up Papa's old grief by asking about her mother.

Silently she scolded herself for having considered burdening him with her troubles. After all, she was an adult and should be able to deal with her problems like one. But there were so many she didn't know which to address first. Maybe if she just gave herself a chance to soak in the love of her family, the answers would come to her without such effort.

"Thank you, Papa. I just needed to know that you were truly as happy as you look. I guess I also needed to know that you hadn't forgotten Mama."

"You worry too much, daughter. Smile more, embrace the day for it slips by too fast."

Toby laughed as her father gently shooed her out of his study. It was wonderful to be home, but it was also unsettling. She was a visitor, a guest and she didn't belong here anymore.

The next day, Toby decided to resolve one issue that had been nagging her. It was so simple, Toby wondered why she hadn't thought of it before. Dr. Harris, the physician who had delivered every one of the Wells children, would be able to give her a frank explanation as to exactly what had caused her mother's death. Toby had been reading every book she could find on the subject but couldn't piece together a clear answer on why Mama had died. Was it something that Rosie, Gwen and Cleo should be warned about? Toby owed her sisters the truth if it was.

"Mary," Toby said, "I'm afraid I wrenched my knee back in New York and I was wondering if Dr. Harris still saw patients." Toby limped slightly to make her claim appear valid.

"Old Doc? Let me think," Mary said, rubbing the small of her back. "Oh, yes, he moved across town, but Robert knows where he lives. I'll go ask him."

Toby doubted her father would naively accept her story the way Mary had and tried to escape outside, but she didn't get far down the hall before Papa stopped her.

"Wait a minute, miss," he called from the door of the study.

"Yes?"

He crooked his finger, motioning her to return. "I doubt there is anything bothering your knee. Come in here and tell me the real problem," he ordered. Her father was seldom so commanding or, at least, the father she had known was not this assertive, and she had no choice but to obey him. Meekly Toby retraced her steps.

"Being onstage hasn't improved your acting," he said, closing the door behind them. "I haven't noticed you favoring that knee since you've been home. So what's all this poppycock about seeing Dr. Harris?"

"Nothing, Papa. I just haven't been feeling well," she lied.

"You forget, Toby, I *know* when one of my children is ill. I realize you were sick in New York, but you look healthy now. Only you've been moping around here like a lovesick puppy. Your letters were filled with Michael this and Michael that, but you've hardly mentioned him since stepping off the train."

He was unintentionally giving her an opening to broach two of the subjects she had been fussing about. "I've been looking for the right moment to tell you that Michael has asked me to marry him."

Papa shook his head, obviously bewildered. "So why the long February face? Don't you love him?"

"I adore him," Toby said, thrilled her father obviously approved. "Michael Sedaine is the sweetest man on earth next to you." She kissed her father's cheek, hoping to divert his attention from her next announcement. "He also gave me a vaudeville theater." Toby crossed her fingers and squeezed her eyes shut, waiting for her father to explode.

"I'm sorry, Toby," Robert said, lightly pounding on his ear. "I don't think I heard what you said. It sounded like Michael gave you a vaudeville theater."

"The title to The Pantheon is in my name, but actually I have two partners. A wonderful couple named Caleb and Chantelle MacRae."

Toby watched her father pull out his pocket watch and snap it shut. "Mary," he bellowed, "come here please."

The floorboards creaked a little as Mary approached, but there was no other noise in the study. "Yes, Robert?"

"Call Ruth and ask her to cancel my afternoon appointments. Tell her I have business to discuss with Toby that can't wait."

Mary looked at Toby and raised her eyebrows questioningly, but Toby just shrugged her shoulders. The door clicked closed and Robert Wells redirected his attention on his daughter.

"I suggest you start from the beginning and don't think any details are so petty that I'll find them boring. I want to hear the entire story."

Toby curled her feet up under her and made herself comfortable for the long session. She edited some intimate facts out of the recitation but tried to stick as close to the truth as she could without enraging her father.

When she was finished, Robert said, "And you find this a suitable career? Owning a vaudeville theater?"

"Yes, Papa, I do. Michael approves and so does his mother. People are different in New York than in Saint Louis."

"I need time to digest all this," Robert said. "Now, why isn't Michael here? He should be standing in front of me shifting his hat from hand to hand while he convinces me he's good enough for my daughter."

"Because I haven't said yes to his proposal. Besides, isn't that a little old-fashioned?"

"Maybe but it's my prerogative," he insisted. "Send him a wire and invite him down. Have him bring Paul and Suzanne also. If I'm going to be a grandfather I want to meet the children first."

"You are as obstinate as Michael. What if I decide I don't want to marry him? What if I decide I want to be a spinster? I might just like living alone, running the theater and not having to raise children."

"Oh, really? If you believe that then you are lying to yourself, Toby. You are so stubborn you won't even say hello to the truth when it's sitting in your parlor. You send that wire and get that young man down here."

Papa rose up from behind his desk and stood next to Toby, patting her hand. "If there's anything else you want to discuss, I'm always here."

Toby jumped to her feet, laid her head against his shoulder and sighed. "I wish Mama was alive," she blurted out. "I have so many questions."

Robert held Toby away from him and looked at her seriously. "I can't replace her, but I think I might be able to answer the questions the way Irina would."

Inhaling deeply, Toby said, "Do you think Mama would make the same choices if she had known her life would end so young?"

"What do you mean? What did her choices have to do with her death?"

She had waited so long to ask this question that Toby almost stumbled over her words. "Would she have all of us again?"

"That's easy. She loved every one of you."

"But...but..." Toby couldn't voice her final question. She was sure it would sound like an indictment.

Papa lifted her chin so she would look him in the eye. "I'm sorry for a lot of things. If your mother was here she'd apologize, too. Her illness forced you into growing up too fast and I depended on you too much."

"Oh, Papa," Toby said, and dropped her chin, "it would be so much easier if you would just tell me what to do."

"Be brave enough to follow your heart. Happiness has a high price tag, Toby."

Chapter Eighteen

Michael crumpled Toby's telegram up and tossed it into the wastebasket. There was nothing he could read into the few sparse words except the obvious. The three of them, Paul, Suzanne and himself, were invited for a visit. Or was he being summoned for another reason?

The red cover of Toby's notebook was closed, but it was right in the middle of the desk, precisely where he had left it after spending most of the night reading it. When the maid had brought him the belongings Toby had left behind, she had drawn his attention to the journal.

"It was kicked under the bed," the maid explained. "I know it's Miss Toby's. She had a few just like it. Must write in them nearly every day to fill so many."

He didn't breach Toby's privacy until this telegram arrived. The three impersonal lines said nothing really, and yet they screamed at him that Toby had more behind her request than she dared say. Well, he wasn't about to travel all the way to Missouri without a clue as to what was going on in her scattered little head. But Michael had had no idea as to the depth of her misgivings—no, terror—about marriage until he read her secret confession.

No wonder she had shied away from setting the wedding date. If what he had read was true, if Toby's mother really had died due to complications from having children and the weakness could be passed on to Toby, she had every reason to be frightened.

Opening the pages dated November 12, Michael reread her entry. What a fool he had been. How could he have been so blind? The entire time he had been trying to convince her to marry him, stressing how much they all needed her, all she had wanted was to be loved. She had told him and told him, but he hadn't listened. The only thing Toby hadn't done was tell him what a selfish, narrow-minded idiot he was.

The quiet room echoed with his laughter as he recalled Toby calling him just about that exact thing. Yes, she had even stated the obvious, and he still hadn't allowed it to penetrate his prejudice. He had been consumed with his own past, never thinking about her personal history. But he knew it wasn't too late. It couldn't be.

"I love you, Toby Wells," Michael said, and ran his hand tenderly across the lined pages.

Toby was fair and forgiving, and Michael was counting on those qualities to come to his rescue. If his plan to create an oasis for just the two of them succeeded and she loved him half as much as he loved her, he would return to New York with his bride.

He slapped the cover of her diary closed and began listing the chores he had to do before he left. The first thing to do was to answer her telegram and then he'd tackle the other jobs.

He penned his message on a blank form. "Love you, too. Need one or two days for business. Arrive as soon as I can. Suzanne and possibly Paul coming, too. Yours, Michael."

Toby clutched his telegram in her hand, wishing it was Michael she was holding and not just his answer to her invitation. At least she could stay busy while she waited, relieving Mary of her chores so Alex and his wife could hunt for a house. They had saved enough money to buy a small cottage and wanted to be settled before Mary's confinement.

As Toby assumed her former responsibilities, she found it was like stepping into a pair of comfortable old shoes. Being the supportive daughter, the surrogate mother, the understanding sister didn't pinch the way a pair of new shoes did or the way her life in New York had.

The rewards were immediate and appreciated; Mo raved about the cookies she baked, Cleo had an enormous stack of mending for her to do, and Charlie was in dire need of someone to box his ears more often. The longer she was home, the more it felt as if she had never left, and New York became fuzzy, like a dream rather than sharp and clear the way Saint Louis looked.

The night before Michael was scheduled to arrive, Toby broached the subject at dinner. "Papa, would you mind if I didn't return to New York? I think I would rather stay here."

Her father had given up reading at the supper table and was an active participant in the swirling conversation. But all sentences were cut short the moment Toby made her announcement.

"You will always have a home with me, Toby," Robert said. "All my children will."

"But why?" Charlie demanded. "Why would you give up your job at the theater you're so proud of to come back to Saint Louis?"

"Well stated," Robert said.

"Does that mean I have to share a room with Gwen again?" Cleo asked, moaning in mock agony.

"Told you so," Mo teased. "Told you Toby was home for good."

The questions and comments were being fired at her so fast Toby couldn't respond to any of them. "It would be nice if only one person at a time would speak."

"And that one person shall be your father in his den after supper," Robert said, dismissing the subject and warning the rest of his children to discuss another part of their day, anything but Toby.

When she had first thought of the idea, it had been just a momentary reflection, but the longer she weighed the merits of staying the more sensible it became. Michael wanted her to marry him and raise his family when she already had a family who needed her right here in Saint Louis. And she was aware of the pitfalls and idiosyncrasies in the Wells home, but the Sedaine house would hold new and unseen obstacles. Could she do it? Maybe. Did she want to try? No.

"Girls," Robert said, "clear the table for Toby and Mary while I get a few answers. After you, my dear," he said, and motioned Toby ahead of him.

Toby suddenly wondered if she had been too rash and grinned meekly at Charlie for support as she walked by him.

"Good luck, sis," he said, and started laughing.

Robert closed the door to his den and turned to Toby. "Now, what outlandish notion have you hatched in that little coop of yours?"

"Papa!" Toby said. "You don't need to insult me."

"Why not? You sound like Cleo, but she's entitled to be flighty since she's only ten. First you are moving to New York to become a famous songwriter. Next, you are on the stage singing and I get letters of how much you love your new career. Just weeks later you own the theater but aren't performing anymore. Oh, but my daughter is in love and is going to marry Michael Sedaine. Aren't I happy for her? Now she's pitching it all and moving right back where she started. Right where I told her she should be in the first place. Do you realize most cows have more sense than you've been showing?"

"You've never talked to me like this before. What's wrong with you?"

"Maybe you never gave me reason to speak to you this way before. Or, maybe I neglected my paternal duties and let you scoot through life without paying enough attention."

"Papa," Toby said, outraged at her father's inference. "I was a perfect daughter. I did everything you asked."

She watched her father cross his hands across his stomach, hitching his thumbs in his vest pockets, and recognized his lecturing stance.

"Loving? Yes. Responsible up until now? Yes. But, perfect? No. None of us are perfect, Toby."

Toby stood and faced her father. "Then tell me what I should do?"

Robert placed his hands on his daughter's shoulders and looked into her eyes. "You should quit treating your life like a dress shop. You've been trying on one gown after another and tossing them aside if they become dirty or torn. Fabric can be washed and mended, but life needs to be nurtured and sometimes even just endured, not tossed aside on a whim. And, if you aren't cautious, eventually you'll find yourself with an empty closet."

"But you don't understand, Papa," Toby said. "I can't make up my mind. I love Michael and I want to marry him but I'm afraid."

"Afraid of what?"

Tears puddled in the corners of Toby's eyes. She knew precisely what her fears were, but there was no way she could voice the words out loud. "I don't know."

"Don't know or can't admit it? Either way, hiding in Saint Louis isn't the answer. I spent ten years hiding, and it took my oldest daughter running away from home to bring me into the daylight."

"I guess playing hide-and-seek is a family tradition," Toby said, and wiped her eyes.

"I certainly hope not. I want you to carefully consider the decisions you will be making," Robert said. "I don't want you living with me because it's safe and unchallenging. We weren't put on this earth to take the easy path. All of us have a purpose and it's a sin to waste our lives. The worst sin of all."

"Is loving a man always complicated?"

"Almost as mystifying as loving a beautiful woman," Robert said, and left the room.

"Oh, Toby, you have guests," Mary called out from the front porch, where she was sweeping the steps.

Toby raced from the kitchen, wiping her hands on her skirt and wanted to run into Michael's arms but didn't. "I missed you," she said, and gave him a brief hug. However, she swung Suzanne into the air and hugged her enthusiastically. "How was the train ride? Long and boring?

"I stayed up way past my bedtime and watched all the lights go by. I want to drive a train when I get big," Suzanne said.

"Girls can't do that," Paul objected. "Only boys can."

"If she owns the railroad, she'll be able to do anything she wants," Toby said. "And hello to you, too."

Michael glared at his son, but Paul remedied his lack of manners immediately.

"Hello, Toby. Thank you for inviting us. This gift is from *Grand-mère*." Paul stuck a box into Toby's hand and stepped back behind his father.

"Thank you, Paul. I'm glad you changed your mind and decided to make the trip with your father," Toby said.

"*Grand-mère* made him," Suzanne said. "He even hollered at her before she whopped him a good one."

Toby looked over at Michael and could see from his expression Suzanne was telling the truth. "Cleo and Mo will be home from school very soon," she said. "Until then, would you like to have a sandwich and a piece of pie? Mary will fix you anything you want," Toby said, prodding Paul and Suzanne toward the kitchen.

"How long can you stay?" Toby asked Michael as soon as they were alone.

"Just a few days. They can't miss much school and I can't keep dumping my business in Reginald's lap or he'll legitimately own Sedaine Music."

"Then we'll make the most of our time together."

Michael didn't know how to respond to Toby's comment, but her choice of words was ominous. His suspicions about being invited to Saint Louis were being substantiated. This was not a social visit but a summons of dismissal.

"Is there something wrong?" he asked. "I feel like a sick man waiting for the doctor's estimate of how many more days I have to live."

"No, nothing," Toby said, and smiled brightly at him. "We're going to have a wonderful time."

"I hope so," Michael said, but he was worried. Toby Wells had something brewing, and he didn't like the smell of what was in the kettle.

As the rest of the family arrived home, Toby introduced them to Paul and Suzanne, and soon Cleo was proudly showing Suzanne how to hold a rabbit, while Mo allowed Paul into the privacy of his tree house. Seated at the kitchen table over a cup of coffee, Toby watched the two city children, unnecessarily bundled against the winter weather, meander through the yard in awe of what Cleo and Mo took for granted. She had missed what was right under her nose all her life. After a few weeks, would she miss the excitement of New York, the thrill of the audience's roar of approval and the unpleasant but treasured odor of backstage?

"Just look at Paul, Michael. He's laughing and his shirt is dirty," she said. "Leave him here for a month and I'm positive he would give up his soldiers."

Michael leaned over and watched Paul rolling around on the ground, wrestling with the dog. "He does enjoy animals, but there's nothing wrong with Paul's hobby."

"Hobby or obsession?"

"Did I come all this way to argue with you about Paul's fascination with toy soldiers? You sound just like my mother."

Toby shook her head and said, "How's The Pantheon? Caleb and Chantelle still have the seats filled?"

"Great, I guess. I really don't have any reason to be concerned about its nightly count."

"They make a good team," Toby said, refilling their mugs. "All they needed was my name on the deed."

"And what do you mean by that?"

"Just what I said. Come on, I think I hear Papa coming up the steps. He's anxious to see you again," Toby said and pulled Michael to his feet. "He doesn't believe me that Rosie isn't causing any trouble in New York."

The rest of the day was a series of fractured conversations, renewed acquaintances, introductions and confusion, making it impossible for Michael to put Toby's cryptic hints into perspective. Cleo and Mo insisted on playing *tableaux vivants* again after dinner, and before Michael could corner Toby, it was time for him to take Paul and Suzanne to the hotel.

"See you in the morning?" he asked, skimming his fingers across her cheek.

"Come for breakfast," Toby said, and gave him a wisp of a kiss on his cheek.

"Is that all? My daughter is more affectionate than that."

"Good night, Michael."

Michael knew something was wrong. Toby was usually the most loving woman he had ever known, and she was treating him as if he had a disease. He couldn't fault her manner or her words, but they were hollow, empty of any real emotion. Tomorrow he would get her alone and pry the truth out of her.

Toby was still packing the twins' lunches when Michael knocked on the door with Paul and Suzanne.

"I thought you three might sleep in this morning," she said, slamming the door behind them against the chill blast of air.

"Oh, no," Suzanne answered. "We're going to help Mrs. Simpson pick out a puppy at her friend's farm. Her old dog died and she's lonely."

Michael had an innocent smile, but Toby knew he had somehow concocted this scheme. "My, my, Michael," she said, grinning, "you must have been up very early this morning. Such a busy day planned."

"I'm not going with Paul and Suzanne. You and I have a business meeting. It should take the entire day."

"We do? Where?"

"With an attorney. I'm having a contract drawn up and I want your opinion before I sign it."

"And the king of Siam is coming to supper?" Toby said.

"He is?" Suzanne said in awe.

"No," Paul said, and shook his head at his sister's gullibility. "Do you always believe what people say?"

"Of course," Suzanne said, and marched into the kitchen as if she'd lived in the house her entire life.

There was little time for Toby to wonder what Michael had planned since the twins were dawdling about leaving for school, feeling wounded and put upon because Paul and Suzanne had such wonderful adventures planned for the day. As Toby argued with Mo, she placed mounded bowls of oatmeal topped with brown sugar in front of all three Sedaines.

"I'll fix your eggs in a minute," she said to Michael.

"Someday you can come visit us in New York," Michael said to Mo and Cleo between bites, "and we'll visit the Statue of Liberty while Paul and Suzanne are in school."

"Promise?" Mo said.

"I promise."

"We won't name the puppy until you get home," Suzanne added, earning a halfhearted smile from Cleo and a withering glower from Mo.

"Girls are so dumb," Mo groaned, and stomped out the door.

"I'd rather be dumb than smelly," Cleo yelled, and ran after her twin.

Michael and Toby laughed at the insults until Paul asked, "Michael, what will happen if my shoes get muddy when we go to the farm?"

"Rinse them off in the water," his father answered.

"But that will spoil the shine."

"Don't worry, son. If your shoes get ruined, I'll buy you a new pair."

Toby poked Michael and pointed to Suzanne, putting her finger against her lips to silence him. They watched as the six-year-old studiously reached her spoon across the table to the window ledge and fed Gwen's black-and-white kitten. Each pass of the spoon was carefully negotiated and Suzanne was fair, first the kitten and then herself, a bite for the kitten and a bite for Suzanne.

Holding back her laughter, Toby said, "Why don't you give that bowl to Tiger and I'll get you another, Suzanne."

"Did you know that kittens like oatmeal, Papa?"

"I think kittens like sweet cream the very best of all," he said.

By the time she had the dishes washed and Michael had dried them and stacked them on the counter, Ruth appeared to take charge of Paul and Suzanne.

"Have a nice day at the lawyer's office," Ruth said as if she were making a wonderful joke. "You just might get talked into signing your life away."

Toby quizzically looked from Michael to Ruth. "I'll read it over carefully, but Michael's a good businessman."

"Well," Ruth said, and leaned down to kiss the top of Toby's head, "I'm counting on you to represent the Wells name in a worthy manner."

"What are you talking about?" Toby said.

"Ask Michael. He's the man with the answers," Ruth said, and smiled. "Good luck, son."

The moment the door closed, Toby said, "Now, Mr. Sedaine, I demand an explanation."

"Get your bonnet and a warm coat. That's all I can say."

"I am not leaving this house until you tell me what is going on."

Michael rolled his sleeves back down and put his cuffs on. "It might be cold without a coat, but you are coming with me even if I have to put you over my shoulder."

"So considerate of you to give me a choice."

"So wise of you to understand that you have none."

Toby took off her apron and went to the hall closet for her cloak and new hat. Gwen had brought the hat home as a gift, and Toby put the curved brim bonnet on her hair. Pinning it in place, she fussed with the blue mull trim and tucked up the straggling curls from the back of her neck.

"You look outstanding," Michael said, coming up behind her. "Let's not waste any more time. We have a great deal to accomplish in one day."

"When did you make all these elaborate arrangements?"

"Last night. If we're not home for supper, Ruth will be here to help Mary."

Michael grabbed her hand and pulled her out the front door. A hired carriage and driver were waiting and Toby's suspicions rose, but Michael refused to say a word about their destination. He would only comment on the passing scenery, the weather and the business district as they whisked through.

"What are we doing here?" Toby asked when the driver stopped in front of the railroad depot.

"I have some business to attend to."

"Then I'll wait here for you."

"I'd rather you came with me," Michael said, tugging firmly on her arm.

"You're not making any sense."

They were halfway across the platform, twenty yards from an engine belching smoke when Toby had an inkling of what might be happening.

Without saying a word, she dropped her hand and turned to run.

"Not quite," Michael said, and swooped her up into his arms.

"Put me down this instant, Michael Sedaine."

"No."

"Yes," Toby insisted. "If you don't, I'm going to scream and tell people that a depraved criminal is abducting me."

"And I'll tell them that my wife has been confused ever since the accident. I'm taking her to New York for treatments."

"You wouldn't."

"I would."

"But what about Paul and Suzanne?" Toby said, squirming the entire time, hoping to escape.

"Ruth will bring them home in a few days."

"I don't have any luggage."

"Your father delivered both our valises this morning, right after Gwen finished packing yours," Michael said.

Toby was so stunned by her family's conspiracy that she quit fighting. "Why are you doing this?"

"Just climb up the steps and once you're inside, I'll explain."

Michael opened the door of the last coach and Toby walked into a Pullman car, but it was unlike any she had ever seen before. Rather than row after row of upright seats, this one was furnished with upholstered chairs, plush sofas and carved tables. There were reading lamps next to the chairs, a vase of fresh flowers on the small round dining table, and beyond the first doorway she could see a large bed dominating the small private bedroom.

"How did you..." She couldn't finish her question.

She slowly walked back to the bedroom. Across the foot of the bed, her dressing gown was spread out and her hairbrushes were on the nightstand.

"Michael! This must have cost a fortune."

"Almost, but it was a small price to pay to get you alone."

"Where are we going?"

"Home."

Gently he unhooked her cape and tossed it aside. "It was the only way I could think of to get you all to myself, with no risk of you running away and with no chance of interruptions. We have the entire trip to ourselves and nothing to do but plan our future."

Toby was in a daze and wandered back into the main room. She sat down in a chair and put her hands in her lap. "I can't believe my father agreed to this."

"I explained it all to him last night at Ruth's after I left you."

"Is that why it took him so long to walk her home?"

"Yes," Michael said, pouring each of them a glass of champagne. "Here, take a sip."

She picked up the glass and drained it, choking on the bubbles. "Do I get an explanation?"

Michael settled down in the chair next to Toby and began. "I've known for a long time that you love me and I put all my misgivings to rest about being capable of loving you. I know that I will love you for the rest of my life."

"But there are problems you don't know about. Risks you don't understand."

"Like your fear you will never care for Paul the way you think you should? Your terror about having a baby?"

Toby was speechless. She had never told a living soul those things, but somehow Michael knew. It wasn't possible.

Michael set his glass down and said, "I read your diary. You left it behind when you packed in such a rush for Saint Louis."

Jumping to her feet, Toby ran for the door. "Tell the conductor to stop this train. I'm getting off."

He grabbed her around the waist and picked her up, trying to dodge her heels, which were taking direct aim for his shins. "Listen to me. I didn't do it to pry. The maid found it underneath the bed and brought it to me after you had left."

"You didn't have to read it."

"Yes, I did. I would have broken every law in the United States and some that haven't even been created yet to discover why you wouldn't marry me. If you had been honest with me, we could have talked about it, but you kept giving me poor excuses. You underestimated me."

"You are a despicable rodent. If you really loved me, you would have respected my right to my own thoughts."

Michael kissed Toby's neck and whispered, "If I set you down, will you listen?"

"To what? Excuses for your poor manners?"

Toby was startled at the way Michael immediately dropped her.

"I may have poor manners," he hollered, "but at least I don't hide my feelings and I don't lie. I was always honest with you even if it hurt your feelings. You don't understand the meaning of the word *honesty*."

"Then why do you love me? Why didn't you just let me stay in Saint Louis where I was happy?"

"Your father asked me the same question and I'll be damned if I could give him an answer. Is that what love means? Caring about a woman even though there is no logical reason or explanation for your feelings. Getting up in the morning with a headache because you've spent the entire night worrying about her even though she treats you like a pile of rubbish or worse, a brother. Not being able to think, eat or sleep."

Michael paused for a moment to catch his breath. "If that's an accurate and fair description of what my future with you will be like, then I'm not exactly thrilled about being in love with you, either, Miss Wells."

Chapter Nineteen

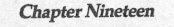

Toby flounced back to the sofa and sat down in a huff. She propped her heels on the chair next to her so Michael couldn't sit too close and crossed her arms across her chest in a defiant posture.

"And who asked you to love me? I certainly didn't," Toby said. "I don't want any man cluttering my life."

Michael took off his coat and threw it across the coach. "You have to be the most exasperating woman in the state of Missouri."

"We probably aren't in Missouri any longer," Toby said. "I think we're in Illinois."

"Thank you for your correction, Miss Wells." Michael struggled to control his temper and not jump off the train himself. "Toby," he said, and took a gulp of air, "do you love me?"

"Yes, unfortunately."

"And I love you, but you need to grow up," he said.

His tone of voice would have frozen hell, and Toby wasn't sure she had heard him correctly. "Grow up?"

"Simple words. Do you want me to spell them? I expect to marry a woman, not a sniveling child who runs away if every day isn't like Christmas eve. I want a woman—shall I spell that word, too?—who will confront her problems, her fears as they appear. I do *not* want a partner who cowers at the unknown, who runs away from the truth because it might be painful." Michael heaved a huge sigh and continued, "A wife like that will one day turn on me at some little misunderstanding because she hasn't the courage to talk to me directly.''

"I would never do that, Michael," she said, and stepped over to him, reaching out to stroke his face.

He stepped back. "Don't."

She flinched at his uncharacteristic detachment and at the ugly portrait he had painted of her—an embittered, petulant child, a spineless woman and a potentially vindictive companion. For years, as a substitute mother, she had seen herself as heroic, self-sacrificing and charitable, but Michael had knocked her off the pedestal, demanding she be accessible and real and equal to him. She had to take the chance that he would understand all her fears and together they would be strong enough to conquer them. Otherwise Toby knew she would never see Michael again after they reached New York.

She stared up at the man she was expecting to work miracles for her, and the light from the brass lamps highlighted his face. Had she once described him as handsome? If so, it had been an understatement. Michael was princely with his aquiline nose, his high, regal cheekbones and his strong jawline.

"Can I have your promise you will never tell another soul what I'm going to tell you?"

"At last," Michael said, and glanced up to the ceiling. "Thank you." He guided her to the sofa and sat down next to her. "I won't ever repeat a word, but before you begin, I have one question. Do you realize how stubborn you are?"

"Mulish," Toby said, and grinned.

"That's the exact word your father used to describe your mother."

Toby started at the comparison. "Papa talked about her? What did he say?"

"That you're just like her. Much more so than any of your brothers or sisters."

Years of stifled rage poured out. "How could he have allowed her to have so many children? Why insist she sacrifice herself for us?"

"Your diary was full of words like that," Michael said. "That's the reason I made arrangements to see your father. We talked most of last night. He never knew how you felt, Toby. You expect people to read your mind and respond to your thoughts, but we can't. We're humans and we can only react to the information you give us."

"My mother was a martyr. Her children were her life and her death."

Michael stroked her head and started to rub her shoulders, hoping the physical comfort would make what he was going to say a bit easier to accept. "That's not what Robert said. Cleo and Mo were the reason she lived months longer than expected. She fought to stay alive to give birth to them."

"But I heard Dr. Harris say Mama shouldn't be having another child!"

"Because he didn't think she was strong enough, given her malignancy, to carry the baby full term," Michael said, and kept massaging her neck.

"Malignancy? What was wrong with Mama? Papa never, ever, told me." Toby was furious at the years of secrecy and misunderstanding.

"She had a tumor here," he said, placing his hand on her breast.

"But why didn't he tell me?" Toby repeated.

Michael took a few seconds to respond. "Your mother believed as long as she denied her disease it wouldn't conquer her."

"Why not tell me after she died?"

"I guess he thought you knew. You acted so mature, so wise it never occurred to him you didn't understand."

"Well, I didn't!" Toby screamed. "I thought Mama died because she was too weak from having all of us. I was afraid the same thing would happen to me."

Michael pulled Toby to him, encouraging her to let the tears she should have shed years ago flow. Patting her back, he said, "I'm sorry, Angel Eyes. He didn't know. Robert was so consumed with his own pain, he didn't have room to acknowledge anyone else's. If it's any consolation, he told me to tell you how sorry he is for hurting you."

Toby choked on her words. "I—I was s-stupid."

"Hush," Michael crooned. "You were a little girl who took snippets of information and pieced them together wrong."

The drama of the day had drained her strength, her emotional reserves were empty and Toby cried until just a soft, gentle hiccup and an occasional shudder were all that she had left to give.

"And I don't want you to worry about Paul," Michael said. "He'll give up his soldiers when he's ready and feels secure. I understand how annoying he is but, trust me, he can be a delightful boy."

"I don't dislike him," Toby said. "I'm afraid I can't help him. He's so angry."

"Can you blame him? He lost his mother, and his father all but abandoned him. Now that I've removed my blinders, I'm positive Paul's problems will be resolved given a little time, some patience and a great deal of love. Mother and I had a long conversation about it and she's in complete agreement. Suzanne and Paul need you. No, they love you."

"But can I do it?" Toby asked.

"You only have to spend a few hours a week at the theater during the evening. We'll hire a housekeeper and a cook and with my help, it should be easy."

Toby drew back and looked into Michael's eyes. "Are you saying I don't need to quit working?"

"Of course not," Michael said. "And I am in love with a one-of-a-kind woman. So why would I think you would act like anyone else? I like you just the way you are. Sassy and feisty, affectionate and wise."

"You really think I'll make a good mother for Paul and Suzanne?"

"They love you, Toby. Neither one of them made a peep about our plan and they knew all about it."

"Even Paul? He was so, so…"

"So much like Paul? Wouldn't you have been just a teensy bit suspicious if he had run into the kitchen and thrown his arms around you?"

"Yes," Toby said and giggled softly.

"It is so wonderful to hear you laugh again. That's your best composition."

Toby buried her face in Michael's chest and gripped him fiercely. How had she ever thought she could survive without him? It was as crazy as a gardener assuming a flower could bloom without the sun, fresh rain and rich soil. Most men would have let her skitter back home and would not have bothered to chase after her but Michael loved her enough to break his code of ethics and read her journal in search of the truth.

She tried to recall all that she had written on the ruled pages since she met him and her face turned red. Michael knew her most intimate secrets. The thought was unnerving and reassuring. He knew the worst and the best, he had learned what gave her joy and what terrified her and still loved her. Michael knew more about her than any person, living or dead, and she was relieved she didn't have to hide. All the years of keeping her secrets were over.

"When did you change your mind about burying your heart with Lillian?" she said, afraid to ask but determined to know the truth.

Toby sat upright and watched Michael's forehead wrinkle in concentration.

"I'm sorry," he said, and shook his head. "I don't understand what you're asking me."

"Ansel claims that's what you said after Lillian's death."

"Oh," Michael said, the misunderstanding fading from his eyes. "He elected to believe I was grieving for Lillian and could never love another woman. The truth is I thought I was incapable of keeping any woman happy. Ansel couldn't accept the fact that his sister was just as disillusioned with me as I was with her."

"But all those times you told me about Lillian, I thought you were still in love with her."

"Then you have a very selective memory. I explained my feelings, but you chose to lock what Ansel said into that incredibly thick head of yours," Michael said.

"You did, didn't you," Toby said, recalling the evening before she got sick when she had walked home from the theater and how Michael had claimed their love, his for

Lillian and hers for him, had ended long before their marriage. How many other times when they were arguing had she remembered only what she wanted to?

"I tried to make you understand," Michael said, and playfully pinched the end of her cute little nose. "But, you haven't been too good at listening, Miss Wells."

"I need to hear you tell me again," Toby whispered.

His hand was across her waist and Toby stroked his fingers. They were strong but sensitive, just like the man, and she delighted in her fortune of being lucky enough to have found him.

"Toby, my very own Angel Eyes, I have never loved a woman the way I love you. I love every square inch of your stubborn, beautiful, inviting body."

"Then haven't we waited long enough?" Toby boldly asked, and riveted her eyes toward the bedroom.

Without wasting a moment, Michael picked Toby up and twirled around the room. "Far too long," he said, spinning them in circles across the room until they were next to the bed.

"I love you, Toby Wells, and we have the entire evening to ourselves. No children, no interruptions, no brothers or sisters and no reason to wait."

"Do I need to pretend?" Toby asked, tilting away from Michael.

"Pretend? About what?"

"I know nice ladies are supposed to be shy, act frightened the first time and lay stiff as a board on the bed."

"I love you, but I've never thought you were a nice lady," Michael said, and started to laugh. "The woman want in my arms is Toby Wells, not some stiff impostor."

"Good," Toby said, and jumped from Michael's arm to pop under the blankets.

He joined her after kicking his boots off. "We have so many layers of clothing between us, we might as well be Puritans separated by a bundle board."

"Not in my bed," Toby said, and giggled. She dove under the covers and pulled his socks off, tickling his toes for a brief moment.

Michael laughed at the squirming mound of bedclothes, amazed at how she could be so sensuous, so unafraid. His laughter died when he felt her groping in the dark at his belt. Toby deftly unbuckled it and pulled his trousers down. Her impatience was apparent as she madly peeled off the rest of his clothes until he was nude.

"My turn," he said in a husky voice.

The difference in Michael's technique was tantalizing. He deliberately extended undressing Toby, savoring each inch of bare skin as he uncovered first one shoulder, then the next. He delighted in tormenting her senses by avoiding any contact with her breasts even though she was straining toward him, begging him to touch her.

It was exquisite agony the way Michael was prolonging their lovemaking. Part of her was on fire, imploring him to join their bodies, but another part wanted to luxuriate forever in the ecstasy. She surrendered to his enchanting caresses, willing herself to accept his skilled attention.

He shifted to her legs, peeling away her skirt and exposing the tender inner surface of her thighs. Hypnotized by his gentle onslaught, Toby was unaware of how the rest of her garments were removed. Her entire focus was on his hands, his lips and the way his tongue savored her skin.

"You are so incredibly beautiful," he said, laying his head on the pillow next to her and using his hands to map the hills of her breasts and the plain of her stomach. Michael closed his eyes, concentrating on her marvelous warm texture. Nuzzling his face into her curls, he inhaled Toby's dulcet scent. Nothing smelled as sweet as his future bride.

She ruffled his shiny black hair and imprinted this moment in her mind. Every detail, each sensation, was tucked away to be recalled later when her heart needed nurturing. No matter how many nights she and Michael frolicked together under the covers and regardless of how many years they had the joy of sharing, none would ever be so clearly etched as this one.

Throwing the covers aside, she bared him so she could investigate his broad chest, the way his muscles curled from his shoulder to his biceps and how his narrow waist sloped neatly to his firm hips.

Heated by just the sight of him, the December chill in the room no longer mattered. "I've wanted to do this," she said, stretching her body on top of his, breast to breast, until she felt as though they were one.

Michael cupped her rounded little buttocks and initiated a gentle rocking of their hips. Instinctively Toby began to open her thighs, but he delayed his entry by clamping his legs around hers. Imprisoned together, he tested them both to the limit of their endurance.

"You are wonderful." She sighed, astounded at how Michael let her set the pace and didn't rush even though she knew he had been struggling to control his passion for months.

Releasing his grip, Michael eased Toby over so she was beneath him. "I've just begun," he promised, kissing her breasts, alternately drawing her nipples into his mouth.

"You can do that forever," she murmured, tingling at the thrill of his succulent nursing.

Michael delighted in Toby's natural passion and sat back on his heels to admire her beauty: the silky smoothness of her skin, the graceful curves of her hips, the slim ivory of her legs. He had never seen such exquisite breasts with rosy pink nipples and he traced his fingers around their fullness to her waist and beyond to the triangle of blond curls between the creamy curve of her thighs.

"Are you really mine?" he murmured in awe.

Toby leaned forward on her knees and drew his tongue into her mouth, tenderly, persuasively, holding him in her arms so that she was not too close and just their lips touched. She felt Michael shudder and explored the taut muscles of his neck and shoulders with inquiring, beguiling fingertips. He sighed a low moan of pleasure and she could feel her own body responding, her blood pounding in her ears while every nerve rejoiced.

Inflamed by her adoration, Michael attempted to coax her onto her back so he could unite with her and consummate their passion.

"Oh, no, my love," she said, halting momentarily. "Just ignore me if you can't be patient."

For the rest of the day, Michael and Toby tested the boundaries of their desire until there wasn't an unexplored, unadored inch on either of their bodies.

"More coffee?" Toby asked, grinning across the supper table at Michael.

Neither of them had eaten since breakfast, and Michael had ordered a huge meal served in their car. "Isn't this marvelous?"

"Before you say anything more, Michael," Toby said, determined to end the last deception between them, "I have one more subject to discuss with you."

"Which one?"

"My appointment with the doctor. I know you read about it in my diary but you've never mentioned it. I'm still going to keep it."

"I didn't think it needed to be discussed," Michael said, and took a bite of his steak. "I know you aren't ready to have a baby and I don't want you to just yet. I feel very selfish about sharing you any more than I already do."

"What if I never want to have a baby? Will you resent my decision?"

"No. That decision is yours to make. As I said earlier, I just want to spend the next fifty or sixty years making love to you," Michael said, and leered at her.

"We're the only couple I have ever heard of that took our honeymoon before the wedding," Toby said.

Michael knew Toby might feel guilty and was ready with ammunition to destroy any remorse. "I saved a special surprise for you. This is from your father."

She watched him lay a gold wedding band on the table and slowly picked it up. It wasn't new and shiny like she'd expected, and Toby was puzzled. Holding it up for closer inspection, she saw an inscription. "ILC & RGW United 2/1/77."

"This is my mother's. How..."

"Your father gave it to me along with his blessing. In his eyes, Toby, the moment you put that ring on your finger we're man and wife. Our wedding day will just be a legal ceremony."

"Will you, please?" she said, and held the ring out to him.

Michael took the ring, came around the table and knelt next to her chair. As he started to slide it up her finger, he said, "Toby Wells Sedaine for the rest of my life I intend to show you how much I love you. You own my heart, my faith and my fidelity. Whatever challenges we have to face, we'll do it side by side, hand in hand."

Toby took her free hand and placed it over her mouth, her fingers wet with tears of joy. When she could speak, she said, "Michael Sedaine, I promise you my heart, my faith and my fidelity. Not only have you blessed me with your love, but you've given me a priceless treasure, two bright, healthy children."

Toby saw Michael swallow hard. All the ghosts between them had been vanquished, and they were free to start their life together, unfettered by yesterday and unafraid of tomorrow.

"Would you care to celebrate our wedding day?" Toby said, untying the sash of Michael's robe. She ran her fingers down his bare chest and across the clenched muscles of his stomach.

"Are you always this sassy, Miss Wells?" Michael said as he slowly stood up, enthralled by the way her hand roamed his body.

"Yes, Mr. Sedaine, I am."

* * * * *

HARLEQUIN
Romance

A Christmas tradition...

Imagine spending Christmas in New
Orleans with a blind stranger and his aged
guide dog—when you're supposed to be
there on your honeymoon!
#3163 Every Kind of Heaven
by Bethany Campbell

Imagine spending Christmas with a man
you once "married"—in a mock ceremony
at the age of eight!
#3166 The Forgetful Bride
by Debbie Macomber

*Available in December 1991, wherever
Harlequin books are sold.*

HARLEQUIN

Romance®

**This November,
travel to England with
Harlequin Romance
FIRST CLASS title #3159,
AN ANSWER FROM THE HEART
by Claudia Jameson**

It was unsettling enough that the company she worked for
was being taken over, but Maxine was appalled at the
prospect of having Kurt Raynor as her new boss. She was
quite content with things the way they were, even if the
arrogant, dynamic Mr. Raynor had other ideas and was
expecting her to be there whenever he whistled. However
Maxine wasn't about to hand in her notice yet; Kurt had
offered her a challenge and she was going to rise to it—after
all, he wasn't asking her to change her whole life . . . was
he?

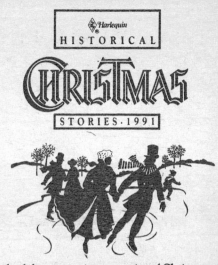